THE REBEL AND THE ROSE

ALSO BY
CATHERINE DOYLE

The Dagger and the Flame

THE REBEL AND THE ROSE

CATHERINE DOYLE

Margaret K. McElderry Books
New York Amsterdam/Antwerp London
Toronto Sydney/Melbourne New Delhi

MARGARET K. McELDERRY BOOKS
An imprint of Simon & Schuster Children's Publishing Division
1230 Avenue of the Americas, New York, New York 10020

Originally published in Great Britain in 2025 by Simon & Schuster UK Ltd

Jacket design by Debra Sfetsios-Conover

The text for this book was set in Adobe Garamond Pro.
Manufactured in the United States of America
First Edition
2 4 6 8 10 9 7 5 3 1
CIP data for this book is available from the Library of Congress.
ISBN 9781665955140
ISBN 9781665955164 (ebook)

For Ali, and
your rebel heart
❤

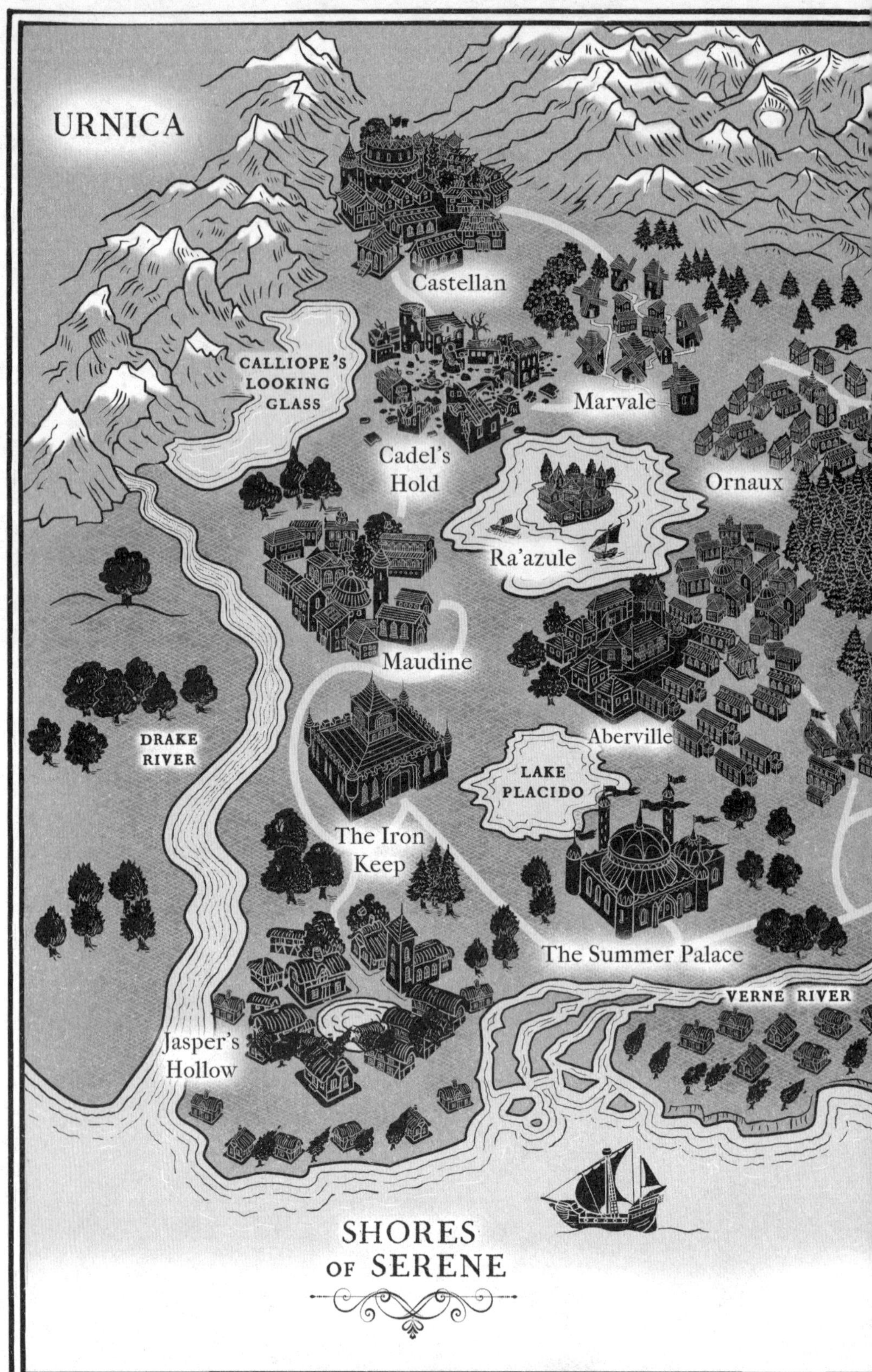
URNICA
Castellan
CALLIOPE'S LOOKING GLASS
Marvale
Cadel's Hold
Ornaux
Ra'azule
Maudine
DRAKE RIVER
Aberville
LAKE PLACIDO
The Iron Keep
The Summer Palace
VERNE RIVER
Jasper's Hollow
SHORES OF SERENE

FARBERG
Halbracht
Silvercrests
Frederic's Rest
The Pinetops
HELLERBEND RIVER
FROGRUN RIVER
The Plains
Appoline University
Bellevue Castle
Mauranus
Montmarie
FANTOME
SILVER SHORE
THE SOUTH SEA
THE KINGDOM OF VALTERRE

List of Players

ORDER OF THE FLAMES

Seraphine Marchant, *Co-Founder of the Order of the Flames*

Theodore Branch, *Co-Founder of the Order of the Flames*

Valerie, *Co-Founder of the Order of the Flames*

Sabine Fraser, *Co-Founder of the Order of the Flames*

ORDER OF THE DAGGERS

Hugo Ralphe Versini, *Founder of the Order of the Daggers*

Gaspard Dufort, *Former Head of the Order of the Daggers (deceased)*

Ransom Hale, *Head of the Order of the Daggers*

Nadia Raine, *Dagger, Second in Command*

Caruso Dantes, *Dagger, Third in Command*

ORDER OF THE CLOAKS

Armand Versini, *Founder of the Order of the Cloaks*

Madame Cordelia Mercure, *Head of the Order of the Cloaks*

Madame Josephine Fontaine, *Former Head of the Order of the Cloaks*

HOUSE OF RAYERE, THEIR ROYAL HIGHNESSES

Bertrand IV, King of Valterre

Odette I, Queen of Valterre

Andreas Mondragon Rayere, *Prince of Valterre, Bertrand's nephew*

SAINTS OF VALTERRE

Calvin, *Saint of Death*

Celiana, *Saint of Song and Poetry*

Frederic, *Saint of Farmers and Hunters*

Maud, *Saint of Lost Hope*

Maurius, *Saint of Travelers and Seafarers*

Oriel, *Saint of Destiny*

Serene, *Saint of Animals*

Alisa, *Saint of the Sick*

Cadel, *Saint of Warriors*

Calliope, *Saint of Beauty and Youth*

Placido, *Saint of Peace*

Jasper, *Saint of Artisans*

Lucille Versini, *Saint of Scholars*

Part I

Centuries of man-made dark,
Will shatter with a lightning spark.
The storm will choose new saints to crown,
Where three stone towers crumble down.

For one who's not content to wait,
The will of magic denies fate.
They will grasp for their own gain,
For greed thrives where power rains.

Yet not all magic weighs the same.
Beware the maker in this game,
Another chosen by the land,
Will act as destiny's right hand.

Old Valterre will soon divide,
When sword and rose come to collide.
Alliances will be betrayed,
And the Kingdom of the Saints remade.

THE LAST PROPHECY OF ORIEL BEAUREGARD
SAINT OF DESTINY

The Storm

The storm pounded Fantome with a fury that shook the entire city. Even the river trembled. The sky wept and thunder roared, as though it had something vital to say. Up north, where the oldest university in Valterre overlooked the sprawling capital, a young scholar listened intently.

Prince Andreas Mondragon Rayere sat on the windowsill of his dormitory with his forehead pressed against the glass, watching the sky thrash. For years he had waited for this night, and now, at last, it was upon him.

This storm.

This spark.

This grand changing of fate.

He grinned as he hopped off the sill, fetching his rain cloak from a hook on the wall. Shrugging it on, he slipped out into the stone hallway. Oil lamps flickered encouragingly as he rushed down the corridor, swinging around the corner and taking the stairwell three steps at a time. Outside, the storm raged on, and yet the hallowed halls of the Appoline University were eerily silent. The other scholars had tucked themselves away for the night, to read alone in their bedchambers or snatch another hour or two of research in the companionable warmth of the library.

Andreas had spent so many sleepless nights studying among the towering stacks, he could picture every gilded spine in his mind's eye, had even molded the cushions of his favorite wing-backed chair to his liking. All those years of dogged research, chasing the lost words of Saint Oriel felt like mere days now. Here and gone in the blink of an eye.

He had arrived at the Appoline University almost six years ago to the day. A pampered prince of barely sixteen, with soft hands and starry eyes, nine trunks of fine clothes and polished boots, and enough books to build a replica of the Aurore Tower in his bedchamber.

He was a scholar now. His room was littered with hundreds of journals, the feverish scribbles of his findings gathering in an endless swell of parchment. The pads of his fingers were permanently stained with ink, his fair hair had grown long and unkempt, and all his boots were scuffed from long walks in the woodlands that surrounded the university.

From the day Andreas had stepped out of the royal carriage and onto the steps of the Appoline, he had spent every spare moment immersed in the lives of the saints, tirelessly researching the fragments of the last prophecy of Saint Oriel, piecing them together like a jigsaw.

He hoped this was the night he'd been waiting for.

The start of the Second Coming.

Lightning struck, casting the courtyard in stark silver light. The storm was getting angrier. The prince quickened his steps. Down one flight of stairs and then another, the door at the end of the long hall giving way to the sodden quadrangle. Rain kissed his cheeks and slicked his hair as he jogged across it.

Dimly, he was aware of faces watching him from the windows.

At the north end of the courtyard, the door to the clock tower was swinging on its hinges. A sign from Saint Oriel, great diviner of fate! On the large moon-white clock face, the smaller hand was inching toward midnight. Heart thundering, he took the spiraling stone steps three at a time, winding up toward the bells.

His mind reeled with thoughts of what lay beyond tonight. The possibilities . . .

The *power.*

The prince's father—the king's only brother and once-revered commander of Valterre's royal army—had long scorned his son's fanatical interest in the saints. He thought himself cursed with a weak, distractible heir, this boy born for greatness on the battlefield but who had instead lost himself to tattered scrolls and half-forgotten murmurings. A stain on the family crest. A cause for Maud, Saint of Lost Hope.

Ever the contrarian, and a royal princess of neighboring Urnica in her own right, the prince's mother had welcomed her son's academic preoccupations with relief, gladly nudging her only child toward books instead of war. And so, when he'd asked, at sixteen, to go to the Appoline, she had pried open the royal coffers and made it so.

His father couldn't wait to get rid of him, of course.

Many years had passed since the day they'd bid farewell on the steps of the Appoline. The prince had not seen his father since, learned only of his exploits in the missives that came regularly from his mother. And then of his death on the battlefield in the Sunday penny papers.

Good riddance.

Panting now, he reached the top of the clock tower. The narrow door there was unbolted—for what scholar in their right mind would think to climb out in a storm, or indeed at all?

The prince stepped onto the narrow walkway. The clock face crowned him like a halo as he looked west toward the Aurore Tower. It flickered like a candle in the night.

Overhead, lightning forked.

Using the metal hands as footholds, the prince climbed up the clock face.

Shouts reached him from below.

Andreas, you fool, come down from there!

Andreas, you'll fall!

The prince has finally lost his mind!

Andreas! Andreas!

Scholars were gathering on the green of the courtyard. Andreas kept his eyes on the sky, climbing hand over hand and foot over foot until he heaved himself onto the steepled roof of the clock tower. A quick glance over his shoulder revealed the Aurore exploding into a golden blaze. It was brighter than it had been a moment ago—brighter than he had ever seen it.

Magic.

Magic sung in the rising wind.

He stood on trembling legs, planting a foot on either side of the sloping roof.

Below him, echoes of his name gathered in a shrieking chorus.

Andreas!

Andreas!

Andreas!

The sky lit up, a fork of lightning shearing the clouds in two. The prince flung his hands up, reaching for the storm.

"ORIEL, BLESS ME!" he roared as loud as the thunder. "I GIVE MYSELF TO YOU!"

The lightning forked past him, reaching for Fantome like a crooked finger. It slammed into the Aurore, and he watched in horrified wonder as the tower fell before his eyes.

A manic laugh burst from his chest. "The first tower has fallen! The prophecy is coming true!"

The storm swallowed his cries.

He reached toward the next fork of lightning. "ORIEL, CHOOSE ME!"

This one arced over him, too, spearing west, toward the low hanging mists of Ra'azule. Nerves gripped him, his heartbeat so loud, he could hardly hear the terrified screams of his fellow scholars, his professors . . . even the provost, the prince's own stalwart mentor, had come running in his nightcap and dressing gown.

The prince didn't dare take his eyes from the sky. He knew the last prophecy like the lines on his palms. Some days it felt like Oriel had scrawled its promise on the fabric of his soul. One more strike to go. One last chance. He told himself he would not beg. A prince of Valterre wouldn't dare, but desperation got the better of him.

He rose to his tiptoes. "ORIEL, PLEASE!"

The clock tower began to chime. For a moment, it sounded like the heavens were crying out.

Gong!

Gong!

Gong!

Darkness enfolded the Appoline until the prince felt entirely alone in the world. The hair on his head rose in every direction. Even the fine blond wisps on his arms and the back of his neck lifted. His mouth filled with the taste of coppers, and a bead of blood dripped from his nose.

Slowly, the clouds above him parted, as though Saint Maurius himself was peeling them apart. From within, came a spear of jagged silver light.

The prince opened his mouth to swallow it.

It shot through him like a poker.

Back arching now, the agony of it wrenched a scream so loud it stole his voice.

The world turned silver as heat consumed him, chewing his bones to ash. His heart was a volcano, pumping lava through his blood.

No. *No.*

It was too hot. Too bright. Too painful.

He couldn't bear it.

He couldn't *stop* it.

His legs gave out as the clock tower began to crumble, and he slipped down the side of the roof. He grasped feebly at the slates, the stone scraping his back as he slid off the edge like a raindrop.

And plummeted to earth.

When the hard slap of grass came, he didn't feel it. Nor did he hear the horrified screams of his peers as they picked through the fallen rubble to get to him. The prince was lost in the blackness that came after, snared by an ancient, golden gaze that watched him from the shadows of his mind.

Saint Oriel, weaver of fate.

She whispered, *"Thief."*

Three months later

Chapter 1

Seraphine

Seraphine Marchant stood trembling beneath the storm's blinding fury, reaching desperately for the sky. A bell rang under her feet, signaling the changing of the hour.

Gong!

Gong!

Gong!

Lightning skewered her like an arrow, lancing through her in a shock of bone-melting heat. Pain erupted, the world spinning as she fell. In the center of it all, shone a moon-white clock face, slowly tick-ticking on.

Screams rang out, calling her name.

Only it was not her name.

Not my memory.

Not me at all.

Then came the hard slap of earth—

Waking with a strangled gasp, Sera shot upright in her seat. Pippin, who had been napping on her lap, pricked his ears up, a low growl rumbling in his chest. On the bench across from her, Bibi pitched forward, grabbing her hand. "You're all right," she said, squeezing gently. "You were just dreaming."

Still panting, Sera swept the ribbons of her blond hair back from her face. "I must have dozed off."

Bibi's blue eyes pooled with concern. "Was it the same one again?"

Sera frowned, nodding. "The clock tower."

It was almost always the clock tower, those screams that didn't know her, that place she didn't recognize.

"We're here," said Bibi, tugging her away from the memory. "Take a look."

Peering out of the back of the wagon, Sera watched the sleepy village of Aberville unfurl like a setting from a storybook. This quaint town of winding cobbled streets and stone cottages, charming shopfronts crowned in frilled awnings, and the clustering pine forests that cradled it from the chaos of Fantome. The last of the winter frost made everything glitter, crusting the windows and clinging to the rooftops like diamond teardrops.

Nestled in the rolling countryside, Aberville was a considerable journey from the northern mountain village of Halbracht, where they had made their home these past three months. Not that Sera had been bored on the way down here, with Bibi and her beloved mutt Pip for company.

They had passed the days playing cards in the back of the

wagon, Pip chewing happily on Sera's bootlaces while Bibi insisted on a game of I spy whenever they passed through a town or village. They spent their nights in whichever local inn was closest to them when the horses began to tire, Sera smuggling Pippin in underneath her coat, before devouring whatever local stew was on offer.

Bibi leaned out of the window as they came to a stop outside the yellow-bricked cottage that belonged to Othilde Eberhard, the most seasoned smuggler in Valterre. "Look at the size of that garden. I think I see a lake back there."

Outside, birds chirped in the trees, heralding the coming of spring. It had been months since Sera had heard that sound. The mountain hawks of Halbracht preferred to shriek, and if a rogue robin ever chirped, it was quickly outmatched by the braying horses and bleating goats. She took it as a good omen.

They hopped out of the wagon, Sera calling to Remy, their driver, "We won't be long. An hour. Maybe two."

"Show time," muttered Bibi, just as Pippin jumped out after them.

The smuggler's scowling face watched them from the window.

Scooping him up before he could urinate on the snowdrops, Sera cradled Pippin in her arms, hoping to all hell Othilde Eberhard liked dogs.

An hour later, Sera found herself pacing by the lake at the bottom of Othilde Eberhard's garden. She could practically feel the old woman's eyes on the back of her head, watching from her kitchen window. Contemplating the offer Sera and Bibi had just made. In essence, this:

Leave behind the only trade you've ever known.

Wager everything you have on Lightfire.

Lightfire, the antidote to Shade. A golden dust-like substance that could easily nullify the power of Shade's lethal shadows. After managing to sweet-talk themselves into Othilde's cottage, they had presented their offer to her, along with a precious vial. The smuggler had heard about the monsters of Fantome and the power of Lightfire already, and had been intrigued by their offer, listening intently as they explained how they had first discovered the ancient magical antidote to Shade and then what they planned to do with it: perfect the final recipe and flood the city of Fantome until every single person had a store of Lightfire at their fingertips. Protection against the Daggers would weaken their hold on the capital, and eventually banish the dark power of Shade magic for good.

They weren't just presenting a new vocation. They were presenting a new Order. A new world. And they wanted Othilde, who was seasoned and clever and quick with her hands, to be a part of it. Not only as an asset to the Order of Flames but as a vital loss to the Order of Daggers.

After all, fewer smugglers meant less Shade in circulation.

Othilde had broken her silence to call them a pair of disruptors, nicknamed Sera *Trouble* (with begrudging affection), and then shooed them from her house so she could think.

The minutes crawled. Flinging a stick for Pippin, Sera

watched the three-legged terrier run after it like a little gray bullet. Her lips curled into a slow smile. The smell of the pine trees and the long grass brushing against her shins, the trill of birdsong, and the wide bowl of the pale sky all reminded her of home. Closing her eyes, she imagined herself back in the plains, standing in the garden of her old life, playing fetch with Pip. Somewhere behind her, Mama was tending to her flower baskets, pruning the dead leaves and planting daffodil bulbs to flower in the spring.

It was so real this memory. This feeling. Home. *Happiness.* Sera's chest warmed, her cheeks prickling with the sudden nearness of her magic. This strange, unpredictable force had taken root inside her three months ago atop the Aurore Tower. She had come to know it as a kind of fire. A flame lit from within, though she did not understand how it worked, or what it wanted from her. Sometimes, when she was sad or scared or angry, it burned like a bonfire in her heart. But at other times, it was cold and slumbering somewhere beyond her reach.

A gift she couldn't quite unwrap.

A magic that fascinated and confounded her in equal measure.

A secret only her closest friends knew about.

"Mind you don't fall into my lake, Trouble. Old Othilde won't be fishing you out. I have not bent these creaky knees in twenty years."

Her eyes flying open, Sera spun around. Othilde Eberhard was standing in the reeds, wearing a pair of bright red rain boots. Thin as a rake and short as one too, the rest of her was swaddled in an oversized plaid coat. Her long white hair was stark against her olive skin and billowing freely in the wind.

"I have come to my decision."

Seraphine blinked. "That was quick."

Was it? How long *had* she been standing out here, lost in thought? And where had Bibi wandered off to?

Othilde crooked a pale brow. "How long did the other smugglers take to consider your offer?"

"I haven't visited very many," Sera admitted. After she'd fled Fantome and found refuge in Halbracht with Bibi, Val, and Theo, she'd barely had time to catch her breath. Within a matter of weeks, winter had whipped up with such a fury, it had made travel down from Halbracht almost impossible. Her grand plans for Lightfire—for Fantome—had only recently kicked up again. "But the one before you chased me from his garden with an iron skillet, so . . ."

"So, clever old Othilde was not on top of your recruitment list, then."

Really, it wasn't a matter of preference but proximity. "How does top five sound?"

"Sounds like horse manure." Othilde jerked her head, as Pippin came striding back, stick in mouth. He dropped it at her feet. She surrendered a dusty smile. "Did you bring the mutt to sway me?"

"That depends . . . Did it work?"

She picked up the stick and threw it. "All my life, I have lived by the man-made darkness of this kingdom," said Othilde, as

Pip took off again. "But I have heard the whispers of Lightfire. Rumors of a Fantome that might have been, if Lucille Versini had had her way." She shook her head, regret misting her brown eyes. "I never believed those stories until the monsters came. If I had known . . ." She trailed off, her lips twisting. "Perhaps I would have devoted my life to a better cause. A better world. The one our saints left behind."

"There's still time to reach for that world," said Sera, without judgment. It was never simple, the business of Shade smuggling. For many, it simply meant surviving. Crawling out of poverty and pain and hardship and clinging onto life by your fingertips. She would not judge Othilde for the same choices her own mother had made. "There's still time to make your mark on Fantome, Othilde."

They had Mama to thank for that. Sylvie Marchant had given her life to the pursuit of Lightfire. In the end, she had died because of it, nearly dragging Fantome down with her. Months had passed since the monsters she had poisoned began their reign of terror in the city. Hundreds of families were still in mourning. And as for the Order of Daggers . . . Sera still had no idea how many had perished on the night the monsters ripped through the catacombs . . . How many would still be alive if she had climbed the Aurore Tower when she was supposed to and set all those monsters free.

She tried not to think about it. At least when she was awake. When she slept, nightmares plagued her. When she wasn't falling from that clock tower, she relived that awful day on the Aurore over and over again, recalling all too vividly the moment she had been struck by lightning up on the tower, how she had pressed her hand against the chest of the Dagger that had come to kill her.

Lark Delano.

She had scoured him to death with her touch.

Seraphine was no Dagger.

But she *was* a murderer.

Her fingers twitched at the memory.

Othilde's shrewd brown eyes missed nothing. "I think there's time enough for both of us."

Sera's smile was strained. "You should know, the Daggers will be displeased at losing another smuggler. The Cloaks, too. They'll see your decision as an act of—"

"Treason?" Othilde snorted. "What do I care?" She turned to watch Pip emerge from the reeds, this time with three sticks in his mouth. Enterprising little thing. "I chart my own course. And Dufort is dead. Ignorant brute that he was. Never bothered to wipe his feet when he came here. Slurped his tea like a dog. I hardly know the one who usurped him. And I sure as hell don't fear him."

"Ransom." Something inside her lurched at his name, but Sera could never tell if it was hope or dread that caused the strange tugging sensation in her chest. "He's called Ransom."

Her hand twitched again, like it was reaching for the memory of him.

She looked to the water to hide the color in her cheeks. Illicit memories crowded in on her, and for a fleeting moment, she was back in that alleyway, pressed against the cool stone wall as he trailed his lips along her neck, kissing the sensitive spot beneath her ear.

Ransom. *Bastian.* Those autumn eyes. That scar-flecked smile. Shadows crawling up his legs, wreathing his chest . . .

Killer. Lover. Enemy.

She would save him, too.

Whether he liked it or not.

"You worry about Ransom, Trouble, and I'll worry about my stiff joints."

Sera laughed, despite herself. She liked the old smuggler more than she was expecting to.

"Tell me, is Halbracht as beautiful as Aberville?" asked Othilde.

Seraphine weighed her answer. "It's wilder than here. There are waterfalls and evergreens, cliffs and caves, and even the occasional brown bear. The animals there roam freely. I suppose it's less like a fairy tale and more like . . . a great adventure."

The smuggler's dark eyes glittered.

"It's quite a journey from here. Three days at best. And that's if the frost up north continues to melt . . ."

Othilde was already turning from her. "I'll gather my things. You gather your thoughts."

Sighing, Sera watched her go. How badly she wished someone had made this same offer to her—to Mama—before everything spiraled out of hand. She would have leaped at the chance to rewrite their destiny. Hell, she would have dragged Mama out of their farmhouse if she had to.

Her chest warmed, a familiar flare of frustration stoking her magic. Sparks danced along her palms. *Maker,* whispered that ancient voice inside her. The one she had first heard the night the Aurore came down—the night she fell with it. *Choose me. Use me.*

Addled by an all-too-familiar confusion, Sera plucked a weed from the reeds and turned it in her hands. Watched it change from green to gold, the wide, flat head twisting into the delicate petals of a rose.

It glittered in the sunlight, the strange magic holding its shape as she tossed it onto the frozen lake. A fleeting trick. But that voice inside Sera had gone quiet again, seeming satisfied.

These flowers were no great creation, but they were the best she could make. *All* she could make. Sometimes she gifted one to Theo when he was hard at work in the barn back at Halbracht, to Bibi when she was sad and missing House Armand, or to Val, whenever she wanted to piss her off.

"Have I caught you mooning over your reflection?" Bibi called, coming out of the trees, her long red hair tangling in the wind. She adjusted her scarf, allowing Sera a glimpse of the golden teardrop necklace around her neck. A precious bead of Lightfire worn by every member of their Order of Flames, whenever they strayed beyond the safety of Halbracht.

"More like basking in our success," Sera called back. "Othilde is coming back with us."

Bibi did a victory skip, before leaning down to ruffle Pippin's fur. Her brows lowered when she spotted the golden rose sitting on the lake. "Who is that one for?"

Sera shrugged, turning from the lake. "Saint Oriel can decide."

Bibi cut her eyes at her. "You should know better than anyone, Sera . . . taunting a Dagger is like playing with fire."

A smile danced along Sera's lips.

Some things, she just couldn't help.

Chapter 2

Ransom

Othilde Eberhard was as old as the hills of Valterre. A seasoned trader with good prices and prompt delivery, her reliability made her one of the best in the trade. Even at eighty years old and with gnarled hands and fading eyesight, she never missed a shipment.

Until after the Aurore fell.

Ransom didn't notice at first. Barely a few months into his new role as Head of the Order of Daggers, he had other matters to worry about. Like explaining to the King of Valterre how Gaspard Dufort *and* the Aurore Tower—Valterre's long-treasured symbol of light and hope—had both met their end on the same night. And of course, there was also the matter of the terrifying swarm of monsters that had marched through the city and ransacked the catacombs, decimating almost a third of the Order of Daggers and lighting the spark of a rebellion that continued to worsen by the week.

Unease festered across Fantome. And it was catching.

No, Ransom was not thinking about Othilde Eberhard at all.

A rainswept autumn had bled into an unforgiving winter, the snow falling so thick and fast it froze the Verne and crusted the rooftops of Fantome like powdered sugar. Ransom had the fireplace in the Cavern repaired in time for Saintsmas, but the chill still found the Daggers deep in the underbelly of Fantome, making their teeth chatter as they gathered around the crackling flames to drink whiskey and exchange trinkets.

No one mentioned Dufort.

No one sat in his chair.

Caruso suggested burning it for warmth.

While the stores of Shade in Hugo's Passage were full, Ransom didn't spare a thought for the comings and goings of his network of smugglers. He focused, instead, on rebuilding the Order and meeting their clients' growing demands, earning back the trust of his comrades and grieving the loss of his best friend. The dirt on Lark's grave froze too, the nearby statue of Saint Lucille weeping crystalline tears as winter gripped Fantome in its icy grasp and refused to let go.

Slowly, reluctantly, Ransom rose to the challenge of the position he had never truly wanted. Seeking solace in the familiar lick of Shade, in the bone-deep sting of every new shadowmark, he pretended his destiny was always meant to play out in the bowels of Fantome under the ancient eye of Calvin, Saint of Death.

Those first few months were long, and the nights were often sleepless.

But when he dreamed, he dreamed of her.

Seraphine.

The spitfire who had torn down the Aurore and made an enemy of herself. To the Daggers and the Cloaks, to the city and the king himself.

There had been no sign nor word of her since the morning after the Aurore fell, when she had fled north with her trio of fellow Cloaks, her little dog scurrying alongside her.

Ransom was glad Seraphine was gone. Far from the chaos rumbling in the capital, and the danger of his own Order.

And yet . . .

Sometimes he woke from dreams of her with such longing pain lanced through his chest.

For the sake of his sanity he shut all thoughts of her away, allowed his memories to freeze in the endless cold snap that followed her departure and hardened his heart like the ice that slicked the streets of Old Haven.

It worked for a time.

Then, one morning in late winter, Lisette banged on the door to Ransom's bedchamber to tell him their stores of Shade were beginning to dwindle. In the last couple of weeks several of their most prolific traders had vanished, seemingly overnight.

The first disappearance had struck Ransom as unfortunate.

The second had made him suspicious.

By the time Othilde Eberhard went quiet, Ransom knew

something was amiss. And he was sure as hell going to find out what.

He had intended to make the journey to Othilde's place by himself, but as his Second, Nadia insisted on joining him, and when Caruso met them coming out of Hugo's Passage on his way home from a job, he invited himself along for the journey.

As the rising sun dragged itself over the snow-swept city of Fantome, the three Daggers took a carriage out of the city and traveled west toward the village of Aberville.

The journey was long and slow, the winding roads made treacherous with melting frost. Spring was coming but it was taking its damn time.

In the back of the carriage Caruso and Nadia sat next to each other, with their boots kicked up on either side of Ransom. Built like a bear and as tall as one too, Caruso crowded the narrow seat, nudging Nadia over toward the window. Absently, she toyed with the drapes as they traded theories about their disappearing smugglers.

"Maybe it's a matter of loyalty?" Nadia suggested, her frown just visible over the high collar of her wool coat. "Now Dufort's gone, they don't have the stomach for it anymore."

Caruso snorted. "People don't lose their appetite for coin. And they all hated Dufort. He was a callous prick."

"And that's coming from you," said Nadia, with a snort.

Caruso had always been a wildcard. Restless, destructive, forever angry at the world. He was quick to lash out and never one to apologize. He would have been a killer either way. Even if Dufort hadn't put that first vial of Shade in his hands at thirteen years old. Saints knew, he was built like one, and he never fell victim to paltry feelings like regret, or remorse. Or so Ransom assumed. If Caruso was capable of human emotion, he certainly hid it well.

But he was loyal to the bone.

The Daggers were all Caruso had.

The Order was all any of them had.

"At least I'm self-aware," Caruso remarked now. "Dufort thought the sun shone out of his own ass. He wore the shadowmarks on his face like a badge of honor." He jerked his chin toward Ransom, who was staring vacantly out of the window, only half listening. "Our pretty boy here is far more palatable. Polite as a prince. And look at those pearly teeth. You'd never know he was a ruthless bastard."

Ransom gave him the middle finger.

"Everyone's been on edge since the Aurore came down," Nadia went on, as if she hadn't heard him. "Most nights, people are rioting in the streets. I reckon some of our smugglers got spooked too."

"Not Othilde. The old crone once killed a bear with a flying pitchfork. Didn't even blink," said Caruso, admiration simmering in his icy-blue eyes. "She *does* the spooking. Half the village call her a witch. But never to her face." He offered the ghost of a smirk. "Cowards."

"They probably don't want to get pitchforked," muttered Ransom.

"He speaks!" Caruso prodded Ransom with the toe of his

boot. “Now that you’re done sulking, why don’t your share some of your own theories?”

“She’s probably dead,” said Ransom distantly. “It was a harsh winter. Othilde is old and lives alone.”

“Tragic,” murmured Nadia.

“More like boring,” said Caruso with a sprawling yawn. “And that still doesn’t explain the other disappearances.”

Ransom turned his face to the snow-laden fields. He spied smoke up ahead, a whisper of life rising above a stretch of dark spindly trees. The truth was, he had another theory about who had been getting to his smugglers, but he didn’t dare utter it aloud. Nadia had finally stopped obsessing over Seraphine Marchant and her role in Lark’s death, and Ransom was not about to stoke that fire again.

And anyway, it was only a hunch.

A tug of paranoia he had been trying very hard to ignore.

“We’ll figure it out soon enough,” he said, gesturing to the plumes in the distance. “We’re almost there.”

“Finally,” grunted Caruso, shifting in his seat. “My ass is numb.”

“Then how are you still speaking out of it?” said Nadia.

Ransom sighed. “Behave, children. You’re giving me a headache.”

As they hopped out of the carriage and sauntered up the stone path that led to Othilde Eberhard’s cottage, Ransom felt like they were walking into a painting. In the front garden snowdrops bowed under the weight of the morning dew frost. Empty flower baskets hung on either side of the blue front door, where frozen spiderwebs sparkled in the sun.

There was no smoke coming from the chimney, no lights flickering inside.

Caruso peered in the front windows, while Nadia tracked around the back of the house.

Ransom thumped his fist against the front door. "Othilde?"

After a minute of silence he kicked it in.

Caruso stepped over the threshold after him, inhaling through his nose. "Stale smoke." Another sniff. "Curdled milk. Hmm . . . no decomposing corpse."

"Why do you sound so disappointed?" said Ransom.

Caruso whistled to himself as he moved about the kitchen, methodically ransacking his way through every single cupboard. Ransom noted an empty pot in the sink and an old loaf in the bread bin. Covered in mold. The milk in the jug on the table had indeed curdled and the apples were rotten.

He left Caruso and wandered through the adjacent sitting room. There was a ball of wool on the chair by the window, a half-knitted green scarf trailing from it. A cold pipe in the ashtray. He continued upstairs, searching the pokey bedrooms.

No sign of Othilde.

Or her corpse.

Unease stirred in Ransom's gut.

When he returned downstairs, Caruso had torn up some of the floorboards. The crawl space underneath the kitchen was empty, save for three cracked vials.

When Nadia returned from the garden, she was frowning.

"There's nothing left. Not a root or a leaf. Even her compost heap has been emptied."

Caruso bit off a curse. "Where the hell did she go?"

Nadia stared out of the window toward the trees. Her brown eyes took on a familiar vacant look, and Ransom knew that she was thinking of Lark. She was always thinking of Lark, her best friend, her lover. They had had a plan to run away together. She'd confessed it, three whiskeys deep, to Ransom over Saintsmas. They were going to lose themselves in a place like Aberville, marry and build a farm. Build a life far from the catacombs and leave the business of killing behind them.

Now Lark was dead.

And so was the plan.

Ransom came to her side.

"We should have buried him back home," she murmured. "By the trees on his mother's farm. He loved it there. He would have wanted that."

Ransom's stomach twisted. "We can visit him in Old Haven."

Not that he ever did. He couldn't bring himself to.

"And talk to the frozen grass." She gave a mirthless snort. "Corpses don't talk back."

"That's my favorite thing about them," said Caruso.

Ransom tossed him a warning look. "Not helpful."

"Neither is this depressing heart-to-heart." Caruso stretched, passing a hand over his shaved head. He had had to cut off his wild dark hair the night the monsters ripped his skull open down in the catacombs. As the sun rose over the weeping city of Fantome, Caruso had stood, bloodless and half dead, in front of the mirror and sewed the wound shut. Badly. Now he had a gruesome scar above his left ear to show for it.

"And you wonder why you sleep alone, Caruso." Nadia's voice hardened as she stepped away from the window. "We should search the forest."

"Why?" Caruso cocked his head. "Do you think the old bat went out there to lay eggs?"

She glared at him. "Maybe a monster took her."

"The monsters are dead," said Ransom.

"How do you know they're all gone?" She turned her pointed glare on him. "*We* didn't make them. And we sure as hell didn't kill them."

"You hardly think they've been playing hide-and-seek in that creepy forest this entire time?" said Caruso. "You're supposed to be the smart one, Nadia."

"And you were supposed to stay home today." She punched him in the arm. "I don't see you coming up with any bright ideas."

"I'm not the ideas guy. I'm the murder guy."

"We're *all* the murder guy," she reminded him.

"Only until the last of our Shade runs dry. Then I'll just use my hands." Caruso cracked his knuckles, the olive skin there covered in shadow-marks, just like the rest of him. "The question is, what will *you* do, princess?"

"I'll jam my stiletto heel through your left eye."

He arched a dark brow. "You know it turns me on when you talk like that."

“You are insufferable,” she huffed.

Ransom left them to their bickering, glad to hear the bite returning to Nadia’s voice. He preferred it over the grief that so often lingered there. The *blame.* Slipping out of the back door, he did his own patrol of the garden. It was eerily quiet outside, the forest making a stark outline against the white sky.

The back of his neck began to prickle as he scanned the trees. Grabbing a vial from his pocket, he took the barest sip of Shade. Just enough to light up the shadows and to keep his own close in case he needed them.

He had come too far, survived too much, to die to a flying pitchfork.

The forest winked to light. It was still. He scrubbed his hands through his hair, ashamed of his own paranoia.

Stalking onward, he headed toward the slow-swaying trees, where the frozen lake reflected the pallid sky. The first time Ransom had come here more than six years ago, as part of a negotiation trip with Dufort, there were swans in this lake.

Two of them.

He had stood in this very same spot, thinking of his mother and his sister, Anouk, as he watched them gliding back and forth on the water.

Now the lake was empty, and Ransom was thinking of someone else. Closing his eyes, he could almost scent her on the wind—a whisper of lemon blossoms and, just beneath it, the barest hint of gunpowder. He could almost feel the ghost of her standing beside him, looking into the same lake. Humming. Plotting.

He snapped his eyes open, finding his own reflection staring back him.

Seraphine.

What are you up to?

Something flickered at the edge of his vision. A flower glowing on the ice. Frowning, he trudged around the edge of the lake to reach it.

It was a golden rose. Artificial and perfect and perched on the ice as though someone had left it there just for him.

Steadying himself with a whip of shadow, he reached over the sheen of ice to pluck it.

His fingers tingled, the familiar brush of magic drawing a sharp inhale. It shot through him like a ray of sunlight, licking the Shade from his bones and shredding the shadows around him. The rose crumbled. The stem first and then the head, falling away in petals of gold and amber, until, for the briefest moment, it looked like a flame kissing the palm of his hand.

Shining flecks of ash sifted through his fingers, and then they were gone too.

Struck still at the edge of the lake, he stared down at his own reflection. There was a wildness in his eyes now, a wildness beating in his chest.

Sera hadn't just been here; she had left a calling card for him.

An invitation to a new game.

His smile curled, slow and lethal.

Saint Oriel was not yet done with them.

Chapter 3

Seraphine

The mountain wind whistled in Seraphine's ears as she pitched forward in her saddle and vaulted across the treeline. The last of the pines fell away as the land spilled out before her, the rolling meadow seeming to go on and on. In the far-off distance, the towering Silvercrests clustered together like craggy elders, their stony peaks crowned by the last dusting of winter's snow.

Not long after returning home from Aberville, spring had exploded across the secluded mountain village of Halbracht in a riot of blooming color. Sera had been starving for it, eager to gulp down the warm air while the sun tanned her face, scattering freckles across the bridge of her nose.

Sensing her restlessness, Paola Versini, Theo's aunt, had lent Sera her horse before leaving for the city with their first trial shipment of Lightfire, a modest crate of two hundred vials.

After spending weeks on the road visiting smugglers, Sera had jumped at the chance to ride away her stress and take a break from official Order business for a couple of hours.

She rose to her haunches. "Yah! Fly, Trapper!"

Trapper was like an arrow beneath her, the black stallion's strides lengthening with ease. Welcoming the giddiness of this fleeting freedom, she inhaled the scent of the wildflowers as she trampled them, letting the wind thread her hair like soft fingers. For the first time in months, her mind emptied of all thought and worry. There was only the thunder of hooves, then—the joy of riding, so pure and simple, it bubbled into laughter.

Bunching the reins in one hand, she flung the other out wide, grinning at the cloudless sky. With her long blond hair streaking through the air behind her, she imagined she was flying like one of the hawks overhead, the world whipping past in whorls of blue and green and gold.

The sudden spike of joy roused the magic in her soul. It flared to life, filling her with a familiar rush of warmth.

Maker, it whispered, as if saying hello.

Not now. She shoved it back. *Not while I'm riding.*

Sera tightened her hold on the reins. A wooden fence edged into view. Beyond it, stood the large red barn where Theo was working side by side with Othilde and some of the other smugglers they had convinced to join their cause. Grinding and mixing the heaping vats of Lightfire, perfecting the bulk recipe they had been poring over for months.

"Faster!" cried Sera.

Trapper obliged, his hooves flying so swiftly they barely

touched the ground. Her magic grew hotter, the well inside her tunneling deeper.

No, no, no.

Sparks danced around her like fireflies, and her eyes began to burn.

Maker, came that whisper again. *Choose me. Use me.*

Frustration needled Sera, her stomach twisting at the heat rising inside her. She was struck by the frightening realization that she was losing control. It was too much, this fire licking at her ribcage, this ring of embers in her throat. She didn't know how to shove it down. How to put it out.

She didn't know what it wanted.

The reins started to sizzle.

Cursing, she dropped them. The strap, now sheared in two, tumbled to the ground before she could snatch it.

Pitching forward, she reached for the bridle. "Whoa there!"

Trapper jolted, his strides growing unsteady.

"EASY, TRAPPER!" Sera shouted but when she fisted her hands in his mane, the horse's coarse dark hair began to sizzle. Panic shot through her as she snapped her hands away.

Oh no. No, no, no, no.

Hunching forward, she curled her hands into fists, trying to keep her balance. Fear stoked her magic, the force of it overriding all logical thought. The heat of it filled her mouth, made her nose run.

Trapper tossed his head about, his brown eyes wide and frightened.

"Slow down! Please!" She was desperately trying not to hurt

him. Not to hurt herself. But she was a living flame, and she couldn't put herself out.

Trapper bucked.

Sera screamed as she was thrown backward. The world reeled, the sky giving way to solid grass, then the painful thud of the earth.

She woke to the screeching of a hawk. Planting her hands in the dirt, she tried to hoist herself up, but she was too winded. She sucked down a labored breath. And another. Like a cat slinking away, the heat inside her vanished. The force of her landing must have knocked her magic back into submission.

Good.

Less good: her left shoulder was throbbing awfully, and there was grass between her teeth. *"Ugh."*

The distant rattle of hoofbeats told her that Trapper was still bolting. The poor creature must be terrified of her. Sera didn't blame him. She was terrified of herself.

And *sore.*

Hurried footsteps sounded nearby. "Hell's teeth, Sera. Are you all right?"

She managed to lift her head. Theo was jogging toward her. His loose white shirt was rolled up at the sleeves, showing his tanned arms, and there was a streak of gunpowder on his cheek. His silver hair was tied into a knot on the crown of his head, which meant she could perfectly see the horror in his turquoise eyes.

"Been better," she managed to eke out. "I fell." She spat out a blade of grass. "Spectacularly."

"Uh-huh. I saw. And heard." He hunkered down beside her. "You told me you could ride a horse upside down with your eyes closed."

"That was before I got stuffed full of this stupid magic." She managed to sit up. Her head was spinning and her shoulder was definitely dislocated. "I was having too much fun, so it decided to bubble up and ruin my day. Poor Trapper."

Theo was frowning, his eyes on the grass where she had been laying.

She followed his gaze to the handprint she had burned into the dirt. The grass around it was white, the earth completely scoured. Dead. For a heartbeat, she was seized by the memory of the same print on Lark's bare chest, right before she killed him.

What if this time it had been Trapper? Or Theo?

Scrabbling backward, she said, "It's getting worse, Theo. I don't know how to control it. I don't know what it wants from me."

Only that it wanted *something.*

Maker, echoed that ancient voice in her soul.

She wished she could rip it out and strangle it, *demand* to know what the hell it wanted.

Theo scrubbed a hand across his jaw. "You'll figure it out, Sera. We'll work on it."

"We've *been* working on it."

Sera was tired of failing. Of standing in fields with Theo,

trying to make her magic do *something*, only for it to sit like lead in her bones. Tired of sitting in the stillness of the pine forest, forcing her thoughts inward, searching the maze of her own mind, only to be met with painful memories and locked doors, dark rooms full of prowling fears. She was tired of watching Theo huff impatiently as he paced back and forth, unable to hide the frustration on his face. They had spent months trying to figure out the power in her veins. And the only conclusion Sera had come to was this: "It feels like it's growing . . . restless."

He frowned. "You just have to try harder."

She glared at him.

He opened his mouth, then closed it again, thinking better of whatever he was going to say. "We'll talk about it later. Get yourself down to the healer. I'll go and find some apples and bribe Trapper into the stables before Paola gets back from the city. I swear she loves that horse more than me."

"That's because Trapper doesn't complain about her cooking."

"That was *one* time," he muttered, sauntering off. "She knows I hate beets."

Sera lumbered back up the hill, with her shoulder cradled in a sling. She made for the barn, which, with the permission of Paola Versini and the village elders, they had converted to their headquarters shortly after their arrival at Halbracht. It was a far cry from the grandeur of House Armand, but what the Order of Flames needed most—beyond music rooms and luxurious dining quarters—was a place for huge vats and wooden barrels, crates and workbenches, and . . . well, covert experimentation.

The barn was perfect.

In the evenings, they ate and slept in Paola's house, a three-bedroom wooden cabin nestled up mountain, on an outcropping that overlooked the entire village. Bibi, Val and Seraphine shared the bedroom at the back, while Theo bunked with his younger cousin, Tobias. The house was cozy and warm, and thanks to Paola's impressive culinary skills, often smelled like stew.

Inside the old red barn, the atmosphere was pleasantly industrious. Othilde was at her workbench, inspecting the boneshade Tobias had harvested earlier that day. The other reformed smugglers were sitting outside on their break, sharing a sandwich.

Sunlight streamed in through the high windows, making the golden blooms of boneshade glimmer. They were already crisping around the edges, ready to be baked and crushed into Lightfire.

"That better not be your grinding arm," said Othilde, giving Sera a quick glance-over. Her knife came down with a satisfying *thwack*, perfectly shearing a head of boneshade in two without even looking.

"Please contain your concern for my health, Othilde," said Sera dryly. "It should heal up in a couple of days."

"I can grind!" said Tobias, making a point to flex his nonexistent biceps. "Look at these weapons."

Othilde prodded one. "If by weapon you mean toothpick."

"Hey!"

"Hey, yourself!" She mussed his hair. "You're thirteen, boy. Don't be in such a rush to grow up. We already have our hands full with that one."

She gestured to where Theo was sitting on the edge of the largest vat in the barn. Tobias was like a miniature version of his cousin. They shared the same silver hair and wide turquoise eyes. Versini eyes. Same mischievous spirit, too. Mere days after her arrival at Halbracht, Tobias had used his charm to worm his way into Othilde's affections, appointing himself as her prized apprentice. He had even convinced her to help him make fireworks for the upcoming King's Day celebrations, despite the elders' law that expressly forbade them.

"Frankly, the more of me around here, the better," said Theo as he leaned over the pool of Lightfire, using a long stick to pop the bubbles on top. "I think we might have put too much gunpowder in this batch."

"Careful!" Sera lunged, grabbing the end of his shirt. "The last time you did that, the whole barrel exploded."

"Afraid I'll absorb all this volatile magic?" he teased. "Maybe I'll give you a run for your money."

She rolled her eyes. "Because two walking infernos are better than one."

"Danger loves company."

"Can I have a go of the big knife?" asked Tobias.

Othilde snorted. "When I am dead and buried under the trees."

"But I want—"

"*Phwist!* No talking when Othilde is chopping."

Sera was looking for a way to make herself useful when Val stalked into the barn, looking livid. And damp. Her purple-tinted dark curls were plastered to the sides of her face and her traveling cloak was soaking wet. Even her nose ring was askew.

Her ankle boots squelched with each stomp. Glancing at Sera's sling, she said, "Whatever happened to you today, there's no *way* it was worse than what Bibi and I just endured."

Theo hopped down from his perch. "Don't tell me you drowned someone."

"Wish I did." Val shrugged off her travelling cloak, revealing a wrinkled blouse. "Bibi and I went to see Farrah Varnel."

Another smuggler on their list. According to Othilde, Varnel was open-minded enough to be reasoned with, and ambitious enough to warrant a house call.

"Waste of our time," Val huffed.

"Did Varnel throw you in the river?" asked Tobias.

"Worse," she grumbled. "The minute she spied us at her gate, she charged like a bull. Said the Daggers would have our heads and hers too if we took another step. I guess they had already paid her a visit. When we tried to talk her around, she shouted for her farmhands." She stopped abruptly, inhaling through her nostrils like she was working up to the next part. "They threw *manure* at us."

Sera flinched. "Oh, Val . . ."

Tobias burst into laughter.

Othilde flicked his ear.

Grabbing one of the large drying sheets from the rack, Sera

threw it around Val's shoulders. "I'm sorry, Val. The Daggers must have spooked her pretty badly."

She should have known Ransom wouldn't take any of this lying down. A part of Sera didn't *want* him to, but now she regretted fanning the flames of his ire. Taunting him with that rose back at Aberville. If only she had known her friends were going to pay for it . . . In *manure.*

"Save your pity for Bibi. She's still trying to get the cow shit out of her dress. And the wagon is a complete mess. We jumped in the Hellerbend the minute we got back."

"You should go for another swim," crowed Tobias. "You've still got shit in your hair!"

Othilde clipped him again. "Next time, I will put soap in your mouth."

"You can hardly tell," said Theo, smoothly. "You still look good to me."

Val always looked good. With her smooth brown skin scattered with freckles, high cheekbones, and those large brown eyes, she was a study in beauty. Even when damp. And despairing.

"Where is your better half?" Val demanded now. "You're not working nearly hard enough to cheer me up. I need the mutt."

"Pip's up at the cabin," said Sera. "Go on up and change."

"There's gin in the tall cupboard by the sink," added Theo. "That'll take the edge off."

Grumbling her thanks, Val stomped off.

"Farrah Varnel should have flipped while she had the

chance," said Theo, once the barn door had groaned shut. "Once we flood Fantome with Lightfire, Shade will lose its sway over the people there. Its value to the smugglers will plummet. Varnel will be destitute."

"Let's see how the trial shipment goes first," said Sera, keeping a wary eye on that bubbling vat. Best not get ahead of themselves just yet. Today had been a loss, on more fronts than one. Bibi and Val were hurt *and* humiliated, her magic was more volatile than ever, and despite her strongest efforts, she was thinking of Ransom. Again.

Ugh.

"When is Paola due back?"

"A week or so. She's going to stick around and monitor the Lightfire shipment."

"That means a week of bad dinners," groused Tobias.

"Which reminds me, you're cooking tonight," said Theo, patting Sera on the back.

She rounded on him. "My shoulder's dislocated!"

He smiled blandly. "*Was* dislocated."

"I hate cooking."

"Remember our agreement? Total equality in the Order of Flames."

"Fine." She stormed off, tossing a parting threat over her shoulder. "But we're having beets."

Chapter 4

Ransom

The midnight air thrummed with distant hoofbeats as Ransom prowled along the Verne, treading an all-too familiar path. Nightguards patrolled the city, trying to stamp out the rising flames of rebellion. But dissent was spreading across Fantome, and it was catching in the outlying towns and villages too.

The people were unsettled, unsafe. Without their beloved Aurore, they believed the fate of the kingdom was changing. That King Bertrand himself had deserted them during their hour of need, sitting safe and cossetted in one of his many castles while a plague of ravenous monsters had stalked the city, leaving a trail of death and destruction in their wake.

Even now, they feared the monsters would return to Fantome.

And there would be no one to protect them when they did.

All along the riverbank, the royal banners burned. On clear nights, fires flickered across the rooftops like stars, as effigies of the king hung from some of the oldest buildings in Valterre. A clear-throated message from its people:

Fantome no longer bows before its king.

Rebellion had taken root in the heart of the kingdom, which meant the king's enemies were growing in number every week. The Daggers had never been busier. And all the while, Seraphine Marchant was working tirelessly against them, paying calculated visits to Ransom's network of smugglers in a bid to lure them to her side and choke his supply of Shade. She was a different, more dangerous kind of threat. She wasn't running around his city, burning flags and desecrating royal statues. She was stripping away the age-old man-made power of Fantome, bit by bit.

Clever. Taunting.

He should have resented her for it. And yet, there was a part of him that enjoyed the challenge, that relished the creeping sense that their paths might cross once more. What had become of his once-innocent farmgirl in the months since he'd last seen her? This calculating creature remade with vengeance and Lightfire. If he saw her again, would she burn him? Would he let her come close enough to try?

Dangerous thoughts.

A cat darting from a nearby alley jolted Ransom from his thoughts. The city returned in a flood of noise and color. When he looked up, he was standing outside the townhouse that belonged to Benoit Renard, one of the richest merchants in

Valterre. An oil lamp flickered in a window on the fourth floor, casting shadows on the drapes. Renard was about to meet one more.

Downing a vial of Shade, Ransom barely registered the acrid taste as he yanked a shadow from the drainpipe and climbed up the trim redbrick exterior. The sash window was wide open, saving him the trouble of kicking it in. He slipped inside, parting the drapes, like a reaper coming through the gates of hell.

And was met with a stifled curse.

Renard was standing at the end of his bed in his nightcap and gown, brandishing a brass poker. "Figured you'd show up sooner or later," he said, in a voice that was commendably even.

Pulling a shadow off the wall, Ransom said, "That's what happens when you plot to kill your king, Renard."

Renard's pale face went translucent. The poor fool really thought he would get away with it.

"Next time you pay a gang of toothless mercenaries to assassinate the most protected man in Valterre, make sure they're not a bunch of blabbering drunkards," said Ransom, slowly winding the shadow into a noose. "Actually, never mind. There won't be a next time."

Renard found his voice. "Perhaps not for me. But others will try. The king's days are numbered. The People's Saint is coming. His followers grow by the day. You cannot kill us all."

Despite his urgency to get this over with, Ransom paused. *The People's Saint.* This was the second time in less than a week that a mark had pledged their dying allegiance to a saint that Ransom had never even heard of.

Renard's yellowed teeth glowed in the dimness. "The old ways are changing, Dagger. The king has failed his people, failed the memory of our blessed saints. Fate has given us a new one. He who will stand up to monsters and protect his people. Courage is catching throughout Valterre." He dared a sneer. "I suspect it will be bad for your business."

"Maybe." Ransom feigned a shrug, shoving his curiosity aside. A distracted Dagger made for a runaway mark. "But not quite yet."

He tossed the shadow-noose, tightening the shadows around Renard's throat just as the wily trader whipped a vial from his pocket. It smashed on the floorboards between them, scorching the bedchamber with blinding bright light.

The Shade left Ransom like a swift and violent wind.

"Fuck," he hissed, falling to his knees.

Fuck.

As the light cleared, he spied the broken vial on the floor, the label as small as his thumbnail. A single burning flame. He blinked up at Renard just as the bastard swung the brass poker. It smashed into the side of Ransom's head. He sagged against the bedpost, barely dodging the next blow. Staggering to his feet, he stumbled backward, hitting the windowsill.

"Where did you get that Lightfire?" he said, half slurring.

Renard paused, poker raised. "Bought it from a trusted trader yesterday morning. Cost a pretty penny. Though I've been assured the next batch will be cheaper."

Seraphine. Ransom swallowed the name like a bitter pill as he slipped another vial of Shade from his pocket. *Always bring a spare.* He resented the waste, but he was not losing his mark tonight.

Renard reached for another vial. This one exploded in his pocket. He cursed, desperately swinging his poker.

Ransom ducked. By the time Renard swung again, the Shade was already working its way down Ransom's gullet. Renard drew back, his hands trembling. All out of Lightfire, then.

Ransom pulled every shadow off the wall and smothered the screaming merchant, brass poker and all. He collapsed in a sea of blackness.

Rubbing the growing welt on his head, Ransom perched on the windowsill and counted to ten.

When he pulled the shadows off, the whites of Renard's eyes were black, his mouth still open mid-scream. Ransom looked away, his stomach turning. Every kill—every mark—took him one step further from the freedom he had almost won all those months ago. From the one who had believed he was worth saving.

How wrong she had been about him.

"Where is your precious People's Saint now?" he muttered, bending down to take Renard's signet ring. A gift for the king. He pocketed it, then paused, taking a piece of the broken vial of Lightfire too. On the way home, he stuffed his hands into his coat pockets, idly running the pad of his thumb over that tiny golden flame.

So, Lightfire had finally made its way to the city. He wondered how long it would be until it flooded the streets, filling the cupboards and pockets of criminals and townsfolk alike. Until it suppressed Shade for ever.

A familiar bronze-flecked cerulean gaze flooded his mind, his thoughts turning to the music of her laugh and that smart, curving mouth. His spitfire was quicker than he thought . . . but for all her boldness, she was not yet winning. The Order of Daggers had never been busier. With the growing unrest caused by the monsters of Fantome, and the rise of the mysterious People's Saint, enemies of the Crown were cropping up like cockroaches, and the king was keen to stomp them all out. Ransom was the boot, and the coin had never been better. It would take more than a few vials of Lightfire to topple the Daggers.

But Seraphine was clever enough to know that.

And strangely, he found himself welcoming her next move.

It gave him something to look forward to.

As he neared Old Haven, his thoughts returned to Renard, whose dying threat had sounded so eerily similar to the last words of Ravi Dyrren. Dyrren was a prisoner who had spent over a decade in the king's dungeon, and a decade more on the king's battlefield before that. War had turned him bitter, the lack of coin that came after a gruesome leg injury on the Urnica border igniting a desperation that made him dangerous to the Crown. Dangerous to the city. He was one of many former soldiers who nursed long-worn grudges against the king.

Dyrren had been in the Iron Keep, the oldest prison in Valterre, until two weeks ago, when out of the blue, the doors had been thrown open, the head guard freeing hundreds of prisoners and scattering seasoned mercenaries and deadly enemies of the Crown across the plains of Valterre.

He'd been hanged for it the next day, but by then it was too late.

Like Renard, Dyrren had gone down swinging, spittle foaming through the gaps of his missing teeth as his eyes turned black. And still he managed to hiss a parting shot that now haunted Ransom.

Where one of us falls, ten more will rise.
The Age of Kings is coming to an end.
The People's Saint is rising,
And we will follow him into fire and death.

Well, Dyrren had been right about the death part. But had a brand-new saint truly come? Could such a magic be real? Or did they have a trickster on their hands?

The question nipped at his heels as he neared the catacombs. Already Ransom could feel his new shadow-mark taking root. It licked the skin of his lower left rib like a cold flame. A familiar hollowness yawned inside him, turning his steps sluggish.

The clouds over Old Haven were soft, the air balmy with the beginnings of spring. But there was a coldness here that had nothing to do with the seasons and everything to do with death: the nearness of it in the graveyards, the promise of it slumbering down in the catacombs.

Up ahead, the statue of Saint Lucille edged into view. Ransom stripped a shadow from a nearby lamppost and cast it around her neck. A sharp tug revealed the entrance to Hugo's Passage, the doorway groaning as it opened.

"Wait!" There came a sharp, panicked cry, and from the

dark behind the statue, a boy leaped into his path.

Ransom skidded to a stop. "What the hell are you doing?"

The boy gasped a breath as he looked up at him. He couldn't have been any more than ten years old. Short and scrawny, with a mop of black hair and wan skin. "Wait," he said again. "Please."

"Have you lost your mind, kid?" Ransom stepped backward, conscious of the spill of shadows between them. "Do you know what I am?"

"Ransom Hale," said the boy, without blinking. He did well to keep the tremor from his voice, but his glassy eyes were wide and fearful. "Head of the Order of Daggers."

A trap, surely. A trick of some sort. Ransom whipped his head around, searching the night for others who might be lying in wait.

All was still.

"I came by myself," said the boy, reading the suspicion on his face. "I've been waiting all night."

Ransom cocked his head. "Are you looking to die?"

He shook his head. "I want to be a Dagger."

Hell's teeth.

Saint Oriel had a twisted sense of humor. Or was this the work of Maud, Saint of Lost Hope, sending a tremulous child to his door?

"Step back. Into the light."

The boy nearly tripped over himself in his eagerness to obey. In the flickering lamplight, Ransom could better study him. He noted the tattered hem of his stained shirt, the scuff of his shoes. There was a faded yellowed bruise under his left eye, another along his jaw.

Ransom's gut twisted. It felt for a moment like he was staring down the barrel of his own childhood, seeing himself the day Dufort had plucked him from the banks of the Verne like a discarded penny.

"What's your name?"

"Fabian," the boy said.

"Where have you come from?"

"Nowhere, really."

Ransom arched a brow. "Where are your parents?"

"Don't have any."

Ransom folded his arms across his chest.

The boy blushed. "Mama died last summer."

"And your father?"

"He ain't no father. We don't fit. Him and me."

Ransom didn't press the matter. It was sketched well enough on the boy's face. "I see."

The boy raised his chin, hands fisted by his sides. "Can I stay?"

Ransom almost laughed. "Obviously not."

Frowning, the boy began to plead. "I can help you. I can—"

"No." The word was crisp and final. Ransom had done a great many terrible things—made cruel, unforgivable choices in life—but he would not become what Dufort had been to him. "Run along. The orphanage will have you."

"I can spy!" cried the boy. "Nobody notices me in the taverns! Down in the harbor, the sailors guzzle their beer and shoot their mouths off. King's days are numbered, they say!"

"Shut your mouth!" hissed Ransom. He almost grabbed the boy to shake some sense into him, but then he'd be dead in ten heartbeats, and Ransom was not in the business of killing children. "Careful what you say about the king in these streets. Fantome is crawling with nightguards. And Daggers." He gave him a meaningful glare. "Even careless words are punishable by death. Don't you know that?"

The boy swallowed. "I was only saying—"

"Don't," said Ransom. "Mind your tongue or you'll be belly up in the Verne before you know it. You're too young for this life."

Fabian's eyes flashed. "You don't know me."

Ransom gave a mirthless huff. The boy was him, ten years ago on the banks of the Verne. All anger and desperation, too eager to barter his soul for a hot meal and a warm bed. For a chance not to feel afraid anymore.

"Go." Arcing around him, Ransom headed for the stone steps. "I won't tell you again."

The boy trailed after him. "Go where? I can't go back home."

"There is no future for you here, Fabian. Only darkness."

Fabian jutted out his chin. "I ain't afraid of no darkness."

"You will be when it gets its claws into you. When it chokes you as you sleep and fills your head with monsters you can never outrun."

Fabian swallowed, fear making his lip tremble. "Please," he whispered.

Ransom paused with his foot on the step. He wavered for a

moment, some quiet maddened part of himself truly considering taking the child in, before he remembered . . .

He was a killer, tied to an unforgiving fate. Not a life raft but an anchor that would only drag the boy down. If he took this child in, he'd be no better than Dufort.

"Head east to the Hollows," he told the boy. "Run until the streetlamps wink out, and then look up. Wait for the shadows to bend. The shape in the dark is House Armand, home of the Order of Cloaks." He glanced toward the parting clouds. "The moon is generous tonight. Knock if you can find a door. Scream if you can't."

The boy nodded, taking it all in.

"Ask for Cordelia Mercure. Plead your case. Show her those nimble hands and that steely spirit. Don't say I sent you."

Again, the boy nodded.

"I don't ever want to see you in Old Haven again," said Ransom, adding a cruel bite to his voice. "If I do, that whip of shadow is going around your neck." He sold the lie through bared teeth. "Understood?"

The boy gulped, backing up.

"One last thing," said Ransom, before thinking better of it. "Your father. Tell me his name. Where he lives."

The boy did, and Ransom added the name to the list in his head. *The marked and the damned.* This one he would do for free. So someday, when he was big enough and strong enough, Fabian wouldn't have to. What was one more shadow-mark among the many new ones on his ribs, his chest? By the time the Order was done with him, his body would be a tapestry of death. And nothing more.

"Now run like your life depends on it."

When the boy hesitated, Ransom ripped the shadows from the cobbles and sent them chasing after him.

He never screamed but he bolted like a deer into the night.

Ransom waited until his footfall faded, then he blew out a long breath, and turned once more for the steps.

"We could have used him, Ransom." Nadia was standing at the entrance, haloed by a banner of skulls. "Our numbers are down."

Ransom glared at her. "He's a child, Nadia."

"We were all children when we came here."

Ransom stalked past her. "And look how that turned out."

"He'll meet his death on the streets," she called after him.

"At least he won't go to hell when he does," he called back.

She said nothing, then, and he welcomed the damp, stony silence.

He was not in the mood to talk morality with Nadia tonight. He was not in the mood to talk at all. Sleep was gnawing at his edges, and with it, the nightmares that chased him into oblivion.

Chapter 5

Seraphine

Sera raced through the winding catacombs of Hugo's Passage, desperately trying to find her way out. Her feet squelched, the endless puddles of blood clinging to her boots like oil. Somewhere close by, a monster roared.

She pivoted, turning into a narrow side passage, and came upon Gaspard Dufort. Her father. Silver-eyed and seething, he was on his knees, choking on his own blood.

"Traitor!" *he hissed at her.* "Murderer!"

Panicking, Sera spun around. She tried to retrace her steps but the tunnels were changing. The walls huddled closer, darkness enveloping her like a shroud. When it cleared, she was alone again. Standing in the crypt of Lucille Versini, looking down at the skeleton of a long-dead girl. The tiara on her head still glittered.

Sera reached out to take it.

"Spitfire." She froze as familiar hands came around her waist,

drawing her backward. Ransom's warm breath caressed the shell of her ear, his voice gruff with want. "Let's play again."

She closed her eyes. "You were supposed to come to me."

"I'm here now, Seraphine." His lips brushed against her neck. "Can't you feel me?"

Desire seized her, stoking the heat of her magic. She whirled around, twisting her fingers in his collar. "Ransom, I—"

A scream built in her throat, and she stumbled backward, away from the arms that held her.

Lark Delano stood before her, bare-chested and sneering. "Murderer."

Blood seeped through his teeth, and that golden handprint on his skin flared, pricking tears in her eyes. "He'll kill you before he'll have you."

He lunged and she recoiled, hitting the edge of the coffin. She had forgotten about it entirely, but now she was stumbling.

No, falling—

Something crackled underneath her, soft velvet caressing her arms as she tried to sit up. There were bones everywhere. She tried to claw her way out, but the spindly arms of Lucille's skeleton folded around her.

She was tugged down into the coffin.

"Murderer," the skull of Lucille Versini whispered in her ear. "You are no better than them."

The coffin lid slammed shut.

Darkness swept in, the smell of wet earth and rotting wood filling her nostrils. Sera opened her mouth to scream, but dirt poured in, muffling the sound. There was a terrible burning in her chest, as though the skin there had caught fire. Her lungs swelled with the damp earth, and still she breathed, clawing desperately at the wood above her until her fingernails bled. Ice seeped into her bones, freezing her hands and numbing her toes.

"I'm not dead," she choked out, in a voice that did not belong to her. "Let me out!

Let me out! Let me out! Let me out!"

Sera woke with a jolt, her hand coming to her mouth just in time to strangle her scream. It eked out in a pathetic whimper. Silent tears streamed down her cheeks as her magic rioted inside her.

Maker, it hissed. *Let me out!*

A burning scent filled her nose, and she looked down to find a blackened hole in her sheets. She must have fisted them in a panic. Stifling a curse, she glanced around the bedroom. Silvered moonlight streamed in through a gap in the curtains, illuminating her best friends' faces.

Val and Bibi were fast asleep in their bunks. Val was snoring softly, and Bibi's slackened jaw was just visible through her spill of red hair.

On his little bedroll between them, Pippin was wide awake, his shaggy head cocked in concern.

Sera waited for the sparks in her hands to wink out. When her magic quieted, she leaned over to scratch behind his ears. "It's all right, Pip," she whispered. "It was just a nightmare."

She should have been used to them by now. But this one was new . . . Her breath rattled in the yawning silence, as though that cloying wet earth still clung to the insides of her lungs.

She rolled out of bed and shrugged on her dressing gown. In the kitchen, she fetched a glass of water and gulped it down, but her heart was still beating wildly. Air. She needed air. She crept outside into the back garden and stood on the wooden deck, silently begging the midnight wind to tug her back to herself. Looking up at the spill of silver peaks, she let herself feel small and insignificant.

Seraphine. Just Seraphine.

Spitfire.

Fragments of her nightmare floated at the edges of her mind. It hadn't been all bad. There had been a moment when she'd felt Ransom's hands on her, the nearness of his lips like a promise that still ached somewhere deep inside her. She had wanted that kiss, those breathy words in her ear. If she was honest with herself, she wanted them even now.

Her cheeks warmed at the memory—false and fleeting as it was. If he ever saw her again, he'd likely throttle her. If she didn't throttle him first. Her hands tingled.

Maker, whispered her magic. Soft and keening. *Please.*

"Please, *what*?" she hissed at herself. *Saints,* she was exhausted, and the last thing she needed was this *thing* inside pulling at her. Slumping onto the wooden steps, she picked up a rough gray stone. Closing her eyes, she held the stone in her fist, letting it ground her as she stilled her mind.

That insistent tug found her again, born of this strange other force that now lived inside her. She was pulled inward, through the addled maze of her own worries. Down, down,

down, she tunneled, through pain and grief and loss and hope as delicate as a bee's wing. She reached beyond it all, searching for a whisper of the magic that slumbered in her soul.

Where are you? she called into the unending dark. *What are you?*

As if in answer, memories crowded in on her. That night on the Aurore replayed itself in sharp, searing clarity. She smelled the rain on the wind, glimpsed the lightning streaking above the tower, then the menacing glint of Lark's teeth as he bore down on her. She felt the pulse of her hand against his chest, the *push* of something else moving between them. Death. *Magic.* That strange heat in her bones, cradling her as she fell . . .

The memories washed over her like a tide of shadows. And there, in the darkness of all that pain, she sensed a gossamer thread of light. Tugging on it, she followed it down, and down again. Deeper than she'd ever gone before. Lost to the world far above her, she tiptoed around the edges of her own soul. There was a door here. And in front of it, a little girl, sitting with her knees tucked into her chest. Blond hair and scrawny limbs, eyes as blue as the sky, save for a fleck of bronze. Sera peered down at her younger self, recognizing all too well the fear shining in those wide, bright eyes.

The door behind her was ajar, magic streaming through a crack there.

Look and learn, it purred. *Let me out.*

Sera reached for the handle, imagined herself shoving it open, but the little girl shot to her feet, slamming it shut.

Frustration hissed from deep within.

"No, no, no," cried the girl. "It's too much. Too soon."

Sera made to try again.

"I can't—" pleaded the girl. "We can't."

The girl was weeping now, and the sound was so gut-wrenchingly familiar, Sera drew back from it. Into the winding dark of her childhood, where her parents' screams echoed in the stillness. There was grief here, and it was clawing at her.

She was afraid now. Scared of the world that once bowed to her father. Frightened of a world without her mother, and the weight of what Sera was destined to become in her absence. Something so much more than what she once was. Something even Mama had never dreamed of.

But *what*?

And *how*?

That door inside her was bolted shut now, the little girl pressed against it like a starfish. Her fear was a fog between them. Sera lost herself to it. She *became* it.

Too much.

Too soon.

Backpedaling now, she turned from the search, and the cloying shadows of her own mind, and reached up, up, up, to the cool kiss of the midnight wind and the scent of pine trees, the night call of the loon, and the hardness of the wood under her bare feet.

She was gasping when she opened her eyes, her cheeks damp as the great bowl of the stars poured their silvered light over her. Good light. Safe light. Starlight.

Coward.

Failure.

Scrubbing the wet of her cheeks, she shook away the shame of another failed meditation, the uneasy sense that her magic was angry at her.

In the warmth of her fist, the stone had changed from gray to gold. It hadn't been for nothing, then. But it didn't feel like nearly enough, either.

"Is this what you wanted?" she said, holding the golden stone up to the sky.

There was such a silence inside her now, the stillness unnerving in its own way. She tossed the stone into the grass, where it shone like a nugget in the earth. Another cheap trick, just like the rose. A morsel of light that would eventually crumble to ash. When she tried to make another, nothing happened. Her magic had gone quiet again, that door inside her firmly closed.

What was the point of it?

Was there a point at all?

"Did I just see you shaking your fist at the sky?" Sera jumped at the sound of Theo's laughter. "What did that bastard moon do now?"

Saints, save me. "You're hallucinating," she said, turning to look at him. "What are you doing up?"

Theo was in his nightshirt and a pair of cotton trousers, his feet bare on the wooden slats. "Paola returned from the city an hour ago. We were talking in her bedroom."

Sera perked up at this morsel of news. "How did the trial shipment go?"

"Do you want the good news or the bad news?" When she didn't answer, only groaned, he said, "Half the batch made it to the city. The other half exploded on the drive."

"It's still too volatile," muttered Sera.

Theo lowered himself down to the step. "We'll keep working on the recipe. Decrease the batch size until we get it right."

She chewed on a hangnail. It was hard not to feel impatient, to spend so long on a batch only to have it fail at the first hurdle. If they flooded the city with exploding vials, the Daggers would laugh at them. The king's eye would turn on their Order, and the people of Fantome would lose trust in the Order of Flames before they even learned of their true purpose.

"The good news is, demand is even higher than we thought," Theo went on. "Paola says rebellion is brewing in Fantome. The king is losing his grip on his people. Ever since the Aurore fell, trust in the royal family has plummeted. The people are frightened. They feel betrayed. The Iron Keep has been all but emptied and the city is crawling with overzealous nightguards. Word on Merchant's Way is the Daggers are busier than ever. Killing anyone who dares speak ill of the king."

Sera's stomach twisted. "If the people are starting to revolt against him, then the rest of Valterre will soon follow."

What did that mean for her Order's mission? For the very fate of the kingdom?

Not for the first time, Sera felt the threads of destiny twining around her.

Theo rubbed at the dent between his brows. "It does beg

the question . . . is now a good time to put a new weapon in the hands of the people of Fantome?"

"When else but now?" she shot back. "I can't think of a better time to empower them. To give them something to fight back with. To *protect* themselves with."

"If the Daggers cede their control of the city, the people there could overthrow the king," said Theo. "I'm no monarchist, but the House of Rayere has ruled Valterre for hundreds of years. The king's army secures our borders from the grasping hands of Urnica and Farberg. A kingdom needs a leader. To topple the Daggers is one thing, but to move against the king—"

"We're not moving against the king." At least not deliberately. And what did they care for the House of Rayere, greedy and self-interested as it had always been? "Let the king keep his army. We're only moving against the power of Shade. Fantome has been in darkness for far too long. It's time to set it free."

Wasn't that reasonable?

Wasn't it about time?

Theo hummed. "There's more."

Of course there was.

Sera braced herself.

His gaze was fixed on that shining nugget in the grass. "Paola says there are rumors of a new revolutionary stirring in Fantome. Someone who intends to unite the people of Valterre. They're calling him the People's Saint."

Sera stilled, the echo of her own heartbeat thrumming in her ears.

"Many are looking to him to lead them out of rebellion.

Into a new age." Slowly, he turned to look at her.

"A *saint*," she repeated weakly. "How absurd."

"Is it?" he said quietly.

No, came a whispering from behind the door inside her.

Yes, screamed the girl that guarded it.

"The saints are dead, Theo."

He looked at her for a long moment, curiosity and trepidation warring in his gaze. And there was something else there, too. A kind of hunger that made the turquoise of his eyes shine a little brighter. Then he said, in a whisper, "Haven't you ever considered the possibility of a new age? Haven't you wondered about the power inside you? What it truly *means*?"

Sera stared at him, waiting for that rogue dimple, a flash of teeth in the dark, but he was more serious now than she had ever seen him, carefully plucking at the thread of her own suspicions . . . her own fear.

No.

No.

She was the same Sera she'd always been. Wasn't she?

Was she?

Theo went on, oblivious to the tornado spinning inside her. "When I was a young boy growing up in Halbracht, the elders here spoke of the Second Coming of the saints. A lasting antidote to the man-made darkness that has plagued Fantome for centuries. The darkness that began in our village . . . that grew from the ambitious minds of Hugo and Armand Versini." His lip curled over his ancestors' names.

"Before my grandmother died, sometimes she would sit

outside and watch the clouds on restless nights. So certain that one day a storm would come, and that it would change everything. My father said it was because she ate the wild mushrooms down by the river, but my grandmother never seemed mad to me. Just . . . hopeful, in the way that hope can be maddening sometimes."

"I know that feeling," murmured Sera, thinking of her mother.

"My grandmother believed in the last prophecy of Saint Oriel. The last words uttered by the Saint of Destiny on her deathbed. When she spoke of the Second Coming of the saints." He swept his silver hair back from his face, looking at the single golden nugget. "It's only recently I've begun to wonder if it might be true."

Sera looked at her hands, so small and pale in the moonlight. *Could it be true?* Was it madness to even consider the possibility? She shook her head vigorously. "I can't be a saint, Theo. Whatever this is . . . it feels like a mistake."

"Maybe that's because you're afraid of it."

She opened her mouth to argue, but the words died in her throat. Theo was right. She *was* afraid, and she couldn't seem to break the spell of that fear, to trust the magic in her veins not to hurt her. Or the people she cared about. Because if she *was* a saint, she was a broken one—her magic rebelling against her. Perhaps it had been meant for someone else, someone worthier.

"Let's keep trying to understand it," said Theo for the hundredth time. "We can have our sessions in the mornings before anyone else—"

"We've *tried*. Doing breathwork with you in knee-high grass isn't going to get us anywhere."

Not unless he could plunge his hand inside her and rip out her fear. Shake some bravery into that little girl who trembled before the door to her magic, and the secrets that glittered therein.

"Something vital changed for you that night on the Aurore, Sera. Something vital changed for the whole bloody kingdom." He couldn't keep the bite from his voice, the frustration from curling his fists. "You owe it to yourself and Valterre to figure it out. You owe it to *us*."

Raking her hands through her hair to keep from shoving him, she swallowed back her retort. He was right and a part of her hated him for it. Failure was a boulder in her stomach, and the weight of it made her feel unbearably tired suddenly. Between the nightmares and the gnawing waking anxiety, Sera felt more at sea than ever.

Who could help her now?

Who would pull her back to shore?

Somewhere in the distance, a bird cackled, the sound just like a madwoman's laugh. She jerked her chin up, an idea striking her like an arrow. Perhaps she didn't have the answers. But she knew someone who might.

She turned to Theo. "Hear me out . . ."

"Three dangerous words," he said warily.

"I want to return to Fantome. I think there's someone there who can help me figure this out."

His face darkened. "You're not seeing him, Sera. Over my dead body."

"Not Ransom," she said, punching his shoulder. Even if, secretly, recklessly, she had let herself imagine what it would be like to stalk into the heart of Old Haven and find him there.

Would he kill her?

Kiss her?

Curse her?

"I want to go to House Armand."

Understanding dawned across his face. "You want to talk to Madame Fontaine."

"The old crone might be halfway out of her mind and as sour as a shriveled lemon, but she has a connection to Saint Oriel," said Sera. "You know it. Val and Bibi know it. When I was a Cloak, Fontaine knew things about me she shouldn't have. It's like her tarot cards were whispering to her."

He scrubbed his jaw, mulling it over. "It's not the worst idea you've ever had. Though it is going to be fraught with untold peril." At her look of guilt, he summoned a grin. "Lucky for you that's my favorite kind of adventure."

She mirrored his smile. "Mine, too."

Chapter 6

Ransom

Ransom jolted awake at the brush of a hand on his neck. He struck out, hitting someone in the dark. They cursed, stumbling backward.

Springing upright, he reached for the oil lamp on the wall. The sudden flare of light illuminated his friend's withering grimace.

"What the hell are you doing in here?" he demanded.

"Waking you!" Nadia made a point of rubbing her shoulder. "Next time, I'll just throw something at you. Save myself the bruise."

"Sorry." He ran a hand through his hair, sweeping the unruly black strands from his eyes. "I thought you were strangling me."

"I was *prodding* you. You couldn't hear me. You were thrashing and groaning. I thought you'd been poisoned."

Ransom rubbed the bridge of his nose, trying to remember what he had been dreaming about. There was nothing but the usual shadows pooling in the corners of his mind and the slow curling dread that often chased him from sleep.

"I hope that wasn't some kind of sexy dream," she added as an afterthought. "Ugh. Now I feel gross."

He gave her a bland smile. "Maybe next time you'll think twice about waltzing in here unannounced."

"Maybe you'll start locking your door, like any sane Head of the Order of Daggers would."

Ransom snorted. Was there such a thing as a sane Head Dagger? He hadn't even moved bedchambers since he'd taken on Dufort's role, preferring to stay in the small damp room he had been assigned at ten years old. He had no interest in the grand trappings of Dufort's former chamber in the east passage, or the ghost of the man that lingered there. Lisette, ever the opportunist, had jumped at the chance to take it, and Ransom had let her, if only to assure her wavering loyalty.

The fewer vipers in the nest, the better.

"What time is it?" he said, taking a slug of water from the glass on his bedside table. His eyes adjusted to the dim light and he noticed Nadia's drawn face and the dark circles under her eyes. There was a tightness to her mouth, her shoulders, too.

"Dawn," she said.

Ransom frowned. Rare was the Dagger acquainted with dawn. They carried out their work in the dead of the night for a reason, and as a consequence, slept long past the rising sun.

Which made this whole interruption even more disconcerting.

"Why are you in my bedchamber at dawn?"

"Because your little bitch is back in Fantome." All traces of amusement drained from her voice. "And when I find her, I'm going to wring her scrawny neck and hang her from the Bridge of Tears."

Ransom was on his feet so fast, his head spun. Last night had been a long one. Three back-to-back angry, spitting marks, all runaway prisoners decked out with every weapon they could find, including a damn soup ladle. No Lightfire, at least. Still, consuming three vials of Shade had nearly sent Ransom slipping into the Verne on his way home. The after-cloud of it sat heavy in his head now, making it throb. Which was why he must have heard Nadia incorrectly.

"Say that again."

She ignored the request. "Get dressed and follow me."

Ransom grabbed the sweater hanging on the back of his chair and pulled it over his head. He shrugged on his trousers, his fingers flying through his bootlaces as he tied them in a rush. There wasn't time to splash water on his face, but it hardly mattered. He was wide awake.

When he left his bedchamber, Nadia was halfway down the passage, marching with a fury he hadn't seen in some time.

He jogged after her. "Hell's teeth, Nadia, slow down! What's happened?"

She stalked on, her words flying over her shoulder. "Words won't do this justice. I want to *show* you what she's done. I want to see your face when you realize you should have killed that manipulative little murderer in the Saints' Quarter four months ago."

Ransom's fingers twitched as he walked. A part of him yearned for a vial of Shade to dull the edges of his anxiety.

Just a taste. A mere press against the lips.

A dangerous impulse Dufort had readily given in to, time and again.

Breathing slowly through his nose, he shoved the instinct down. Whatever had spooked Nadia, they would handle it together. *He* would handle it. Just as soon as she started making sense.

Outside, dawn light bled across the sky in streaks of amber and pink. Old Haven was fast asleep, the statue of Lucille Versini staring blank-eyed toward Primrose Square, where a low-hanging cloud filled the space where the Aurore Tower had once stood. The only sound was the soft whistle of the morning breeze, and a robin chirping in the nearby trees.

Nadia was waiting for him at the top of the stone steps, tapping her foot impatiently.

"What?" he said, growing impatient himself.

She simply turned sharply and headed straight for the graveyard.

Guilt tugged at Ransom as he stepped through the gate after her. He hadn't been here in months. He spent so much time around death, he hated to sit in the aftermath of it. He despised the eerie stillness. The rotting flowers. The stench of the mossy headstones. The reminder that his best friend, Lark, was dead because of him. That he was stuck here without him.

Nadia came here every evening before she went to work. She had spent her birthday sitting at the foot of Lark's grave, reading his favorite book. Lisette had told Ransom that, with a sneer of her usual judgment, and coward that he was, he had never asked Nadia where she'd been that day. He simply left a cream bun and a card in her bedchamber, and that was that.

She made for Lark's grave now, winding her way toward the south-east corner of the ancient graveyard. Steeling himself, Ransom followed her, averting his eyes as he passed under the statue of Calvin, Saint of Death.

By the time they finally came to Lark's row, Nadia was silent. Fresh tears striped her cheeks as she wordlessly pointed toward the graveside. Ransom understood then why she couldn't speak, because when he followed her gaze, words left him too.

Lark's grave was open.

A pit yawned in Ransom's stomach as he stumbled forward, trying to make sense of it.

Six feet down, the walnut coffin Nadia had carefully chosen was wide open. The crimson velvet lining was covered in dirt and the upper panel had split in two, as though someone had jammed their foot through it. Over and over again.

Lark's body was gone.

Ransom swayed on his feet, anger and confusion careening over him. *"When?"* he managed.

Beside him, Nadia was as stiff as a statue. "Some time in the night." She stepped back, the empty grave so unsettling she had to steady herself against the bench Ransom had had erected by the grave. For her. "Caruso and I were here at sundown yesterday."

Ransom looked up at that. *"Caruso?"*

"He walks here sometimes. I think it's because dead people don't require anything of him. Like interesting conversation. Or the barest shred of empathy."

Well, at least she had retained her dark sense of humor.

"Lark's grave was fine last night," she went on. "I left peonies." She gestured to the shredded bouquet, its delicate pink petals now strewn across the grass like confetti. "He used to buy them in the Rascalle every Sunday to take home to his mother . . ." She trailed off, her fists scrunching like she was trying to force the tears back inside herself. "I couldn't sleep so I got up early. When I came here, he was gone."

A grave robber in Old Haven.

Ransom scoured the surrounding grass, looking for footsteps.

"There's nothing," she said, from where she watched him. "I searched the whole graveyard, even the trees beyond. Whoever took him was in and out like the wind. Quick, careful. Silent." A meaningful pause. "Like a Cloak."

He shook his head. "Nadia . . . Seraphine wouldn't do something like this."

"She's the one who killed him in the first place, Ransom. She's been disrupting our trade for months. Luring our smugglers away. Trickling Lightfire through the city like a leaky tap. Practically *daring* you to come after her." She threw up her hands in frustration. "Open your eyes."

Ransom scrubbed his jaw, trying to untangle his thoughts from his feelings. Everything Nadia was saying was true but what business did Seraphine Marchant have with Lark Delano's dead body?

"She's five foot nothing, Nadia. Even if she wanted to do something depraved like this, she wouldn't be able to."

"She has her own Order now," she reminded him. "The Flames barter in Lightfire and seek the destruction of Shade. Of *us*."

Ransom's sigh whistled through his nose. He knew all this, had trodden this conversation so many times he was sick of it. "But she hasn't destroyed us, Nadia. The city is in chaos. We've never been busier." He had the shadow-marks to prove it. "Hang the turncoats, who want to work with Marchant. Where one smuggler walks away from us, another will come running." He turned back to the grave. "This . . . she wouldn't do *this*. I know her."

"Do you?" said Nadia, bitterly.

No, said a quiet voice inside him.

The falling of the Aurore had changed everything.

He did not know this Seraphine at all.

He did not know what she was capable of.

So, why, then was he still protecting her?

Because you are a fool, Bastian.

"Marchant has people under her who can do her bidding now." Nadia glanced pointedly at the open coffin. "If she wanted to pull Lark from his grave to mess with us, she sure as hell has the means. The motive. The muscle." Her nostrils flared, and she drew a breath. "And she's *here*. In the city."

Ransom turned from the empty grave. "What are you talking about?"

"The river traders saw her in the north quarter yesterday evening." She tilted her chin, watching him just as closely as he was watching her. "I'd asked them to keep an eye out."

No. It was a mistake. Seraphine was not reckless enough to set foot in this city after he'd warned her to stay away. After everything she did with those monsters . . .

Such arrogance.

Such *recklessness.*

"She wouldn't . . ." he began, but then he thought of that golden rose at Othilde's house. Not just a taunt but an invitation.

Was *this* the game? Was this her move?

Grave robbing right under his nose?

He swallowed a curse. Had she lost all sense of herself entirely? He turned back to the empty grave, if only to save himself from Nadia's penetrating glare. His heart galloped, confusion spilling into anger. She wouldn't . . . *would she*?

"She wasn't alone," Nadia said. "The Shadowsmith was with her. And the other two. The redhead and the one with the nose ring."

Ransom ground his jaw, staring so hard at the headstone, his eyes blurred.

HERE LIES LARK DELANO

FOREVER BELOVED

Was she trying to draw him out?

How far would the spitfire go to get his attention?

To desecrate a grave right under his nose . . .

No, it was absurd.

Wasn't it?

Was it?

Nadia was still talking but Ransom's mind was reeling.

The Daggers had enemies. Hundreds, perhaps more. But none of those enemies would have known what this grave meant to Ransom. To Nadia. To Seraphine.

Only her.

Sitting down, he let his legs slide into the open grave. Bracing himself, he leaned over the hole, trying to find a clue to what had happened here. The wind stirred, blowing petals across the grass. And something strange yet familiar tickled the inside of his nose. There: a tang of lemon blossoms on the wind. The barest taste of magic. Of *her*.

Fuck.

Her scent lingered; the same one that had clung to him the last time he'd seen her. When she'd kissed his palm and shattered the Shade inside him, that strange golden light flickering behind her eyes. He told himself he'd imagined it, that it was an impossibility. But for weeks after, he swore he could still smell her on his skin. He'd wanted to stamp the scent there forever.

Yes, something had changed the night the Aurore came down . . .

Perhaps Nadia was right.

Maybe Seraphine *was* screwing with them. As callous and cruel as any enemy.

He flopped backward, splaying his arms as he stared up at the sky. "Well, shit."

Nadia's face appeared above him. "Finally coming to your senses?"

He turned his head, inhaling a lungful of dirt to chase the scent of her away.

"Better late than never, I suppose." She stomped away.

He called after her. "Where are you going?"

"To get a vial of Shade. So I can find her. And kill her."

She turned to glare at him, daring him to stop her.

Ransom opened his mouth. Closed it. He couldn't let this slide. He shouldn't *want* to let this slide.

He was Head of the Order of Daggers, and this wasn't just business.

It was personal.

He got to his feet. "I'll go with you."

They walked back in strained silence, both lost in thoughts of anger and revenge. When they reached Hugo's Passage, a pair of dayguards were waiting by the statue of Lucille Versini. Dressed in official uniform, with their longswords glinting at their hips and the royal insignia of Valterre emblazoned on their chests—a rose crossed with two swords—they had the good sense, at least, to dip their chins in deference as Ransom stalked to meet them.

It was rare for a soldier of the Crown to interact with a Dagger in broad daylight. The king preferred to conduct his affairs—and assassinations—in private. Usually after dark, or, on occasion, in one of his grand castles.

These were desperate times indeed.

"Morning," said Ransom, flatly. "What's this about?"

The soldiers dispensed with false pleasantries, the one on the left struggling to meet his gaze when he reached into his breast pocket and produced a letter bearing the king's seal.

Ransom swiped it from him and tore it open, his mouth twisting as he read.

"What is it?" said Nadia, peering around his left shoulder.

Ransom's frown deepened. "We've been summoned to the Summer Palace."

Chapter 7

Seraphine

In the darkest corner of the Rose and Crown, Sera sat with her three best friends eating a rib-eye steak as big as her head. Somewhere outside, the sun was finally setting, and the taverns on Merchant's Way were springing to life. The promise of chaos lingered in the air, the distant thrum of patrolling cavalry adding an ominous backdrop to their dinner.

They had arrived in Fantome yesterday evening, just in time to see a flaming scarecrow king swinging from the top of Traveler's Arch, and a pair of nightguards beating the rebel who had put it there to a bloody pulp with the hilts of their swords. On the way to their inn, they watched six more rabble-rousers get chucked into the Verne, while fires raged all along the riverbank.

Fantome was on its knees. It was hard to tell who exactly was in control, only that danger hung thickly in the air, and that both sides were clearly frightened. Violent. Desperate.

Though Sera was eager to get in and out of the city before one of them accidentally wandered into a brawl or landed belly up in the Verne, they could not readily stroll into House Armand and request a meeting with Madame Fontaine without repercussions. They had resolved to wait a day while Bibi sent word to her contact on the inside. Alaina, the pastry chef there, was a long-time friend and occasional lover of hers, and, after some back and forth, had agreed to leave out a key for them tonight.

Now it was simply a matter of waiting . . . and then secretly ambushing Fontaine in her bedchamber.

Sera was less convinced about the second part of their plan, but Theo was sure he could talk the old Cloak around faster than she could squawk for Madame Mercure, the head of the House. Still, they'd need wine for courage, dirt cheap and watery as it was.

Returning from the bar, Theo made sure to fill their glasses to the brim.

"Careful you don't eat the bone, Marchant."

She flicked a pea at him. "Eyes on your own plate, Branch. And I always save the bone for Pip."

She regretted having to leave him behind this time but the atmosphere in Fantome was too volatile for a curious mutt like Pip. He was better served back in the mountains, chasing the volatile fireworks Tobias loved experimenting with. Yes, Halbracht was a much safer place for Pip. Fantome was bubbling over, the flames of rebellions hissing and spreading. It wasn't safe for any of them here.

Last night, they had retired early to sleep, and had kept to themselves all day, moving about in their hooded cloaks. Even now, Sera couldn't help glancing at the doorway. It was not the nightguards or the wayward rebels that made her nerves swill. It was the Daggers that dogged her fears. She wasn't foolish enough to think the Order she'd almost decimated four months ago would be so casually unconcerned with her comings and goings. That Ransom Hale, and his second, Nadia Raine, didn't have eyes on every entry point in the city.

But beyond her own increased wariness, there wasn't much she could do about it. So she polished off her steak, and with another hour or so to kill, decided to order dessert—a sinfully gooey slice of fudge cake. She shared it with Bibi, while Val went to the bathroom and Theo brooded over his second glass of wine, no doubt thinking about their return to House Armand.

Val returned waving a copy of the Sunday penny papers about. "Look what I just swiped from that drunk old man over there."

Once a Cloak, always a Cloak.

She set the newspaper down on the table, and they crowded around to read the front page.

GRAND VERSINI LIBRARY
BURNS ON THE ANNIVERSARY
OF FOUNDER'S DEATH

EXACTLY 350 YEARS after the death of Hugo Versini, the notorious founder of the Order of Daggers, the Grand Versini

> Library went up in flames. Last night, the skies over the Scholars' Quarter burned amber, though whether the act of arson was in tribute or scorn to one of the most reviled gang leaders in recent history, one cannot know for sure.
>
> As the fires of rebellion continue to raze the city, and vandals stalk the streets at night, the heart of Valterre has never felt further from peace. Our beloved Aurore has been toppled, our most sacred buildings are burning, and our neighbors are rioting, while the flag of Valterre hangs in tatters from every flagpole across the four quarters.
>
> We, the people, are crying out in fear, terrified another plague of monsters will soon sweep through our streets.
>
> Who will save us then?
>
> Can you hear us, Your Majesty?
>
> Do the windows of your grand palaces not rattle with the echoes of our pleas?
>
> Does your heart not bleed for your people, and the darkness that threatens to swallow us? *[. . . continued on p. 3]*

"The Grand Versini is a pillar of this city." Theo sighed. "Corrupt, Shade-addicted founding ancestors notwithstanding. I hope they rebuild it."

The others were stone silent, likely staring at the same thing Sera was. Not the article but the sketch beneath it. It was a portrait of Hugo Versini.

Theo made to turn the page, but Val's hand shot out to stop him. "Not so fast. We are obviously going to have to talk about this."

Feigning ignorance, he simply said, "What?"

"Eh, the fact you look *exactly* like your ancestor Hugo?" She glanced at Bibi. "How did we never know this? Seriously, *how*?"

In his portrait, Hugo was standing on the front steps of the Grand Versini. Though he was clearly several years older than Theo, he had the same light hair and keen eyes, a hard-edged jaw and lips that curved as though he was about to tell a joke. It was uncanny. Unnerving. If there weren't hundreds of years between them, they could have been twins.

"It's not exactly something I brag about," said Theo, turning the paper over. "Thankfully, Armand was far vainer than his older brother. There aren't many portraits of Hugo floating about and that's how I like it."

It belatedly occurred to Sera that while she had grown up hearing horror stories of Hugo Versini's ruthless grip on the underworld, she had never seen his face before. They knew Armand well enough. His portrait hung in the dining room at House Armand, his tousled dark hair and expressive brown eyes making him seem handsome. And more than that—human.

"Good thing you've kept your hood up tonight," said Bibi, sneaking the paper toward her to take another peek. "The last thing we need is for the people of Fantome to think Hugo Versini has risen from the dead. Things are bad enough here already."

Theo frowned. "It's not *that* uncanny, is it?"

They exchanged a bemused look.

"It's not like he was ugly," reasoned Sera. "There's no need to be so upset about it."

"I don't want anything to do with him." Theo took another generous slug of wine before slamming the glass

Humming to herself, Fontaine said, "It would appear so. The Second Coming is finally upon us. I was hoping I'd be dead by now."

"Why do I feel like you're going to outlive us all?" muttered Val.

Fontaine kept her penetrating gaze on Sera, like she could see the war raging inside her head: fear giving way to wonder, only to be snatched away again. "No need to look so disturbed. You haven't made any choices worth making yet. And for that matter, neither have the rest of you."

"What does that mean?" said Sera warily.

"It means in this new age you don't know what kind of player you are. Or what you're truly capable of." A long pause then, her lips twisting and twisting. "And neither do I." She leaned back against the window, setting her pipe to one side. "I will tell you what I know about the Second Coming. If only to keep you from seeking the same answers from those who would use you for their own nefarious means."

Without meaning to, Sera drifted closer.

"The original twelve saints of Fantome were made under the same storm over a thousand years ago. Each one struck down and remade by the kind of lightning that cleaved the entire sky in two, erupting from the ether like a long golden finger," Fontaine began, looking up to the stars as she weaved her tale.

Sera's cheeks prickled at the memory of the fork of lightning that had skewered her just the same not half a year ago. She had never wondered how the saints of Valterre had come to be, only that they *were*, and that they had lived with the soul of the

Without preamble, Sera said, "What do you know about Saint Oriel's final prophecy?"

Fontaine's brows rose. "What makes you think I know anything about it?"

So she was going to toy with them first. Great.

"You're a descendant of Oriel Beauregard," said Val flatly. "All the years I was at House Armand, you never let me forget it. I swear I used to think you could read my mind."

Fontaine smirked.

"The cards you play with," said Sera. "They tell you things."

"You seem to know a lot about me."

"Not as much as you seem to know about me."

Fontaine gave a rasping chuckle. "I suppose it makes sense . . . this sudden *eagerness* to learn of our great saints. Or indeed the ones yet to come."

"Why do you say that?" said Theo warily.

"Look at her." Fontaine didn't take her milky eyes off Sera. "You couldn't hide that new blood in your veins even if you tried, Seraphine. I can see the sheen of it behind your eyes." She bared her graying teeth. "Gold blood, they used to call it. The blood of the saints. Fate has bound you with its thread." With surprising sprightliness, she pitched forward, blowing a ring of smoke right in her face. "And it *terrifies* you."

Sera took a step back, the grass whispering under her feet. Just like the other night with Theo, a part of her wanted to outrun the accusation—the inherent truth she felt in it—but another part of her was eager to grasp for more.

Theo inhaled. "So Sera is a saint."

yet . . . "Give it up, then. I don't have all night."

Theo was the first to remove his cloak. "Caught," he said, with his usual good-natured charm.

Val went next. Then Bibi, freeing her spill of long red hair. "It's good to see you, Madame—"

"You lie like a lazy cat, Sabine. I read your note, remember? *You* are not here to see me at all."

Bibi knew better than to correct her. She was, in fact, chiefly here to see Alaina.

Fontaine rolled her eyes, then gestured with her walking stick, dismissing her.

Tossing an awkward smile over her shoulder, Bibi promptly scooted off around the side of the building, leaving the three of them to deal with Fontaine.

Seraphine was still considering whether or not to remove her Cloak when Fontaine blew a ring of smoke directly at her.

"If you think I can't see the fire in your eyes, you're a witless wonder, Seraphine Marchant. There is no disguise that can hide you from me now."

Sera cast off her cloak. "Better?"

"Not particularly," said Fontaine. "I'd rather you weren't here at all."

"I came to see you."

"No shit." She beckoned them closer. They stopped a cane's length from her. Just in case she tried to swat them. Fontaine took a long drag of her pipe. The smoke was sweet and cloying, and it made Sera's stomach turn. "Well? Get to it, turncoats."

Armand flickered into view. Moonlight danced along the yellowed leaves, tracing the contours of the towering manor house. According to her note, Alaina had left a key under a flowerpot in the back garden.

"Which one is it?" hissed Val as they slipped through the front gate.

"The big blue one," Bibi hissed back. "She even drew a diagram for us."

"Good," said Theo. "I pity the fool who tries to break into House Armand without a cleverly thought out—"

"Then you are a fool indeed, Theodore Branch." A familiar croaky voice made them jump.

"Madame Fontaine?" Bibi whispered. "Are you out here somewhere?"

"Sabine Fraser, you shameless sneak. I taught you better than this."

"This is exactly what you taught us," Val piped up. "Sneaking. Spying. General subterfuge."

"Which is why you little miscreants should know I intercept all mail that comes and goes at House Armand."

At their shared looks of alarm, the old crone cackled. The sound scattered a nightingale in the back garden.

"Well, now I feel like a prized idiot," muttered Bibi.

"You should." The clouds parted, and a slant of moonlight danced across the garden. They saw her then, as clear as a specter. The old bat was sitting on a windowsill, smoking her pipe.

She eyed the space where they were standing, like she could spy them through their Shade-coated cloaks. Impossible. And down. "I hate him. Who he was, and what he did to the city. To our family. Our legacy. Every time I look in the mirror, I have to see his face. It's like some kind of cruel joke." Lips twisting, his voice quieted as he glanced away. "And what if it's worse than that? What if I share more with Hugo Versini than the slope of his nose and the shade of his hair?"

Sera frowned. "What do you mean?"

"I mean, what if the same darkness that moved inside him lives in me, too?"

Sera's frown deepened. Of course Theo was ambitious. He was quick and clever, a natural-born artificer with a whirring mind and a desire to leave his mark on the kingdom. They were *all* ambitious. They had vats of Lightfire, a brand-new Order, and a missing Aurore Tower to prove it. But that didn't make them bad-minded or dangerous.

It made them hungry for change.

And change was good.

Wasn't it?

"That's not how it works, Theo. You are not destined to become Hugo Versini, just as I am not going to become my father."

"I don't even *know* who my father is," Val was quick to point out. "So, if you ask me, we all get a clean slate."

Bibi clinked her glass. "It's not about what's in your blood. It's about what drives your spirit. We make our own choices. Carve our own paths."

Sera smiled. "For the better."

"For the better," the others echoed.

To Theo, she added, "And don't worry, if you start showing signs of moral decay, I'll knock some sense into you."

He managed a smile. "Thank the saints for good friends."

"And big schemes." Val drained her glass. "Speaking of, I believe it's about time for a little breaking and entering."

They set out for House Armand as the clock tower above the Marlowe struck nine, making their way there on foot. The Hollows was more alive than Seraphine had ever seen it, revelers spilling out of every tavern and bordello, where they crowded the streets, singing and dancing and vomiting.

"Rebellion abounds in the north and south quarters but everyone still parties in the Hollows," mused Theo as they crept along the shadowed streets.

"The folk here never really had anything to root for. What do they care about who rules Valterre?" said Val. "It's not like the king ever cared about us."

When the streetlamps winked out and the midnight ruckus died away, Sera knew they were getting close. She drew her cloak tighter, trying to stave off the sudden chill. Nerves fisted her stomach, a rush of her anxiety stoking the magic inside her.

"Careful," hissed Bibi. "Your eyes are glowing."

Of all the inconvenient times . . . Closing her eyes and counting out her breaths, Sera shoved her magic down. *Not now. Go away.*

Up ahead, the ivy that hugged the invisible façade of House

kingdom in their hearts, striving always to protect and serve its people in their own varied ways.

"During the first coming of the saints, the storm raged for three days and three nights, as though a vengeful god was shaking the heavens. In that time, twelve strikes skewered the kingdom. Twelve different magical gifts were gifted to twelve plain folk. Golden-gazed and gold-blooded, they rose up, one by one, discovered the new power slumbering inside them, and eventually became the saints of Valterre."

In barely more than a whisper, Sera said, "How did they know what they were meant to be? What magic they possessed?"

"They opened their souls," said Fontaine, like it was as simple as that. "They *welcomed* their gifts with gratitude for what it meant for their kingdom, not the small-minded of fear of what it meant for them."

The barb stung all the worse because it was unintentional. And it was true. Sera couldn't see how to change that, to welcome the very thing her own consciousness rebelled against. How to tame a beast that so easily overwhelmed her. How to trust it.

All her life, she had never known a benevolent power. Not the cold deadly dust of Shade that used to stain her mother's fingers, or the kind her own father, Gaspard Dufort, wielded over Fantome as Head of the Order of Daggers.

How could Sera trust the power that now slumbered inside her? The twisting, burning, hissing thing that she didn't understand? If her own father had turned on her, what was to say the magic inside her wouldn't, too?

Reaching into her shawl, Fontaine removed her tarot deck.

The gilded cards shimmered in the moonlight. She closed her eyes as she shuffled, her lips tightening.

They stepped in close, drawn to the whispering cards.

"The storm will choose new saints to crown, where three stone towers crumble down . . ." Fontaine muttered, her frown deepening. "Let's see what shapes our figures take . . ."

Fontaine drew three cards and placed them on the windowsill.

The silence thickened as they stared down at them. The first card portrayed a figure in a plain brown tunic, kneeling over a slab of clay, with an axe in one hand and a chisel in the other.

"The Stone Maiden," said Fontaine, distantly. "Both builder and breaker of clay."

It meant little to Sera.

The second card revealed a skeletal figure dressed in rags.

"The Necromancer," Theo read the words at the bottom.

"Death's right hand." Fontaine suppressed a shudder. Then, more to herself, she muttered, "Different saints this time around . . . different tasks, perhaps . . . hmm . . ."

"That one sounds more like a curse than a gift," said Theo under his breath.

The third card was a man with tousled hair and wide, gleaming teeth. He was staring right out of the portrait, like he could see them.

"The Silver-tongue," read Sera.

"A charmer versed in the art of persuasion," said Fontaine. "Intriguing."

"I don't think that's our Sera." Val patted her on the shoulder. "No offense."

Sera's gaze remained on the cards. Her eyes burned, as though her magic was peering out too. "Is one of these supposed to be me?"

The crevices in Fontaine's face shifted until she looked impossibly old. "There is a wrongness in this reading. Something hidden. Something missing . . ." She snapped her chin up, her milky gaze narrowing. "Or perhaps it is *you* who feels wrong."

Sera took a step backward. "I haven't done anything."

Like a marble in the pit of her soul, her magic roiled, as if to say, *That's the problem.*

Fontaine's eyes glazed over. Her lips moved soundlessly, as though she was having an argument with someone inside her own head.

Sera tried to look at the cards again, but Theo had already pocketed them.

"Draw one more," she pleaded. "It might make things clearer."

Fontaine returned to herself with a withering scowl. To Sera's surprise, she shoved the deck at her, then took a long drag of her pipe. "Draw for yourself. The cards are addled."

Sera shuffled clumsily. She didn't know when to stop or where to pull from, but then a card leaped from the deck all by itself. Val snatched it in mid-air, turning it over.

It was a single red rose.

Not a figure this time but a symbol.

Fontaine canted her head. "The rose," she said, tracing the gilded petals. "The official flower of Valterre. A symbol of rebirth and renewal." She traced the thorns along the stem, miming pricking her finger. "But not without pain. Without sacrifice."

She snapped her gaze up, and the darkness that gathered there made Sera shuffle closer to Theo. "The rose is both soft and dangerous. It can mean great beauty or untold destruction. It depends on the soil in which it grows. The forces that surround it."

Sera wanted to ask her more, about the cards and the saints and the prophecy—about what it meant for Valterre, and for her—but Bibi reappeared at that same moment, coming around the side of House Armand with a look of stark worry on her face. "I'm afraid we've been rumbled."

Theo stiffened, his hand flying to Sera's elbow. She jerked her chin, following his gaze, and caught sight of Madame Mercure's withering grimace in a second-story window. There was no mistaking the threat in her dark eyes.

"We should get out of here," Theo said, urgently. "Looks like we've outstayed our welcome."

"You never had one to begin with," said Fontaine, returning to her snarky form with impressive ease. "Cordelia has had eyes on you since you set foot in her garden."

"We'll go," said Sera, backing away now. "We really don't want any trouble."

The others turned, promptly bolting from the garden, just as Fontaine called after her. "Seraphine!"

Sera realized she was still holding the tarot deck.

She doubled back to return it. "Honest mistake."

"You seem to be full of those."

Sera bit back her retort. No point. No time. Leaving the wily old Cloak with the last word, she turned to go, but Fontaine pitched forward, dropping her voice until she alone could hear it.

"Fear is a fog you cannot see through. Only the light of bravery can banish it," she said, urgently. "When you decide what you're willing to sacrifice for your gift—your unwritten destiny, your own self-control—it will reveal itself to you."

The others were at the gate, calling for her.

"I don't know how to do that," said Sera, desperately.

"Think less. Look to the future, not the past. Otherwise, you'll be lost in the fog forever." Madame Fontaine made a shooing motion with her hands. "Now run. Before it's too late."

Sera caught up with the others out on the street. They broke into a jog, forgoing the cloaks they kept tucked under their arms.

"I don't know why we're running so hard," said Val, between gasps. "Mercure isn't going to chase us. She's too dignified for that kind of thing."

"And she doesn't have the right kind of shoes," added Bibi.

Even so, Sera quickened her pace. She was eager to get back to the Rose and Crown so they could pick through Fontaine's words, and look more closely at the cards Theo had swiped. She was so focused on getting out of the Hollows that she barely registered the carriage trundling toward them.

It screeched to a halt.

Bibi lunged, grabbing her arm. "Something's wrong."

They spun around, looking for Val and Theo, several steps behind. "Put your cloaks on," said Sera, urgently.

Too late. Footsteps pounded through the dark.

Theo yelled, "RUN!"

Sera turned back a heartbeat too late. Something hard slammed into the side of her head. The world turned sideways as the ground rose to meet her. Someone caught her before she fell, a breathy chuckle raking down her spine. Somewhere nearby, Bibi screamed. Theo's shouts grew more distant.

Bucking blindly, Sera kicked her legs and swung her fists. Her captor hissed as she connected with his jaw. "You little bitch."

She reared up just as he slammed his head down, cracking her nose. Pain spiderwebbed across her face, making her eyes stream.

"*Nnngh.* Get. Off." She bucked again, but a broad hand closed around her throat, choking the air from her. Her thoughts swam, the stars in the faraway sky slowly winking out.

Blackness rose like a wave, until there was only the dying shouts of her best friends and the cruel laughter of their captors rippling over her.

In those final moments of flickering awareness, Sera realized she'd been kidnapped. Amid her panic and confusion, she couldn't tell whether the enemy who had moved against her was a Cloak or a Dagger.

She hoped she lived long enough to find out.

Part II

"Those who move against the House of Rayere
Will die for their designs.
For there is no master greater than the king,
No power stronger than the Crown."

BY ORDER OF KING BERTRAND IV OF VALTERRE,
HOUSE OF RAYERE

Chapter 8

Seraphine

Plink.

Plink.

Pink.

First, there was darkness. Then pain, blooming like a flower in her skull. Noise filtered in, with a slow and steady dripping. And with it, the scent of seaweed and brine.

Plink.

Plink.

Plink.

There came a low, furious clacking. By the time Sera realized it was her own chattering teeth, she was finally coming to. Her cloak was gone, her bare arms half frozen. Beneath her cheek, the ground was cold and damp. Roughened stone scraped her as she turned. Sitting up was a struggle. Everything hurt. Her nose. Her jaw. Her wrists. She *ached*. Her hands were bound in front of her, the roughened rope chafing her skin.

Rising with a grunt, she came to her knees. It was dim here, almost black. In the distance, an oil lamp flickered on a stone wall. But there were bars between Sera and that solitary kernel of light. Thick metal bars.

She was in a cell.

Great.

She whipped her head around, regretting the quickness of the movement. Her head screamed in protest, her nose so blocked it was surely broken. The cell was small and windowless, and yet the smell of the sea seeped through the walls, borne on a howling wind. Salt water dripped from the ceiling and pooled in puddles around her.

This place was too damp to be the catacombs.

And Hugo's Passage didn't smell like this . . . like piss and sweat and brine. A dungeon, then. A hell she had not been to before. She scoured her aching mind for fragments of her last memory: Theo and Bibi shouting as a group of men descended upon them. Triumphant guffaws, the errant glint of a sword, the heel of a tall black boot . . . then the rattle of carriage wheels over stone.

Panic shot through Sera. Where the hell was she? And where were her friends?

"Hello?" she croaked out. Her *throat* ached. She could feel bruises there too. "Val? Theo? Bibi?"

There was scrabbling nearby, followed by a pained grunt. "Sera? Are you here?"

Theo! Theo was here. And he sounded just as sore as she was.

"I'm here!"

"Are you all right?" His voice was a low rasp.

"Been better." Inching toward the bars, she laid her forehead against them, letting the cool iron soothe the pain along the bridge of her nose. When she spoke again, her voice carried a little further, into the narrow walkway and toward his neighboring cell. "What happened?"

She hated how her voice broke on the question, like she was no more than a child cowering under her bed. She wanted to be strong for her friend, but she was aching and frightened and failing not to panic.

She heard him shuffling on the other side of the wall, making his way to the bars. "Whatever the hell that was, we survived it," he said, steady now, playing the role of protector. "And whatever else comes, we'll survive that too."

She closed her eyes, willing a flicker of courage into her heart.

"I glimpsed the royal crest when they shoved me into the carriage," said Theo. "Right before they knocked me out. Looks like we're in one of the king's dungeons. By the smell of seaweed coming through the walls, I'd bet we're under the Summer Palace."

Southwest of Fantome, then. Near the mouth of the Verne.

"Bibi? Val?" Sera's voice cracked from the strain.

No answer.

Theo rattled the bars of his cell. "BIBI!" he bellowed, the call echoing around them and reaching into the shadowy bowels of the dungeon. "VAL!"

“SHUT THE FUCK UP!” a gruff male-sounding voice called back.

“Where are they?” hissed Sera.

“Probably still out cold,” said Theo, a note of hope in his voice when he added, “Or maybe they got away. I never saw them get dragged in. Did you?”

“I think I heard Bibi scream. I don’t know about Val.” It had all happened so fast. Sera’s lips twisted. She felt a cut there, too. “Do you think it was Mercure who tipped the soldiers off?”

He ground out a curse. “I don’t know.”

Regret needled Sera. It had been a mistake going to House Armand. They had played with fire and paid for it.

“I’m sorry,” she whispered, weakly.

“Don’t be. We’ll figure this out.”

“Any opening suggestions?”

“Start chewing on your binds. If we can get our hands free, at least we’ll be ready for whatever happens next.”

With little else to do, Sera started chewing on the rope around her wrists. It was damp and it stank, and she had a vague image of herself like a rat gnawing through wood. Definitely a low point. But at least they were in the gutter together.

Theo went quiet for a while, doing the same. Every so often, one of them would stop to call out Val and Bibi’s names. When no answer came, they’d return to their task, the time passing in the steadily dripping water around them.

Sera was down to the final threads around her wrists when bootsteps sounded nearby. She scrabbled backward, hitting the wall of her cell just as they came to a stop. A tremor ran through her at the sight of two towering nightguards leering in at her. Longswords glinted at their hips and by the matching hostile glint in their eyes, she sensed these were the same soldiers who had kidnapped her.

"Look who woke up early," sneered the one on the right. A bald man with red cheeks and a high forehead.

"Guess you didn't hit me hard enough," said Sera, bitterly.

The other one snorted, his thick moustache twitching. "Look in a mirror and say that again."

Grant me one and I'll crack it over your thick head.

Rage rushed through her, making her palms spark expectantly. She looked down, accidentally drawing their attention to the rope fraying around her wrists.

The cell door swung open and they stomped inside. Sera reared backward but there was nowhere to go. She kicked out as they rebound her wrists tighter than before. Her hands were pressed inward, her fingers interlacing. Her magic, now turned against itself, winked out.

Useless.

Not that she knew how to use it anyhow.

Still struggling with the binds, she was too distracted to fight off the cloth they balled up and stuffed in her mouth. Panic surged again. With her nose broken, it was already hard to breathe. Her head grew both light and heavy at once.

Next door, Theo was shouting.

"The Shadowsmith is awake," grunted the bald soldier, taking off in a clatter of footsteps.

"The Shadowsmith has questions!" Theo roared. "Like,

what the hell are we doing here? Where are our friends? And what are you going to do with that—" He broke off, descending into a string of muffled swears.

The other soldier remained, looming over Sera like a reaper. A sack was tugged roughly over her head. Her protests turned to frustrated whimpers as she struggled to suck in air around the gag. Soot marred her lips and filled her nostrils, the stained fabric sitting heavy against her tongue.

Bound and unseeing, Sera was dragged to her feet. With her airflow restricted, her head throbbed even worse than before. From the cell next door, she heard a similar scuffle. Theo was still hissing and cursing, fighting the guard that dragged him down the narrow walkway alongside her. Any relief at leaving the dungeons was short-lived.

Now she had to worry about what awaited them beyond it. The gallows or the noose. Or maybe they'd put blocks around their feet and chuck them into the Verne, let them wash up on the shore in three days' time like the rebels across Fantome.

Sera stopped fighting the guard's hold on her. Better to preserve her energy for wherever they were headed. She wondered what crime they had pulled her in for.

Had word of her involvement with the monsters of Fantome reached the king, or was it their recent trial shipment of exploding Lightfire that had drawn his ire? Or had it been a vengeful Cordelia Mercure, watching them from the windows of House Armand, who'd used one of her ravens to send a missive to the nightguards?

Perhaps it had been a trap all along.

Theo stopped fighting too, both of them falling silent as they were dragged up a winding flight of stairs. On and on they climbed, away from the dank squalor of the dungeons to lamplight and warm air and the faint smell of the sea. Distantly, Sera heard waves crashing against the rocks. She pictured the Summer Palace in her mind, the decadent white-stone castle that sat on a sloping cliff overlooking the South Sea. It was one of several extravagant royal dwellings throughout Valterre, but the one the king favored when the last of the winter frost melted and the weather brightened.

Doors groaned as they were opened for them, soldiers muttering under their breath. Their surrounds grew warmer still, the scent of fresh lilies trickling in. The floor changed from rough stone to polished tile, the rooms they passed through growing larger and grander. Sera could tell by the echo of her own footsteps.

Finally, they came to stop, the door closing behind them with a thud. Plush carpet softened Sera's footsteps as she drew a shallow soot-choked breath. Her lungs screamed for air, her head swimming dangerously from the exertion of getting here. Wherever *here* was.

This room felt smaller than the others. Closer, somehow. Though her head was covered, she glimpsed firelight flickering through the grainy sack, felt its heat rippling along her bare arms. And yet, she still shivered with an uncomfortable mix of anger and fear.

She felt, rather than saw, the sharpened attention of others in the room. Their breaths were loud in the silence as she was maneuvered in smaller steps. Her hip bumped the edge of a table.

Her guard's voice then, too close to her ear. "*Behave.* Or I have orders to run you through with my sword."

Sera resisted the urge to jerk her head back and shatter his nose as his hands came to her shoulders, shoving her roughly into a chair.

Beside her, Theo received the same treatment.

The sack was ripped from her head, taking several strands of hair with it. Wincing at the flare of light, she blinked furiously, catching quick glimpses of her surroundings. A dining room more splendid than any she had ever seen. Lush forest-green wallpaper and gilt-framed oil paintings. A crackling fireplace and a three-tiered chandelier dripping from a high corniced ceiling.

Across the table, someone cleared their throat.

Sera jerked her chin down.

What little breath she had left her.

Ransom Hale was sitting directly across from her.

There was a Dagger on either side of him, a woman Sera knew as Nadia Raine, and a tall lethal-looking man she couldn't place. She paid them little mind, the sudden violent tug in her chest dragging her attention back to *him*. It was like seeing the sun rise after an endless night, his handsomeness so acute that for a moment, she felt punched through with longing.

But those eyes . . . *Saints.* Those honeyed eyes that had once looked upon her with such naked desire now burned with firelight and rage.

All of it for her.

Confusion careened over Sera. Why in Saint Oriel's name was Ransom Hale sitting across from her in the king's royal dining room? Looking thoroughly *unaccosted*—well kempt and well rested, without a single dark hair out of place. He looked good. Too good.

On his right-hand-side, Nadia looked good too. Apart from the vicious scowl on her face. The other Dagger looked faintly amused. A thick scar spiderwebbed the entire left side of his shorn head, but it was not a recent injury.

Was Ransom behind her kidnapping? Had he ordered the bruises that now marred her face in revenge for the smugglers she had stolen from under his nose? For the Lightfire that would soon destroy his hold on the city?

Did he think her a rebel too?

The deep sting of betrayal made her stiffen in her seat. Shoving down her traitorous simmering attraction to him, she returned his glare with as much ferocity as she could muster. She wanted to tell him to wipe that murderous look off his face. He had no right to judge her for anything she had done these last few months. Not while those hands of his were covered in fresh shadow-marks. And there were more still through the V of his shirt. At least twice as many kills than weeks since they had last seen each other.

Theo grunted as the bag was removed from his head. A quick side-glance revealed his silver hair was stained red from an ugly gash on his forehead. A deep bruise marred the underside of his jaw and his shirt had been ripped down to his breastbone.

His turquoise eyes were narrowed, filled with the same hatred that shone at them from across the table.

Three Daggers. Two Flames. Four soldiers standing straight-backed against the walls, silently observing them.

Ransom's attention remained entirely on Sera, his eyes flicking along her face, like he was counting her cuts and bruises. Cataloguing his victories, no doubt. She bit down on her gag, hating her forced silence.

Last autumn, they had spent weeks trying to kill each other across the quarters of Fantome, traded vicious insults and even bloodied wounds. And yet, in all that time, she had never seen the Dagger look so . . . *feral.*

And his eyes weren't even silver.

Without a lick of Shade in his system, Ransom Hale was entirely himself. Clear-headed and hazel-gazed, and all the more menacing for it.

"Red *really* is your color, Seraphine." Breaking the strained silence, Nadia offered a leering smirk. "I love how all that blood turns your hair pink."

Theo grunted around his gag.

Sera let the barb wash over her. She knew she was blood-soaked. It was hardly a surprise that the Dagger would enjoy the sight of it, after what had happened with Lark at the Aurore. She refused to give her the satisfaction of flinching.

Ransom's fingers slowly curled into fists, drawing Sera's attention to the gaudy skull ring on his left hand. The same ring her father had worn as Head of the Daggers. Revulsion prickled along her skin. She looked away, toward the empty seat at the top of the table. It was high-backed and lined in red velvet. Guarded, even now, by two stern-faced soldiers.

Was the king truly coming? Or was this spectacle some kind of grand power play arranged by the Daggers? In the fog of her mind, she didn't know which was worse. Only that she was seated too close to the fireplace. Smoke thinned the air, snatching away the oxygen she so desperately needed.

She inhaled sharply, her lungs contracting as they struggled for breath. Nadia was still talking. Ransom was silent. Seething. Theo was struggling against his binds.

Sera's vision started to blur.

The Dagger beside Ransom reclined in his chair, folding his arms over his chest. "I see it, you know," he remarked. "Even under all that caked blood. Actually, the blood makes her hotter. But that's probably just me."

A muscle ticked in Ransom's jaw. "Shut the fuck up, Caruso."

"Oh, do you prefer the strained silence where we all just death-stare each other?" Caruso turned on Theo then, arching a dark brow. "And by the way, what the fuck is Hugo Versini doing at the table? Did someone dig up that grave too?"

Nadia bristled. "Do *not* joke about that."

What did *that* mean? Sera's curiosity swiftly flittered away. She was trying too hard not to pass out.

Caruso leaned across the table. "Are you sure you're sitting on the right side of things here, Versini?"

Theo jerked, letting out a string of muffled curses. If that gag wasn't stuffed halfway down his throat, he would have eviscerated Caruso, even if this particular Dagger, with his icy bright eyes and savage smile, looked as wild and lethal as a wolf.

"Did you really think you'd get away with it?" said Nadia, turning her venom back on Sera. "That we wouldn't know it was you who took him after what you did at the Aurore?"

The haze in Sera's head thickened. She blinked, slow and heavy, trying to fight the sluggishness in her mind. Her head lolled to one side, the effort of holding it up suddenly too great.

"Remove her gag," Ransom ordered the soldiers, his eyes never leaving hers. "She's suffocating."

"Let her choke," said Nadia.

No one moved.

Theo slammed his bound hands against the table.

Sera heaved, desperately seeking a morsel of air. The soot stung her eyes. She was embarrassed at how tears streaked her cheeks, mingling with the dried blood there. In all the ways she had envisioned her reunion with the Head of the Daggers, not once had she ever imagined herself like this: bloody and beaten and slowly suffocating.

Black spots swarmed her vision. She was so spent she didn't even flinch when Ransom lunged across the table. He steadied her jaw with one hand—his grip deceptively gentle, despite the violence in his eyes, and with the other, deftly yanked the gag from her mouth.

"*Breathe*, Seraphine," he said in a low, hurried voice. "Come on."

Gasping down a ragged inhale, Sera threw her head back, greedily filling her aching lungs. Fresh tears streamed down her cheeks, and she let them fall, no longer caring. When she looked back again, Ransom was already back in his chair. Sitting as stiff as a statue, as though he hadn't just sprung across the table to help her.

"Very gallant," remarked Caruso. "Should I do the same for Versini, or do you think he'll bite me?"

"Why gag me in the first place?" croaked Sera. "Am I supposed to be grateful now?"

Ransom ignored her, moving his glare to the guard that stood nearest Theo. "Here's a tip, soldier. Next time you're tasked with transporting the king's prisoners, don't suffocate them at his dinner table before he shows up." He bared his teeth, his voice becoming a low growl. "Or beat them to a bloody fucking pulp without instruction."

She supposed she had her answer, even if he hadn't bothered to direct it at her. This was not Ransom's doing after all. She was embarrassed by the silent rush of her relief.

Lip curling, she said, "I imagine that was part of their fun."

"More like a necessary means," sneered the soldier. "The firebrands gave chase."

"You ambushed us!"

The soldier simply snorted, not even bothering to deny it.

Ignoring them, Sera turned to help Theo with his gag. With her hands bound, she had to twist fully in her seat to reach the knot at the back of his head, but even with trembling fingers, she managed to undo it.

He spat the rag out, and a string of curses with it. Most were directed at the leering soldiers, but he reserved a few choice words for Caruso, who weathered it all with a big shit-eating grin.

Ransom bolted to his feet.

Sera whipped her head around, sure she had missed something vital in the exchange.

Nadia glowered up at him. "Leave it, Ransom."

"He can't help himself," said Caruso, with a chuckle.

"What are you talking about?" rasped Sera.

It was Caruso who answered, dragging a finger along the front of his neck. She thought it was a threat but then Theo said in a quiet, furious voice, "There are fingerprints all over your neck."

Ah. That'd be the attempted strangulation. It wasn't like Sera wasn't already keenly aware of the bruises. Ransom must have seen them when she'd twisted to untie Theo's gag.

He rounded the dining table, like a beast on the hunt. On instinct, Sera huddled closer to Theo, but for once, the Dagger wasn't glaring at her. All that rippling hatred was fixed on the soldiers that had carted them up here only moments ago.

They drew their swords. "At ease, Dagger."

"I'm surprised you're familiar with that term," he spat.

The first soldier raised his sword, and Sera was pleased to see that it trembled a little.

"Word to the unwise," Caruso called out. "I'd stow that ceremonial toothpick, before he shoves it up your ass."

Ransom lunged, swiping the sword without so much as a tussle. In the next instant, it was pressed against the soldier's neck. Sera was just starting to enjoy herself when Nadia moved, sliding across the table like a cat on the prowl.

She grabbed her bloodstained collar, yanking her up from her seat. "Where did you take him?" she hissed. "Tell me or I swear I'll gut you right here on this table."

Sera headbutted her, knocking her back. "What the hell are you talking about?"

Nadia rose to her knees on the table, but Theo was on his feet then, swinging his bound hands like a club. Nadia dodged the blow, but it seemed to activate Caruso, who prowled around to the other side of the table. "Let the ladies work this out, Versini, or I'll add an inch to that nasty gash on your forehead."

Sera registered a faint cracking sound as Ransom smashed his fist into the face of the soldier behind her. Her eyes remained on Nadia, who was coming at her again. This time, Sera hinged backward, nearly toppling from her chair as she dodged the seething Dagger. Theo surrendered his fight with Caruso to grab a butter knife from the table.

Nadia, meanwhile, palmed a fork and placed it under Sera's chin. "Start talking, grave robber."

Sera stiffened as the prongs bit into her skin, pressing her back against the chair. Behind her, an all-out brawl had broken out. Caruso jumped into the fray as the other three soldiers swarmed Ransom, trying to wrangle him into submission.

Chaos descended in a fury. Sera couldn't hear Nadia's threats over the sudden chorus of shouts, but the fork was slowly biting into her skin. Theo, who had worked his hands free with the knife now, knocked the makeshift weapon from Nadia's hands, just as the door to the dining room swung open.

In walked the King of Valterre.

Chapter 9

Seraphine

King Bertrand IV of Valterre took one look at the chaos before him and barked a furious command. His personal guards drew their swords, rushing forward.

The tussle fell apart with remarkable speed. Ransom and Caruso backed away, moving around the table with their hands raised. Ransom looked a little worse for wear now, which made Sera feel somewhat better. Strands of his thick black hair dipped into his eyes, and there were smudges of blood on his left cheek and on the collar of his shirt.

It was not his own.

Caruso was bright-eyed and panting, like a wolf who had just taken down a deer. Or indeed a Dagger who had just beaten the shit out of a pair of the king's soldiers in his own damn palace. Not a hint of remorse on his face. Nadia slid back into her own chair with leonine grace, absently smoothing the flyaway strands of her sleek ponytail as though she hadn't just forked Sera in the jugular.

"What in the name of Valterre is going on in here?" demanded the king. "If you insist on scrapping like a pack of stray dogs, you can take it to the streets."

His thick black moustache twitched in anger. It matched the fullness of his beard and considerable sideburns, the rich hair there running into a mass of tumbling curls that crowned the rest of his large round head. The wig did nothing for him.

The king was portlier than his official portrait suggested, with puffed-up ruddy cheeks, deep-set gray eyes, and a bulbous nose. He was dressed formally in a black-and-gold frock coat lined in thick ermine, striped with a crimson sash that ran from his right shoulder to his left hip. A line of seven ribbons—his ceremonial war medals—occupied the left side of his upper chest and swayed as he approached the dining table.

Four somber-faced figures dressed in courtly attire entered behind the king, and stood behind his chair, their keen eyes assessing everything. Sera guessed by their age and finery that they were the king's royal council of advisers. *The silent quartet*, as they were known in the penny papers.

"Apologies, Your Majesty," said Ransom, who had the good grace to look ashamed. Or at least, fake it. "There was a misunderstanding in your absence."

The king quirked a brow. "Of what sort?"

"Your soldiers ran into my fist. Several times."

Sera's eyes widened. Had Ransom lost his mind, speaking that way to the most powerful man in—

King Bertrand chuckled. The ripples of it raised the hairs on her arms, but his amusement seemed to set everyone else in the room at ease. Even one of his stern-faced advisers cracked a smile. Still smarting, the brawling soldiers resumed their spots against the walls. The king looked them over. "Next time, I'll set some house rules for my prized Daggers. I suppose you'll tell me they deserved it, Hale."

"Yes, Your Majesty," he said coldly.

The king gave Sera a once-over. "Did the girl run into your fist too, Ransom?"

That muscle in his jaw ticked. "The handiwork of your soldiers."

The king's eyes flashed with intrigue. He sat back in his chair, glancing between them. "I see."

Sera took his utter lack of surprise at her injuries to mean he had likely ordered his soldiers to rough them up—or at the very least, didn't tell them *not* to—which meant he was exactly the careless asshole she figured he was. Perhaps he deserved his own brewing rebellion.

By the murderous look on Theo's face, she guessed he was thinking the same.

They were in dangerous territory now. They would have to tread carefully, keep the mutinous expressions from their faces, and bite their tongues until they figured out what the hell was going on here.

Returning his attention to Ransom, the king said, "If only Dufort could see you now. What a beast he has raised. Brawling at the Summer Palace against the king's own guards. Arrogant and unrepentant to the last. I expect he would be pleased with his successor."

Despite the roaring fire, the temperature in the room plummeted.

Sera shuddered.

Ransom swallowed.

The king clicked his fingers, summoning refreshments, before turning his beady eyes on Theo. "Here sits Cordelia Mercure's prized Shadowsmith," he said, stroking his beard. "No longer a student of Shade but of *Lightfire*, it seems . . . Tell me, Mr. Branch, or should I say *Versini*, was House Armand not exciting enough for you? Or are you often led astray by pretty little creatures?"

Sera fought the urge to gag. This man might well be King of Valterre but he was singularly revolting.

Theo kept his voice even. "I am merely a student of innovation, Your Majesty."

The king *hmm'd.* "Just like your *illustrious* ancestors."

Behind him, his quartet whispered furiously to one another.

Theo bristled, his lips pressed together so tightly, they lost their color. Sera squeezed his knee under the table—three quick pulses: *Keep it together.*

Presently, a servant arrived with a tray full of wine goblets and a platter of cured meats, fresh bread rolls, and grapes, and more kinds of cheese than Sera had ever seen before.

She knew she must be hungry since she couldn't remember the last time she ate, but as the king took a deep swig from his goblet, her stomach twisted at the blood-red wine dribbling down his beard. Shoving a wedge of mottled blue cheese into his mouth, he twisted in his seat, settling the fullness of his attention on her.

She hated how his eyes roamed, his tongue darting out to wet his stained lips. "Seraphine Marchant." He tipped his goblet at her. "At last, we meet."

She could speak. Now it was Theo's turn to squeeze her knee.

She offered a demure smile. "I didn't realize we were overdue, Your Majesty."

"Well, you have been busy, according to my spies."

"Spring is an industrious time," she said, coolly. "Just look at how busy the birds are."

She felt his advisers' attentions sharpen, their mirrored frowns making them look eerily similar. The room had fallen deathly quiet now, the Daggers watching their exchange like a trio of hawks.

The king took another languid sup of wine. "For months now, I've longed to meet the firebrand who saved my capital from ruin . . ."

There was a hardness in his eyes that belied his words. A challenge was brewing there, as though in doing something about it, she had overstepped her mark. Made him look bad.

"As I understand it, you managed to rid our hideous plague of sewer monsters with your innovative jars of Lightfire . . . Or so you have been telling people." The king cast a knowing glance toward his nearest adviser, a pale elderly man with a long silver beard.

Sera kept her expression blank, but unease prickled under her skin. He was a lot better versed than she'd suspected. Then again, they had been up and down the length and breadth of Valterre spouting about Lightfire to any smuggler who would hear them. She had been naive to think he wouldn't hear about it—or indeed *care* about it.

"The question is, what do you plan to do with your special brand of magic now?" His voice fell to a deadly low. "I hear your first shipment has reached the streets of Fantome. Some of your vials have found their way into the hands of those who seek to harm me. They are using your magic to protect themselves from the consequences of their own traitorous actions."

There was a heavy, daunting silence.

Sera's heart thundered furiously, panic scrambling her thoughts.

This was bad. Very bad.

"So I *must* ask," he went on, with a flat, sinister smile, "what else does your Order have in mind for my rioting capital? Do you count yourselves among the rebels who seek to dethrone me?"

"No." The word whooshed out on a staggered breath. "No, of course not."

"We harbor no ill will toward the Crown," added Theo, quickly.

The king's eyes darkened. Very slowly, he said, "Then why are you *arming* my rebels?"

Sera grasped for something to say that was not about to get them killed. "Lightfire is not a weapon, Your Majesty. It's simply a way for the good people of Valterre to protect themselves from Shade. To feel safe in their own city."

Caruso snorted.

The king's advisers exchanged a series of bemused glances.

The king canted his head. "Would you prefer that your own king feels unsafe in his kingdom?"

A dangerous question.

Sera could see now how deeply the king and the Daggers were intertwined, how he relied on more than just his soldiers to keep his restless subjects in line. Ransom and his Order had their own part to play in the king's secret undercourt, and Sera's Order of Flames was plainly disrupting it.

All she could do now was plead ignorance.

"I'm no rebel, Your Majesty," she said, firmly. "We only want what's good for the kingdom." She swallowed. "And our king."

Theo nodded emphatically. "We made the Lightfire to save Fantome from those monsters." This, at least, was true. And by the way Theo's eyes shone with conviction, Sera hoped the king would believe it. "We would never knowingly move against the Crown."

"Bullshit," muttered Nadia.

The king sat back in his chair, momentarily surrendering his ire for a slab of cured ham, shoving the entire thing into his mouth in one bite. Swallowing thickly, he said, "Let us put your stirring convictions to the test, then. I'm sure you are wondering why I invited you here."

Sera exchanged a side-glance with Theo. *Invited* was one way of putting it.

"I have a task for you." He paused meaningfully, his gaze roving across the table. "*All* of you."

The Daggers shifted uncomfortably.

"You are well aware of the dissent festering across my kingdom." The king's expression turned grave, the high color fading from his cheeks. "The fall of the Aurore has marked a change in the fortunes of this kingdom. A change that some believe was foretold by Saint Oriel one thousand years ago."

Behind him, his quartet dipped their heads in perfect unison, wariness alighting on their withered faces.

"In their fear and ignorance, the people of Valterre are holding me accountable for this act of divinity. In the wake of those monsters, and the destruction of their great symbol of light, they believe my time as king is at an end. That they need a different leader." He barked a mirthless laugh. "Simple minds will reach for simple explanations, but I have done nothing these past few months to earn such flagrant, violent ungratefulness."

Perhaps that's the problem, thought Sera.

The king hadn't shown his face once in Fantome since the monsters had ripped through it, or even issued a letter of strength and solidarity to his people. Not before or after the Aurore fell. He had willingly neglected the chaos in the capital, letting the wave of paranoia swell, and only cared about it now that the tide was finally reaching him in his castle.

It was an effort to keep these thoughts from her face, but she did her best, pressing her lips together until her teeth bit into them.

"There is an agitator, of course. Every uprising needs a

leader. Someone to seize upon their terror and whip them into a fury that cannot be contained by force alone."

Not that he hadn't tried, evidently.

The king steepled his hands, bringing them to his lips. "I cannot quell the flames of rebellion if I do not first fell the dragon."

"Who is the dragon?" asked Sera, carefully.

It was Ransom who answered. "The People's Saint."

The king grimaced. "The insurgent in question is my wayward nephew Prince Andreas Rayere." He drummed his fingers along the table, adding a percussion to the rising wave of his anger. "The ungrateful bastard son of my late brother, Hector. Regrettably, Andreas's mother is a first cousin of Rafael Mondragon."

"As in . . . the newly crowned King of Urnica?" said Theo.

"Very astute, Versini," remarked the king drolly. "Someone is keeping up with their penny papers."

Sera noted the subtle change of atmosphere. No longer was the king leering at them with veiled threats and insidious questions. Rather, he was holding court with them, betraying his frustrations as though they were an extension of his trusted quartet and not two warring factions who had been scrapping like hyenas in the dirt not thirty minutes ago.

"So your nephew has ties to Mondragon's court," said Nadia.

The king gave an affirming grunt. "A court that already has designs on conquering my kingdom."

That much Sera knew. As neighboring kingdoms and long-standing rivals, Valterre and Urnica shared a long and bloodied history. In recent decades, they had been enjoying a rare spate of hard-fought peace, but Sera knew from the maps that once papered the walls of her old bedroom, there was nutrient-rich land in the southwest of this kingdom that had, centuries ago, belonged to Urnica. Land that the new Mondragon king no doubt intended to reclaim. King Rafael was young and thirsty, more brutal than his predecessor, and by all accounts, eager to make a name for himself on the wider continent.

"So war is coming to Valterre," said Ransom darkly.

"War is already here," murmured Sera.

Fury simmered in the Dagger's gaze, casting the rest of the room and its occupants in sudden shadow. For a moment, it felt like it was just the two of them, trading silent accusations across the table. Oh yes, war had been here all winter. It thrummed between them even now.

She looked away, biting her lip to focus her thoughts. Dutifully ignoring the hard line of his jaw and the careless sweep of his dark hair, the white scar that bisected his lip and the memory of how she had once licked it.

Something far greater than their enmity was quickly coming to the fore. Something urgent and vital and growing by the day—an uprising that could change everything.

"Do you understand my concern?" The king's question jolted her from her thoughts.

Theo answered. "Valterre has a formidable army, but if war comes to our kingdom, you are better off using those forces along our borders. With your eyes on Urnica, it will make it difficult to defend Valterre from within . . . From this *People's*

Saint, and whatever power he possesses. Not to mention whatever deal he may strike with his cousin, Mondragon."

The king tipped his goblet in answer. "You were right," he remarked to his advisers. "It is indeed gratifying to watch a Versini mind at work."

"So this Andreas has to go," said Ransom, coolly.

"Why do you need those two?" Caruso jutted his thumb in Sera's direction. "This is clearly a task for the Daggers."

The advisers canted their heads, watching through hooded gazes as the king no doubt parroted what they had discussed in private before now.

"All magic in this kingdom answers to the King of Valterre," he said, pointedly. "That goes for Shade *and* Lightfire. The Daggers have a seasoned reputation for finding and killing enemies of the Crown. But the two people sitting across from you destroyed an army of monsters never before seen in Fantome with a kind of new magic that rivals the very power of Shade." Peeling his lips back in challenge, he looked now to Sera. "If there is to be a new Order in my kingdom, it will bend the knee to me."

It was not hard to miss the implied *or else . . .*

"The Flames are not to be trusted," said Nadia quickly. "Seraphine Marchant is no innocent."

The king gave a dismissive flick of his wrist. "I don't concern myself with matters of morality, Dagger. Only victory."

He ignored their burgeoning looks of discomfort. "Andreas has always been a battle-shy bookworm who can barely hoist a sword, let alone wield one. He sequestered himself at the

Appoline for the better part of the last decade, kissing the feet of our dead saints and forsaking his destiny on the battlefield. Indeed, he did not even deign to make the journey home to honor his father upon his death. No, there is no true blood of Valterre in that boy's veins. Andreas was born an Urnica turncoat and coward."

The king tapped his goblet, and a servant scurried to refill it. "It seems that as of recently Andreas has acquired not just a measure of actual personality, but the kind of influence that can sway even hardened battle-worn prisoners to his cause. Which is, as you may have guessed, overthrowing *me*."

"Alas," said Sera under her breath.

Ransom shot her a warning look.

"Andreas had a fall on the night of the great storm," the king went on. "According to his fellow scholars at the Appoline, he climbed the clock-tower that night and got struck by lightning. Somehow, he survived the ordeal. When he awoke on the lawn, his eyes were glowing." The king drew a long breath, glancing back to his advisers. "Shortly after, Andreas surrendered his royal title. He now styles himself as a saint."

Sera had gone perfectly still. She swore she knew that memory—the sound of a bell chiming, the poker-hot shriek of lightning running through her bones. A falling tower. A fading clock face. She had dreamed it over and over again. She had *felt* it.

She reached for Theo's hands under the table.

He squeezed her fingers four times.

Don't. Say. A. Word.

"My advisers believe that Andreas is the first saint of the

Second Coming," added the king, with great derision. "Blessed with the fortitude and charisma of a natural leader, or so rumors abound."

"A true prince charming," remarked Nadia.

The Silver-tongue.

Fontaine's tarot card danced in Seraphine's head. Her heart galloped, heat rushing through her blood. Open talk of the saints was drawing her magic out, like it wanted to listen in or claim a role for itself.

Please behave.

Squeezing her eyes shut, she blew out a careful breath.

Please, please, please.

"Seraphine."

She looked up at the sound of Ransom's voice. His brows were drawn low, his lips parted. "Are you all right?"

A hush had come over the room.

The king cocked his head. "You do look hideously pale."

Sera reached for a lie, something to chase off the suspicion she was bringing down upon herself, but her mind kept snagging on that word: *saint.*

She and Andreas were the same.

Not only was she not alone in this new destiny, but fate had tossed the identity of another right into her lap. Someone who was not afraid to embrace their new powers.

She swallowed, quickly looking away. "It's just . . . a lot to take in."

Ransom was silent then. Sera didn't dare look at him again. Did he remember their goodbye at Our Sacred Saints' Cathedral all those months ago? How her magic had sparked at his touch? Did he know she was different now too?

"So it's really true, then?" said Caruso. "About the saints coming again?"

"The truth is immaterial." The king's face was stark, his words holding a chilling finality. "Anyone who seeks to overthrow the Crown will meet the sharp end of Valterre's sword." He laid his hands flat on the table, glancing from one side to the other. "Which leads me neatly to the matter at hand. I want you to hunt down my nephew and bring me his dead body."

Chapter 10

Ransom

Ransom had been expecting the king's request from the moment he arrived at the Summer Palace. He was, after all, a trained assassin. The best in Fantome, with an entire Order under his thumb. It was why he'd brought Nadia and Caruso. If the king wanted something done—and that something was *personal*—then Ransom was taking two of his best Daggers with him.

He had not, however, been expecting to come face to face with Seraphine Marchant. As he'd sat drumming his fingers in that sweltering, overwrought dining room, he hadn't been thinking about her at all. For once.

When the door swung open, he'd pitched forward in his seat, as though tugged by some invisible force between them. The sight of the troublesome spitfire, bound and trembling like a prisoner on her way to the gallows, kindled in him a rage so quick and violent his mind had emptied entirely.

When the guard yanked the sack off her head, revealing a gruesome patchwork of cuts and bruises across her bloodless face, a roar of fury gathered in his chest. He fought it with every ounce of his control, even as his fingers itched for the Shade he had surrendered upon his arrival.

He had been doing *so* well.

Until he saw the bruises on her neck.

Something inside him had snapped. A red mist clouded his thoughts, and he forgot what side he was on. In truth, he didn't care. He was on his feet in one heartbeat, squaring up to those soft-jawed brutes in the next, his mind tunneling until all he could hear was the satisfying thwack of his fist striking their faces over and over again.

He could have lost his own head for it and destroyed the Daggers' good standing with the Crown while he was at it, but by the time he was pummeling the breath out of those smarmy assholes, he found he didn't care much for his own head. Seeing the spitfire again had punched a hole in all that careful resentment he had been stockpiling over the winter. One look at her, sitting on the other side of that table with her chin raised like a battle-worn princess, had made him weak for her all over again. Had he taken Shade tonight, every soldier in that room would be dead.

When the king arrived, Ransom's blood was still fizzing with adrenaline.

Bertrand had called him a beast for it.

Ransom had felt like one.

He *still* felt like one.

And try as he did, he could not keep his eyes off *her*. He had been starved of Seraphine Marchant for far too long. Her delicate heart-shaped face. Those searing blue eyes flecked with bronze. That soft, smart mouth.

The spitfire was bad for his concentration. Bad for his blood pressure. Bad for business.

She's the enemy.

Three times, Nadia had pinched his leg under the table. Reminders that Seraphine Marchant was *not* one of their own. All winter, she had been methodically dismantling their trade, screwing with their livelihood, and now the king himself had all but accused her of being a rebel, a potential traitor to the Crown.

No, Seraphine Marchant was no friend of the Daggers.

She was a threat: to the Order and to the kingdom. To his own furious heartbeat.

But there was a greater, more powerful enemy at play now.

"So, just to be clear, you want us to kill someone who might be an actual, literal saint?" said Caruso, with a flatness that told Ransom he was struggling to believe it.

"I want you to kill a traitor," said the king. "Do you have a problem with that, Dagger?"

"No." Caruso shrugged. No great moral quandary there. Saint or sinner, a mark was a mark. "I like a challenge."

"Me too," added Nadia, after a beat. "The sooner the city settles, the better."

"Hale?" asked the king.

They were hardly in a position to refuse, and Ransom was already long past morality. Stamped and damned, and waiting for hell. He dipped his chin. "Consider it done."

Killing the king's nephew wasn't just about money, though the reward would be considerable. It was a matter of their continued protection. The freedom to go on doing whatever the hell they liked, without consequence.

The silence across the table was palpable.

The Shadowsmith's face was like stone, his tanned skin marbled with bruises. *Versini*, the king had called him earlier. He'd plainly hated it. Which made Ransom warm to it.

"Flames?" prompted the king. "Lost your tongues?"

Seraphine hesitated, looking to Versini. "We're not assassins, Your Majesty."

"But she *is* a killer," said Nadia, coldly. "She just does it for free."

Seraphine cut her eyes at her. "I don't hurt people, for sport or coin."

Ransom stifled a groan. Couldn't she see there was no choice here? The king hadn't extended an offer to them; he had given an order. And if she refused it, she wouldn't walk out of this place alive. Hell, she'd barely gotten here in one piece.

"But we can help," said Versini, engaging some actual survival instincts. "Whatever Your Majesty commands. Of course."

"Of course," Seraphine added quietly.

"Very good," grunted the king.

One of his advisers rushed forward, whispering something in his ear.

Nodding, he returned his attention to the table. "Once you are done dealing with my nephew, I want you to take a trip to the Isle of Alisa."

Ransom's brows shot up. Of all the places he was expecting to be sent . . .

The Isle of Alisa was on a small man-made lake in the middle of the village of Ra'azule in west Valterre. Barely the size of the Hollows, the island was home to the reclusive Order of Alisans, priestesses who devoted their lives to Alisa, Saint of the Sick. There they prayed to her, morning, noon, and night, forgoing all manner of nutritious food for bone broth, swearing off all their material possessions, and giving up all possibility of love. Wealthy folk paid good coin for their prayers, believing the Alisans held more sway over their ailing loved ones than even the best physicians in Valterre.

Folly of the rich, his mother used to call it, but the Order had existed for centuries, and in their devout selflessness had become a source of pride for Valterre.

"To repent?" he asked now.

The silent quartet tittered at the suggestion.

The king's face was grave. "There's another mark there in need of urgent attention. A young acolyte, a Sister Marianne, who has been acting out since the storm. According to their Mother Superior, the girl tore down their prayer tower. They found her in the rubble the following morning. For months she's been unconscious, flitting in and out of dreamsleep. Her sisters have been praying for her night and day. Recently, she has awoken and is acting . . . *destructively.* She seems to be developing somewhat . . . *saintly* powers."

"You think this Sister Marianne is a new saint?" asked Ransom carefully.

The king gave an affirming grunt. "She has already killed one of her sisters. The other Alisans are petrified of her. Mother Madeline has written to me personally of her concerns. For now, the girl is being kept under lock and key. But she will need to be dealt with before her power escalates, and the matter buried along with her on that island."

"You mean to kill *another* saint?" said Seraphine, aghast.

"I intend to do away with an agitator and a murderer," said the king darkly. "These *creatures* are not like the saints of the first age. The world is very different now. The meaning of that word has changed."

Seraphine chewed on her lip. Whatever thoughts were dancing behind her eyes, Ransom silently urged her to swallow them.

"We understand," said Versini. "You have made everything plain."

"Except this," the king added. "If you fail to complete the task, or you abscond on the journey, the redhead will pay for it in blood."

Seraphine pitched forward, horror rushing her words together. "You have Bibi?"

"Did you think she evaporated on the journey?"

"Leave her be," she implored. "She's innocent."

"Innocence is a matter of perspective, Miss Marchant. Failure is not." The king came to his feet. He nodded to the soldiers along the wall. "Return them to their cells." Wagging a finger between Seraphine and the Shadowsmith he said, "Think well on your loyalty in the dark. You will depart in the morning."

With his advisers trailing after him, the King of Valterre plodded from the grand dining room, then stalled on the threshold to throw Ransom a backward glance. "A word, Dagger. In private."

Ransom rolled to his feet as the guards moved in to collect their prisoners. There wasn't time to speak to Seraphine, and by the way she turned her back to him, he doubted she was interested in his advice. Which was: *Behave, for fuck's sake.*

A moment later, Ransom stepped into the king's war chamber. He had been here before, four months ago. That fateful day on the cusp of a cruel winter when he had been summoned to see the king. First, to explain what had befallen Gaspard Dufort and the city he once presided over, and secondly, to introduce himself formally, as the next leader of the Daggers. To kiss a new ring and welcome his role as the king's brand-new shadow puppet.

The king awaited him in a chair by the grand stone fireplace, the flames there bracketed by a series of violent battle tapestries. "Next time you strike one of my soldiers, you'll spend the night in my dungeon, Dagger."

Ransom dipped his chin. "Forgive me, Your Majesty."

"That woman is a liability."

"That woman had been beaten to a pulp."

The king rolled his eyes. "Why are Daggers always so dramatic?"

Ransom chewed on his words. For too many years he had sat across from men more powerful than him, trying to swallow back the taste of his own revulsion at their power games, at his own part in them. Without his crown, King Bertrand was not so different from Gaspard Dufort. A greedy, brash man, prone to violence and insecurity. Always grasping for more control, the power in his meaty fists never quite enough.

The king turned his face to the fire, his expression drawn. "Rebellion has its teeth in my kingdom. Rumors of Oriel's final prophecy occupy my advisers' every thought. They speak now of nothing else. They believe these new saints will spell the end of our age. Of kings and Shade, and man-appointed power. As they crop up like weeds, we must stamp them out, before our control over Fantome and its surrounds diminishes entirely. Do you understand the urgency here?"

Ransom understood that the king was scared. Truly, deeply frightened, not just of rebellion but of *change* foretold by an ancient diviner of fate. He was speaking of them as though they faced the same threat, but Ransom was not a slave to power, no matter how often he consumed Shade or how it ate away at his soul. He was not desperate at the thought of losing his standing in Fantome; it was that same power that had robbed him of himself.

Made him Ransom, and not Bastian.

He didn't care for saints or kings, or magic at all. Deep down, all he truly coveted was freedom. Even if the possibility was long gone. And yet, he could see what the king wanted of him in that moment, and so he nodded and said, "I understand, Your Majesty."

The king grunted in approval. "I want Prince Andreas and that acolyte dead, Ransom. And I want it done by King's Day." A flash of yellowed teeth. "Consider it a birthday gift to me."

King's Day would dawn before the next full moon. Ordinarily, this would be ample time to find and kill a couple of marks, but these were no ordinary targets, and by all accounts, the People's Saint was a slippery sort, ever present yet always moving.

Ransom said, "Consider it done."

The king leaned back in his chair. "For the girl and Versini, this is a test."

"I gathered."

"Watch Seraphine Marchant. Keep her close to you." The king drilled his fingers along the armrest. "I want to know the true measure of her loyalty. What she is willing to do for the Crown. How easy she is to command."

Ransom almost laughed. Seraphine Marchant was about as easy to control as an inferno. But if the king knew how slim his chances were of wielding her as his own weapon, she'd never make it out of that dungeon, and Ransom would never get to unravel what she was to this kingdom now. What she was to *him*.

"I'll keep her in line."

The king worried a black curl between his fingers. "You are easier than Dufort," he said, in what Ransom assumed was a compliment. "A good soldier does as he's told and reaps his due."

Ransom's brows lifted.

"When we spoke some months ago, you expressed a fervent interest in finding your family. Your mother, Gisele. Your sister, Anouk."

"Well remembered," said Ransom with some surprise.

Each name was a breath of fresh air in the stifled room. A daring whisper of hope. Last year, Gaspard Dufort had promised Ransom the same thing—that he would enlist the king to find his family, but like most things Dufort had told him in secret, it had turned out to be a lie. When Ransom mentioned his desire to track down his family to the king a few months ago, it was the first the king had ever heard of it.

Ransom couldn't fight the stiffening of his spine now, the galloping in his chest as he leaned toward the king. "You've found them?"

"My spymaster is on their scent." His smirk grew at Ransom's undisguised eagerness. "His search has taken him to the town of Mauranus in the south-east, where a widowed basket weaver called Gisele lived with her daughter some years ago." Though Ransom had never been to Mauranus, he could picture the little fishing town perfectly, the white-washed cottages lining the pebbled shores, the taverns with their blue-striped awnings, the gray gulls circling over the white-capped waves.

"There could be news any day now . . ."

More reason for Ransom to hasten back, of course. King's Day couldn't come soon enough. Two dead saints were the cost of this information, of the two missing shards of his own heart. Not that cost mattered at all. Ransom would have piled ten dead bodies at the king's feet for a chance to embrace his mother, to see how his little sister Anouk had grown up.

"You will have your marks before the month is out," he said. "Dead and gone. I vow it."

The king's smile was elastic. "If the Flames kick up any trouble, kill them on the road."

"I will," said Ransom easily.

"You are dismissed, Dagger."

Ransom stood, bowed low, and left.

Chapter 11

Seraphine

It was several hours from dawn and Sera was back in the dungeon of the Summer Palace, trying to fathom how on earth they had gotten themselves into this mess.

Theo, meanwhile, was working on what they could gain from it.

"Think of it as a turn of fate," he reasoned from the next cell. "It's not like we *have* to kill the king's marks, but at least this way, we'll be able to find our way to them."

Sera's mind whirled. Were there really two more saints, like her, turned loose in the kingdom? Presented to her on the very night she had wished to know if there were others out there?

She couldn't shake the feeling that fate's hand was resting on her shoulder. That this awful night—this grand *task*—was no coincidence. But the plan was far from straightforward.

"Once we find them, the Daggers will kill them." Of this, Sera was unerringly sure.

What did Ransom Hale and his ilk care for saints, when they already enjoyed the protection of the king and the enduring power of Shade?

This prince posed a threat to the Dagger too. If he survived, he might change everything. And who knew what kind of secret power bloomed on the misted Isle of Alisa?

Her heart sank. "We might not even get the chance to speak to Andreas before they strike."

And saints, she *wanted* to. Desperately. Whatever magic Prince Andreas had gained in that storm seemed to be working just fine for him. He had managed to whip up a fervor never before seen in the capital and amass a band of devoted followers to his cause. The prison break had clearly helped, gifting him an army of disgruntled mercenaries who had their own scores to settle against the King of Valterre.

Yes, Prince Andreas had grabbed onto his new-found power with both hands. And now the King of Valterre was sweating about what he was going to do with those hands. Or indeed who he was going to extend them to.

"I doubt he'll go down easy," mused Theo, and Sera realized that might be true too. Her hopes brightened. "The Daggers are going to try and kill him whether we come along or not. At least this way we'll have a chance to speak to him. Perhaps even help him."

Or join him.

Sera's heart raced at the thought. To work with a traitor to the Crown was tantamount to signing her own death sentence. But it was clear to her now that being a saint already afforded her one. If the king ever found out about her true power, she'd be hanged. Or maybe this time, Ransom really would kill her.

He was different than he was before. Still irritatingly handsome, but sharper somehow. Shade-bitten. Hardened by the last few months, the shadow-marks on him had created a new and devastating tapestry. A reaper made flesh.

In any case, the more salient truth of the matter was this: if they tracked down Prince Andreas, perhaps *he* could help *her*.

She would have to consider her allegiance carefully. After all, Andreas could end up being more powerful than any ruler that had come before him. A revolutionary *and* a saint. Maybe even a king one day.

Who was he? What would he do with that kind of power?

Questions swirled inside her head, anxiety and anticipation making her thoughts heavy. Her lids too. Sighing deeply, she laid her forehead against the bars.

They had been fed, at least. A crusted bread roll stuffed with stringy gammon and hard cheese. Nothing like the platter the king had feasted on during their late-night meeting. Still, she had devoured the stale bread in six bites, washing it down with a canteen of cold water.

"Of course we have to keep Bibi in mind," Theo said, quietly.

Sera frowned. It was an impossible dilemma. Whatever their feelings about Prince Andreas and the rogue Alisan, they had no choice but to play along with the king's plan for now. To defer to Ransom and his Daggers. Until they could figure out a better way forward. A way to save themselves and their friend.

At least Val had gotten away. Sera was sure if they'd managed to capture her, too, the king would be dangling her fate over them just as keenly as he was dangling Bibi.

A small mercy.

"Try and sleep," said Theo, through a sprawling yawn. "Dawn will be here before we know it."

Sera eyed the narrow bedroll in the corner of her cell. The servants had brought those too. She shuffled over to it now, but she couldn't bring herself to lie down. She hugged her knees against her chest and sat with her back against the damp wall, willing sleep to come.

Sooner than expected, she nodded off. Her head lolled, jolting her from nightmare to nightmare, where she found herself falling—always falling—down, down, down . . .

Then choking, the dirt so thick in her mouth, she couldn't scream.

Get me out! Get me out! Get me out!

She woke at the sound of approaching footsteps.

It was still dark outside, the only light flickering from the oil lamp beyond her cell. She couldn't tell how long she'd been asleep for, only that she felt groggy and sore.

The footsteps drew closer, and then stopped abruptly. A shadow loomed outside her cell. She stared blearily at it, thinking it was some kind of apparition. A leftover remnant of her nightmares.

"Seraphine." Ransom's voice trickled through her like warm

water. A pair of large shadow-marked hands curled around the bars of her cell. "Are you awake?"

She lurched forward without meaning to, leaving her bedroll and crawling toward him like he was a life raft bobbing in a violent sea. Dimly, she knew she was out of her senses. There wasn't supposed to be anything comforting about seasoned assassin Ransom Hale, Head of the Order of Daggers and sworn enemy of the Order of Flames. Of her.

Except for the way he uttered her name like a prayer in the dark. It stirred something deep inside her, like a coin tossed into the pool of her soul.

When she reached the front of her cell, he came to his knees, his hands sliding down the bars until his fists framed the sides of her face.

"What the hell are you doing here?" she hissed. Now that he was no longer standing to block it out, lamplight poured over them, illuminating his face. It was stark.

"Making sure you're not planning to do something reckless tomorrow," he said in a low voice.

Sera narrowed her eyes. "Can you be more specific?"

"Like shoot off that smart mouth of yours and refuse the King of Valterre."

"Are you saying that's an option?"

"This isn't funny, Seraphine."

"You think I find *any* of this funny?" she said, jutting her face forward, until his curled fingers brushed her temples. "*Look* at my face. Am I laughing?"

Voice strained, he said, "It makes me feel murderous."

"You're always murderous."

He huffed a sigh.

And just like that they were bickering again. Home sweet home.

"I'm pissed at you," she said. "Just so you are aware."

He gave her a flat look. "You're one to talk."

"Oh, don't tell me you didn't see me coming. You hardly thought I'd retire the secrets of Lightfire once I saved my own ass? Let you get on with your little reign of terror?" she scoffed. "Leadership obviously suits you. You're *covered* in shadowmarks." She drew back, running the pad of her finger along the marks on his knuckles, not missing the way he shivered at her touch. "And after I went to all that trouble to erase them."

Momentarily, she was seized by the memory of that reckless, heady kiss in the alleyway near Hugo's Passage, how he had groaned against her neck, slid his hand down her trousers, and shattered her whole world. How the Lightfire in her cloak had responded to the swell of her pleasure, running through him like a current and shredding all the Shade festering inside him. It had been perfect, before everything went to hell.

By the way his eyes darkened, she knew he was succumbing to the same memory. "Don't talk like that when there are bars between us."

She regretted it herself. Her heart was like a volcano, spewing heat through her blood. She could feel her magic waking up, getting ready to erupt into an inconvenient and possibly deadly spectacle.

She scrunched her hands, schooled her breathing.

Not here. Not now.

She'd never make it out alive.

Think of something else. Anything else. "How many kills have you notched up since I last saw you?"

There. An ice-cold bucket of reality to douse the bonfire of her lust.

"Where are my prized smugglers?" he parried. "You know, the ones you stole from me?"

She rolled her eyes. "I hardly stuffed them into a big sack and ran off with them into the night. I offered them a different path. And better coin."

"And Lark?" His voice turned cold, his eyes too. "What about him?"

Sera pulled back from the bars. "You know what happened with Lark. He tried to kill me."

"I'm not talking about the night at the Aurore."

"Then what *are* you talking about?"

He said nothing. He just watched her in that unnerving way, like he was waiting for something.

Let him wait. "If you came down here to speak in riddles, you can piss off. My head aches enough already."

He frowned, shaking off whatever strangeness had come over him. "We'll talk in the morning. Once you officially offer your services to the King of Valterre and thank him for the opportunity to prove yourself."

"I'll kiss his feet too, shall I?"

He gave her a stark look. "Play the game, Seraphine. You've always been good at that."

She narrowed her eyes. "Why, so Nadia can strangle me out on the road the first chance she gets?"

"Leave Nadia to me."

"My gallant knight," she taunted. "I thought you hated me."

He rested his forehead against the bars until those firelit hazel eyes were all she could see.

"Not enough to watch you suffer, Seraphine." He reached through the bars, his voice gentling as he traced the bruise on her cheek.

She jerked away. Too close. Too dangerous. The familiar scent of him came rushing back, heady notes of woodsmoke and sage surrounding her in a mist. She hadn't realized how starved for it she'd been. How some vital part of her had been slumbering in his absence.

Her magic was sparking again.

She hinged backward, afraid he would see the gold fire burning behind her eyes.

He curled his fingers into a fist. Regret flickered in his eyes, and she realized what she must look like to him, bruised and bloodied inside her cell. Perhaps he had wanted to comfort her, or simply remind himself that she was still alive. Still breathing. Still fighting.

His face turned serious. "The king is wary of you, Seraphine. He fears what your Order stands for. Fears that it might one day stand against him."

Just wait until he learns what I really am.

"The king kills all that he fears." Ransom ground his jaw. "I should know."

She gave a mirthless huff. Of course. He was the one who killed them, after all.

"Don't give him anything else to be wary of," he said, holding her gaze. Letting the silence carry the rest of his words. She heard the warning loud and clear.

Ransom knew, or at least suspected, that there was magic inside her now. He must still remember the hint she had betrayed all those months ago when they had endured a strained goodbye in the Saints' Quarter, how her palm had sparked against his lips when he kissed her goodbye.

He had seen the handprint burned into Lark's chest. The golden scorch mark on his best friend's lifeless corpse. Her doing. Her magic. A thing that thrashed and roiled inside her, longing to be free. But how could she free a thing she could not understand? A beast that seemed not to answer to her?

"I don't plan on drawing any more attention to myself," she said carefully.

"Does this mean you're going to do as you're told on the road?"

She snorted. Avoiding the king's sharpened attention while in his dungeon and diverting from his orders while out in the wilds of Valterre were two different things entirely. And what was Ransom expecting? That she'd bend her knee to *him*? "Or what? This time, you'll really kill me?"

"Maybe I will."

"I guess some threats never get old."

They regarded each other in the uneasy silence, everything that had happened over the last four months filling the space between them. The truth was that despite their enmity, Sera had fled the city with his permission. Even after killing his best friend, he had let her go. He had taken over the Order of Daggers just to keep them from chasing her. That had been their agreement. Her freedom, for his own.

She would run and he would stay.

And kill, and kill, and kill.

He looked so drained now. So unhappy.

Perhaps that's why the words flew from her mouth. "I thought you would come to me. I thought you would find me again."

His smile turned rueful. "That's because you're an idealist."

"And what are you, Ransom?"

"You know what I am, Seraphine."

A killer. Cold-blooded and clear-eyed. That's how he saw himself. But she had once known the man beneath the Shade. Bastian, his mother had named him. Raised for a gentler sort of life, before his father had chased her off with his fists. Because her father had found him on the banks of the Verne. Made him a killer.

Sera curled her fingers around the bars of her cell. "We are all more than just one thing."

"Not when the thing you are is a Dagger."

Footsteps sounded nearby. The guards were doing their rounds. Spurred by a rising urgency, Sera said, "I need you to find Bibi for me. I have to know that she's all right. That she knows what's happening. I don't want her to think we've just left her to rot here."

"Do you want a tea tray while I'm at it? I don't exactly have free rein around here."

"You're the king's prized assassin. I think you'll survive." He quirked a brow. *"Please,"* she said, dispensing with her sarcasm if only for Bibi. "You're the only one who can help me."

He raked a hand through his hair, unsettling the thick black strands.

Footsteps drew closer.

"I really need—"

"You know I will." Rolling to his feet, he dusted the dirt from his trousers. "I'll find your friend."

Sera stood too. She clutched the bars. He leaned down until they were almost nose to nose, the metal stark and cold between them.

"See you at dawn, Seraphine." His words were a taunt against her lips. "And remember . . . *behave.*"

She rolled her eyes.

He huffed a quiet laugh, pulling away.

She stepped back into the shadows, letting the darkness enfold her. The soldiers were coming her way, and she didn't want them to see she was awake. Ransom took off in the opposite direction, winding his way down into the darkest reaches of the dungeon, without breaking his assured stride.

Closing her eyes, she listened to his fading steps, hoping they would lead him to Bibi. Once the soldiers had come and gone, she turned her nose into her collar, breathing in his scent.

"You shouldn't do that, you know." Theo's voice filled the echoing silence.

She jerked her chin up. "Do what?"

"Make the Dagger think he still has a chance with you."

Sera chewed on her bottom lip, unsure of what to say.

"The king has shown his hand, Sera. He intends to kill anyone he deems more powerful than him. He fears a new Age of Saints more than anyone else in this kingdom. If he hears of more . . . *of others* . . . He'll do everything in his power to kill them too."

He'll kill you.

Sera's heart pounded like a war drum. Theo was right. If they were clever enough to find their way to Prince Andreas, they wouldn't be killing him. They'd likely be joining him.

Against the king.

Against the Daggers.

Against Ransom.

If she lost sight of that, she'd lose herself, and everything she had worked for—everything Mama had worked for—her whole life.

A better kingdom.

A better world.

So long as Ransom was a Dagger, he would always be her enemy.

And yet, if she was going to betray him and the king's mission, he mustn't see it coming. He mustn't know what she was truly capable of.

Even if she didn't quite yet know herself.

Chapter 12

Ransom

It was an hour past dawn, and Ransom was pacing in the south courtyard of the Summer Palace. Its towering white-stone turrets wound up to brush the blushing sky while the rising sun kissed the South Sea. The waves glistened, the eager gray gulls swooping low over the water, hunting for fish. In the air, the tang of seaweed mingled with the sweet scent of the queen's prized rosebushes.

A nearby tinkling fountain added a sense of peace to the morning. But a war waged inside Ransom. Where the hell were Seraphine and Versini?

Outside the towering palace gates, by the leafy arch that led into the royal graveyard of Valterre, three large black carriages were waiting. Though gleaming and pulled by the finest of coach horses, each one was conspicuously absent of the official royal crest—a rose crossed with two swords. From the Summer

Palace, they were to turn their backs to the sea and travel north undercover, lest any eagle-eyed rebel spies find out the king's nefarious plans for his nephew.

In his ten years as a Dagger, the job had rarely taken Ransom beyond the bounds of the capital, and the marks that led him further astray were never more than an hour or two by carriage. But this mark was mercurial and fast-moving. Prince Andreas could be anywhere in Valterre, as close as the taverns in east Fantome or as far as the low hills that bordered Urnica.

They would begin their search at the Appoline, the university where Prince Andreas had spent the last few years of his life, no doubt coming up with plans for the eventual usurpation of his uncle. From there, the trail could go cold at once, or branch off into several new directions.

There were concerns to consider, like how well Lisette would run the Order in Ransom's and Nadia's absence and whether its remaining members would be able to withstand the rising demands brought about by the chaos in the capital. At least with Seraphine under his supervision, her next shipment of Lightfire would be delayed, allowing the Daggers the upper hand once more. He hated to admit they needed it, that eventually the swelling rebellion would become too much for them and the Shade at their disposal.

Pushing those worries aside, Ransom focused on his impatience, glaring at the doors to the Summer Palace with an intensity that made his head throb.

"Keep staring. That'll definitely make her appear faster," remarked Caruso, who was kicking the rounded heads off the king's Buxus plants. They soared over the rosebushes and into the garden pond, where Nadia was skimming pebbles so violently it looked like she was trying to wound the water.

A bored Dagger made for a destructive Dagger.

A pair of nearby sentries gave Caruso an admonishing glare, but neither moved to rebuke him. Only a fool would square up to one of the king's assassins.

"Can you not vandalize everything you lay your eyes on?" said Ransom, like he was scolding a child. "Believe me, you wouldn't like the dungeons here."

Caruso barked a laugh. "Like they'd dare drag me down there."

"They will if you piss off the queen. These are her gardens."

"She has a hundred gardens. And she's not even in residence here. The maids say she's back at Bellevue Castle with her little gremlins. Probably thinks the king is a pig. Did you see the way he eats? Doesn't even chew his food."

"Speak louder. I don't think they heard you down in the servants' quarters."

"How much longer do we have to wait?"

"Go and bother Nadia if you're bored."

"Why, so you can brood in peace?"

"I'm not brooding. I'm thinking."

About her.

He replayed their conversation from last night. The fire in her eyes so at odds with the bruises marring her face. That barbed tongue and smart mouth, the softness of her skin under his cruel, callused hands. The anger he had tried so hard to cling to had fractured at the sight of her sitting in the dark. The confusion on her face when he'd questioned her about Lark. It had seemed genuine.

Ransom had reported it to Nadia this morning over breakfast. She had rolled her eyes as she sipped her coffee, tossing him that piteous look he had grown to hate, the one that relegated him to some addled lovesick fool.

She's a slight little thing, Caruso had reasoned, around a mouthful of bacon. *I can't imagine her lugging a skeleton out of the ground. And her man's got clean fingernails. Versinis don't like to get their hands dirty.*

Unless you count all the killing they used to do, Ransom had reminded him, with a bite in his voice. *And he's not her man,* he'd wanted to add, but what did he know? And what did it matter to Caruso?

Nothing dirty about killing if you do it right, said Caruso, downing his coffee.

Nadia had done the same. *Next time, let me do the interrogation.*

Fine, he'd relented.

There would be plenty of time on their journey.

And the truth was, even if Ransom did believe her about Lark, he still couldn't trust her. What loyalty did Seraphine Marchant have toward the King of Valterre, a man who had dragged her off the streets of Fantome and had her beaten black and blue? Threatened her in full view of his Daggers and remained wary of her, even now.

The only thing tying her to this mission—and her word—was

the fate of one of her best friends, Bibi. But Seraphine was a mercurial creature and a Versini always had a plot up his sleeve. Ransom would have to watch them both closely to keep them in line.

At last, the palace doors groaned open and Seraphine came down the stone steps. The Shadowsmith was with her, both of them washed and dressed in clean clothes, and carrying matching satchels presumably with supplies for the journey ahead. Someone had stitched closed the cut on Versini's forehead, and applied tinctures to the rest of their wounds.

Seraphine's bruises were already fading from purple to yellow, the swelling around her eye abating overnight. Compared to Versini, she was faring a hell of a lot better. Ransom fisted his hands as that *thing* in his chest tugged.

Was it the work of Saint Oriel or his own twisted desire?

She is not to be trusted.

She is your enemy.

This was just *business*. His business. *Royal* business. They would work together for a time, kill the prince and bury the acolyte, and come home to kiss the king's ring, before going their separate ways again. For good. Seraphine would live under the Crown's protection, and Ransom would return to the fate he had resigned himself to.

Yes. Good. Fine.

Fine.

Seraphine surged forward, leaving Versini and their accompanying soldiers trailing down the steps behind her. She stomped toward him, and at once, Ransom was drawn to the strand of wheat-blond hair that had slipped free of her braid.

He folded his arms to keep from reaching for it. "Ready to quest, spitfire?"

"Did you find Bibi?"

"She's in the lower dungeon. Scared half stiff. Though she seems to have fared a lot better than you and Versini."

"Call him Theo."

Make me.

Versini was glaring at him. Standing six paces back with his arms folded like some kind of war general. "Let's not start off on the wrong foot, Tunnel Rat."

Ransom cocked his head. "Do you always talk to trained assassins this way, or just the ones who already want to kill you?"

Seraphine swatted him. "Don't start. It's too early."

"Accosting the Head of the Daggers in front of his underlings." Caruso whistled. "You must have a death wish, little dragon."

"It's all right, Caruso. That's just her way of flirting."

"Bibi," she said impatiently. "Tell me."

Right, right. The king's bait. "As I said, she's alive. Well fed, and somewhat rested. As far as hostages go. When I found her, she attempted to claw my eyes out through the bars of her cell. I think she thought I had killed you both." Sera flinched. *He* had flinched. It had taken several minutes to calm Bibi down, to convince her to trust him. "I tried to put her mind at ease."

"Did it work?"

He weighed his answer. The truth was *definitely not.* Bibi had burst into tears, almost immediately, then begged him to free her. "I told her you and I were going on a little quest. And that when we return, she'll be free to go."

She chewed on her bottom lip. The cut there had crusted over in the night, the cherry red of her blood a shade lighter than the rest of her mouth.

That mouth.

"All right," she said, more to herself than him, but she seemed unsure. Versini was wearing the same look of unease.

"You are coming on our quest?" said Ransom.

She cut her eyes at him. "We're here, aren't we?"

Across the courtyard, the palace gates opened. Three coachmen arrived presently, loading the carriages with provisions, before checking the horses. Then came four of the king's favored soldiers dressed in plain clothing. Two of them Ransom had bloodied up last night. They avoided his gaze now. With more than enough Shade to last them, they were hardly in need of such paltry backup, but he suspected they were here as an extension of the king himself, to cast a wary eye over the mission and make sure nothing went terribly awry.

As long as they didn't get in his way, Ransom didn't care.

They drifted through the gates. Four soldiers. Three Daggers. Two Flames. And a whole lot of unfinished business.

Versini and Seraphine made a beeline for the first coach.

"Bye, then," Ransom called after them.

Seraphine waggled her fingers without turning around.

"See you at the Appoline, Tunnel Rat," called the Shadowsmith.

"I'm decking him for that when we stop for lunch," said Ransom.

"As far as public rejection goes, I wouldn't take that personally," mused Caruso, coming to stand beside him. "If she sits anywhere near Nadia, she'll get her throat slit before we reach the next village."

Nadia rolled her eyes, prodding him toward the second carriage. "You know I don't kill before my second coffee of the day. You two can have the pleasure of my company if you promise to shut your mouths until I drink it."

"Only if you play cards with me. I haven't fleeced you in months," said Caruso.

They bickered their way into the second carriage. Their retinue of soldiers, which included a red-haired woman with a stern face, called Maelle; a stockier, bald soldier called Bram, whose nose Ransom had rearranged last night; a beanpole with a push-broom moustache called Ribauld; and a ghostly pale blond called Kasper were collectively wise enough to leave the Daggers to their own carriage and made instead for the third coach.

The sentries saw them off, but Ransom's eyes were on the white-stone balcony above, where the king himself stood watching, his fists curled tight around the balustrade like he could hold onto his palace—and all that inherited power—through sheer will alone.

It occurred to him that the future of Valterre as they knew it now rested squarely on their shoulders. The coming weeks would decide what kind of kingdom would emerge from this brewing uprising. A land of dangerous untried saints or one that continued to kneel under the boot of a self-concerned king.

The thought was oddly . . . *wearying.* Or perhaps it was the lack of sleep from a night spent traipsing through the king's dungeons, trying to save the life of a woman he was not supposed to care about.

Caruso parted his hands, flicking an entire deck of cards between them. "Twenty-one. You want in?"

"I'll take your money later." Ransom kicked his feet up on the opposite bench and slid down in his seat, tucking his chin into the collar of his coat. "Wake me when it's time for lunch."

Ransom woke to the sound of screaming. He was up like a shot and out of the carriage before he could process where he even was. One blink revealed the sun, ripe and golden in a cloudless sky. It must have been an hour or so after noon. Another blink revealed a bustling market square, packed with wooden stalls draped in colorful banners.

That scream came again.

He whirled, catching sight of Nadia and Caruso standing among a gathering crowd of onlookers. They were both laughing, glued to the senseless brawl unfolding right in front of them. Likely a pair of violent, drunken—

Hell's teeth.

Through a break in the crowd, Ransom spied a familiar blond hair braid. Seraphine was scrapping with one of the king's soldiers. Or, more accurately, she was swinging from Ribauld's neck. The soldier was half crouched over the body of . . . well, shit. Was that the Shadowsmith sprawled out in the square?

Ribauld had his sword drawn, the point dangerously close to Versini's neck. Versini had gone completely still.

Good. *Easy does it.*

Seraphine didn't *quite* get the idea. She was pummeling Ribauld from behind, yelling at him to drop his sword.

Stifling a curse, Ransom lunged, pushing through a sea of shoulders only to stumble into a sudden flare of blinding bright. Another scream ripped through the square. This one belonged to Ribauld. Ransom blinked the floating black spots from his vision to find the soldier rolling around on the ground, holding his left ear.

Seraphine was scrabbling away from him. The market crowd broke into startled cries, the spectators drawing back as the stench of burning flesh filled the air. Another glimpse at the soldier's ear revealed the lobe had been seared clean off, the skin on his cheek bubbling into angry blisters.

Unease snaked through Ransom.

The Shadowsmith paled as he got to his feet.

"What the hell was that?" said Caruso, stalking forward.

Nadia pulled him back by his collar. "Don't go near her."

The rest of the crowd was watching the writhing soldier, trying to figure out where the rogue fire had sprung from.

Ransom was watching Sera.

She was crouched on the edge of the circle, trying to slow her ratcheting breath. Her eyes burned bright gold. She blinked and the glow winked out, but not fast enough.

Ransom made his way toward her.

Nadia slid in front of him. "Don't you dare touch her."

"Someone has to get her out of here."

"That was no vial of Lightfire," she said in a low voice. "That was *her*."

"The more reason to get her away from all these people," he said pointedly.

The other soldiers were already descending on Seraphine. By the time Ransom reached her, they were binding her wrists.

"Leave her to me."

"She struck a royal guard," hissed Maelle. "Can't let that go unpunished."

Seraphine instinctively covered her head. "He started it!" she spat from the cradle of her arms. "He went for Theo! I was only trying to get him off."

"You lit one of them firecrackers!" accused Kasper. "Shoved it in Ribauld's ear!"

"Did not!"

"It hardly burned itself off!" shouted Bram. "Bloody Flames. Knew you were trouble from the off."

With a sharp sigh, Ransom withdrew a jar of Shade from his pocket. One mouthful and every shadow in the square was his to command. He pulled them from the ground, like slithering vipers.

The crowd scattered in terror.

"Subtle," remarked Caruso.

The soldiers jerked their heads up, their chins quivering at the sight of all that encroaching darkness. Slipping his hands into his pockets, Ransom cocked his head in a lazy threat. "Like I said, I'll take it from here."

Sera peered up at him from her spot on the ground, the only one among them who wasn't remotely afraid of the shadows that now moved across his skin. Nor the ones that pooled like ink at his feet. It wasn't like they could hurt her, thanks to the strange fire in her blood. That much was more than clear to him now. He had been wondering when he would get a glimpse of it again.

"Send Ribauld back to the barracks," he said. "He can't travel any further without treatment. As for the rest of us, let's get back on the road before we end up in the local penny papers."

Hardly an auspicious start to their journey.

Versini shoved his way into their huddle. "This whole thing was Ribauld's fault." The soldier, who had finally staggered to his feet, moaned weakly in protest. "I slipped away to send a missive back to Halbracht, and he jumped me. Thought I was doing a runner."

"Save the monologue, Versini," said Ransom in a bored voice. "Can you play cards?"

"What?"

"Cards. Twenty-one. Saint or sinner. Go fish. Can you play?"

Narrowing his eyes, he said, "Obviously."

"Good." Ransom called to Caruso. "Versini and I are going to swap places for the next leg. Reckons himself a card shark. Feel free to take all the coin he's made trying to put us out of business."

Caruso's teeth gleamed. "Finally. New blood."

"I'm getting snacks first," said Nadia, heading across the

now deserted square. "I need a bucket of caramel fudge to take the edge off this shitshow."

Ransom was about to help Seraphine to her feet when Versini jostled in front of him. They bent their heads together, exchanging a short, furious conversation on their way back to the carriages.

"Promise me," said the Shadowsmith, pulling away.

"I know," she said, shooing him.

She marched toward the first carriage, tossing a challenging look over her shoulder. "I want to play cards too, Dagger."

"You'll have to wait," said Ransom, stalking after her. "You and I are going to play a different game, spitfire."

Her brows shot up. "What kind of game?"

"Truth or dare."

Chapter 13

Seraphine

"Make yourself comfortable," said the Dagger, seating himself across from her. "But do try not to set anything on fire."

She glared at him. "Don't tempt me."

"I *live* to tempt you, spitfire."

So he had chosen flirting. Fine. It was better than an interrogation. Sera didn't know how to explain what had just happened in the square. Only that her anger had gotten the better of her. *Again.*

Think less, Fontaine had advised her.

This was *exactly* what happened when Sera surrendered all rational thought for raw feeling. That door inside her flew open and all that magic came barreling out, white hot and lethal. The sight of Ribauld whaling on Theo had kindled a quick and violent panic that had made thinking impossible. Before she knew it, she was swinging from him like a spider monkey. When the heat rushed her, she couldn't stop it, couldn't wrench herself away quick enough.

Still, she didn't fully regret it. Theo's neck had been *inches* from Ribauld's sword and if her recent kidnapping had taught her anything, it was how impulsive the king's soldiers were.

Of course Ransom had witnessed the whole thing.

He watched her intently now, his silver eyes gleaming in the dimness. He seemed even taller in here, those broad shoulders commanding half the carriage bench. Shadows darted across his olive skin as the rest of his Shade leisurely worked its way through him. Head canted as he studied her, he absently licked the scar on his bottom lip, and, Saints help her, it made her blood heat.

Here he sat like a dark god looming over his prey.

With the curtains drawn and the wheels moving swiftly beneath them, the carriage felt too small, the air between them too close. Under her finely woven cardigan—a parting gift from the royal house of Rayere—Sera's skin grew clammy. She raked the stray strands back from her face, resisting the urge to fan herself.

"Too hot, Seraphine?"

"Usually."

"Do you often catch fire?"

She pressed her lips together, diverting her gaze to the threading on her sleeve.

Don't say a word about your magic, Theo had warned her back at the marketplace. *He works for the king. He'll only use it against you.*

The silence lingered, the Dagger's gaze like a brand on her forehead.

Clearing her throat, she gestured to the shadows wreathing his shoulders. "Can you rein those in?"

"Bothering you, are they?"

"No." She shrugged. "They just *really* wash you out."

"Good thing I'm not vain."

Just hideously observant. Which, frankly, was worse. She did not want to have this conversation with Ransom, but she didn't know how to avoid it either.

"A copper for your thoughts, spitfire."

She tapped her chin. "Do you think Nadia will share her fudge with me if I ask nicely?"

"Only if she thought you'd choke on it."

Sighing, she tipped her head back to the ceiling. She hoped Theo was holding his own with the other Daggers.

Ransom hinged forward, narrowing the space between them. He was too close now, the scent of woodsmoke and sage making her cheeks prickle. His voice was soft and lethal. "What happened back at the marketplace, Seraphine?"

She flattened herself against the bench, unnerved by the ravenous look on his face. It was as though the Shade was speaking for him. This beast that moved under his skin. "That soldier got lairy with Theo. Started flinging threats and swinging his sword about. So I threw myself at him and then he got . . . a little . . ." She rolled her hand.

"Earless?"

"I was going to say irreparably scalded."

"I love it when you talk dirty."

She resisted the urge to kick him.

"Shall we get to our game, then?" Shadows wreathed his fingers, kissing that gaudy ring that shone just as brightly as his eyes. A stark reminder of what he had become these past few months: her father's predecessor, a man she had despised above all others. A man whose memory haunted her, even now.

Determined to hold her own, she said, "Assassins first."

"Truth or dare, Seraphine."

Why did that question feel more deadly than the shadows swirling around them?

"Dare," she said.

"I dare you to tell me the truth about your magic."

She snorted. "Nice try, Dagger."

"All right, we'll warm up to it," he said, lazily. "I dare you to take off that cardigan."

She arched a brow. *"Seriously?"*

"For your own comfort." When she didn't immediately rip her cardigan off and fling it at him, he said, "Your cheeks are burning up. So either it's hot in here, or you're hot for me."

Right on both counts. She played it off, lest his ego swallow up the rest of the space in here. With an exaggerated eyeroll, she shrugged her sweater off. Beneath it, she wore a cream chemise. The breeze kissed her collarbones, wrenching a sigh from her.

She heard him swallow.

"Truth or dare, Dagger?"

"Truth."

Seraphine's mind went . . . blank. Utterly, completely. It was the way he was looking at her, with that unnerving intensity . . . the sudden simmering weight of expectation. Too much pressure. She went for something light. "Did you miss me?"

"Wretchedly," he said at once.

She blinked. *Well . . .*

"Did you miss me, spitfire?"

"Too busy trying to dismantle your life's work," she lied. "And before you ask, I choose dare again."

Leaning back now, he stroked his jaw. "I dare you to say something nice about me."

Another eyeroll. "You're tall."

He gave her a flat look. "That's a fact."

"My turn," she chirped. "Truth or dare?"

Conceding, he said, "Truth."

Sera frowned. "Truth *again*."

"I'm afraid if you want to take my clothes off, you'll have to do it yourself."

She flung a cushion at him, inwardly delighting when it hit him in the face. He'd let her do it, of course. Meditating for a moment on her next question—and wanting to make it count—she sat forward, close enough to reach through the pool of shadows between them and trace the dark whorls on his hands if she wanted to. Perhaps too softly, she asked, "Why have you done this to yourself all over again, Ransom?"

His face tightened. "Can you be more specific?"

Fine, then. "I'm talking about all the mindless killing. You know, the continued willful wrecking of your one eternal soul.

All that Shade is eating away at you. Even now, I can sense it like a beast under your skin."

And it frightens me.

He gave a rueful smile, the playful glint in his eyes guttering out. "Because this is what I'm good for, Seraphine."

"Give me a better answer. One I might actually believe."

"All right," he said, with a bite. "I did it to forget you, and the dream of another life."

The one they had promised each other before Lark died and the Aurore fell.

It felt like a lie—or perhaps not the whole truth. But why did it sting so badly? "And how did that work out for you?"

"It was going well until you started to ransack my trade. It's hard to ignore a horsefly constantly buzzing around my head."

"What did you expect me to do, Ransom? Toss the recipe for Lightfire in the Verne and forget about it? Let the city continue to cower under my father's legacy?"

His eyes flashed. "I expected you to *run*, Seraphine."

"I did run!" she snapped.

You made me run! You nearly tore down a damn cathedral!

"But you didn't hide," he said, his voice climbing to match hers. Gone was the ease of their game, and here was the frustration and resentment they had been harboring toward each other; broken promises, diverging destinies, and the barb of dangerous lingering feelings.

And all that Shade was still feasting on his humanity, the tender parts that made him Bastian.

Shadows pooled as his composure shattered, crawling up the

sides of the carriage and stealing the last of the window light. Here was the real truth—his anger, as plain as the darkness that swaddled them. "You made a spectacle of yourself *everywhere* you went," he said through his teeth. "There isn't a smuggler in Valterre who hasn't heard of you. The ones you didn't manage to lure back to Halbracht are out to get you for fucking with their livelihoods, and that's to say nothing of the gang lords up and down this kingdom who have heard about that first shipment of Lightfire. Do you have *any idea* how many people have come to me about you these last few months? How many of my regulars have put a price on your pretty little head?"

"Are we including your Second in this figure?"

"Nadia would kill you for free."

Of course Sera knew her Order would end up pissing people off. She was upending the most prolific trade in Fantome, casting a flame into its dark underbelly and flushing out all who thrived there. She just hadn't imagined it would coincide with a city in revolt, or that there'd be quite so *many* active bounties on her head. That Ransom Hale would be the sole arbiter of her fate.

It occurred to her that he was just one quick kill away from being a *very* rich man.

She raised her chin. "Why drag this out any longer? Here's your free shot."

"That would be counterintuitive."

"Why?"

He threw her a contemptuous look. "Because I'm the one *protecting* you," he said like it was the most obvious thing in the world. "I've been protecting you for *months*. I'm *still* protecting you." He held up his stained hands, turning them from front to back. Even his palms were riddled. At her continued silence, he ripped the top three buttons of his shirt, revealing the shadow-marks there. They looked deep, and painful, as bad as the ones on his forearms when he rolled up his sleeves to show those too. Marked, all of him. Damned, every bit of him. Much worse than before—so much worse. *Saints above,* how was there any humanity left in him at all?

"I willfully *wreck my one eternal soul*—as you so creatively put it—because it keeps me in power. And when I'm the one in power, *you* are allowed to live. Wherever the hell you feel like, doing whatever the hell you want." He shook his head, his lip curling. "*Hell's teeth,* Seraphine. What part of that don't you get? You are *free*. And I'm the one paying for it."

"That's not fair!" Her own anger burst out of her. "I asked you to come with me. To leave the Daggers behind. I *begged* you." His choices were his alone. His *kills* were his, even if they were in some kind of twisted service to her. She had never asked him to protect her. She had never wanted *this*.

She was breathing too fast, her heart hammering like a drum. Beneath her anger, guilt pricked at her. She *was* free, and he was her living sacrifice. But this wasn't her fault . . . it wasn't her doing . . .

It wasn't *fair*.

Magic yawned inside her, heat kissing her blood. She felt it in her throat, hot and insistent. Impatiently, it roiled, and for an absurd moment, she felt like a dragon, ready to spit fire.

Maker, it crooned.

Take him.

Make him.

"You're right." The resignation in Ransom's voice cut through the chaos inside her, the wounded look in his eyes quelling the bite of her rage. "My undoing is my own." He slumped in his seat, dragging his hands across his face. "I never used to get angry like this. Sometimes I feel like I'm losing control of myself. Losing the man I used to be."

She couldn't tear her gaze from the marks on his hands. They were changing him. Ruining him.

Regret needled her. She had been too cavalier with her words, too free with her judgment. Wounded him because the sight of that skull ring flashing on his left hand wounded her. It wasn't fair. It wasn't simple. That was the problem.

Opening the curtains, he turned to watch the countryside flitting by, like the sheep there were of sudden fascination.

"I shouldn't have said that stuff about your soul," she said quietly. "I wasn't trying to hurt you . . . It's just . . . whenever I see that ring on your hand, I feel like I'm back in the catacombs looking at my father."

Ransom's eyes were glazed. Was he even listening to her?

"Hey?" She leaned forward without thinking. His shadows parted, like they were afraid of her. When she touched his knee, her fingers sparked. The darkness disintegrated, there and gone in the blink of an eye.

She reeled backward, caught in the sudden flood of afternoon light.

Ransom swung his head around. *"Your eyes."*

Bright gold. She could feel the heat behind them. Touching Ransom's Shade had brought her magic rushing to the fore. She squeezed her eyes shut, willing it to go away again.

"Seraphine." The seat creaked as he moved closer, a quiet command in his voice. "Look at me."

She shook her head, keeping her eyes shut. "No thanks."

He drew closer still, his broad hands bracketing her thighs on the bench. "Seraphine," he whispered. "I dare you to let me look longingly into your eyes."

A shiver went through her.

He was way too close, his thumbs brushing the thin material of her trousers, his breath warm against her lips. "I know what you are, Seraphine."

"What, hungry?" she said, weakly.

That heat flared again, like her magic was rising to his challenge.

Maker, it begged, like an animal prowling in its cage.

Go away, she hissed back. The last thing she wanted was to scald Ransom's stupidly perfect face. But her magic thrashed until it became uncomfortably hot, a sun burning in her chest. Fire spewed through her blood. It was reacting to his nearness, dancing to the furious beat of her own heart.

"I didn't understand at first, the way the barest touch of your skin shattered my Shade," he said in a low voice. "But hearing about Prince Andreas. And that acolyte on the Isle of Alisa . . . the rumors of a Second Coming."

Sera held her breath without meaning to.

"I'm thinking . . . you're a . . . saint," he said, deathly quiet.

Panic struck.

Lie.

Play it off.

Save your ass.

"That *scent*." He inhaled, breathing her in. "Like lemon blossoms . . ."

She swallowed a whimper, her hands absently curling in the collar of his shirt. She had meant to shove him off, to put some distance between him and her unruly magic before it struck out, but his nearness was so intoxicating, she couldn't think clearly.

"Careful," she warned. "If what you think is true, you really have no idea what I'm capable of."

There was a shift in temperature. He drew back from her, flattening himself against the bench.

She opened her eyes.

"What do you mean by that?" he said.

The heat inside her vanished, replaced by a sudden wash of cold. It was the way he was looking at her now . . . with suspicion. And . . . *disgust*.

Theo had warned her not to reveal anything more about her magic, and this was exactly why.

"Nothing. I didn't mean anything."

Too late. It was too late to take any of it back.

He stared at her.

She folded her arms. "Are you going to tell the king about me? Will I be next on your list?"

He didn't even blink. "That depends, what kind of saint are you, Seraphine?"

"What kind of question is that?"

One she couldn't answer.

He said, "The only one that matters."

"I'm still waiting on my letter of instruction from Saint Oriel," she said, reaching for sarcasm. "Right now, I kind of just char stuff. Let me know if you ever want a steak cooked."

That look of suspicion remained.

"What you did back there at the marketplace—"

"Was an accident. Not that I entirely regret it."

"And what about Lark?"

Lark *again*. "You already know what happened with—"

"Did you go to his grave?"

Surprise cut through her frustration. "What are you talking about?"

He chewed on his response. Where once the carriage had been too close to think straight, now it felt cold. *She* was cold. Outside, the sun was dimming as heavy storm clouds rolled in from the east. She reached for her cardigan.

He watched her shrug it on, a muscle working in his jaw. Was he really so disgusted by the idea of her accidental sainthood, or was he wrestling with his sworn duty to the king? He was, after all, Bertrand's appointed saint-killer. And here she sat, within choking distance.

She watched his hands twitch.

Let him try it.

She'd go down swinging.

"Why would I go to Lark's grave?" she pressed. "It's bad enough that I killed him. Every time I think about that night, it makes me sick."

"Someone disturbed it." He drew out each word, carefully studying her reaction. "The grass there . . . it smelled just like lemon blossoms."

"Like magic, you mean."

"Like *you*, Seraphine."

For goodness' sake! She rolled her eyes. "Like I don't have better things to do than go around vandalizing people's graves. *Saints*, Ransom. Give me a little credit."

"They took his body."

She froze. "What?"

"They came in the night and stole his body," he said again. "His grave is empty. Nadia nearly lost her mind."

Sera's stomach lurched. Her thoughts turned to Fontaine's tarot cards, the same ones she and Theo had been poring over in the carriage that very morning. They were burning a hole in her pocket. Her fingers itched to draw them out, to look upon one card in particular. *The Necromancer*—Death's right hand. Was Fontaine's fortune-telling holding true? Was there another saint prowling around Fantome, yanking bodies from their graves?

The silence thickened. Ransom was still watching her in that calculating way, like he was waiting for her to break.

All hell . . . Was this how he truly thought of her? Some depraved grave robber who would wrench the body of his dead best friend from the earth just to screw with him? Words failed her. She couldn't think past the storm of her own confusion and anger . . . her *hurt*.

"I want to pull over," she managed. "You can switch places with Theo."

He jerked his chin. "Why?"

She had to work to keep her voice steady. "Because apparently you think I'm a *fucking grave robber*."

"Your eyes are glowing again."

"Good," she hissed. "Wait another minute and they might actually incinerate you."

Right now, it didn't feel like the worst outcome.

"You wouldn't," he said.

"You have no idea what I can do, Ransom." *And neither do I.*

"But you *clearly* have a wild imagination," she added.

"Calm down," he said, raising his hands. Now that she had passed his little grave robber test, he was all sunshine and smirks again. Too bad. She was not about to forget the insult. "It was a misunderstanding. The lemon blossoms . . . I had forgotten. I just needed to be sure."

"Go to hell," she snapped.

"Seraphine, I had to ask."

She folded her arms. "Congratulations on your new-found common sense. No, I did not steal the corpse of your dead best friend. Any other depraved accusations you'd like to level at me before I shove you out into that rain?" Something else occurred to her. "Is that what your provocative little game of truth or dare was really about?"

"It was more about getting your cardigan off."

She offered her middle finger. "Stay here another minute and we'll find out what else I can rip off . . ." She glared pointedly at his crotch.

"Oh good, we're back to flirting."

She kicked his shin. *Saints*, her eyes burned. What was it about this Dagger that made her feel like a lit match?

He canted his head. "Huh, it seems like your magic is tied to your emotions."

"This one is anger, in case you didn't realize."

"It must accelerate your healing, too. The bruise along your jaw is almost gone."

Shame she couldn't say the same for her bruised feelings. If this carriage ride had taught her anything, it was how little he thought of her. Why would she ever confide in him when he held such a dim view of her? Why would she even *want* to?

What did it matter anyway? She was going to jump ship the moment they found Prince Andreas. It would be easier this way.

She slammed her fist against the ceiling, yelling for the coachman to pull over.

As the carriage trundled to a stop, she kicked the door open. "Either you get out, or I will."

Ransom gave her a flat look. "It's a long way to the Appoline, Seraphine. No more games, I promise. We'll think of something else to do."

"In your dreams."

"Admittedly, yes."

"Get out, Ransom."

To her surprise he did, offering her one last doleful look

over his shoulder before disappearing into the rain.

A moment later, Theo returned, his brows pinched in concern as he clambered inside the carriage.

He looked her over. "Did you fight?"

"Of course," she huffed. "What did you three talk about?"

"Not much." He slumped onto the bench, sliding a little to one side. "We were playing cards."

Sera sniffed, then narrowed her eyes. "Why do you smell like whiskey?"

He offered a lopsided grin. "We were doing forfeits."

"And what? You lost?"

"Oh no," he said, kicking his legs up and settling in for a snooze. "I won."

Chapter 14

Ransom

For three long days on the road, Ransom barely made eye contact with Seraphine. After their argument in the carriage, which had come hot on the heels of her little inferno at the marketplace, she had made a point of avoiding him.

Whenever they stopped to stretch their legs, she stomped off on her own, feigning interest in a nearby oak tree or lingering at a street stall filled with forgettable trinkets. When they ventured further afield for refreshments, stopping in a local tavern, Seraphine always sat at a different table with Versini, keeping her back to Ransom and three of the king's soldiers between them. Once, to test the waters, Ransom asked to borrow her saltshaker, and she had roundly fired it at his head.

Caruso had nearly pissed himself laughing.

Nadia had fired it back, clipping Versini in the ear.

Seraphine had met Nadia glare for glare across the all but deserted tavern, before offering Ransom her middle finger.

So she was holding a grudge.

At least now he could be sure she wasn't their grave robber. Which begged the question . . . who the hell had taken Lark's body? And to what aim?

Beneath it, another question stirred: what kind of saint *was* Seraphine Marchant, and where did her loyalty truly lie? He wasn't fool enough to think they were on the same side just because they were on the same journey.

On the nights when they stopped to rest at inns, Seraphine shared a room with Versini on an entirely different floor to the Daggers.

It sent Ransom half mad with jealousy, thinking of them sharing a bed, imagining her peeling off her chemise after a long day of travel, cozying up to that arrogant Versini prick. He spent those nights ignoring the furious tugging in his chest by staying up far too late and necking whatever Caruso slammed down on the table in front of him. Nothing helped, but the screaming hangover made for a nice distraction the following day. As the hours wore on, and they entered the northwest province of Valterre, Nadia's worsening mood began to rival his own. With every mile closer to the Appoline, she grew antsy, restless. It didn't take a scholar to figure out what was eating away at her. And it had nothing to do with their troublesome prince.

Nadia wasn't satisfied with Ransom's recounting of his argument with Seraphine—or her staunch outright denial about Lark's grave. She wanted to have it out with Seraphine herself. If not for the grave robbery, then for Lark's death.

Resentment simmered.

Sooner or later, it would come to a boil.

On the fourth day, they reached the Appoline University. Ransom could tell by the generous tree-lined driveway that now cloistered them from the rest of the countryside, the oaken leaves whispering as they watched them go by. Up ahead, he spied towering black gates, the verdant university grounds spilling out beyond. Over the high stone walls, ivy-wreathed turrets jutted up like stakes.

His heart gave a painful thud. In another life his destiny might have led him here. To a haven of learning to study the great artists of old. To paint his own landscapes, first under the tutelage of the masters, and later, across the far-flung lands of the continent, where he would answer to no one but his paintbrush. It was the dream his mother had fostered in him long ago, the life they whispered about at bedtime, when the oil lamp flickered low, and her burnished eyes made him feel like anything was possible.

You will be one of the great artists, my darling boy.

You will paint a world far lovelier than this one.

Ten years on and the only thing Ransom had managed to paint was his own body, the dark marks on his skin burrowing deeply and painfully. What would his mother and his sister think of him now? If the king truly did manage to track them down, how could Ransom ever face them? How could he explain the monster he had become? Late at night, when his thoughts turned from Seraphine, they always settled on his family, on the scouring need to find them again, and the fear that they might not love the man he had become in their absence.

Who could stand him, when he could barely stand himself?

Who could love him, when he hated himself?

Seraphine had said it well enough. All this *willful wrecking of his eternal soul* would leave him hollow in the end, with nothing but the residue of Shade in his bones and the nightmares in his head. Already it was so much worse than before, the pathway back to himself so dark and twisting he was losing sight of it.

As ancient trees towered over them, blotting out the sinking sun, Ransom clenched his hands into fists. The hideous skull ring glinted up at him. He imagined it laughing in the deep baritone of Gaspard Dufort. Long before he became a Dagger, Ransom's father had trampled his dreams beyond recognition. Dufort had simply finished the job.

You have made yourself the canvas, Ransom.

And marred it all with shadow.

"Uh-oh. He's brooding again." Caruso's voice cut through his reverie.

Nadia nudged Ransom with the toe of her boot. "What's wrong?"

Everything.

"Hangover," he said, raking his hair back. "That's the last time I play saint or sinner with Caruso."

At last, the carriage trundled to a stop, pulling into a narrow side bank under a gnarled hawthorn tree. Just ahead, the black gates glimmered.

Seraphine and Versini had already disembarked. The soldiers got out to stretch, joining the coachmen in the long grass to smoke cigarillos. They would not be accompanying Ransom and the others inside the Appoline. Since this was not an *official* royal visit.

Smoothing the lapels of his long black coat, Ransom stalked toward the Flames. They were waiting by the gates.

For the first time in three days, Seraphine deigned to speak to him. "Well, Dagger, what's the grand plan?"

"So now you want my advice? Two days ago, you flung a saltshaker at my head."

"Not my fault you have poor reflexes," she said, with a shrug. "And anyway, salt is bad for your health."

"Something you have in common with it."

"Enough flirting," said Caruso in a bored voice. "Go behind that giant tree and screw this out of your system so we can get on with it."

Seraphine's cheeks turned a furious shade of pink.

Ransom rewarded Caruso with a blistering glare.

Versini huffed an impatient sigh. "Visitor entry to the Appoline is by personal invitation of the provost. I'm assuming we don't have one of those?"

"Well reasoned," said Ransom drolly.

"Why doesn't fire-fingers over here melt the gates like she melted Ribauld's ear?" said Nadia. "Better yet, why don't you melt the gatekeepers too? You do love to make a scene."

Seraphine was doing a remarkably good job of holding her tongue. Which made Ransom . . . nervous. Or perhaps she hadn't heard Nadia, since her gaze was trained on the turrets behind them, her lips parted in quiet wonder.

"Enough bickering," he said wearily. "Just leave the talking to me."

The most prestigious university in all of Valterre, the Appoline, had been built in honor of Saint Oriel herself, gifted by one of the many kings who had loved her during her lifetime more than a thousand years ago. Once a place that was open to every eager scholar, now the university was a playground for the wealthy, guarded by literal and metaphorical gatekeepers, who walked the perimeter of the high stone walls, manning the black gates all day and night.

It struck Ransom as a bit much. But then, he did live inside a skull-lined catacomb, guarded by the ancient statue of a dead saint. Each to their own.

Dressed in hooded brown robes tied with a thin golden sash, and carrying longswords donated by the descendants of Cadel, Saint of Warriors, a pair of gatekeepers watched them through the iron bars as they approached.

In what he was dimly aware was an unnecessary move, Ransom removed a vial of Shade from his pocket and took a sip. The black dust danced along his tongue, burning all the way down. His eyes heated, flickering to silver. When the keepers stumbled back from the gates, he knew he had their attention.

And more importantly, their fear.

"I don't know why I expected this to go civilly," muttered Versini.

Ransom strode forward, pulling shadows from the stones and sending them skittering through the bars.

The keeper on the right began to tremble.

The other raised her sword, and cried out, "Who goes there?"

Ransom gave his customary savage smile. "Surely, introductions are not warranted? You are not so far from Fantome that you haven't heard of me."

Shadows wreathed the metal bars like dark fists, making them rattle.

The keepers swallowed thickly. Their hoods were deep and gaping, shielding their faces.

The one with the raised sword spoke again, her voice quaking, "W-what b-business do the Daggers have at the Appoline? This is a place of learning. And *peace*."

"I fancy a tour," said Ransom, with a casual flick of his wrist. A move meant to show off his ring. Not just *a* Dagger. But *the* Dagger. "Open these gates before I wrench them apart."

They hesitated.

"Maybe you should try saying 'please,'" said Seraphine.

Too late for niceties. The Shade had its claws in him now. Pretending not to hear her, Ransom cocked his head. "Unless you'd like your ribs wrenched apart too?" With a curl of his fingers, he cracked the nearest shadow like a whip.

The keepers yelped, leaping away from it.

"Now," he growled.

The gates groaned open.

He stalked inside. "Fetch the provost," he demanded. "Have him meet us in the inner courtyard."

The gatekeepers scurried off, leaving them to make their way down a stone path bordered by neatly pruned rosebushes. The cobbles led them right through the arched foreground of the Appoline, and onto the grassy quadrangle within. Shadows prowled alongside Ransom, keeping pace with his steps. The others remained at his back, silently taking in the grandeur.

The Appoline was a palace all of its own. Towering ivy-clad walls made a perfect square four stories high with wide gilded windows that looked out over the generous courtyard, welcoming the sunlight of each new day. History seeped from every stone, wept from every ancient willow they passed. They emerged at last into the central courtyard. The grass here was neatly shorn, bordered by rows of lavender and long-stemmed daisies. Wooden benches occupied the middle, where scholars had gathered to picnic, or to read in the late-afternoon sun. Some looked up as they approached, clocked the sea of shadows that moved with Ransom and fled, leaving their satchels and half-eaten sandwiches behind.

"And you thought *I* made a scene at the marketplace," remarked Seraphine, plucking a book from the grass and idly thumbing through it. "You're creating mass hysteria."

Ransom glanced at her over his shoulder. "I'm nothing if not efficient."

"Just try not to kill the provost when he arrives."

He pretended to mull it over. "Unless he's rude to me."

"Not funny."

"What makes you think it was a joke?" Caruso piped up.

"Don't talk to them, Sera," said Versini, under his breath. "They clearly get off on it."

Faces gathered at the windows as frightened scholars cowered in their dorms, waiting for the big bad wolf to leave. Ransom hated how he envied them.

Wasn't this power more intoxicating? Wasn't he richer than all of them put together?

Then why do I feel so empty?

Caruso picked up an abandoned sandwich and devoured it. "These fuckers eat well," he said, licking mustard from his fingers. "Brain food, I suppose."

"They sure as hell pay enough money to come here." Nadia grabbed a discarded apple and practiced aiming it at the nearest window. "This provost has three minutes to show his face, or I'm smashing something."

Fortunately for the venerated university, the provost arrived in two, hurrying across the lawn in a long black robe and with a face like thunder. He was tall and as narrow as a rake, with a drawn pale face, a crop of wiry gray hair, and a short gray beard.

Somewhat surprisingly, he didn't look scared. Just completely incandescent.

"Enough of this terror!" he bellowed. "What brings you to these hallowed grounds? We have an accord with the Daggers!"

Ransom's brows shot up. He hadn't known that. Maybe brute force hadn't been the best choice here. Leashing his shadows, he cleared his throat and said, "Calm yourself, Provost. We don't mean any harm."

"Yet," added Caruso.

"We won't cause any trouble," said Versini, who had the *gall* to step in front of Ransom. Skirting those shadows as if, in his heightened state, Ransom wouldn't flick one at him on a whim. "Thank you for coming here so promptly, Provost Ambrose, we really appreciate your time." He stuck his hand out.

What an insufferable, simpering—

"A little decorum. Very good." The provost shook his hand, offering a flat smile. "Whatever this is about, I'm sure we can handle it like civilized adults."

Despite the forced air of politeness, tension simmered.

Ransom cut to the chase. "We're looking for Prince Andreas."

The provost went paler still. "You seek to kill a prince of the realm?"

"Not necessarily," he lied.

The provost took a measured step backward. Looking between them, he said, "Andreas left us months ago. Not long after the unfortunate clock tower incident." He pointed past them, toward the north end of the square. They all turned, craning their necks as they took in the remains of what must have been the clock tower. The top half, including the clock face and the heavy brass bell, had been destroyed. The rest of the stone had caved in on itself, forming a mound of rubble atop the roof.

"How on earth did he survive that fall?" said Nadia.

"Sainthood, I suppose," said Ransom.

He glanced at Seraphine. She was chewing on her thumbnail,

staring up at the broken clock tower like she was looking at a ghost.

"What exactly happened here?" asked Versini.

The provost took a moment to answer. "A sort of madness came over Andreas. He climbed the clock tower in the middle of the storm. The lightning struck him in the mouth. It went through him like a current."

"Didn't anyone try and stop him?"

Brow furrowing, the provost said, "Andreas was single-minded in this, as he was in all his endeavors."

"When did he leave?" asked Ransom.

"Within the fortnight. Once the worst of his injuries had healed. He slipped out of his bedchamber some time in the middle of the night, grabbed his personal effects, and waved goodbye to the gatekeepers. Never summoned a carriage. He must have walked for hours."

"To where?" Nadia pressed.

The provost shifted from one foot to the other. "I couldn't say."

"Take a guess," urged Ransom.

"What is it that you want with Andreas?" asked the provost baldly.

"Tea and scones," said Caruso, dryly. "What the fuck do you think, old-timer?"

Versini cut in, his voice laced with concern. "Rebellion is stirring across Valterre. Fantome has fallen into lawlessness. Innocents are fighting in the streets. They are dying for a cause that has sprung up as if from nowhere . . ." If the provost was surprised by any of this, he didn't show it. The Appoline might be tucked away in its own leafy pocket of the kingdom, but they had hundreds of seasoned scribes at their disposal, scholars whose sole vocation was to catalogue every single thing that happened in Valterre, from the disputes reported in the daily penny papers to the changeable weather.

"There are rumors that Prince Andreas is behind this uprising. We'd like to see for ourselves."

The provost's frown deepened. "I am no rebel," he said, taking another step back, as if to distance himself from the implication. "The prince was discharged from the Appoline the moment he left through those black gates. His movements are his own."

"What about his thoughts?" Ransom watched the old man squirm. "Weren't you the prince's personal mentor while he was here?"

"We shared an interest in the saints," said the provost, in a clipped tone. "Like most of the scholars here."

"What about overthrowing the king?" said Caruso, a cat toying with a skittish mouse.

The provost spluttered in horror. "Certainly not!"

"Stop it," chided Seraphine, nudging Caruso to one side. "We haven't come here to interrogate you, Provost Ambrose. We understand you have a university to preside over and have no interest in stoking a rebellion far beyond these walls. And though none of us have had the pleasure of your tutelage, you can rest assured that *most* of us are intelligent enough to know"—she spared a pointed glance at Caruso—"that you're not hiding Prince Andreas in the pocket of your robe."

Taking the provost by the arm, she smiled sweetly at him. Even though Ransom knew it was as fake as all hell, he liked how it softened her eyes.

The provost seemed to like it too. He rolled his shoulders back, seeming to relax a little.

"To save time, and more droning questions, could you please show us to his old study quarters?" she asked, gently tugging him away from the others. "There might be something there that will help us make sense of all of this. What Andreas was planning, or where he might have gone. We'll be out of your hair before you know it."

"It is not customary to let visitors roam these halls . . ."

Ransom flicked his fingers.

The provost's gaze dropped to the shadows now inching toward his shiny black shoes.

Seraphine twisted, putting her body between him and that menacing puddle of darkness. "We'll be in and out in an hour. Once we've had a look at his chambers, you can return to the important work you do here, and rest easy knowing you'll never hear from us ever again . . ."

Swallowing hard, the provost said, "I could show you to his desk. Andreas hardly ever left it. But his more recent work, his writings . . . they're more like ramblings."

Seraphine summoned that saccharine smile. "Lead on, Provost. We'll be right behind you." She released his arm with a wink. "Keeping a safe distance, of course."

The provost vaulted ahead, clearly eager to be rid of them.

Ransom hung back, falling into step with her. "Well played, spitfire. Who knew you could be such a darling?"

"It's called common decency. Try it sometime. Your people skills are appalling."

"I'm better with corpses."

She rolled her eyes. "If you threaten our first and only lead, we'll never find another one. Do you want to find the prince or not?"

"You mean *kill* the prince."

"Right. Same thing." She scurried ahead, passing under the stone arch and turning left toward a set of doors that led into the east wing of the Appoline.

"Is it?" he said, striding to keep up.

She stopped abruptly, letting the others slip inside ahead of her. Turning to face him, her eyes grew wide and searching. "You tell me, Dagger."

Ransom stilled, angling his body toward hers. Shadows pooled around them, blotting out the world. "Are you having second thoughts, Seraphine?"

Biting her lip, she raised her gaze, the bronze fleck there glimmering. "Right now, I'm having . . . *other* thoughts," she said, in a low, breathy voice.

Ah. His gaze dipped from her eyes to the bow of her lips. The cut on her mouth was a faded pink line. He wanted to press his lips against it. "I'm all ears, spitfire."

"Good," she murmured, sliding her hands up his chest. "Because I need something from you. Rather *urgently*."

His heart gave a deep, insistent thud, as if to say, *Anything.*

Her eyes gleamed as gold as sunlight as her fingers dipped beneath his open collar, lightly tracing the shadow-marks there.

Magic met magic. Dimly, he was aware of the Shade leaving him. More overtly, he didn't give a shit.

He stifled a groan, every nerve ending in his body firing under her touch. That thread in his chest was so taut, one tug would yank his heart right out. "I need something too," he said, hoarsely.

You. Now.

Always.

She smirked.

He leaned in, desperate to taste that smile, but she was already side-stepping away.

He turned, blinking at her in confusion.

"There." Her smile grew. "*Much* better."

Ransom looked down at himself, noting the distinct lack of shadows at his feet. *Ah.* The brazen spitfire had shredded his power. She had put a muzzle on the attack dog, who had been too busy drooling over her to notice.

"We're in a hallowed place of learning," she said, in an entirely different tone. One he did not particularly enjoy. "So stop threatening everyone like a slack-brained brute and start acting like it."

He bit back a curse. "I knew it was too good to be true."

She arched a brow, pushing past him. "Eyes on the prize, Dagger."

They are, he thought to himself as he stalked inside after her.

Chapter 15

Seraphine

Stepping into the library at the Appoline was like straying into a dream. Vaulted ceilings crowned stone walls hung with beautiful oil paintings, each one depicting a venerated Saint of Valterre. Arched stained-glass windows looked out over the courtyard below, their generous sills lined with velvet cushions.

Oil lamps flickered on the low reading tables, casting shadows across endless rows of walnut shelves. They towered so high, each bookshelf had its own reeling ladder to reach all the way to the top. The wooden floors were polished to shine and carpeted with generous woven rugs, and the air was heavy with the scent of beeswax and parchment.

This place was a cathedral of learning, brimming with so many leather-bound books and weighty tomes, a part of Sera wanted to curl up and stay here forever. No wonder Mama always dreamed of this place. It was a haven for scholars, a place that smelled like history and secrets and possibilities.

She fell behind, idly trailing her fingers across a wing-backed reading chair. Tipping her head back, she let the stained sunlight dance along her face, and imagined the library was welcoming her. *Come and gaze upon our treasures. Come and see what secrets we hold.*

All around the grand chamber, dedicated scholars did their best to continue their work, despite the gawking visitors in their midst.

"If I lived here, I don't think I'd ever want to leave," said Theo, as he wandered next to her. "No wonder this was Oriel's Sanctuary. They say most of her prophecies are stored here."

"Been brushing up on the saints, then?"

He gave her a knowing look. "The old and the new."

She thought again of Fontaine's tarot cards.

Stone Maiden, Necromancer, Silver-tongue.

They played over and over in her head, these clues that prowled at the edges of her mind.

Sera and Theo weren't the only ones ignoring the impatiently beckoning provost. Ransom and Nadia had drifted toward an oil painting of Calvin, Saint of Death, an unnervingly handsome figure with ice-pale skin, thick black hair, and green eyes. And yet, despite his unsettling beauty, the saint's face was grave, those green eyes haunted.

It occurred to Sera that not all powers are blessings. That to oversee death was a curse in itself.

She turned away, weathering a twist of discomfort. She tried not to wonder if she had been cursed too, if she would be able to endure the full flush of whatever magic lived inside her. Perhaps that was why it often hid from her, only emerging in answer to the nearness of Shade or her own rioting emotions.

Brushing past her, Caruso wandered over to Cadel, Saint of Warriors, gazing up at him the way a child might regard a lion at the Menagerie Zoo.

A black cat watched him from a nearby windowsill, holding court beside the tapestry of Serene, Saint of Animals. Sera found herself drifting toward a tapestry of Saint Oriel. It was three times her own height, and so intricately braided it must have taken years to complete. The oracle's beauty shone out from every strand, the delicate folds of her pale gold dress cascading along her lithe form. Her deep brown skin was unlined, her black hair falling to her waist in thin beaded braids. She wore a simple gold necklace, and around her arm a circlet that looked like three waves rising from the sea.

In her right hand, she held a single red rose, the oldest symbol of Valterre. Not of the kingdom but the land itself, the true soul of the country. Sera's cheeks prickled, her thoughts turning to the tarot card she had pulled from Fontaine's deck.

The rose is both soft and dangerous. It can mean great beauty or untold destruction. It depends on the soil in which it grows.

Oriel was smiling in her portrait, the light in her burnished brown eyes hinting at all the secrets she kept. Or perhaps it was simply a show of her ease—with herself and her destiny. Sera stared up at the saint, wondering how she could ever be worthy of a tapestry such as this. A reputation that spanned centuries.

She was just a barefooted farmgirl from the plains, an orphan and a chancer. A smuggler, even now.

The mere idea of sainthood made a laugh bubble out of her.

The black cat offered a scolding meow.

"Sorry," she said, sheepishly.

The provost, who had been barely enduring their slow-footed curiosity up until now, cleared his throat, pointedly. A fair protest. They had all but prodded him here under duress, and now they were perusing the library like tourists in a museum.

"This way, please. Time is of the essence."

They followed him down to the lower chamber of the library. Here was a more modest space, which housed a row of private alcoves, and at the back of the room, a large sequestered hall where the scribes of the Appoline worked from noon to night, preserving the living history of the kingdom.

Provost Ambrose stopped at the third alcove, gesturing toward the room inside. It was a small study chamber, the desk here littered with papers and ledgers. A satchel hung from a hook on the wall and a crumpled cashmere sweater had been slung over the back of the wooden chair.

"You may look at your own discretion. I'll be back within the *hour*." He leaned on the last word, making his intention more than clear. "In the meantime, please keep your voices down. There are scribes at work down here."

"Don't worry, Provost. The Daggers are nothing if not discreet," said Ransom, waving him off.

Now that he wasn't wreathed in all those menacing shadows, he was more like himself. Unhurried, easy-going . . . almost normal. This was the version of Ransom Seraphine found herself most drawn to, the one she watched from the corner of her eye when she was supposed to be ignoring him. The one she dreamed of kissing whenever she nodded off in her carriage, her skin growing clammy at the thought.

Left to their own devices, they started rifling through the prince's effects, looking for clues of his grand plans for Valterre, and where he might have disappeared to. The tight space was improved by the swift exit of Caruso, who cried boredom after three minutes and went off to chase the black cat who had come by to spy on them.

Most of Prince Andreas's scribblings were indeed illegible, ordinary sentences trailing off into feverish ramblings, while in places entire paragraphs were repeated. It soon become clear that before his disappearance, the prince had been trapped in a kind of loop—one that began and ended with the saints. Pages upon pages of parchment had been dedicated to their birthplaces and early childhoods, their familial relationships and notable feats of power, as well as any rumors that had circulated around them during their lives.

There were maps, too. So many they littered the floor.

Ransom looked up from the ledger he was thumbing through. "This whole book is full of Beauregards. Births and deaths. Their final resting places."

"Saint Oriel's descendants," said Sera. She wondered if Fontaine was in there somewhere.

"Maybe he was after her final prophecy. He was clearly obsessed with the Second Coming," said Nadia, who had just pulled a biography about Saint Oriel from the prince's satchel. "Spare me these spoiled rich men and their never-ending quests for greatness."

Theo leaned in to have a look, his shoulder brushing hers as he examined the cover. Annoyance prickled at Sera. Whatever merriment he had enjoyed with Caruso and Nadia in their carriage three days ago had dissolved their ire toward him. But every time Nadia locked eyes with her, Sera felt like the Dagger was imagining her slow and painful demise.

"So many Havelocks," Theo muttered, turning back to the ledger he had been flicking through. "Why is that name so familiar?"

"It's the family name of Saint Maurius," said Ransom, setting down a raft of papers.

Sera's brows rose. If Oriel was her own favored saint, then Maurius, Saint of Seafarers and Travelers, was Ransom's. She had watched him pray to him once, in Our Sacred Saints' Cathedral. Not for himself but for his mother and his sister, Anouk. That they had found safe haven somewhere far beyond the cruel fists of his father and the dark underbelly of Fantome, that one day he might be reunited with them again. As the Head of the Daggers, and a slave to the thrall of Shade, he was further from that dream than ever.

Theo scrubbed his jaw. "The Oriel obsession makes sense to me, but why the interest in Maurius?"

Again, it was Ransom who answered. "Maurius was Oriel's scribe. In the last days of her life, he came back to her, here in the Appoline. Maurius wrote down Oriel's final prophecy when she was too weak to write it herself."

"Why?" said Nadia.

Ransom looked right at Seraphine. "Because they were lovers."

Oh.

She looked away, sharply. It was strange to imagine Saint Oriel like that. Not as some untouchable, divine being, but as a hot-blooded woman who was loved and cherished by another, kissed and caressed, and even tended to by him in the last hours of her life. There was something so gently human about it.

"How do you even know that?" said Theo.

Ransom shrugged. "My mother told me a long time ago." And then quieter, as if more to himself, he added, "She was a hopeless romantic."

Theo was stunned into silence. Sera couldn't tell if it was the revelation about Maurius and Oriel, or the fact that Ransom Hale had just revealed something incredibly personal to a man he openly loathed. In a handful of words, he had revealed the glimpse of a mother who had once confided things in him. Someone who had loved him, when he was a boy and not a Dagger.

Returning to his search, Theo unfurled another map. A double spread of Valterre marred with several black crosses. He spread it against the wall.

"He's marked all the towers in the kingdom." Sera recalled Fontaine's fevered murmurings. *The storm will choose new saints to crown, where three stone towers crumble down.* "He must have known the storm would change everything. He was probably waiting for it his whole life."

"Waiting for power," said Nadia. "And now he's using it to tear the kingdom apart."

Maybe he has a good reason. A better vision.

She kept those mutinous thoughts to herself. But Nadia rounded on her, like she could hear them. "What about you? What magic did you wrench from that storm?"

"I didn't take anything," said Sera, stiffening.

At least not on purpose.

"More lies from our own resident saint," Nadia spat. "Did you really think I wouldn't notice what you did to Ribauld back at the market? That I wouldn't put two and two together after the golden handprint you scoured into Lark's chest?"

"Nadia," warned Ransom. "Keep your voice down."

"Why?" she challenged. "It's not like she doesn't know what she is."

"It's complicated." Theo's eyes darted to the entryway, like he was afraid a rogue scribe might be listening in. "Now is not the time or place to get into it."

Nadia folded her arms. "When were you planning on dealing with this conflict of interest?" she challenged, without bothering to keep her voice. "Before or after we murder the other living saints of Valterre? It seems to me that you and Andreas are cut from the same cloth."

Sera kept her face blank, even as her heart smashed against her ribcage.

Nadia stepped in close, her dark eyes flashing. "Tell us, Seraphine. Are you planning to kill the prince, or work with him against the king? Against *us*?"

"Back off, Nadia," said Theo through his teeth.

"I don't know anything about Prince Andreas," said Sera carefully. "I didn't even know he existed until a few days ago."

There. An easy truth. Something she could sell.

Nadia curled her lip. Not buying it.

Ransom had gone silent, his gaze on Seraphine's face, like he was searching for the same betrayal that seemed so apparent to Nadia.

"I don't know anything about Andreas," Sera repeated, this time with bite. "I have no idea what he's capable of."

"Just like we don't know what you're capable of," Nadia shot back.

"That sounds a lot like your problem."

"Not if we kill you too, *saint.*"

Sera's cheeks were prickling, her magic rearing up at the threat.

She squeezed her hands into fists. *Not now.*

Too late. She felt her eyes flash, glimpsed the golden glint in the reflection of Nadia's pupils as they widened.

Nadia canted her head, her lip curling. "Exactly what kind of saint are you?"

Fontaine's tarot cards flashed through Sera's mind: *Stone Maiden, Necromancer, Silver-tongue.*

She wanted to scream, *I don't know!*

"A confused one," said Ransom, with dawning realization.

"Let her talk," said Nadia without looking at him. "What *exactly* can you do?"

Sera sensed what this was really about. Or rather, *who.*

"Why don't I save us all this mindless interrogation. I'll tell you what I don't do," she said, slowly, even viciously. "I don't steal bodies out of graves."

Nostrils flaring, Nadia took a step closer. "Why don't I believe you?"

"Because you have deep-rooted trust issues?"

Too far. Too much. Nadia was angry, still grieving. Sera was on the back foot, and *pissed*.

The tension was so thick it was clouding her head. Sera needed to get out of this room and breathe.

But Nadia blocked the doorway. Her eyes were wild now, her breath hitching. "It wasn't enough that you killed him, you had to wrench his body from the earth, too."

Sera narrowed her eyes, the last of her patience evaporating. "Drop it, before you really start to piss me off. Whatever happened to Lark's body has *nothing* to do with me. Maybe you should have kept a better eye on it."

Nadia jerked like she had been slapped. "How dare you!"

Sera would have regretted those words if her blood wasn't boiling. A part of her knew she should slow down, take a breath—and a walk—but her tongue was loose and that fire inside her was hot, so she said, through her teeth, "I'll do whatever the hell I like. You can't stop me, Dagger."

Nadia pounced, fast and hard. Sera was on the floor, half winded, before anyone in the room even registered the hit.

Nadia pinned her there with her knees. "Say that again," she hissed, jamming the side of her face into the wooden boards. "I *dare* you."

Sera bucked madly. "Get. Off. Me!"

"Admit what you did! Admit what you took from me!"

"Go to hell!" Sera slammed her knee into Nadia's back. It *crunched.* Fear and rage entangled in her chest, stoking her magic like a poker. That roiling heat raced through her, until she felt it in her palms. Power consumed her, and this time, she let it. Now the Dagger would pay. She swung, reaching for the end of Nadia's ponytail.

"SERA, NO!" yelled Theo.

Sera's fingers met with thin air as Nadia was yanked off her. Ransom swung her behind him. She was still spitting when Theo moved in to restrain her.

Sera collapsed to the ground, trying to catch her breath.

Ransom peered down at her, horror-stricken. "What the fuck was that?"

"Self-defense," huffed Sera, but her voice was small. She was trembling now, her magic rushing out of her as quickly as it had reared its head. She got to her feet, furiously scrubbing the tears that leaked from her eyes. A moment ago, she had felt feral. *Dangerous.* Now she felt like a cornered mouse, frightened of the dragon that lived inside her. The monster that she had almost unleashed on Nadia. All but proving her point.

"I'm not scared of you," said Nadia, from behind the wall of Theo's body. "Try that again and I'll jam my heel through your skull."

Before Sera could reply, Ransom spun her around, promptly marching her out of the alcove.

She fought against his hold, but his hands on her shoulders

were a vise, steering her through the towering stacks. His voice was low and hard in her ear. "If I'm not allowed kill innocent scholars with my Shade, you're not allowed to scald my second-in-command."

"What are you doing?" she said, swatting at him.

"Putting you on ice, little firecracker."

The gall! She jerked her head back, aiming for his nose.

He chuckled, easily avoiding the blow.

She continued her weakening protests.

"Easy, spitfire," he murmured. "Let's not do a murder."

"She started it!"

"By all means, command the moral high ground, like I didn't just watch you try to burn her scalp off."

"I was going for her ponytail!"

"Nadia would tell you that's just as grievous."

No shit.

He swung her into an abandoned alcove at the end of the row. This one was smaller and darker than the one they had come from, with barely enough room for a desk. Folding her arms, she slumped against it. Still heaving. *Seething.*

"Should we do some breathing exercises?"

She had to crane her neck to glower at him. "You must have a death wish."

"Something like that," he said, flashing his teeth.

"Ugh." She flung a paperweight at him. It bounced off his hard chest. He didn't even flinch, his hazel eyes warming like he found it endearing.

In their tiny alcove his scent surrounded her, that heady

rush of woodsmoke and sage snatching at the edges of her anger, making her damn knees weak.

As if sensing she was about to sag, he picked her up, lifting her easily onto the desk.

"Feel better?" he said, bracing his hands on either side of her. Caging her in. "Or would you like to throw that ink pot at me too?"

"I'm seriously considering it," she mumbled.

"Just . . . take a breath."

She didn't want to breathe too deeply or think too hard about what had just happened. The truth was, she felt . . . wretched. Embarrassed by what had transpired with Nadia, terrified of what she'd almost done in the mist of her own rage. And then there was Ransom's nearness, wreaking havoc on her heartbeat. It was the heat of him, the slow tilt of his head and the curve of his lips as he watched her.

He moved closer and, saints help her, she spread her legs, allowing him to stand between them.

"I've just figured you out, spitfire."

Arching a brow, she looked up at him. His eyes were on her lips.

"You can't tell Nadia what kind of saint you are, can you?"

"Maybe I don't want to."

"Maybe you don't know." He hooked his finger under her chin, tilting her head back. "Maybe that terrifies you."

Magic roared through her blood, that thread in her chest going taut.

He smiled, like he could feel it. "Tell me I'm right."

She wrestled for control of her own body. "You're unprofessional."

"Only a little," he said, soft and low. At the warmth of his breath against her lips, her lids fell to half mast. All thought eddied away, the warning shouts in her head growing fainter, until it was just the two of them, teetering on the edge of that bonfire of lust. She twisted her hands in his collar, yanking him closer. "And it's none of your business," she said, through her teeth.

"I'm a saint-killer," he said, in that same seductive rumble. "I'm afraid it's entirely my business."

How could one man make murder sound so damn appealing? She really was losing her mind. Her heart thundered madly, magic crackling on her lips.

Brushing his thumb there, he murmured, "Fascinating."

Thwack!

Ransom reared backward, his hand flying to the back of his head. "What the fuck?"

Caruso was standing in the narrow doorway. He was cradling the black cat, and by the looks of things, had just fired a thesaurus at Ransom's head. "What's going on in here?"

"Nothing." Sera raked her hands through her hair, hastily settling the unruly strands . . . trying to hide the disappointment guttering through her. Not that hurling herself at the Head of the Daggers would have made for a particularly good decision, given she was planning on betraying him—and their entire mission—fairly soon, but in that charged moment, with his lips so close to hers, his heart thundering just a few inches away, it had felt like the right move. The only move. She could have sworn her magic had wanted it just as badly.

"This'd better be important," snapped Ransom.

"The provost is back. I think we've officially outstayed our welcome."

Sera slid off the desk. "Good. We're done anyway."

"Uh-huh," drawled Caruso, languidly petting the cat in his arms.

They returned to the others. Theo was talking to the provost, probably trying to smooth over the scene they just created down here. Nadia was keeping her distance, still stewing somewhere in the stacks. Ransom went to speak to her, while Sera drifted toward Theo.

"Nothing of much use in here, I'm afraid . . ." Theo was saying. "Unless you count his fevered obsession with the saints."

"That's all Andreas was in the end." The provost rubbed his forehead as he looked into the alcove, his gaze flitting over all those ledgers and loose papers. "We shared a common interest in Saint Oriel's prophecies, though I admit I did not expect the Second Coming to begin quite this soon. Or even in my lifetime. Many of us here at the Appoline have been waiting for it." His brow furrowed as he looked away. "Some more urgently than others."

An ominous feeling came over Sera, raising the hairs on her arms.

"Are you unhappy now that it's finally here?" she said, reading the strain on the provost's face.

He looked between them, weighing his words. Perhaps it

was the absence of the Daggers, who were out of earshot, or the earnest curiosity on their faces, that made him relent. "My studies lead me to believe this new Age of Saints will not like be like the last one. This time, fate will play a different hand. Power will be given, and power will be taken. Some saints will fall into their destiny, while others will chase it."

"Do you mean that some will be more worthy than others?" said Theo, glancing at Sera. What was that shadowed look in his eyes just now? Was he thinking the same thing that she was—that she was some kind of divine accident, a saint unworthy of the power in her veins? Was that why her magic refused to listen to her?

"Who can know for sure? The kingdom is teetering on the cusp of this new age. We are at the beginning of change, not the outcome of it. We must wait for the dice to settle." The provost passed a hand over his beard, tugging at the wiry strands. "Although there is one thing I am sure of. There is a difference between power and goodness. One does not beget the other."

"Perhaps it depends on the gift," reasoned Theo. He was careful not to look at Sera now, as though afraid even a glance would cast her in a glow of sudden suspicion. "Is there a way to know what powers will present themselves in this new Age of Saints?"

"Not so," said the provost, who had plainly considered it at great length. "I believe the gifts will act on the person as they did during the first age. We know that Alisa, Saint of the Sick, was a nurse before the storm struck. Her gift of healing seemed to be the most natural outcome. Maurius had been a sailor, so he knew the ways of the wind long before his magic enabled him to corral it. And Cadel was a venerated soldier in the royal army before his true prowess in war manifested. Calvin grew up with a mother who practiced seances, so to commune with the dead was no great stretch for him. And Saint Oriel, of course, was prone to daydreaming, even as a child . . . There is no telling how precisely power will manifest before the magic itself settles. It is the alchemy of the soul and the divine that decides it. Just as before."

Sera's breath was coming sharp and fast, curiosity piling a hundred more questions on her tongue. About the saints of old, and the ones still to come. Fontaine's tarot cards were like lead in her pocket. A part of her wanted to draw them out and wave them in the provost's face, beg him to examine them just as closely, to tell her what she had become in that storm—or who she was supposed to be—but the Daggers were coming their way, clearly growing impatient.

So, too, was the provost. He seemed to snap back into himself, stepping away from their conversation and stiffening his shoulders. "I believe your search is at an end," he announced to all of them. "I'll show you out."

Chapter 16

Ransom

As they left the lower chamber of the Appoline library, with nothing to show for their journey but more bad blood, Versini made a point of walking between Nadia and Seraphine, lest one of them decide to kill the other. Again. Despite his ongoing disdain for the Shadowsmith, Ransom appreciated his foresight.

As they wound their way back through halls of the Appoline, scholars watched them from the shadows, peering out from behind statues and pillars. Still carting that black cat around with him, Caruso pretended to lunge at one every so often.

Eventually, they were shooed out of the front door, the provost offering a stilted goodbye as the gatekeepers peeled far away from them. Ransom was halfway down the path when he realized Seraphine was not with them. She had lagged behind, her golden hair just visible through the crack in the front door.

Retracing his steps, he silently stepped into the shadows on the other side.

She was standing in the foyer with the provost, her voice low and edged with concern. Despite his obvious disgust for the Daggers, the old scholar seemed to have taken a shine to Seraphine. He was standing with his arms folded and head bent, listening intently.

". . . that it's troubling me," she was saying. "It feels like it's all happening so quickly."

He *hmm*'d in agreement. "Such is the nature of great change. It is the after that will decide the fate of the kingdom."

"Provost, is there such a thing as a bad saint?" she said, in a small nervous voice.

The scholar scrubbed his jaw. Seraphine wrung her hands as she awaited his answer, her anxiety so palpable it made Ransom's heart thrum.

"That I do not know," the provost admitted, with a heavy shrug. "But I will admit that it is my greatest fear."

"Mine too." Seraphine's voice was so quiet Ransom had to lean in to hear her. He stood now with one foot in the doorway and one foot out, the gatekeepers' curious gazes boring into his back.

"Although some of my best scholars would argue that goodness, or indeed badness, is a matter of perspective," the provost reasoned. "The saints of old were not without fault, Seraphine. They were human long before they were blessed. But what they shared with each other was an implicit understanding, a bond born out of the uniqueness of their circumstances, despite the differences in their gifts. The pull to each other was always stronger than the pull of ambition, but of course, with all power, the temptation for *more* is always there . . ." He trailed off. "In that way, I don't believe we can judge Andreas until the rest of the saints reveal themselves. However many there may be this time around."

"I admit I'm curious about the other saints," she said, so very carefully. "I wonder whether they will find their way to the prince."

She was fishing.

And damn if it wasn't working.

The provost looked at her, his hawkish eyes narrowing. Ransom wondered if he could glimpse the fire in her, if all those decades he'd spent researching the saints of Valterre had prepared him for a moment like this. To look beyond what was most obvious, to the hidden truth therein.

Seraphine turned her face up to him, like she was willing him to see her. To trust her.

Unease needled Ransom. He had to fight the urge to stalk inside and pull her away from the provost, to keep her from unravelling the greatest—and most dangerous—secret of her life to a man who owed her no loyalty. But then, Seraphine was cleverer than Ransom was, cunning in a way that often caught him off guard. Perhaps she had a plan even now, a deeper reason for this hushed conversation.

And then the provost spoke again, and Ransom almost laughed at how easily she had snared him.

"If they were *really* curious, they could always look for him in the town of Marvale."

So the wily old bastard knew exactly where Andreas was—he had known this whole time.

"Marvale," echoed Seraphine, a hitch of excitement in her voice. "That's where Oriel Beauregard was born."

The provost nodded. "Andreas believes the other saints will find him there. That is his greatest hope."

She pressed a hand to her heart, like she was storing the information there. "Thank you, Provost Ambrose." She sounded sincere . . . almost *relieved.*

"Be careful what you do with that information," he said, stepping away from her.

She dipped her chin, conviction rippling in her words when she answered, "You can trust me, Provost."

But can I? Ransom wondered.

The twist in his gut told him the answer.

Stepping back, Ransom flattened himself against the outer wall of the Appoline as Seraphine came striding out, wearing a smile that made her entire face light up. Spying Versini passing through the black gates up ahead, she hurried to catch up with him.

Ransom went after her. "There you are!" he called out. "I thought you'd been kidnapped by a scribe."

She spun around, her lashes fluttering in surprise. "Where on earth did you just come from?" she said, half breathless.

"I asked you first."

"No, you didn't."

"Tell me anyway," he said, offering the challenge.

Come on, Seraphine. Tell me the truth.

He watched the lie form behind her eyes, her teeth nipping her lower lip when she said, "I had to use the bathroom."

Frustration curled his lip and made him itch for a taste of Shade to take the edge off. Canting his head, he said, "How is it that you trust a wily old scholar more than the man that's been keeping your head off a pike for the last four months?"

Her face fell. "You were spying on me!"

"You were sneaking around," he hissed, walking her back against a nearby stone pillar.

She flattened herself against it, fuming. "It's called having a private conversation."

He leaned over her, dropping his voice to a deadly quiet. "What were you planning to do, steal one of our carriages and peel off into the night with Versini? Find your way to Marvale and throw yourself at the prince's feet? Beg like a dog for a place on his court?"

She prodded his chest. "Watch your mouth, Dagger."

"Watch *yours*," he growled. "You're playing with fire."

"Good thing it's my favorite element."

He resisted the urge to take her by the shoulders and shake some sense into her. "You're going to get yourself killed."

"By who? *You?*"

"You made a deal with the King of Valterre, Seraphine. If you intend to survive, then you have to start trusting me."

"Why would I?" She jutted out her chin, blowing a stray strand from her eyes. "The second he finds out what I am, I'll be your mark."

"You've been my mark for as long as I've known you." Ransom

threw his hands up. "And look at you. More alive than ever."

She eyed him with unconcealed suspicion, her survival instincts making her shoulders stiff, her voice clipped, when she asked, "What exactly has the king promised you for this quest? You know, the dead bodies of two newly minted saints, the premature ending of an era divined by Oriel herself. It's no small thing, Ransom."

No, indeed it was not. That much was not lost on him. But a good Dagger didn't indulge in moral quandaries. Therein madness lay. A good Dagger killed, and killed, and killed again. Let the gloom take him at the end of a long night, and he would rise again the following day, with death prowling at his side.

When he didn't answer, she pressed again. "It's not coin. It can't be coin."

"No," he admitted. "Not coin."

Something far more valuable, and a hell of a lot more tenuous. His past. His family. A chance to know that they were all right, that Anouk had grown up and Mama had grown happy. Even if he might never be able to face them again, even if he was too scared to show them what he had become in their absence. This tapestry of death. This unholy reaper.

Her brows raised. "So what, then?"

He hesitated, not wanting to say. To give her something she could hold over him, when she had lied to him so readily just now, revealed so little of her true intentions.

No, they were not confidants. Not by a long shot.

Her smile was mirthless. "I guess the lack of trust is mutual, then."

"I guess it is."

They could be honest, at least, about that.

And yet, he could have sworn he glimpsed a glimmer of hurt in her eyes. She shrugged it off, arcing around him to where Versini was waiting by the gates, firing invisible daggers at Ransom's head.

Stalking after her, Ransom called out, "Good news! It seems fate has dealt us a new lead. We'll continue north to Marvale."

Chapter 17

Seraphine

Sera was still smarting when she climbed into the carriage after Theo. Arrogant, interfering Dagger, with his stupidly perfect face. Why did he insist on scrambling her thoughts before she had a chance to sift through them herself? She hadn't even decided what she was going to do about the provost's tip before he'd yanked it out of her hands and waved it around for all to see.

"He caught me in a lie," she groaned into her hands. And he was pissed. Worse—*hurt*. And more emboldened than ever. "Marvale is going to be a bloodbath."

"It was always going to go like this," said Theo, calmly. "He'd be a fool to think you were on the same side. The minute we find Andreas, things are going to get messy."

"Didn't you see what happened with Nadia back there?" she felt compelled to remind him. "Things are already messy."

"They're only going to get worse," he said, darkly. "Ransom might be indulging his protective side right now, but when all that Shade finally eats through the last of his humanity, that will change. The black stuff already has its claws in him, Sera. You can't count on his feelings for you. Not above loyalty to his Order. His king." His brows knitted, his voice softening when he added, "With everything that happened with your father, you know that better than anyone."

Slumping back in her seat, she gave no argument. Her thoughts turned to what the king had promised Ransom, and the secret deal they had struck in the shadows. Was it worth more or less than her life to him? And how long would it take before his predilection for Shade chewed that up too?

The carriage in front screeched to a sudden halt. Outside, voices rose to an angry pitch. Sera stuck her head out of the window to find Ransom marching Caruso back up the driveway, looking furious.

He yelled over his shoulder, "He stole the damn cat! I'm making him take it back."

Despite their souring mood, Theo barked a laugh. "You should have been a Cloak, Caruso!"

Caruso stuck his middle finger up. "Too talented for common thievery, Versini."

Belatedly, Sera noticed the black cat tucked snugly under his left arm. "Didn't take him for an animal person."

They had barely resumed their journey when the carriage screeched to a halt again. More commotion outside, as a coachman shouted, "Madwoman on the road!"

Theo set down the journal he had been scribbling in. "What *now*?"

Sera hopped out of the carriage just as Caruso was confronting their obstacle. The three soldiers had disembarked too, and were edging closer with their hands on their swords. Caruso was so tall and broad, Sera couldn't see around him, but when a familiar shriek rang out, she stumbled in shock.

"I'm NOT moving off this road until I see my friends!" At once, Sera recognized the human hurricane that was Val, her furious anger like music to her ears. "I swear to Saint Calvin, if you have laid a *finger* on any one of them, I will gut you where you stand, ice man."

Caruso cocked his head. "*Ice* man?"

Sera pushed through the soldiers and rounded Caruso to see Val brandishing a rusty corkscrew at the menacing Dagger. Saints help her, Caruso was going to chew her up and spit her out. Not that Val seemed remotely afraid. "Icy eyes to match your icy heart, fucker. I know you're a Dagger, so you'd better move the hell out of— ALL HELL, SERA! YOU'RE ALIVE!"

Sera darted forward, sweeping her friend into a hug. Pressing her face into Val's shoulder, she inhaled a lungful of jasmine perfume, telling herself that Val was real. She was here. She was *safe*.

"I'm so glad you're all right," she said, pulling back to look her over. Her dark curls fell wildly about her face, which was paler than usual. Her trousers and sweater were dusty from her travels, and she was carrying a satchel on her back. Apart from looking tired and travel-worn—and vaguely furious—she was in good condition.

"I knew you'd make it back to us," said Theo, hurrying to join them. "You're too scrappy to go down without a fight. You never even got picked up, did you?"

Val shook her head, looking vaguely guilty. "I got my cloak on just in time. I ran for the shadows when the nightguards came, then returned to House Armand. I didn't know what else to do, so I hid in a bush until Fontaine came poking around with her walking stick and found me."

Figures. "I bet she's the one who turned us in in the first place," said Sera.

"It was Mercure." Val's expression soured. "At the king's request, apparently. He's been after the Flames ever since our first shipment of Lightfire dropped." She looked between them, then over their shoulders to where the Daggers and soldiers had gathered. "And where's Bibi?"

"We'll fill you in," said Sera grimly.

Ransom approached their huddle. "How did you manage to track us down?"

"The morning after the soldiers came, I took a wagon out of the city. I was going to travel to the Summer Palace, but Fontaine said it was a hangman's mission. Said she had a hunch you'd end up here sooner or later. So I took the risk."

Sera squeezed her hand. "I'm really glad you did."

Now she had one less person to worry about, and another ally at her side, for whatever lay ahead.

Val summoned a shaky smile. "Better than going back to Paola and telling her I'd bolted like a coward that night and lost all my friends."

Theo was still struggling to understand it. "Why would Fontaine help you after Mercure sold us down the river?"

Val shrugged. "She's always liked me best. We have a hate-hate relationship. That's her love language." She swiped a hand through her unruly curls, only unsettling them further. "And I think she felt bad about the way it all went down. Not sure she saw those beatings in her precious tarot cards."

"So let me get this straight," said Ransom, who was still hovering—entirely unwelcome—on the edge of their conversation. "You came here based on nothing but a mercurial, potentially insane soothsayer's guess to try and rescue your friends from an errand you still know nothing about?"

Caruso butted in, "With that shitty corkscrew in your tiny ineffectual fist?" I was four seconds away from flinging you into that tree over there."

Val pointed the corkscrew at him. "And I was *three* seconds away from shoving this into your jugular, Dagger. Watch me use that Adam's apple like a bull's-eye."

Caruso blinked in utter astonishment.

Ransom muttered, "Hell's teeth."

Val resettled her attention on Sera. "What exactly is going on? The cryptic old crone never mentioned this villainous lot." She craned her neck. "Don't tell me Bibi's napping through our reunion."

"Bibi's not here," said Sera, with a swift rush of guilt.

"What do you mean 'not here'?"

"As in, your friend is currently *rotting in the king's dungeon*," Caruso supplied.

This time, Val didn't even look his way. "Seriously, who *is* that? Can I punch him?"

"I wouldn't recommend it," said Theo. "He's thoroughly unhinged."

"Start explaining," she said, folding her arms. "Why were you at the Appoline with our literal mortal enemies? And how come you haven't killed each other yet?"

"We'll get around to it," said Nadia, breaking her stony silence.

Sera tugged Val by the sleeve. "Come on. I'll tell you everything on the road."

Val bared her teeth at Caruso as she passed him. He raised his brows, betraying what Sera thought might actually be a dim simmering of respect. "I feel better about giving the cat back now," he remarked to no one in particular. "This vicious little creature is going to be a *lot* more fun."

"I'm going to punch him," said Val loudly, following Sera into the carriage.

Chapter 18

Seraphine

As they rode north toward Marvale, Sera and Theo filled Val in on everything that had happened since the night they parted outside House Armand. She listened in horrified silence, barely biting back her anger when they explained what had happened to poor Bibi.

Once they had finished, she leaned back in her seat. "It sounds pretty simple to me, then. We kill a couple of marks. We get our friend back. We go home."

"Prince Andreas is a saint," Theo reminded her.

"So what?"

"So it might not be in our best interests to kill him. He could prove helpful to Sera."

"But he's a mark. He's the key to Bibi's freedom."

"Maybe he can help her, too," said Sera.

Val's lips twisted. "That's a big maybe."

The weight of that maybe sat heavily on Sera's shoulders, but one thing she was sure of was there was more than one way to storm a dungeon, and she didn't trust the King of Valterre any further than she could toss him.

Taking out Fontaine's tarot cards, Sera studied them in the waning light. Idly, she traced her finger along their edges, like they might tell her a secret if she waited long enough. Val yawned, laying her head on her shoulder.

"Do you two smell smoke?" Across the bench, Theo pulled the window curtain back. The sky was a haze of pink and orange, but the clouds in the distance were darker than usual. "I think something's burning."

Sera stuck her head out of the window. Though she could detect a faint whiff of smoke on the wind and see the graying sky well enough, she was distracted by the trill of jaunty music and the high-pitched squall of children's laughter. She drew the rest of the curtain back, revealing a big wooden wheel.

"There's a carnival up ahead," said Val, pointing to where food stalls were dotted around the fairground. There were games of skill and chance, a carousel filled with white horses, and what appeared to be a small petting zoo, full of harried-looking animals and overexcited children.

Sera's stomach grumbled. "I smell doughnuts."

"I smell pony shit," said Val.

"What about the smoke?" said Theo, still frowning. "It looks like it's spreading."

"It's coming from beyond the carnival," said Sera, returning her gaze to the sky. "Let's pull over. I have an idea."

A short while later, they disembarked their carriage. The others arrived in various states of confusion, the coachmen seizing the opportunity to slip away for another cigarillo.

Ransom sauntered over. "Looking to ride the ponies or just delaying the inevitable? We're kind of on the clock here."

"Calm down," said Sera, breezily. "We won't be long."

"Why don't you go shove a little icing sugar in your face?" Val suggested. "It might help you lighten up."

"Thanks for the advice. I think I'll stick to my actual job."

Val tapped her chin, looking around. "I doubt you'll find any princes to kill here, but best of luck."

They took off as a trio, making their way into the heart of the carnival where boisterous music filled the air, and giddy children with sticky hands chased each other around the pens. Sera didn't have to turn around to know that the Daggers were following. The soldiers too. For all their grimacing, they must be hungry. And the smell of spiced sausage and fried potatoes was hard to ignore.

"I'm getting a doughnut," said Val. "And I might see about petting those donkeys over there too. Come and find me after."

She waved them off toward the turning wheel. Sera had only been on one once before, when she was six years old and a traveling carnival had set up in a field not far from her house in the plains. She had spent the entire day at the fair with Mama, stuffing her face with doughnuts and whipped ice cream, riding the carousel round and round until she was too dizzy to stand. After, they found a stall offering teddy bears as prizes. She spent a fruitless hour fishing for rubber ducks, until Mama had emptied her coin purse and bought a bear straight off the rack, pressing it into her arms like treasure.

Her heart gave a pang as they approached the wooden wheel. This one was so much larger than the ride in her memories. At least as tall as Our Sacred Saints' Cathedral, it would allow them to see far and wide across the northern plains of the kingdom and find out where all that smoke was coming from.

They paid a copper and hopped into a gondola, the wooden seat creaking as it slowly lifted into the air. Sera clutched the sides, reminding herself to breathe.

Theo glanced sidelong at her. "Didn't I *just* watch you scale the Aurore? I thought you weren't afraid of heights."

"There's heights, and then there's *floating in the air on a flimsy creaking bench*," she said, between labored huffs. "Turns out, there's a difference."

"Just don't look down."

Too late. Like a magnet, her gaze was drawn to Ransom. Leaning against a gaming stall with his arms folded, he was looking up at her with an utterly bewildered expression on his face. To him, it must have looked like an impromptu lovers' outing, Theo and Sera stealing a moment together to overlook the tapestry of their kingdom.

She waggled her fingers at him.

He pointed at Theo, then dragged his forefinger across his neck.

Clucking his tongue, Theo muttered, "So childish."

The wind picked up, the bench groaning as it swayed. Beneath them, the land unfurled in a patchwork of bucolic farmland, neat thatch villages and bustling gray-walled towns. The slow-sinking sun bled across the faraway treetops, painting the lakes and rivers gold. But it was marred—all of it—by the smoke. The higher they climbed, the thicker it became. Soon, Sera's eyes began to prickle.

"All hell," said Theo, under his breath. "That's a lot of fires."

The smoke was coming from all over the northwest, the fires—too many to count—scattered across towns and villages. Some blazed through the surrounding forest too, while others were as high and bright as beacons, lapping greedily at the sky.

Smoke made a choking canopy of clouds that floated southward on the wind. Toward them.

Sera's heart sank. "Is this what I think it is?"

"Rebellion is catching in the north," said Theo uneasily.

More effigies, more burning messages to the king. The northwest was turning its back on the House of Rayere. And there, beyond those menacing pockets of flames, jutting up along the horizon were the famed red mills of Marvale. The birthplace of Saint Oriel.

And if Provost Ambrose spoke truly, the place they would find the People's Saint.

Andreas.

It was surely no coincidence.

"Looks like the prince's message is spreading," said Theo, in a low voice. "The king is losing his footing outside Fantome too. Andreas has a stronghold in the north."

The turning wheel dipped, slowly returning them to the fairground. And yet, those fires burned behind Sera's eyes, the smoke clinging to her nostrils. She shifted in her seat, growing restless. The kingdom was already changing, and she couldn't shake the feeling that she was late to the party.

Curiosity was tugging her toward those red mills and the saint who was waiting for her there. But the impulse vanished at the sudden sound of screaming. Terror gripped the carnival, sending Theo and Sera leaping from their gondola and into the scattering crowd. The root of the commotion was over by the gaming stalls. As they fought their way through the fleeing carnival-goers, Val crashed into them.

Grabbing Sera by the shoulders, she yelled, "He's a madman! He hanged the guy with his own shadow!"

Alarm guttered through Sera. "What guy? Who did?" But the crowd was parting now. The worker manning the bull's-eye game was lying face up on the grass. Dead. The whites of his eyes were as black as coal. Kasper, the youngest of the three remaining soldiers, was curled up in a ball beside him clutching his head in his hands. Alive but whimpering.

Ransom was standing ten feet away, with his arms folded. His jaw was so tight it looked like he was chewing glass.

Sera stalked right up to him. "What the hell happened?"

He turned to look at her. "I see you're back from your date," he said, coolly. "Did your little carnival excursion amount to everything you hoped it would?"

She shoved him in the chest. "Did you do this to get my attention?" When he didn't answer, she shoved him again. "What is *wrong* with you?"

He caught her hands, trapping them under his own. "Check

your ego, spitfire. Do you really think me so unhinged?"

Belatedly, she realized his eyes were their usual shade of hazel. He hadn't taken any Shade. Which meant he hadn't killed the man. A quick glance over her shoulder revealed a stressed-looking Nadia and a silver-eyed Caruso ranting at Bram and Maelle.

"Oh."

"Yes. *Oh*," said Ransom, releasing her. He stepped back, folding his arms again. "Now that you've hopped off your pedestal, would you like to know what happened?"

"Not in that shit-eating superior tone of yours," she snapped. "Your Dagger just killed an innocent man. And by the looks of things, decked a soldier while he was at it! At least have the basic decency to look put out about it."

"Actually, Nadia decked the soldier."

"Like it matters."

Val and Theo were at her side now, providing silent backup. Not that she needed it. Her magic was a firestorm in her chest, ready to erupt. Tamping it down, she said through her teeth, "What *exactly* happened?"

"You and Versini decided to derail our journey for a jaunt on the turn-wheel," he said, with a flat smile. "Caruso decided he wanted to win a goldfish. He played six rounds before he realized the game was rigged . . . And I'm sure you can divine the rest."

"And where were you?" accused Theo.

"Shaking my fist at the sky in jealousy," he said, drolly. "I was getting food, since I'm starving." He returned his attention to

Sera. "Kasper tried to jump in and wrench Caruso away, nearly killing himself accidentally in the process. Nadia dragged him off and knocked him out for his own good. End of fairy tale."

Sera looked back at Kasper's crumpled form. Maelle and Bram were crouched beside him, trying to rouse him. The corpse remained where it had fallen, like a piece of discarded refuse.

Nausea gathered in the pit of her stomach. How many children had witnessed the horrifying kill?

"What now?" said Val, looking around helplessly.

"Now Caruso gets his goldfish and we continue on our way," said Ransom. "Unless Sera wants to have a little go on the carousel first."

Sera glared at him.

He glared right back.

"Let him handle it," said Val, tugging her away. "It's his mess."

"You go on," said Sera, squeezing her hand. "I'll be right behind you."

As Val and Theo returned to the carriage, Sera hung back, watching Ransom approach the king's soldiers. He bent down to check on Kasper, tapping the boy's cheek. He told Maelle to wait with him until he came to, then return with him to the barracks. Sera could tell by Maelle's expression of relief that she was eager to put some distance between herself and Caruso.

Sera didn't blame her. That Dagger walked around like a lit fuse.

Ransom wandered over to Nadia and Caruso then, the

conversation too low for her to overhear. Setting her rage aside, Sera approached the dead body. She stared down at the stranger's Shade-mottled skin, those black eyes like twin coals in his haggard face, and couldn't help but think of poor Mama, who had met the same fate.

The dead man had a wiry frame and unkempt brown hair. Sera wondered if he had family working here at the fairground, if his children had seen him hang from Caruso's makeshift noose, had counted those ten endless seconds before his heartbeats ran out. The fairground was empty now, the other workers long since fled. A part of her wanted to flee too. From this place, this task, this looming cloud of destiny.

A terrible shiver tore through her as she clambered into the stall, searching for something to cover him with. In the end, she had to rip down the awning and spread it over his body. She went to the edge of the grass and knelt there, picking a small bouquet of wildflowers. She returned and laid it on his chest, feeling guilty at how paltry it looked.

Roused by the nearness of his Shade-ravaged body, her magic flickered to life. That door inside her opened again. Only a crack now.

Maker, it called, like it was trying to comfort her.

She grabbed a dandelion and held it in her fist.

"Make something of this," she whispered. "Please."

Her palm sparked. The weed changed from a flat yellow dandelion to a golden rose. A gift of magic, come too late to save him. She laid the rose on his chest. It was a promise. Some day Lightfire would flood every town in Valterre, and no one in this beautiful ancient kingdom would have to fear the dark reaches of Shade again.

"What are you doing?"

Sera turned around to find Ransom watching her. His eyes were hooded, his hands dug into his pockets. The other Daggers must have returned to the carriage.

She said, "Cleaning up your mess."

He arched a brow. "It's a little late for that, don't you think?"

"Oh, piss off, Ransom." She shoved past him.

He followed her. "Hey, wait."

She ignored him.

He grabbed her hand.

She spun around, jabbing him hard in the chest. "An innocent man just died for *no reason*. I'm not about to stand here and let you make fun of me for showing his dead body a basic shred of respect. It might mean nothing to you, but it means something to me. And it sure as hell will mean something to his people when they come to collect his body."

He stared at her for a long moment, a muscle working in his jaw. Then quietly, he said, "All right."

"All right?" She prodded him again. "Is that all you have to say?"

"What do you want me to say, Seraphine?"

"That you're going to punish Caruso. That what he did was unforgivable. That it *bothers* you." Standing back from the heat of his body, she scraped her hands through her hair. "*Saints*, Ransom. Why the hell doesn't it bother you?"

"What makes you think it doesn't?" he said, evenly.

"Everything I know about you."

He jerked like she had hit him.

She turned around again, ignoring the furious thudding in her chest. A part of her wanted to cry. She didn't know if it was the sudden nearness of her own grief or the reminder that the man she liked beyond reason was a cruel and deadly killer—that he might always be just that.

"Hey." He jogged to keep up. "Talk to me." His voice was soft now, his expression imploring.

She stopped beside the deserted doughnut stall, where the grass was powdered with sugar, and the rest of the carnival felt miles away. Her throat bobbed, her tears threatening to spill over. She rubbed her chest, trying to soothe the ache there.

Her magic flared again, that door inside her widening.

Maker, it whispered. She felt it reaching out. Not for her. For him.

She shoved it back. *No.*

Ransom was looking at her again, his dark brows knitting. "Tell me what's wrong."

Huffing, she thew her hands up. Where to begin? How to explain that she felt like a player in a game she didn't understand. Like every move she was making was the wrong one. That she was hurting the people around her, drawn to a man who would always be wed to the darkness. A man who might one day turn into the monster her father had become. A man who had sworn to murder the only two people in Valterre—the only two saints—who had any shred of an inkling about what she was going through. About what lay on the other side of all this confusion.

"I hate this," she said. "All this death and fear and *terror*. I feel like I can't relax. Like I'll never get away from it."

He canted his head. "Do you feel afraid, Seraphine?"

It was worse than that. "I feel *hopeless*."

He moved closer, crowding out the rest of the fairground until it was just the two of them, and the honeyed softness of his eyes. "Let me help."

Her laugh was a bitter thing. "How can you help when you're part of the problem?"

This, of everything she had hurled at him, seemed to wound him the most. Looking away, he scrubbed a hand across his jaw. "I don't want to be part of the problem. But if you don't tell me what's going on with you, then how can I solve it?" He was so close now, close enough that she could feel the warmth rolling off his body, smell the peppermint on his breath.

She swayed, wondering what he would do if she confided in him about her magic, about her deep, tunneling fear of the beast that slumbered inside her. If she asked him, here and now, to spare Prince Andreas. To spare the acolyte on the Isle of Alisa. To give up the lure of Shade and hang his loyalty to the Crown. To his friends. Let the saints of Valterre live. Let the new age dawn, so that she might find her place in it.

It was madness to even consider it. And yet . . . she wavered.

He was still standing there, his hands flexing like he wanted to reach for her. "If you just let me *in* . . ."

Without meaning to, she laid her hand against his chest,

not to prod this time. Or to shove. Just to feel the thrum of his heart beneath her fingers, to remind herself that he was human. Still Bastian. The Shade had not yet erased him. "I don't know how," she whispered.

He took her hand in his, her magic leaping at his touch. Lifting her hand to his mouth, he brushed his lips against it. "Yes, you do," he said, pressing a kiss to her knuckles. To the hand that had killed Lark, had maimed Ribauld. His touch was soft, so very gentle, like he was trying to show her what he was capable of. "You're just afraid to try."

And that was the truth, simple and stark.

Sera wanted to trust him, but she was afraid of the leap. Afraid of the fall. By the time she was ready to respond, he had already turned from her, his strides lengthening as he made his way back to the carriage.

Chapter 19

Ransom

As they continued north, Ransom replayed his conversation at the fairground with Seraphine. How lost she had looked as she gazed up at him, her voice little more than a broken whisper.

I feel hopeless.

Those words were like a knife in his chest. At the carnival, he had taken one look at that black-eyed corpse and felt almost nothing. Sera had looked upon the dead man and thought to cover him with a blanket. Laid a flower on his chest. A spark of magic used to comfort, not to kill.

Because she is a saint.

And you are a monster.

Of course Ransom had chewed Caruso out at the carnival, twisted his hands in his collar and threatened to send him back to Fantome before Nadia had intervened. They had come this far already. In another day or so, they'd be at Marvale with the first of their marks finally in sight.

Soon, it would be over.

It would all be over.

Caruso had had the good sense to feign a *modicum* of remorse over his impulsivity, but guilt was a foreign concept to him. To down a jar of Shade in a carnival full of children was one thing, but to then hang a man with his own shadow in plain sight of them was a whole other level of unhinged.

Seraphine had been right to lose her temper at Ransom. It had taken every strand of his composure to keep from losing it himself. He was the Head of the Order of Daggers and he had no control over the violent whims of this Third. How could Seraphine trust him to rule himself, when Ransom couldn't even keep Caruso in line? No wonder she couldn't bring herself to confide in him.

He was so lost to his own frustration, Nadia had to kick his shin to get his attention. "Look!" she said, drawing back the curtain.

They were coming upon Ornaux, a farming village halfway between the Appoline and Marvale. Streetlamps flickered up ahead, marking the bridge that led into the quaint stone village. Along the walls, the royal banners had all been ripped down, and the smell of smoke sat heavy on the wind.

The People's Saint was close at hand.

The lazy river burbled, beckoning them onward, but Nadia was pointing toward a modest graveyard on the outskirts of the town.

Ransom had to stick his face out of the window to be sure of what he was seeing. Under the sparse oil lamps, several graves appeared to have been disturbed. Mounds of dirt mottled the gray headstones and manicured grass, while flowers had been strewn over the wall.

"Maybe they're new graves," he said, ignoring the twist in his gut. "Dug, but not yet filled."

"I can count eleven," said Nadia. "Unless Ornaux just had a plague we haven't heard about, I find that hard to believe."

"The people here are in revolt. They might be dead rebels."

"The king's soldiers don't bury dead rebels. And look, there." Caruso pointed out a pair of nightguards lingering by one of the graves. Ransom spied another pair walking through the graveyard, their hands fastened to the pommels of their swords, like they were waiting to strike.

A disturbance in the cemetery.

Or rather, several.

A familiar sense of unease festered.

"Let's continue into town," said Ransom, not wanting to stop again so soon. Or draw unnecessary suspicion upon themselves. "We can look into it from there."

Nadia slumped in her seat, equally disquieted. Twirling a black strand around her finger, her dark eyes turned vacant. Troubled. Despite the evening breeze whispering through the windows, the air inside the carriage grew close. Heavy.

She was thinking of Lark. They were all thinking of Lark. Of that open grave back in Old Haven, and how sickeningly familiar this moment felt.

...

Ransom was sitting so rigidly by the time the carriage came to a stop, the muscles in his back throbbed. Their destination, the Bellflower Inn, was a welcome sight: a tall well-tended building strung with purple flowers and crowned with gleaming white gables, with enough stables for their horses. Oil lamps flickered in the windows, and gentle string music wafted out from within.

After securing their rooms and depositing their satchels, Ransom washed and changed his clothes before joining Nadia and Caruso in the eatery downstairs. Val and Seraphine were there too, sitting in the back corner of the restaurant. As far away from them as possible.

No sign of Versini.

Ransom joined his friends at their table. They were too busy inhaling their food to make conversation. Nadia gave him a look that said, *Eat first, catastrophize later.* Talk of the graveyard would have to wait, thanks to a combination of the cook's fragrant lamb stew and the bottle of aged whiskey Caruso had commandeered from the bar for saints knew how much.

As he ate, Ransom kept one eye on Seraphine's table. Versini returned before long, his face unusually grave. Immediately setting down their forks, Val and Seraphine leaned across the little round table, all three of them whispering furiously, like a coven of witches.

Ransom was still watching them when Seraphine looked up sharply, catching his eye.

He raised his brows. *Everything OK?*

She stood and made her way toward their table. The others followed.

Reluctantly setting their whiskey glasses down, the Daggers looked up in bewilderment.

Seraphine said, "Did you see the graveyard on our way in?"

Ransom nodded. "It was somewhat hard to miss."

"Theo's been speaking to the inn-keeper. It seems Ornaux has its own grave robber." She turned on Nadia, her stare turning hard, as if to say, *And it's not me.*

Nadia arched a brow. "Is that why you've come stomping over here? To plead your innocence?"

"Ornaux is one of several graveyards in the area that have been recently disturbed," Versini supplied before Seraphine could fling the retort that was no doubt dancing on the tip of her tongue. "Someone has been taking corpses from their graves and moving them about in the night."

Grimacing, Nadia reached for her whiskey, gulping it down.

"To what end?" said Ransom, struggling to keep his own revulsion in check.

Versini shrugged. "Innkeeper says it's a mystery."

"More like a horror," muttered Val. "It sounds like the bodies get up to take a walk, then collapse again somewhere nearby."

"Could be local rebels," mused Caruso. "We've seen the same thing happen in Fantome."

Albeit a more personal grave robbing. It was certainly an effective way to sow terror.

The Flames exchanged a loaded glance.

"We shouldn't stay here any longer than we have to," said Versini, looking between them. "We intend to leave at first light."

"Fine by me," said Ransom.

The others gave no argument.

Ornaux gave them all the creeps.

Something in common, at last.

Perhaps it was that which made Ransom push back his chair, making room at the table. "It's been a long day. Do you want to join us for a drink?"

The Shadowsmith canted his head. "That depends. Are you buying?"

"If you promise not to annoy me."

Smirking, Versini pulled up a chair, making a point of seating himself between Ransom and Seraphine. So much for their deal. Caruso went to get more glasses from the bar, filling them with whiskey. Soon, their more serious talk of uprisings and renegade saints turned to lighter stories from House Armand and Hugo's Passage, the former Cloaks and current Daggers swapping tales, almost as if they were old friends and not age-old nemeses. Then followed the card games and wagers that called for more drinking until most of them were too bleary-eyed to remember their enmity at all, and far too tired to care.

The other diners cleared out, the coachmen trudging upstairs to their rooms until it was just the Flames and the Daggers, and Bram, the remaining soldier, necking spirits at the bar while he watched them. Given there was no love lost between Bram and the others, he had the good sense to keep to himself.

Halfway through a rousing game of saint or sinner when everyone but Nadia and Val had surrendered all their coin to the pot, Seraphine stood up, announcing she was too exhausted to lose any more games.

She slipped around the table, squeezing Ransom's hand as she passed. And there it was again—that insistent tug in his chest that made him want to trail after her. It wasn't until she'd disappeared upstairs that he noticed the small wedge of paper in his palm.

He was on his feet before he even opened it.

"Tapping out already?" Caruso clucked his tongue. "We were just about to go double or quits. Versini's a damn shark. And that kitten has claws."

"Say that shit again and I'll take your eye out with one," snapped Val, slamming another copper down.

"Dealer's spread," said Nadia, shuffling the playing cards. "No peeking this time, Caruso."

"Try not to kill each other," said Ransom, stepping away from the table. "I'll see you in the morning."

In the stairwell, he read Seraphine's note.

Ransom,

Come and find me on the roof...

I want to try.

Chapter 20

Ransom

It was almost embarrassing how easily Seraphine Marchant could command him. How fast his feet moved, up one narrow stairwell after another. On the third floor, a warm breeze slipped through the narrow door at the end of the hall. He followed it up a set of rickety steps, where another door gave way to a small roof garden. A modest stone courtyard, cloistered by those white sloping gables.

Troughs of lavender and leafy potted plants made a border around the square and in the middle a large paisley rug lay across the stones. Seraphine was lying on it, her long blond hair fanning around her like a halo. Her eyes were closed, her arms tucked behind her head.

Ransom's heart stuttered.

Without opening her eyes, she said, "I can *feel* you staring at me."

"You look like a painting."

A beauty in repose, bathing in the moonlight.

What he really meant was, *You look like a goddess.*

"So paint me, Dagger." A teasing smile tugged at her lips. He wanted to get on his knees and taste it.

Someday.

In another life, when he had all the time and colors in the world. Where this darkness was behind them, and they were free. He didn't know how to say it, how to promise such a lofty dream. He had done it once before, and she hadn't forgiven him for it.

"Did you like my note?" she said, cracking an eye open.

"You mean your white flag?" he said, drifting toward her.

"Call it what you like."

"What made you write it?"

She hummed, sitting up. In the dark, her eyes were wide and star-flecked. The moon was full and bright above them, so much closer than usual, as though some divine being was looking down at them. "I was thinking after the fairground . . . Maybe you were right about trust. Maybe that's the only way we'll both survive what comes next."

She removed a small stack of cards from her back pocket. Like a dealer in a gambling hell, she set down three in a row.

Ransom slowly lowered himself to the ground, bringing his knees into his chest. "The tarot," he said. "Where did you get those?"

"At House Armand, the night we were ambushed. I went to see Madame Fontaine about the magic inside me. About what it meant." She swallowed thickly. "We spoke of the Second Coming of the saints. These are the cards she drew."

Ransom's brows shot up as he examined each one.

The Silver-tongue.

The Stone Maiden.

The Necromancer.

His gaze snagged on the third tarot, a sharp twist in his gut making him frown. The Necromancer. A puppetmaster of the dead. Some bastardized reincarnation of Calvin, Saint of Death. He thought again of the graveyard on the way in, the hairs on the back of his neck rising.

"Who is this meant to be?" he said, fingering the card.

"I don't know," she admitted. "But I believe whoever stole Lark's body back in Old Haven might be here. Somewhere in the northwest."

Ransom tensed, the muscles in his back straining. "The prince?"

"Perhaps. Perhaps not." She traced the Silver-tongue with her finger. It was a better fit for the prince, according to the rumors in the capital, and the king's own words. "We won't know until we meet him."

"You mean kill him."

She lifted her gaze from the cards. Doubt glistened there. He could see it now, as plain as the moon looking over them. She did not intend to kill the prince at all. And she was ready for him to know it. It wasn't like he had expected her to do it with her own hands; he didn't need her to. But it had never occurred to him that she might try and stop him.

"Seraphine . . ."

"There's one more card," she said hastily, laying down a fourth.

A red rose, gilded at the edges.

Ransom stared at it with mounting confusion.

"Saint Oriel's flower. It's the oldest and truest emblem of Valterre, from a time before this land was conquered by kings and queens, torn apart by war and unrest, rebuilt and flooded with greed and avarice. When the Rayeres came to power, they crossed two swords in front of the rose and made it their crest. A mixing of nature and man, of beauty and force." She traced the petals, like she could feel them. "Madame Fontaine says the rose means a new beginning. A sign that things are changing." A beat of hesitation, then, her words softened like she was telling him a secret. "That perhaps things are *meant* to change."

"How so?" said Ransom, though he sensed where this was going.

"A thousand years ago, Oriel wrote of the Second Coming of the saints. A new era of light for our kingdom, after centuries of man-made dark. Bad magic. Destructive power." She was gazing at his hands now, silently tracing the menacing black whorls there. "If we kill Andreas and the acolyte on the Isle of Alisa, we'll be moving against destiny itself."

Ransom inhaled. "Seraphine—"

"Wait," she pleaded. "Let me say this. I have to." She swallowed hard, and he saw now that her hands were trembling. "I think it was destiny—Saint Oriel herself—who brought us together all those months ago, Ransom." Her eyes were so large now, so soft and full of moonlight. It was like he could see all the way into her soul. He had asked her to let him in, and here she sat, offering him her innermost thoughts with a vulnerability that stilled his tongue. She really believed their coming together was the work of divine intervention, and the truth of it was, a part of him did too. There was nothing ordinary about their connection, or the tug he felt inside himself whenever she was near.

Finally, she understood. They were not meant to be enemies, to constantly push and pull like restless animals. They were destined to find common ground, to survive this quest together. He was beginning to smile, to feel the welcome flutter of relief when she said, "I don't think Oriel wanted us to kill her saints, Ransom. I think she wanted us to save them."

He frowned, surprise rendering him momentarily speechless.

She turned her hands over, absently tracing the lines on her palm. "I don't know where I fit in Fontaine's tarot spread or what this strange magic inside me is yet, but I know I can't use it to harm another saint." A pause then, a sudden fierceness hardening her voice. "Ransom, I *won't*."

He stifled a groan. "It's too late, Seraphine."

"How can it be? We haven't done anything."

It hardly mattered. "The king is testing you. Testing both of us." It was not up to them. It never had been.

She shrugged his words off. "I would rather betray a man like Bertrand Rayere than spit in the face of fate itself. It's not like we'd be the only ones denying him. Soon, the entire kingdom will be in revolt."

Ransom struggled to find that common ground that had seemed so close only a moment ago, but he couldn't fathom the scale of the risk, or why she would want to take it. "You wish to ally yourself with a violent, untried insurgent, who scatters rebels across the kingdom like marbles while remaining safe and cosseted in Marvale?" he said, shaking his head. "An acolyte who murdered her own sister? A *necromancer* who pulls dead bodies from the ground and plays with them like dolls?"

He might have laughed if she didn't look so damn serious. "You have no idea what these people are capable of, Seraphine. Just because they're like you doesn't mean they're the same as you." She was scowling now, the moonlight in her eyes like shards of steel. "You heard what the provost said back at the Appoline. Even he doesn't trust the prince. A man he has known for *years*."

"What if Andreas *is* good, Ransom?" she said, refusing to back down. "What if the kingdom is supposed to change, and he's the catalyst?"

"What if he's not good?" Ransom shot back. "What if he's poisoned by the same ambition as his uncle? Do you want a power-mad emperor instead of a mortal king?"

She threw her hands up. "And what about me? Am I not as bad? I've had months to figure out this magic inside me and I still can't control it. All I've done is hurt people with it." She closed her eyes, shame casting a blush in her cheeks. "Maybe I'm a mistake."

Ransom bristled. "You are not a mistake."

"You don't understand."

"I understand well enough. You're wagering on a better world emerging from a ruthless rebellion and you're gambling with your own life. If you stand with Andreas, you tie your fate to him."

"Look at me," she hissed, those eyes flickering from blue to gold. "I'm already tied to his fate."

"No. *No.* You can't pledge yourself to a man you've never met." He couldn't help his rising voice, his horror at the things he was hearing. "It's madness, Seraphine. And what about Bibi? Do you want her to rot in the king's dungeon for ever? To hang from the royal noose?"

"Of course not," she said, her own voice rising. "We can lie to the king. Tell him the marks are dead. That should buy us enough time to—"

Ransom gave an incredulous laugh. "You can't be serious."

She broke off, glaring at him. "Why are you being so difficult?"

"Why are you so *reckless*?" he returned, just as angrily. "So you don't want to kill a saint. Fine. Sit in the carriage and let me do it. Then post up in a nearby tavern and play cards with Versini while I go to the Isle of Alisa. I don't need you to help me in this, Seraphine. I just need you to stay out of my way."

"I can't just stay out of your way," she shot back. "Everything that's happening right now is a turning point, Ransom. Can't you feel the threads of destiny at work? The kingdom is stretching, changing."

"What does that matter?"

"I think it matters more than anything," she said, an edge

of desperation to her voice. She reached for his hands, pulling them into her lap. His shadow-marks were so dark against the perfect sheen of her skin. He hated them for it. Hated himself. "Ransom, if you kill a saint, I don't think you can come back from it." She brushed the whorl along his thumb, tracing it to the underside of his wrist. "It's bound to change you irrevocably. Shred through you worse than all of these already do."

He dropped his head, lost to her feather-light touch. "It's already too late for me, Seraphine. I can't come back from the wicked things I've done. Let me finish this."

"I don't believe that," she said, threading her fingers through his, squeezing, as though to press her hope into his skin. "Isn't there a part of you that wants to try? What if all of this is some kind of test? A chance to do the right thing and remake your destiny one last time?"

His smile was rueful. "You always were good at fairy tales."

She gently laid his hands down, turning again to the cards. "If kingdoms can be remade, so can destinies." She traced the rose that sat between them. "You spend all this time trying to save me. Can't you see that I'm trying to do the same for you?"

But there was one crucial difference, and despite her pretty words and grand dreams, she must have known it; only one of them was worth saving.

Ransom let the silence settle, too tired to argue over the life of a rebellious prince, though he knew the matter was not yet at rest.

He stayed beside her, stretching his legs out as she gathered up her cards. Glimpses of saints that might yet change the face of the kingdom or drop at the mercy of his Shade. There was too much to think about, and all he wanted to do was talk of something else. Anything else. Take this moment of speech and stretch it out, allow them both a reprieve from the ever-swinging pendulum of death and destiny.

Even if it was fleeting. Even if it wasn't real.

He didn't know how long this would last, the whisper of freedom between them, the sense that the world had stopped turning, if only for a little while. It was a gift to be alone with her, and he didn't want to squander it by arguing.

She must have been having the same thought because she flopped backward, patting the rug beside her. "Lie down, Dagger," she said, with a sigh. "Let's marvel at the moon together. It might tell us what we're supposed to do."

He lay down next to her, one hand tucked behind his head, the other brushing the side of her hip. Absently he threaded his finger in her belt loop, like some part of him was afraid she might float away. He turned to look at her. Her eyes were wide, riveted. "Copper for your thoughts."

She nipped at her bottom lip. "I was just thinking of how tired I am of arguing with you."

"I suggest a truce." He tugged her closer by her belt loop, until their legs were touching, the rest of the courtyard falling away.

"All right. But only until the whiskey wears off."

"You barely even drank any whiskey."

"It tasted like lava." She wrinkled her nose. "I couldn't stomach it."

"But you can stomach this," he said quietly. *"Us."*

Why else would she still be fighting for his future?

"That's never been the problem," she admitted. "I just know that I'm afraid, Ransom. I'm afraid all the time." She turned back to the sky, her brows drawn. "I get these recurring nightmares," she said, in a faraway voice. "Sometimes, I find myself in other people's heads . . . Falling from that clock tower back at the Appoline or trapped and choking in the dirt . . . it makes me feel like I'm going mad."

He took her hand, folding it in his own. He knew little of saints and destiny, but nightmares were second nature to him. He had known them all his life. "If you're mad, then they haven't come up with a word to describe what I am."

She frowned. "What do you mean?"

"When I sleep, I see monsters. Predators with dripping fangs and razor claws, surrounding me in my bed. Snapping at my feet. Tearing at my skin." Lately, the nightmares had been constant. Some nights they were so bad, he refused to sleep at all, sitting red-eyed and exhausted in his bed, waiting for the sun to come up. "Sometimes, I see my father, red-faced and cursing, his cruel fists raised like weapons. I can even smell the spirits on his breath. In those dreams, I'm still a boy, hiding under my bed. And every time he finds me."

"Ransom," she said softly.

"I don't know which monster is worse," he confided. "The one that chased me into this life with his cruel fists. The ones that prowl like panthers in my head as I sleep. Or the one I know I'm becoming."

"You're not a monster." She squeezed his hand, her grip fierce. "Those nightmares are your fears. They're not who you are."

His smile was grim. "What if they're one and the same?"

"You're not a monster," she repeated. "You're just . . . *stuck*." There was a desperation in her voice, like she wanted so badly to unstick him. Like she didn't quite know how. He looked again at their hands, her pale slender fingers so small against the shadow-stained canvas of his own. Her grip as fierce as the look in her eyes. "You are better than this life, Ransom. You are meant for more than the Order of Daggers."

"Once, maybe." But did he deserve it now? Now, after everything he had done. He thought of all the vials he'd downed in his life, how weak he'd been as a child, how desperately he had fought to survive in the underworld. But the moment Dufort died, freedom was his to take. And he had turned his back on it, losing himself once more in Shade. Consuming more than he had ever had before. Enough to cover himself with scars and fill his dreams with monsters he could no longer outrun. He wondered if they would always be a part of him, these ravenous creatures that liked to gnaw at the ribbons of his soul.

"Still," she said. And then again, "You are *still* meant for more than this." She lifted his hand to her mouth, kissing the shadow-mark along his palm. A shudder worked through him, raising the hairs on the back of his neck. "When you are ready to be a rebel and not a Dagger, you will finally be free."

She said it like a spell. He had never wanted to believe in anything so badly.

They were closer now, their heads brushing, their hands intertwined. "Enough about nightmares," she said, turning back to the moon. "I want to talk about dreams."

"I think I'm in one right now."

"Perhaps *you* are the real Silver-tongue," she said, a smile in her voice. "Tell me something true, Ransom. Where would you go with your freedom?"

"Ferrera," he said, without hesitation. A small island about a day's crossing from the south harbor, Ferrera was renowned for its natural, rugged beauty. Over the centuries, it had been a home to some of the greatest artists on the continent, inspiring several of his favorite landscapes. Places he longed to see in the flesh.

"I'd like to visit the orange groves in the east, walk the winding white cliffs and smell the wildflowers on the coast. If the weather holds, I'd take a boat out to the sea caves and see what inspiration I might find there."

She *hmm*'d. "Just you and your paintbrush? How romantic."

And you.

In another life.

"I had a pin in Ferrera," she said, dreamily. "My bedroom used to be covered in maps of the world. I marked all the places I wanted to see before I died."

"Like where?" he said, propping his head on his hand and turning on his side to watch her eyes light up.

"Like everywhere," she said, her breath hitching. "I want to ride the wild horses of Urnica. Explore the bustling market streets of Paresi. Climb the highest Silvercrest and picnic with the hawks. Steal a bicycle in Liefdam and ride along the canals, wear a ballgown to the Festival of Lights in Borea and dance until my feet fall off. And that's just off the top of my head!"

Ransom grinned like a fool, imagining her twirling her way through the Festival of Lights, like a sunbeam come to life.

"Does this mean you're a good dancer?"

A gleeful shake of her head. "No, but that's half the fun of it. Right?"

"Even better when you're good at it," he teased. "And I would know. I am an incredible dancer."

She huffed a laugh. "Why do I find that hard to believe?"

"Because you *insist* on seeing the worst in me."

"No." She rose up, propping her head on her hand. "The real trouble is, I see the best in you. I see Bastian."

She whispered his true name like a prayer. He wanted her to say it again and again, to pull him back to that version of himself.

"You like that," she murmured. "I can see it in your eyes."

"It does something to my chest," he murmured. "Or maybe that's just you."

She drew nearer, magic sparking in her eyes.

And froze.

"It's all right," he said, gently tipping her chin. Her lips were so close, soft and plump and begging to be kissed.

She hesitated. "I don't want to hurt you."

"You won't."

"What makes you so sure?"

"Because you don't want to."

She shook her head. "It's not about what I want."

"That's the thing," he said, brushing his nose against hers. "I think it is. Deep down. I think that's the secret."

The air grew close, the heat of her body rolling against his. She swallowed thickly, wrestling with her desire. Even as it turned her eyes gold, made her cheeks pink. "This . . . feels dangerous."

He smiled against her cheek, pressing a kiss there. "You forget, spitfire. I like to burn."

He felt her lips curve, the soft breath of her words on his mouth. "Let's see if that holds true."

She pressed a trembling palm against his chest, pushing him down to the rug. Her hair fell around them like a curtain, the silver moon haloing her face as she traced his collarbone, lightly fingering the shadow-mark there.

Saints above.

He stifled a groan.

This was one way to burn. Slow and aching and begging for more.

She lowered her head, until her lips hovered an inch from his own.

Ransom's breath punched out of him, all traces of his composure gone in a blink. "Would you like to experiment on me, spitfire?"

She toyed with the first button of his shirt, deftly easing it open. "Would you be amenable?"

The word was ragged. *"Always."*

She nipped at her smile. He raised his thumb to trace it.

Saints help him, she licked the pad of his finger. Then moved south, her hair trailing along his chest as she opened another button. She pressed a kiss to his collarbone, lightly sucking the skin there.

He gasped as the shadow-mark tingled under her power. Dissolving with each brush of her lips, the darkness in him was no match for the power of her Lightfire. She was replacing his mark with a love bite, the realization alone making him harden. Another groan seeped through his teeth.

She stopped, looking up at him from beneath heavy lids. Her eyes were golden, her magic glowing faintly under her skin. So beautiful—and otherworldly—that for a moment, it was like staring into the sun. "Pain?" she whispered.

"Pleasure," he hissed. "Don't stop."

Smiling coyly, she lowered her head and licked the hollow of his collarbone, following another whorl. His skin prickled, the mark dissolving under her wet mouth. His back bowed, and he grabbed hold of her, sliding his hands into her hair.

"Let me kiss you," he said, breathless.

Or I'll die.

"But your marks."

"Forget the marks."

She clucked her tongue. "So impatient."

"Yes," he said, tugging her mouth to his.

The kiss was gasping, crushing. Five long months of forbidden dreams and reckless longing made them fall into each other with fevered abandon. He sat up, reaching for her as she climbed into his lap, hooking her legs around his waist. He slid his hands through her hair, tilting her head back to deepen the kiss. She rocked against him, his answering moans stifled in the heat of her mouth.

This was what he had been yearning for. A greater addiction than Shade. A pure, punishing perfection. Heart-thundering salvation. His spitfire in his arms, her soft gasps in his ear, her hands on his shadow-stained body, both of them holding on to each other so tightly, not even Saint Oriel herself could wrench them apart.

Maybe she could save him.

Maybe they could save each other.

Yes, he could so easily believe it now.

Yes, even just for a moment.

Yes, yes, yes.

Ransom was so lost in her that he didn't hear the distant screams at first.

Seraphine snapped her head up, those golden eyes flaring. "Did you hear that?"

He stilled, panting hard. Closing his eyes, he laid his forehead against hers, and listened.

Somewhere below them, Val was screaming.

Theo was shouting.

And Caruso was . . . laughing.

Fuck.

Downstairs, there was a dead body on the ground. Bram. Although the soldier didn't appear to have met his end via Shade,

Ransom could tell by his bulging eyes that he was fairly dead. Still, Nadia was kneeling beside him, checking his pulse.

"You've got to be kidding me," fumed Seraphine. "Not *again*."

Versini was pacing. "Let's keep our voices down."

The scene was bad enough already. They had been on the road for less than a week and had already managed to lose their entire royal accompaniment. Maybe Seraphine was right. Perhaps fate was moving them away from the king and his orders.

Val was by the bar, utterly stone-faced, with her arms wrapped tightly around herself. Seraphine crossed the room to go to her.

Caruso was standing over the dead body, like a proud wolf. Claiming it.

The ground floor of the inn was otherwise deserted. The Bellflower was full of heavy sleepers. Or drunk ones. Even the innkeeper had made himself scarce.

Ransom gave a long-suffering sigh, looking between his Daggers. "Explain."

Everyone looked to Caruso.

Caruso simply said, "I snapped his neck."

"Yes, I can see that." Ransom pinched the bridge of his nose. Three minutes ago, he had had Seraphine in his arms. Now they were standing with yet another corpse between them, Bram's bulging bloodshot eyes serving as an ever salient reminder that Ransom was a depraved Dagger with hundreds of kills notched on his own blackened soul.

And that was to say nothing of the bureaucratic headache this was going to cause.

"*Why* did you murder the king's prized soldier?" he clarified. "Do you not see how this is going to be a problem for us? We're supposed to be *allies of the Crown.* We've already sent one soldier back without a damn ear and concussed another—and now *this.*"

"This one is definitely the worst," said Versini completely unnecessarily. Either he was taking this unusually well, or he was steaming drunk. A quick glance at the empty bottle of whiskey on the table confirmed the latter.

Caruso remained unmoved. "He was being a prick. Now he's a dead prick."

Ransom glared at him.

"It's true." Val piped up. "Bram was a pig. When I went outside to get some fresh air, he followed me. *Cornered* me . . . I couldn't get free of him." She inched closer, her haunted gaze on the dead man's face. "When he pushed me to the ground, I screamed."

"And I killed him," said Caruso, looking pointedly at Val, like he was expecting her to say *thank you.*

She cut her eyes at him. "Ruthless motherfucker."

There was something in it that almost felt like a thank you.

Nadia rolled to her feet. "Well, he's definitely dead. The question is, what do we do with him?"

Time to salvage the situation. "Grab your things. Drink some water. Sober up," Ransom announced. "We're leaving. Now. We'll take a single carriage and continue north to Marvale." He felt Seraphine bristle, all too aware that they were still at odds about what would happen once they got there. There wasn't time to get into it here.

"We'll take turns sleeping on the road, find a new inn by morning." He turned on Caruso. "*You* can help me with the body."

"All right," said Versini, coming around. "That's a plan."

Brushing past him, Seraphine said, "Fine. Let's get going, then."

Ransom chewed on his frustration. A few moments ago, Seraphine was grinding in his lap. Now he was cleaning up a damn murder scene. Ordinarily, the best thing about being a Dagger was never *having* to clean up afterward. But a dead soldier spelled trouble for all of them. Not that Bram was worth mourning. On that, even the Flames agreed.

For two warring factions, they worked together with remarkable efficiency. Nadia and Versini went to fetch the carriage, while Seraphine and Val volunteered to gather everyone's things, leaving Caruso and Ransom to deal with the body.

Caruso flung it over his shoulder like a sack of grain.

"Wait!" said Val.

Caruso spun so fast, he swung Bram into an oil lamp. It shattered on the ground.

Val stepped over it, rushing up to the body. For a bewildering moment, Ransom thought she was double-checking his pulse to make sure he really was dead . . . Until she snapped his gold watch off and slipped it into her pocket.

"As you were, Daggers," she said, skipping after Seraphine.

They turned to watch her go.

"Little menace," muttered Caruso.

Chapter 21

Seraphine

Ransom was wavering. Not just about the king's quest but the changing of the kingdom and his own place within it. Sure, they had argued on the roof, but he had listened to her too. In sharing her truth—her *fears* about what they were about to do—Sera had rattled his resolve. Pricked a pin in that careful ruthless façade.

But as they absconded from the Bellflower in the middle of the night, leaving a dead soldier in their wake, she sensed the Dagger's will harden again. Time was running out, every mile bringing them one step closer to the People's Saint. Closer to the answers she had so desperately been seeking about herself, and the fear that Ransom might swipe them all away before she could get through to him.

On the way out of Ornaux, the carriage almost crashed three times. Not bad considering Caruso and Nadia, who had volunteered as temporary coachmen, were hopelessly drunk. And had no idea *how* to drive.

"At least the horses are sober," said Theo, digging his hands into the leather bench as they swerved their way into the wilds beyond. The town's flickering lights soon faded into the distance, leaving the silvery moon alone to guide them. In the darkness, all the trees looked like skeletons, creaking in the midnight breeze.

Val, who had stuck her face out of the window to vomit, shrieked when a branch slapped her in the forehead. "VEER LEFT, YOU FOOLS! WE'RE IN THE DAMN TREES!"

Ransom, who was holding on to the back of her shirt in case she tumbled out released her as she slumped back onto the bench beside him. Val was sitting opposite Theo, while Ransom was sitting directly across from Sera. Not for the first time that night, they locked eyes.

What she wouldn't give to be back on the roof of the Bellflower, where, for a moonlit moment, everything between them had been so perfectly, achingly simple. Nothing but dreams and desire. Even now, she felt the shadow of his broad callused hands sliding up her back, his hot mouth against her neck, his throaty words in her ear, promising more. Promising *everything*.

By the way his throat bobbed now, she imagined he was thinking about the same thing.

Take me back.

And leave me there.

"Let me see the welt." Theo leaned across the carriage, tilting Val's face toward him. "It's not too bad. It'll fade in a few days."

"Stupid tree," she mumbled.

"Tell Caruso about it next time we pull over," said Ransom. "Maybe he'll go back and murder the elm for you."

Theo shot him a blistering glare.

Smirking now, Ransom closed his eyes. "Relax, Versini. It was a joke."

"Someone died tonight," Val reminded him. "A terrible brute of a man. But . . . still."

"I'm sure Bram's gold watch will cheer you up."

"Oh, whatever."

Finally, a welcome stretch of silence.

Sera had almost nodded off when Theo piped up. "It was actually a birch tree."

"What?" chorused Val and Sera.

"It was a birch, not an elm," he said, stretching his legs out. "But how would a Tunnel Rat know that? I doubt they have trees in the flaming pits of hell."

Ransom's eyes flew open. "Well, you would know, Versini. Your ancestors are running it."

"*All saints,* would you two idiots shut up?" snapped Val. "If you insist on having a pissing contest, then get out and walk." No sooner had she said it than the carriage vaulted over a ditch, tossing them all head-first into the roof.

Theo slammed his fist against the ceiling. "Pull over before you kill us all!"

Caruso and Nadia ignored him, crowing with laughter as they urged the horses onward, into the darkening night. Sera gripped the bench, holding on for dear life. Defeated, Theo sat back, exhaling through his nose. "Silver lining. At least our concussions will lull us to sleep."

"*Not* funny," said Val.

But he was already out cold.

They neared Marvale as the sun was coming up. Thanks to the worries churning in her stomach, Sera was already wide awake. She was keen to finish her conversation with Ransom about the prince and the saints, but the Dagger was still fast asleep. Making a crack in the curtains, she pressed her face to the carriage window, inhaling a lungful of floral-scented air.

Marvale glimmered in the distance. In the early dawn light, a reddish hue lingered over the village. The buildings were made from the region's unique red sandstone. Red-brick chimneys dotted a landscape of neat, pointed roofs, piping smoke into the blushing sky. At the far end of village, perched along the distant hills, stood the famed red mills, a unique cluster of taverns and dance halls that hosted all manner of merriment from dusk until dawn and back to dusk again. As the stories went, so long as the windmills were turning, there was fun to be made and opportunity to be seized.

At a sharp gasp from behind her, Sera turned in her seat. Ransom jerked awake. He was breathing too fast, his unseeing eyes wide with horror. His fists were clenched on his lap, his body jerking with half-sleep. His nightmare still had its claws in him.

Sera laid a gentle hand on his knee. "Hey," she whispered. "Good morning."

Ransom blinked, quickly clearing the shadows behind his eyes. "Hey," he croaked. He raked a hand through his hair, settling the unruly strands. "I must have fallen asleep."

"Well. That was the idea."

She could tell by his frown he hadn't meant to. Perhaps he was afraid of the nightmares, or, more likely, what the others in the carriage might make of them.

Val woke with a groan, complaining about the crick in her neck. Theo was the last to rouse, indulging in a sprawling yawn as he came to.

Sera drew back the drapes. "We're nearly there."

They crowded the windows, peering out at their destination.

Just up ahead, the birthplace of Saint Oriel glittered like a living, breathing jewel.

Sera's heart hitched—then stuttered in her chest. Her gaze had fallen from the red mills to the street ahead, to where a vaulted stone archway marked the entrance to Marvale. In the middle, etched in stone, were the words,

WELCOME TO THE BIRTHPLACE OF

ORIEL BEAUREGARD,

BLESSED SAINT OF DESTINY

On either side, dead nightguards hung from their polished bootstraps.

"All hell," hissed Theo.

"Look at the flags," whispered Val, quailing at the sight. "They're different too."

With great effort, Sera tore her gaze away from the corpses and settled it on the flags billowing atop the arch. The customary crest of Valterre—a rose crossed with two swords—had been altered. Gone were the steel swords of the Rayere dynasty. There was only the rose now, the stark crimson symbol gilded by the rising sun. Her thoughts turned to Fontaine's rose, the card burning a hole in her back pocket.

No one spoke as they drew closer, and though the carriage slowed as Nadia and Caruso noticed the same gruesome sight, it didn't trundle to a stop. They pushed forward, ducking as they passing under the arch.

The bodies swayed next to Sera's window, close enough to see that their eyes had been gouged out, their slackened mouths carved into blood-tinged smiles.

Stifling a whimper, she drew back into the carriage, finding Val's hand.

At the other window, Ransom's face was like stone. "This is your People's Saint," he said, in a cold, cold voice. "Is he truly better than your king?"

She looked away, doubt eating away at that quiet hope inside her.

Part III

"To be a saint is to give yourself to the tides
of fate.
Surrender, and they will carry you to shore.
Fight, and they will drown you,
Over and over again."

CALVIN VENATOR,
SAINT OF DEATH

Chapter 22

Seraphine

Upon finding that all but one of the inns at Marvale were full, they had little choice but to check into the Paramour, a small inn tucked away on the eastern edge of town, which was bedecked in all manner of tassels and velvet. It seemed they were not the only ones seeking an audience with the People's Saint, which only added to Sera's disquiet. How many people now stood between her and the prince? And would one of them be Ransom?

The bed in Sera's suite was red and frilled and shaped like a heart. Big enough to share with Val, and with a generous love seat for Theo to sleep on. They took their time washing and getting changed before heading downstairs for breakfast.

The Daggers joined them, and over a platter of eggs, bacon and fresh fruit, they worked out their plan, dutifully pretending they were all still on the same side. Since the cobbled streets of

Marvale were deserted, they would spend the day scouring the town for word of the prince. It was early yet, which meant they had time to gather their wits and some new clothes while they were at it. As Nadia was quick to point out, nights in Marvale were long and loud, and the fashions here were flashier than what they were used to back in Fantome.

They would either have to adapt or stick out like sore thumbs. A prospect that was even more off-putting after having glimpsed the mangled bodies hanging from the entrance arch.

"What would you have us dress up as, then?" asked Theo. "Rebels or revelers?"

"Whatever improves that hideous brown jacket," Nadia said, between swigs of coffee. "You look like someone's grandfather."

Theo spluttered in mock offense. "I'll have you know this jacket was a most treasured gift from your king." He gestured to the fading bruises along his jaw. "Along with these."

"Whatever." She shrugged. "Just do better."

"Val and I will see to our new wardrobes. But only if you promise to replace that creepy coat of yours. Nothing screams *I've come to murder you* like an intimidating black trench coat and knife-blade stilettos."

Nadia smirked. "That's typically the idea."

They bickered on, Val and Caruso soon joining in. All the while, Sera kept her eyes on Ransom. And Ransom kept his eyes on her.

Neither of them ate very much, picking at cold strips of bacon as the clock on the wall ticked on, moving ever closer to that fork in the road. The question that still lingered between them:

To kill or not to kill.

"Can we speak alone for a moment?" she asked, when her appetite had deserted her entirely.

He was on his feet at once. They moved into the narrow hallway, where the colored oil lamps cast them in a soft crimson glow.

Sera cut right to the quick. "We never finished our conversation at the Bellflower."

"For what it's worth, I preferred the second part of that interaction," he remarked.

She was too tired—too addled—to snip at him. The stakes were higher now, the strands of destiny tightening around them. "Are you going to kill him?"

He folded his arms. "Are you going to try and stop me?"

The answer was yes, and they both knew it, but she couldn't be with Ransom every second of the day, and she knew if he came upon Andreas before her, it would be too late.

"You don't even *know* him," she said.

"Neither do you," he pointed out. "Although those carved-up nightguards certainly made for a pleasant introduction."

She gave a huff of frustration. "There are rebels hanging all over Fantome."

"I'm the one who kills them." Not even a flinch. "But I don't play with my corpses, Seraphine. I don't pocket their eyes like jewels and carve up their faces."

A tenuous line. And she could hardly defend it. Instead she said, "Don't you care about anything we talked about?"

"I care about all of it." There: a dent in his composure, those tired eyes softening. "I just don't know if I can bring myself to believe that Andreas is worth saving. That your life is worth the gamble."

"Is your soul worth the gamble of killing him?" she shot back.

"Let me worry about my soul, Seraphine."

"Let me worry about my life, Ransom."

Another impasse. Another argument bubbling up inside her. She closed her eyes, wrangling her frustration before she tore her hair out.

"We won't do anything rash for now," he said quietly. "Anything that Oriel might deem . . . unforgivable."

She cracked an eye open, hope fluttering inside her. "What do you mean?"

"I trust you, Seraphine. I want to trust your intuition, too." His throat knotted as he swallowed, working up to a compromise. "The best I can offer is time. When we find Andreas, we'll watch him first. Speak to him, if you like. Get the answers you seek. And then we'll know the worth of the gamble. For both of us."

She practically sagged with relief, the exhaustion of their journey—and all that lay ahead—coming over her in a wave.

It was not a reprieve, but it was a chance.

And it was enough.

After breakfast, they split up. The Daggers made for the artists' district in the west, while Val, Theo, and Sera scoured the south quarter, poking in and out of the boutiques there in search of outfits that would help them blend in once the sun went down.

They returned to the Paramour in the late afternoon. Theo promptly kicked off his boots and took a nap in a sea of satin pillows, while Val rifled through the collection of tiered skirts and fancy corsets, trying to choose her favorite.

Unable to settle, Sera went in search of the Daggers. A knock on Ransom's bedroom door yielded no answer. Outside, the streets echoed with laughter as the city slowly came alive. Sera wandered over the east bridge, where the inns thinned out and the dusty road was bordered by wildflowers and oaks. The air grew crisper, and she welcomed the chill, trying to calm her racing anxiety.

Ransom was fine. He would always be fine. He wouldn't go back on their word, not after they had fought so hard to trust each other again. The Daggers would return by nightfall, as they'd agreed.

She was so lost in thought she didn't notice the graveyard until it was right in front of her. The wooden gate was swinging on its hinges. Just beyond it, among the neat rows of mottled gray headstones, she glimpsed a familiar sweep of long black hair.

Nadia.

She was standing underneath the statue of a weeping angel. Sera hesitated on the threshold to the graveyard, not wanting to disturb her. Or draw her ire. Again. But curiosity soon got the better of her. She slipped inside, announcing herself with a timid, "Hi."

Nadia turned, lightning fast. Her slender brows knitted.

"Has something happened?" she said, urgently. "What's wrong?"

"What? Nothing," said Sera quickly. "I was just walking this way. And I spotted you."

"Oh. Right."

There was a beat of heavy silence.

"What are you doing out here? I thought you were with Ransom and Caruso."

"I was. We went up to the mills and I spotted the graveyard from there. I wanted to check if any of the graves had been disturbed." She tightened the belt on her coat, pulling her arms around herself. "I just had this . . . strange *feeling*."

Sera could relate. Lately, it seemed like her entire life was a collection of strange feelings, nudging her into dangerous situations. She looked around, scanning the graves. Everything appeared normal to her, but Nadia's words had set her on edge. Her magic, too. The hairs on the back of her neck rose as it flickered to life inside her. That crack in the door slowly widening, like someone was peeking out.

"What are *you* doing out here?" said Nadia.

"I don't know," Sera confessed. "I was looking for you three and I sort of ended up here."

But why? she wondered now. There were ten different directions she could have chosen. Wasn't it strange that they would both find themselves here?

Nadia didn't seem to notice, or care particularly. "They're still tracking the prince. According to the locals, Andreas holds court in the evenings. Ransom says you're keen to speak to him before we off him . . ."

Sera shrugged, feigning a casualness she did not feel about the entire affair. "I think a target this vital to the fate of the kingdom should at least be given a chance to explain himself."

"Afraid killing a saint might finally taint that squeaky clean soul of yours?"

Sera glanced sidelong at her. "Aren't *you* afraid? To kill for the king is one thing, but to knowingly unthread the strands of fate is another . . . There are greater enemies than the Crown, you know."

"Tell that to your friend Bibi."

"I'll get her out," said Sera, defiantly.

"Meet your precious saint, then. Kiss his feet if you like. I have nothing to lose either way." Nadia looked away, but not fast enough to hide the shadow behind her eyes. "I've already lost."

Lark.

His life, and then his body.

The specter of him seemed to crowd the space between them.

Feeling a sudden chill in the wind, Sera turned, her gaze lingering on the trees to their left. The branches there were swaying, as if to wave them off. She didn't know what possessed her, why a part of her wanted to dwell in this uncomfortable moment with the Dagger who had made no secret of her hostility toward her, but she didn't feel right leaving her on her own either, so she said, "Should we . . . Do you want to walk a bit?"

Nadia's brows lifted. "And what, try not to kill each other?"

"Novel concept, I know. I'm game, if you are."

Was that a smile on Nadia Raine's face? It occurred to Sera that she really was beautiful. In certain circumstances, that smile would probably be just as deadly as the Shade she carried in her pockets.

They fell into step, ambling through the graveyard like a pair of old friends, and not two people who had brawled in the Appoline barely a few days ago.

"I believe you, you know, about Lark's body," Nadia said after a minute or so. "Ransom told me about the Necromancer. He thinks it's another rogue saint."

Sera was surprised at the flutter of relief in her stomach. "Good."

It was something, at least. Not a bridge, but perhaps the first stone.

"It doesn't mean it's not difficult for me. To be here on this journey. With you."

It's no picnic for me either. Sera swallowed her retort.

Progress. They were making progress.

"I know I'm the reason he's dead. I'm never not aware of that."

She couldn't bring herself to apologize for it. All she had done was defend herself on top of the Aurore that night.

"He tried to kill you that night," said Nadia, as if reading her thoughts. "We both did." Her slender brows hunched and for the first time since Sera had met the enigmatic Dagger, she looked ashamed. "Different sides. Different stakes. We thought it was the right thing."

"Why?"

"Because that's what we were told by Dufort." A mirthless smile. "In truth, we never really thought about right and wrong. That's not how we were raised. Or trained. We just took our orders like soldiers, and spent the coin well."

"Well, at least you're honest about it, I suppose."

"It's easier to grieve Lark when I can blame you for his death," Nadia went on. "It means I don't have to blame myself for egging him on that night. It means I don't have to blame him for the life he chose. The risks he took. It means I don't have to blame Saint Oriel."

But wasn't it always Saint Oriel in the end?

"I get it," said Sera.

And more than that, she didn't blame the Dagger for it. Sera was the villain in Nadia's story, just as Lark was the villain in her own.

"It was a game. The same one Lark and I played every night for nearly ten years. Kill or be killed. This time, you won." She gave a heavy shrug. "And Lark lost."

It didn't feel like absolution, or forgiveness. But Sera wasn't seeking those things from her. "I wish it had all gone differently," she offered. That much, at least, was true.

"So do I."

Nadia kicked a stray pebble, watching it plink off a nearby headstone. "We were going to leave the Order together. We'd been saving up for a patch of farmland. We were going to keep chickens. Sell their eggs at the local market. He wanted cows and sheep, too, but I told him I wasn't made for shoveling shit. My clothes are too fine."

Sera gave no argument. Even here, after days of travel with little rest, Nadia was unbearably chic, clad in a sleek black coat, narrow leather trousers, and a lethal pair of boots.

"I wish I had said yes to it all now." She shook her head, her voice turning rueful. "Maybe we would have left sooner. Maybe we'd be there right now. Shoveling shit. Free of our pain, at last." She turned her hands, tracing the slender shadow-marks there. "I was always the realist. I struggled to see another life beyond the catacombs, but even as a boy, Lark was so sure we could remake ourselves. That we could be something else. Something better."

Sera tried to hide her surprise. She had spent so much of her time with the Daggers thinking about Ransom's desire for freedom, she never imagined the others might feel the same way. That there could be a different life outside the catacombs for Nadia, too. That she might covet it just as badly as he did.

Suddenly, her meeting with Andreas felt more vital than ever.

"You can still strive for something else, Nadia. There's so much waiting for you outside Old Haven. You could do anything. *Be* anything."

Nadia looked away, trailing her fingers along a passing headstone. When she spoke again, her voice was quiet, and Sera got the feeling she was talking to herself as much as her. "Without Lark, what's the point?"

There was such sadness in her now, it made Sera's heart clench. "I used to feel the same way about Mama," she confessed. "After she died, I didn't see the point in going on. It all felt so impossible. The world was so large and so bleak without her."

Nadia glanced sidelong at her. "So what changed?"

"I made friends. I considered the world, not for what it had taken away from me, but for what it might yet give me if I just hung on long enough. Freedom. Family. Purpose." She shrugged. "I suppose I found the point."

Nadia *hmm*'d, digesting the words. She didn't look convinced, but these things, big things—like grief and uncertainty—took time to overcome.

Nadia bent down to pull a weed from a nearby grave. When she stood up, she looked at Seraphine—*really* looked at her for the first time—without an ounce of hostility. The brown of her eyes glimmered in the afternoon sun. "Can I admit something that's probably going to hurt your feelings?"

Sera shrugged. "Only if you promise to say sorry after."

"I wish that night in the storm that Saint Oriel had chosen Lark instead of you."

Sera had braced for the words and found they didn't hurt at all. They were human, and honest. In return, she offered her own truth, "Sometimes, I wish that, too."

Nadia blinked in surprise. "Do you truly despise your magic?"

"I think the problem is I don't understand it," Sera admitted. "It's hard to summon. Except when things get out of hand. It's like it only comes rushing out of that well inside me when I'm not looking, when I'm not ready. It ends up hurting people. *I* hurt people."

"And you're hoping this prince-saint will help you figure it out?"

An affirming nod. "I think he's the only one who can."

Nadia was quiet then, perhaps unconvinced. For a while, the only sound was the crunch of her boots on the gravel. Sera was beginning to regret her honesty when the Dagger said, "It was like that for me at the start. With Shade. I would swallow a vial and then panic. The shadows would go everywhere, like a pit of frightened snakes. Twice, I nearly killed Lark and Ransom. The time I accidentally hit Lisette, she ran to Dufort. He nearly kicked me out of the Order."

"I had no idea it was so complicated."

"It's not supposed to be," said Nadia, a little sheepishly. "I was just afraid. Really, really afraid. My fear became a block. It made the Shade turn back on itself instead of doing what I wanted it to do."

"How did you fix it?"

Nadia smiled. "I got out of my own way."

"Well, that's helpfully vague." Sarcasm tripped through Sera's voice.

"As long as you fear your magic, it will master you. If you learn to embrace it, even the big scary parts, *you* will master your power. Only then will you know what kind of saint you're truly meant to be."

Madame Fontaine's words echoed inside Sera's mind.

Fear is a fog you cannot see through.

"I guess I'll just have to figure out the fearless part."

"Just wait until you're faced with a threat bigger than your magic, saint."

They walked on, coming to the back of the cemetery, where the graves thinned, and the trees thickened. The wind picked up, and the scent of lemon blossoms tickled Sera's nose.

She came to a stop, sure she glimpsed movement in the trees. Or perhaps it was her magic that sensed something. That familiar flare of warmth in her chest grew hotter, more insistent, as if something had roused it.

"Do you see something?" said Nadia.

"I don't know." Sera tried to shake it off. "I just . . . I have the weirdest feeling we're being watched."

Nadia rolled her narrow shoulders, slipping a vial from her pocket. "We're the threat. We have nothing to fear."

"You're right. I'm probably just being—" Sera's foot hit against something. She looked down to find herself staring into two gaping eye sockets. There was a skull in the middle of the path.

Nadia cursed, pulling her toward a nearby headstone. More bones here too. A ribcage. A leg and an arm. Fingers strewn along the row like confetti.

They followed them like breadcrumbs, bile gathering in Sera's throat. "These graves are open."

Not wasting another breath, Nadia downed her vial in one go, putting a foot of space between them. Shadows swarmed her like a cloak. "It's here," she hissed. "It's *practicing.*"

Sera's magic was in her throat now, as hot as lava.

"We should run," she said, with growing urgency.

Nadia planted her feet. "No. We should fight."

Panic roared in Sera's ears. They couldn't fight. Not like this. Not when it was only the two of them. But Nadia refused to budge. The wind cast strands of her ebony hair about her face as she scanned their surroundings. Bringing her hands to her hips, she shouted, "We're not scared of you, grave robber." Shadows billowed around her, making her look fierce and beautiful and deadly. "Come out and face us!"

Sera's heartbeat thrummed, her hands glimmering with the nearness of her magic. Her skin adopted that strange, eerie glow.

She told herself, *Don't be afraid. Don't be afraid. Don't be afraid.*

All hell, she was petrified.

"What exactly are you planning?" she said, through chattering teeth.

"I'm getting answers," said Nadia, gathering more shadows around her. "And then I'm putting that Necromancer into its own grave." She lifted her chin. "ARE YOU FRIGHTENED, GRAVE ROBBER?" She picked up a leg bone and flung it toward the trees. "Come back here and pick up your toy soldiers!"

"You're mad," huffed Sera.

"Absolutely *raging*," said Nadia, tightening her ponytail.

There came a cool rush of wind. Sera's spine went stiff, her magic whispering through her bones.

Don't be afraid. Don't be afraid. Don't be afraid.

The trees rustled, and from the darkness within, a figure lumbered out. They were tall and slim, wearing a long crimson robe that swept the ground. Their hood was low, hiding their face, and they wore a pair of black leather gloves.

They raised one, as if in greeting.

A long finger twitched.

The leg bone Nadia had flung stood on end and then leaped into the air, returning to her as though carried by an invisible dog. As it floated toward them, it gathered more bones, all of them stacking and clicking, until it became a complete skeleton.

It was the most fascinating and terrifying thing Sera had ever seen, the scent of rot—of *death*—making her stomach churn. Here was a saint in full control of their power, and she had nothing to defend them with. Just this choking fire in her belly, and the violent howl of her own terror.

Refusing to be cowed, Nadia sent out a wall of shadow. The skeleton shattered into pieces. "Neat trick," she sneered. "Now give me back Lark Delano's body before I crush the life out of you in ten heartbeats."

So much for not killing any saints.

Rising to her challenge, the Necromancer advanced, their strides lumbering to one side. Raising their hands, they silently readied another assault.

"Have it your way, freak." Nadia sent out another wave of shadows. They crested over the figure and everything that surrounded it, the blackness so sudden and complete, the entire end of the graveyard turned to night.

"Ha— *Shit.*"

The shadows shattered. Night collapsed around them, and Nadia stumbled backward, gasping. The Necromancer remained exactly where they'd stood, hood cocked as if to say, *Is that all you've got?*

Nadia looked at Sera over her shoulder, her brown eyes wide and darting. There wasn't a flicker of silver left. Her Shade was spent. The Necromancer had eaten through it by simply . . . *standing* there.

Sera cursed herself for not realizing sooner. If Shade no longer worked on her, then it stood to reason that the other saints would likely enjoy the same immunity.

The Necromancer must have known that, probably saw this little run-in as a game. They were moving faster now, those leathered hands flung out, like they were reaching for Nadia.

"Run!" yelled Seraphine.

This time, Nadia listened. They made for the other end of the graveyard, the rattle of footsteps behind them getting closer, louder. Halfway there, Nadia's boot caught on something. She tripped, coming down hard on her knees.

The Necromancer closed in, hundreds of bones trailing alongside them like calcified snakes. Nadia staggered to her feet. Too late. The Necromancer lunged.

Without thinking, Sera leaped, a cry bursting out of her as she landed between them. She flung her hand out, welcoming the fullness of her magic as it connected with a hard chest.

There was a blast of heat. The Necromancer fell backward, crashing into a towering headstone. The stone cracked under the weight, the bones around them finally falling still.

The gaping hood slipped back as the Necromancer's head lolled.

Sera's magic was a fuse inside her, that ancient voice louder than ever before.

Maker.

It belongs to you.

Sera yanked the hood back, revealing a shiny gold mask. The skin underneath it was mottled and gray, the Necromancer's collarbones as sharp as knives. With trembling fingers, she reached for the mask. A black glove twitched, stretching for her wrist.

Nadia yanked her back. "Leave it. We're about to be sorely outnumbered."

A salient observation. Since they were in a graveyard teeming with bodies. For a necromancer, that meant soldiers. And for them—deep shit.

Sera's magic was already receding, the heat inside her fading. Like it was done fighting. Done listening.

She staggered to her feet, moving backward.

Nadia's hand in hers was trembling. "We need to go. *Now.*"

They turned and ran.

They were almost back at the Paramour when they ran headlong into Ransom. He was standing outside, scouring the street like he had lost something.

Sera was running so fast she skidded right into him. He flung his hands out to steady her, his eyes darting, frantic. "All right?"

"Just about," Sera managed, between gasps.

Nadia skidded to a stop, bracing herself against a nearby windowsill to catch her breath. "Might vomit," she heaved. "Feet definitely bleeding."

"Where the hell were you two?" said Ransom, looking

between them. "We've been out searching for you. We thought something terrible had happened."

"You mean you thought we'd killed each other," said Nadia, sweeping her sweat-slicked hair back from her face.

He narrowed his eyes. "You both look like you've tried."

"No," said Seraphine, slumping back against the sill. "Worse."

Nadia slumped down beside her. "Way worse."

Arms folded and brows hunched, Ransom stood over them. Both a bodyguard and an inquisitor. "Explain."

Chapter 23

Seraphine

In the low-lit velveteen lounge of the Paramour Inn, Ransom paced back and forth. The others sat around a bar table, watching him while Val reclined on a tasseled chaise longue. It was too risky to return to the graveyard in pursuit of the Necromancer. And besides, what was there to gain, beyond a conflict they were ill prepared for?

For now, their focus was squarely on Prince Andreas.

The hour of their meeting was close at hand.

"It seems when he's not traveling the countryside rallying rebels to his cause or breaking into the king's prisons to add to his burgeoning army, the prince holds court at the Rose Garden up at the red mills," Ransom was saying.

Hope sparked in Sera's chest.

"Did you glean anything else?" Theo asked.

Ransom stopped pacing. "Is that not enough for you, Versini?

While you were off buying a year's worth of feathers, we were tracking down our actual mark."

"Don't be so ungrateful," snapped Val. "You haven't even seen the feathers yet. *And* we got top hats."

"I'm not wearing a top hat," said Ransom.

"You will if you plan on fitting in at the Rose Garden tonight. The goal is to be inconspicuous. Which in Marvale, means the exact opposite."

"Inconspicuousness is what we do," said Ransom. "It's who we are."

"Not when the dress code is *Decadent Delight*," said Val. "And before you bitch about it, just know you'll be expected to wear tails, too. And flashy shoes."

Caruso barked a laugh.

Val jabbed her finger at him. "That goes for you too, brute."

"Outfits aside, we're forgetting one *crucial* point," said Nadia. "Since Andreas is a saint, our Shade will be useless against him. If things go the way they did in that graveyard, we're going to need weapons."

Val nodded at Caruso. "That one can snap his neck like a tree branch."

Caruso flashed a menacing smile. "Thanks, kitten."

She flung a candle at his head and he caught it without flinching.

Before Val could throw something else, Sera rose from the table. "Right, then. Let's get on with it."

...

"I look like a cupcake." Sera surveyed herself in the mirror of their suite at the Paramour. Bedecked in a cascading red skirt and matching laced corset, it took her a moment to recognize herself. Her long blond hair hung in loose curls, and Val had smudged kohl underneath her eyes, adding a touch of rouge to her lips and cheeks.

In the mirror, Val's reflection beamed back at her. "I know. And now for the final touch."

Val slung a lavender feathered scarf around her own neck, twirling for full effect. She was dressed similarly to Sera, except her corset was violet and her skirt was black. Her boots were high, and her hair was bouncier than Sera had ever seen it. Somehow, she carried off the look like a seductive siren, and not a befrilled baked good that had been cursed to life. Although Sera supposed what mattered most was not her own vanity, but that she looked like every other reveler in Marvale tonight, rather than the king's former prisoner turned would-be assassin.

Theo, who was slicking his hair back in the adjoining bathroom, ducked around the doorframe. "If you want a gentleman's opinion, you both look like a pair of haunted dolls."

Turning to glare at him, Sera readied a taunt of her own but as usual, Theo Versini looked damn good. He was wearing a black suit with tails, with shiny, sharp-toed shoes, and a top hat tucked under his arm.

"You look . . ."

"Dashing? Suave? Eye-wateringly handsome?"

"Expensive," she decided.

Val sashayed over to him and stuck a purple feather in his front pocket. "Perfect."

He came to stand beside Sera in the mirror. For a moment, all three of them stood in silence, taking in their reflections.

"We are a long way from Halbracht," said Sera. Yet that voice deep inside told her she was exactly where she was supposed to be.

The Daggers were waiting for them on the street outside. It was three hours until midnight and the town had come alive. The flowery trellis-lined streets were strewn with giggling women in full-tiered skirts and boned corsets, their necks slung with beads and feathered scarves that trailed along the cobbles. Elsewhere, gentlemen ambled about in crooked top hats and tails, pressing their waning luck with beautiful courtesans far beyond their stations. A constant chorus of raucous laughter rang through the vibrant streets, buoying that tenuous hope inside Sera.

She felt Ransom's eyes on her the minute she stepped onto the street. He moved as if shoved by an invisible hand, his shadow stepping into light, until they were so close that she had to remind herself to breathe.

In the half-light, he seemed a little pained. "You look . . ."

"Do not make fun of me," she warned him.

"Like a dream," he said quietly.

She blinked up at him in surprise. "One of your nightmares, you mean?"

A smile danced along his lips. "Definitely not."

She stood back to look him over. He wore no suit or tails. Just plain black trousers, black boots, and a simple double-breasted waistcoat with a silver chain, over a crisp white shirt. His dark hair was lightly tousled and he was freshly shaven.

"I know. No top hat," he said, reading into her silence. "As Head of the Daggers, I have to retain some dignity."

"What about weapons?"

"More than you can possibly imagine, spitfire."

"Let's hope you won't need them."

He nodded, still watching her in that way that made her legs feel like jelly. He plucked a red feather from the end of her scarf and stuck it in the front pocket of his waistcoat. She was surprised by how much she liked it, how it made him look like he belonged to her.

"Stay close to me tonight." His eyes took on a new intensity, glimpses of the hardened Dagger already peeking through. "No matter what."

"All right." Her stomach swooped. Was her corset too tight or was her heart trying to squeeze its way out? She felt her magic more keenly now, unfurling from that deep space inside her, stretching languidly like a cat. What was it about this man that made her feel so vitally present?

Val shoved between them. "Caruso is wearing an actual *cravat*," she said, with a snort. "I didn't think he had it in him."

Without tearing his gaze from Sera, Ransom said, "He plans to strangle Andreas with it at the first sign of trouble."

Val hummed. "That makes it less endearing."

Nadia sauntered over with all the confidence of a queen.

She was dressed just like Sera and Val, her gold corset laced with the same shiny black ribbon that hung from her skirts.

She swished the end of Sera's feathered scarf. "You carry this off, farmgirl."

"I'm not sure if that's a compliment or not."

Nadia smirked. "Honestly, neither am I."

Next to her, Theo fitted his top hat onto his head, then made a show of checking the pocket watch Val had swiped for him that afternoon. "Time to go."

It was a short walk to the mills, the group blending in so seamlessly with the revelers that at times Sera lost sight of Val and Nadia in the thickening crowds. But never Ransom. He stayed so close to her their hands brushed as they walked, every fleeting touch setting the ember of her magic aglow.

As Sera stepped inside the Rose Garden of Marvale, she had the uncanny sensation that she had strayed into a dream. A grand dance hall located on the ground floor of the largest of the red mills, the Rose Garden crowned the north hills of Marvale like a glittering ruby, overlooking the night-kissed sprawl of the village. It was already teeming. The warm night air trilled with music, the lullaby as inviting as the generous garlands that hung from the arched ceiling, casting a floral scent about the hall.

Sharply dressed waiters scurried to and fro, carrying trays of fizzing wine and brightly colored cocktails, while dancers bedecked in feathers and elaborate headdresses sashayed through the crowd, enticing people to get up and dance with them. There were so many people here—more laughter and dancing and kissing and drinking—than she'd ever seen in her life.

And yet, the moment she stepped through those doors, her gaze fell on the prince.

Even seated at the other end of the hall, with his face upturned toward the dancers on the stage, Andreas Mondragon Rayere stuck out like a lit flame. Here was a beacon burning brighter than the spectacle around him, the North Star in a sea of midnight.

And when he turned his head suddenly, as though some innate force inside him had whispered of her arrival, his eyes met hers across the room.

They flickered bright gold.

In a single thudding heartbeat, Sera's magic erupted into life.

The prince smiled.

And she went to him.

Chapter 24

Seraphine

"Seraphine." Ransom's hand tightened around hers. Concern edged his voice. "Where are you going?"

"I'm all right," she said, gently shaking him off. "I'll be all right."

She did not know her magic well, but she knew enough, somehow, to recognize a moment of destiny—an intersection that had been fated to happen since that night on the Aurore. She knew, too, that this path, or at least the last few steps of it, were ones she must now walk alone.

And she was not going to be shy about it.

Striding purposefully toward the prince, she lifted her chin, the heat inside her thrumming like a second heartbeat. Like called to like, magic to magic. Saint to saint. Sera had never felt surer of her own footsteps, or more keenly aware of the strands of fate tightening around her.

Yes, she was right to come here.

Yes, she would find the answers she sought.

As though he could feel the same force working on him, Andreas Mondragon Rayere rose from his chair and stepped away from his table without bothering to finish his conversation. The crowds parted as he moved through them, but he kept his eyes on Sera.

They flickered from gold to blue and back again, as though his own magic could not resist peering out at her. She understood the feeling.

Dimly, Sera noted the prince was classically handsome, reasonably tall with a straight nose and strong cheekbones, a mane of glossy golden hair and a pair of full lips that appeared to be naturally quirked. More Mondragon than Rayere, she decided, for the royals of Urnica were known to look like the old western gods, touched by beauty in construct and savagery at war. Perhaps in another life, the fierce brightness of Andreas's smile would have knocked her sideways, but even in the thrall of her own magic, she was keenly aware of the Dagger at her back, watching over her like an avenging angel. Watching Andreas with the predatorial instincts he was feared for.

One wrong turn from the prince and this whole meeting would go up in Shade, and blood.

They met in the middle of the dance floor. Among a sea of twirling skirts and bubbling laughter, the People's Saint flung open his arms in a welcoming embrace, and said, entirely to her surprise, "Seraphine Marchant! It took you long enough."

Sera jerked at her name in his mouth, any impression of her

having the upper hand flittering away with the music. "You . . . you know me . . . ?"

"*Know* you? I've been waiting for you all my life! Well. Give or take a decade or two." It was a joke, followed by a velveteen laugh more stirring than the music around them. And although the dancers in their midst could not possibly have overheard their conversation—or understood that joke—several of them joined in, guffawing at them like hyenas.

Sera glanced around, uncertainly. "What is happening here?"

"Fate, Seraphine. Fate is what's happening here." As he extended a manicured hand to her, she noted the golden rose embroidered on the sleeve of his fine blue shirt, and thought of the tarot card back in her bedchamber. Fate, indeed.

"Come," he said. "Sit with me."

"I'd like that," she said.

Sera followed Prince Andreas to a secluded spot on the far side of the dance floor, where a scattering of velvet seats clustered around a low glass table. A flick of his wrist chased off the group of revelers that had gathered there, allowing them to speak freely.

A quick glance over her shoulder revealed the tell-tale silver glint of Theo's hair. He was drifting nearby, keeping watch. Though she couldn't spot the others in the low-lit shadows, Sera could feel Ransom's attention like a slant of sunlight on the back of her neck. She offered a quick nod to the room at large, knowing he would see it.

All is well.

With a kind of regal grace lacking in the king himself, the young prince settled into an armchair, crossing one slender leg over the other. He was dressed impeccably, in a deep blue shirt and matching waistcoat, the lapels embroidered with what looked like thorns. The roses he wore on his sleeves, next to a pair of shiny gold cufflinks that bore his initials. Even at rest, he sat with the ease of a man who had known comfort all his life. And he wore it well—the decadence of this place—unlike Sera, who felt like a doll in her stiff corset and ruffled skirt.

Unsure of where to begin, she perched on the edge of the chair beside him. "So, you know me," she said again, now that the shock of his greeting had sunk in. "How?"

His smile was a wedge of white in the dimness. "Saint Oriel's foretelling is stamped on my very soul, Seraphine. You think the Aurore Tower would fall and I wouldn't hear about it? That I wouldn't make it my business to find the woman who fell with it and emerged unscathed from the rubble?" He leaned across the armrest, his voice low and conspiratorial. "We were always meant to find each other, you and I. It is the will of fate."

His words struck true. "I think I've been dreaming of you. The night that you fell from the Appoline."

"Yes, yes, of course you have." He seemed pleased to hear it. And more than that, entirely unsurprised. "Oriel has been guiding you to me all along."

But Sera had been having other dreams too. Glimpses of coffins and bones and soul-rattling panic, the cold wet earth filling her lungs until her screams died inside her. Unease prickled under her skin as she recalled her run-in with the masked saint in the graveyard, likely the same creature that had been trawling through graves across Fantome.

She eyed the prince more closely. In physicality, he did not strike her as that figure, but she knew well enough that senses could be deceiving, and magic, at its best, could be tricky. "What is your true power, Prince Andreas?"

His laughter was a warm caress, chasing her disquiet away. "Isn't it as plain as daylight? I am a bringer of joy." He gestured to the hall around him, where spirits and merriment flowed in equal measure. Even here, secreted away in a low-lit corner of the room, it was impossible to ignore the rampant trills of laughter, the skirts swishing up onstage and the revelers cavorting around them, behaving like they were in their own private bedchambers. "Where I go, paradise blooms."

Sera's brows shot up at his confidence. "But how do you do it?" she pressed, craving specifics, hoping they might help her activate her own magic. "How do you simply *make* people happy?"

His smile curled, threads of gold glimmering in the blue of his eyes. Sera's own magic flickered in answer, like their souls were sharing in some ancient joke. "I simply tell them to be so."

"That's it?" Peering around, she tried to spot the intricate workings of his magic. There was so much laughter. So much dancing. People were constantly moving, flitting about the hall like butterflies. Unwilling to perch for too long, or to welcome even the briefest respite of silence. The room felt alive and strangely dizzying. Whatever magic the prince wielded had seeped into his people.

And they loved it.

They loved *him* for it.

"You mean you persuade them?" She spied a couple in the corner grinding against each other with wanton abandon. Her cheeks heated and she looked away to find the prince watching her with a look of bemusement.

"People by their very nature wish to be happy, Seraphine. It does not take much encouraging."

Truly a silver-tongue, then. A charmer, gifted with a god-like persuasion. And he was damn good at it by the looks of things. But there was more to the prince—more to this—than dancing, surely. Despite her ease in his presence, she would not fall under his spell so easily. She owed it to Ransom—and herself—to be discerning.

"And what about your rebels? What do you tell them to make them set their villages alight? To string up the night-guards by their bootstraps and carve up their smiles?"

Despite a slight stiffening in his shoulders, Andreas's voice was easy, that sureness oozing from every pore in his body. "I tell them to fight for the kingdom they want to live in. To claim the world they wish to leave to their children."

"Is this version of Valterre really so terrible?"

"If it wasn't, would you have founded your Order of Flames?" he parried.

It was a fair question, and it stumped her. He was right—Valterre, and Fantome in particular, could certainly do with some improvement. But all-out rebellion . . . these growing rivers of fire and blood, she remained uncertain about.

As if sensing that uncertainty, he said, "A king who thrives in darkness will never welcome in the light. Even when it's banging on his windows." Reclining in his chair, he gestured to a passing waiter. Two glasses of red wine were set down on the table in front of them. He offered one to her and Sera took it, if only to keep from wringing her hands, when she said, "There is a necromancer in Marvale." Andreas didn't flinch. "We had a run-in."

Of course this came as no surprise to the prince, but his brows twitched, implying the barest hint of frustration. A dent in that easy charm. "I'm afraid my necromancer has yet to familiarize himself with the rules of common courtesy."

"And grave robbing," she was quick to add.

"It is regrettable that he frightened you."

"You speak like he belongs to you," she noted, with a slip of unease. "Does he?"

Again, that musical chuckle. "I only meant that we are of the same making. The same magic." He tipped his glass against hers. "As you are, Seraphine." He drank deeply, the red wine staining his lips. For a fleeting moment, he looked so like his uncle the king, the wine so like the blood that had dripped from those hanging nightguards, that she had to blink the image away.

"I would ask you this . . ." he said, his eyes imploring as leaned toward her. "Don't blame my necromancer for the unpalatable nature of his power. You know as well as I do that we have no control over what kind of magic takes root inside us." There was a glimpse of something then—a shadow passing behind his eyes, his hand tightening around the stalk of his glass. "It seems that part is left up to the divine."

She set her wine aside. "Isn't it all left up to the divine?"

He drank again, draining his glass. "Indeed," he said, setting it down. "Indeed."

She looked at her hands, wondering if now was the time to give voice to her insecurities, to reveal that she knew so little of her own magic she couldn't name her power if she tried. But something was stopping her. Perhaps it was the loudness of the room, or the dizzying spiral of dancers that seemed to prance like ponies around them.

Increasingly, it seemed to her that there was no room for her in Fontaine's foretelling. Here was the Silver-tongue sitting before her. Earlier, she had come upon the Necromancer in the graveyard. The Stone Maiden must be the acolyte, Marianne, trapped on the Isle of Alisa. If Sera wasn't in those cards, then what on earth was she?

And what was the true meaning of the Rose card?

"You're troubled." Andreas's words pulled her back to him. He was frowning in earnest now, his fair brows knitting.

"Confused," she allowed. "I'm so full of questions; sometimes I can't sleep from the noise of them bouncing around in my head."

He smiled in understanding. "Stay with me and I will help you answer them. You will find your place here."

Yes. She wanted to say it, scream it, take him by the shoulders and make him promise it loud enough for the others to hear. But the folk of Marvale were too busy twirling, lost in their own paradise. The atmosphere was so intoxicating, the air thick with sweet-smelling smoke and the light dimmed to whispering candle flames, she almost forgot the world outside it. And everything that had come before this moment:

The trial shipment of Lightfire.

Her brutal kidnapping.

The king's dungeon.

Bibi's incarceration.

Bibi.

Bibi.

She could have slapped herself for forgetting, the urgency of the situation making her pitch forward and dig her nails into the armrest that separated them. "I want to stay here and learn more about you. About the saints. But I need something from you in return."

"Then name your price," he said, the gold in his eyes flaring, like his magic was rising to the challenge. "I am not letting you go."

Seraphine was too focused on Bibi to unpick the strange hunger in those words, the sudden sharpness of his teeth under the flickering lights. "I've heard what happened at the Iron Keep. How you opened the oldest prison in Valterre like a cupboard door and freed five thousand prisoners in one night."

"Rebels," he corrected her. "One man's prisoner is another man's war general."

Like it mattered. "You freed them."

"With ease," he said, betraying a hint of arrogance. "There isn't a prison guard on this continent that I can't sway."

Good. *Good.* "My best friend, Bibi, is in the king's dungeon in the Summer Palace. She's innocent. Only there because of me."

The prince's eyes narrowed, his easy grin twisting into a grimace. For the first time since she had met him, Andreas Mondragon Rayere did not look handsome at all. He looked like a lion, hungry for blood.

"I've been meaning to pay a visit to the Summer Palace. I'll see to it that your friend is freed." She wanted to press the matter, ask him *when* and *how*, to urge him to hurry those plans, but the gift of his help was too recently offered that she was afraid he might take it back. Canting his head, he said, "After all, we are allies now, are we not?"

He might have noticed her beat of hesitation if it hadn't been for the arrival of a young woman, who came sweeping into their bubble. With a veil of hair like spun gold and eyes as green as jade, the sight of her momentarily stole Sera's breath. Her skin was golden tan, and she wore a blue dress of gossamer silk. It fell like waves around her as she came to perch on Andreas's armrest.

"Talisa," Andreas said with a sigh, without looking at her. Annoyance curled his lip, but if Talisa noticed, she didn't care. "I suppose you couldn't resist interrupting."

The woman, who possessed the fine, dainty beauty of a forest nymph, revealed two neat lines of straight white teeth. "You're hogging her, cousin. What did you expect?"

Playful now, he flicked her wrist. "I suppose pampered princesses are not raised to wait their turn."

"Grumbles the pampered prince," she chided, before turning

her curiosity on Sera. "Our precious flower has arrived at last!" The princess's large eyes were glassy and her speech was slurred, so Sera couldn't be sure of her words when she crowed, "Oh, but *when* is she going to bloom? I can hardly wait!"

Sera frowned just as Andreas cut in, "Seraphine, this is my cousin, Talisa Mondragon. Another one who needs a lesson in common courtesy." Another flick of Talisa's wrist, his fingers lingering there this time like a manacle. "Don't spook my guest, cousin. We're still getting to know each other."

"Well, when you're done, you might as well tell her I'm a lot more fun."

Sera couldn't give a rat's tail if Talisa was good company or not. She hadn't come here for friends; she had come for answers. And right now, the drunk Urnican was getting in her way.

If only the king could see her now, fraternizing with the greatest known threat to his reign and a princess of Urnica, gleefully guzzling all his precious Valterran wine. He'd have poor Bibi in the stocks by morning, dead and buried by noon.

Startling her from her thoughts, Talisa pitched forward, snatching Sera's hand. She squeezed hard, her own clammy with sweat. "We'll be great friends, you and I. I'm already so glad to know you."

Andreas yanked his cousin's wrist, drawing her back with a sharp tug. "Don't mind, Talisa." There was an edge to his voice now. "She's hideously overfamiliar with everyone."

Talisa pouted. "Perhaps I'm just bored of twirling my skirts all night."

"And yet the music calls. Go on and dance, butterfly. Be merry." His eyes flashed, and for a second the room felt unbearably bright. Talisa was on her feet then, sashaying away with an unsteadiness that suggested she could fall over at any moment.

Andreas waved her off, like a gnat. "Excitable as a pup, my cousin. Loves a shiny new toy."

"Seems to me that everything here is shiny," said Sera. "I don't know why *I* would hold such fascination."

"No, you don't, do you?" he said, chuckling as he swept a rogue golden lock from his eyes. "I suppose you are yet to discover how special you truly are."

Sera's cheeks prickled, the eagerness to be *seen*, to be known, clashing with another deeper discomfort she could not name. More questions gathered on her tongue, but they were interrupted again, this time by a group of grisly-looking men, who were not at all dressed for the Rose Garden. A collection of stubbled jaws and crooked noses, they wore work shirts and oversized britches, with stomping black boots. Mercenaries, then. Rebels who didn't quite get the dress code, or perhaps shouldn't be in here at all. The one in the middle had his sleeves rolled up, and there was blood splattered on his collar. It was fresh.

The prince held up a cautionary hand before any of them could utter a single word. "One moment, Callum."

He turned back to Sera. "Forgive me. An urgent matter."

"So I see," she said, still eyeing all that blood. "More enemies, I suppose."

Andreas gave a bland smile. "My uncle and his spies. He just can't help himself."

Guilt stiffened Sera's shoulders. She hoped to all hell he hadn't noticed. "Right. Of course."

Summoning that buttery smile once more, the prince rolled to his feet. "Dance, Seraphine. Be merry. I'll return shortly."

His words were easy, enticing even, but they lacked the effect they had had on Talisa. Sera didn't want to dance. She stood up, desperately wanting to ask him about his plans for the kingdom, what else he knew about her, and why he seemed so oddly fascinated by her.

He stilled for a moment, like he could feel her curiosity crowding in on him.

"I can see them," he said, stepping closer. "All those questions burning in your eyes. I will help you, Seraphine. I am the only one who can." Bringing his lips close to her ear, he lifted a hand to her face. "I have to, you see. Because you are more than just a saint." He traced a gentle finger down her cheek, raising every hair on her arms. "You are my rose."

Jarred by his closeness, she stumbled backward. Heat gushed through every part of her. Whether it was his touch or his words that did it, she couldn't tell, but her magic was erupting like a volcano. He was laughing now, like they were sharing a joke.

"Later," he said, his gaze flitting to something over her shoulder. That smile curling and curling. "Everything you seek and more. I promise. In the meantime, you might do me a favor and call off your Daggers."

Dread sliced through Sera like a cold blade. At her look of alarm, he simply clucked his tongue. "I'd hate to have to do it myself." A meaningful pause, those lion teeth flashing. "And believe me, so would you."

Sera turned to find Ransom shoving through the thrum of bodies between them. A vial of Shade already in one hand and a blade in the other. Stalking. *Seething.*

Coming straight for the prince.

She moved like a bolt of lightning, the prince's threat still echoing in her ears as she flung herself at the assassin currently hell-bent on murdering him.

Chapter 25

Ransom

As Ransom watched Seraphine drift toward the prince like a moth to a bonfire, every muscle in his body went taut. His hands itched for the vial in his left pocket, but he stayed the impulse, reminding himself of the promise he had made to her.

I will give the prince a chance.

Why had he made that stupid promise again?

Because Andreas might end up being her salvation.

He might even end up being yours.

Fuck. Fuck. Fuck.

Fine.

The way Andreas approached her, like he was beholding a new jewel for his treasure chest, made Ransom feel . . . well, *feral.* Sweeping a hand through his hair, he took a steadying breath and walked on through the crowds, reminding himself not to do anything rash. He tracked her all the way to the far corner of the dance hall, where she turned, offering a quick nod over her shoulder.

A signal to stand down.

Relax, you hot-headed fool, he told himself.

Seraphine's no shrinking violet.

She can hold her own.

He glanced around for the others, who had obviously got the same message. Nadia was necking shots at the bar, while Caruso swiped a pair of whiskeys from a passing tray. Val was standing at the edge of the dance floor, her face upturned toward the stage, where a slew of dancers were hollering and kicking their feet in the air.

Their mark forgotten—or shoved aside for now—the others were getting into the spirit of Marvale, which seemed to be unfettered hedonism. The Rose Garden was a glamorous canvas of sex and drink and dancing, and the kind of bawdy laughter that spilled out onto the streets. Hardly the lair of an evil prince. Ransom could at least admit that.

The rumors were proving true. Andreas was clearly beloved, and his pleasure hall was a world unto itself, where the troubles of the kingdom seemed a thousand miles away. Or perhaps, a keen glimpse into what the kingdom could one day become, if the People's Saint had his way.

Why, then, was Ransom having trouble relaxing?

Because she looks like a rose in bloom.

And he's leering at her like he wants to pluck her.

Ransom had never considered himself a jealous sort until

the day Seraphine Marchant barreled into his life. Now he was all those things and more—jealous, protective, *consumed* by her, and something about this place was making it all the worse.

"I need a drink," he muttered, looking for a passing waiter. When none appeared he ducked toward the nearest table and yanked a full glass of dark liquor straight out of a man's hand, the old drunkard too plastered to notice.

Ransom downed it in one, relishing the burn. It took the edge off, for about three minutes. Not quite as effective as Shade. Again, that itch in his fingers.

Keeping to old habits, he settled himself in a shadowy corner at the edge of the dance floor, where he leaned against a wooden pillar. Val was dancing nearby, Caruso smiling as he watched her. Nadia was still at the bar, probably ruminating on her run-in at the graveyard. Trying to drink the memory away. Ransom would have gone to her if he wasn't glued to the prince and whatever he was saying that made Seraphine's eyes gleam like that.

"If you're trying not to draw attention to yourself, you are failing miserably." Versini's voice made him jerk his head to the side. "Any drunken fool in here could nail a game of spot-the-jealous-ill-adjusted Dagger."

Versini and that shit-eating grin.

At least it was diverting.

"What do you want?" said Ransom, wearily.

"Just making sure you're not about to go back on your deal and lunge at the prince. Whatever they're talking about seems to be going well."

"I'll reserve my judgment."

"How unlike you."

"Careful," growled Ransom. "I still want to maim something tonight."

That earned him an eyeroll.

"Calm down, guard dog. I'm not your enemy."

Ransom summoned a flat smile and said again, "I'll reserve my judgment."

Scoffing now, Versini turned his gaze on the prince, silently observing his conversation with Seraphine. "She likes him."

Now he really was just trying to piss him off. "She doesn't know him."

The Shadowsmith tossed him a sideways smirk. "That's the whole point of this evening. We get to know him. See what he can teach her about her magic." When Ransom didn't respond, he went on. "Is that really such a horrifying concept to you? The idea that Seraphine is a saint? That she's meant for something more than the life she was born into?"

"Why would that horrify me?"

"Because it's better than any future you could give her."

That needled something between his ribs. "You really do love the sound of your own voice, don't you?"

"I'm just saying . . . let him help her. Let him teach her."

"He can teach her all he likes," Ransom allowed. "As long as he doesn't use her. Whatever Andreas is planning for Valterre, I won't let Seraphine become his weapon."

"Not even if it's what she wants?"

Prickling now, Ransom turned on him. "I don't know what she wants. And neither do you."

Versini only shrugged. "Isn't it worth it, to see what she can really do when she finally unlocks her magic?"

It was a reasonable question, but Ransom was not in a reasonable mood. "So long as it doesn't harm her."

"It's already harming her," said Versini, and that was another truth that rankled him. "But of course you'd prefer to keep her weak. Unable to truly defend herself. That way, she'll always need you."

That vial of Shade in his pocket was becoming harder to resist. He reminded himself that they were not here to brawl but to watch. To wait and see what kind of man—what kind of saint—Andreas proved himself to be. And Seraphine had yet to raise the alarm. Rather, she was enraptured by him. There was a woman sitting with her now, fair-haired like the prince.

"Versini, you must know by now that I would never hurt her."

The Shadowsmith leaned back against the pillar, his arms folded across his chest. "That doesn't make you trustworthy. It just means you want to screw her."

"You do realize you're in stabbing distance?"

He flashed his teeth. "Try it, Tunnel Rat."

This arrogant prick.

And he just kept prodding.

"You know, if you really cared about Sera, you'd find it in yourself to stop constantly threatening me, Ransom."

"I'm wary of you for good reason," he shot back. "You're a Versini."

Tensing, he bit out, “So what?”

Was he really so obtuse? “So you’re a *direct descendent* of Hugo Versini, the most notorious figure in the history of Valterre. Your ancestors changed the face of this kingdom forever, and for the worse. They bastardized Fantome, sucked all the light out of it. They plunged the City of the Saints into darkness, all because of their own insatiable ambition. The need to be better, richer, grander than everyone else.”

“I know the history,” he said curtly.

“*Your* history.” Ransom made a point of clarifying it. “What’s to say you don’t have that same streak inside you? The slow-creeping urge to be greater than your Order? Your friends? Your kingdom? What’s to say that’s not the real reason you want to save the prince, so you can watch how he trains Seraphine, and then find a way to use it to your advantage?”

Versini’s nostrils flared. “You’re reaching, Dagger.”

Now it was Ransom’s turn to smirk. “Then why are you getting so worked up?”

“*You* are the assassin here,” Versini hissed. “You murder for coin and then kiss the king’s ring. You would sooner laugh at the will of the saints and raise a knife to the throat of one of their own than actually consider what might, in fact, be best for the kingdom, or indeed the woman you claim to give a shit about.” He huffed a mirthless laugh. “You’re the Head of Hugo Versini’s depraved little Order and you have the gall to judge *me*, you morally corrupt prick.”

Turning his back to the prince, Ransom rounded on the Shadowsmith, training all his ire on him. “I became a Dagger because I had no other choice. At ten years old with no food and no coin, it was the catacombs or the bottom of the Verne for me. You had a family, a thriving village in Halbracht. You *chose* to become a Cloak. To spend every day with that black dust between your fingers, because it made you feel powerful, and important. Then someone even more powerful came along. Someone in possession of a kind of magic so alluring you just couldn't resist. You followed it like a trail of breadcrumbs."

"I followed *her*." Versini raised an accusing finger, bringing it dangerously close to Ransom's chest. One more inch and that vial was coming out. "While *you* stayed behind to murder your way through the city. Over and over again. Killing rebels who have the nerve to picture a better life, a safer, brighter kingdom than the one you try to ruin every day of your miserable life."

Ransom spoke through his teeth. "Every choice I make is about survival. *Her* survival. Her freedom. That includes when I kill someone. And when I let them breathe a little longer." He gestured behind him, toward the prince. "*You* are a slave to your own ambition, Versini. The question is, just how far will it take you?"

Slipping out from under him, Versini jutted his chin. "You don't know me, Dagger."

"I don't have to know you." Ransom's smile was cold. "As long as there's power in play, a Versini can never truly be trusted."

With a derisive snort, the Shadowsmith took a measured step back. "Keep stewing, Tunnel Rat. When she leaves the prince tonight, you'll still be wearing her dead father's ring, and I'll be the one she confides in."

He sauntered off without a second glance.

When Ransom turned around, Andreas and Seraphine were on their feet. Stepping way too close, the prince leaned in to murmur something in her ear. His eyes flicked to Ransom, his smirk slow and taunting, as he trailed a possessive finger down her cheek.

This fucker.

Ransom was already moving. Crossing the dance hall like a bullet, a vial in one hand and a knife in the other.

Looks like there would be murder tonight after all.

Chapter 26

Seraphine

Ransom was vibrating with rage when Sera reached him. She lunged, pressing her hands against his chest. "Don't you dare." She had to shout over the music to be heard. "Remember our deal!"

Grimacing, he paused to look down at her. "He put his fucking hands on you."

"A finger," she said, pushing him back.

He conceded a step. "That's one finger too many, spitfire."

The prince's overfamiliarity had taken her by surprise too. But she was not about to murder him over it. "There was nothing in it. Andreas has a flair for dramatics."

Ransom's lips twisted, all that latent anger still thrumming against her palms. The prince had slipped away with his mercenaries but there was no telling when he would return, or what Ransom might do with him when he did. Yanking the silver chain on his waistcoat, Sera dragged him into a nearby alcove, where they were hidden by a teeming bouquet of pink roses. "Calm down. You're like a volcano that's about to erupt."

"I am calm," he said, working to keep his voice even. "I'm so fucking calm."

"And *so* convincing," she teased, working the dagger from his grip and sliding it back into his pocket. He let her do it, watching her hands with rapt attention. "I told you I would be all right."

He nodded slowly, relinquishing his Shade next. "Yeah . . ." He rubbed the spot between his brows, trailing off. "I thought he . . . I don't know what I thought."

"You were jealous," she said, hooking her finger around the chain on his waistcoat.

"Obviously."

"And we don't kill people out of jealousy."

His brows lowered. "There's a first time for everything."

"Not tonight there isn't."

"Give me another reason, then."

"I can't." And she was relieved. "Our conversation went . . . well. He's not at all like the king made him seem. He's *human*." But they had barely scratched the surface, and she was eager to know more about him. About what he could do for her. And more than that, Bibi. "I need more time with him. So if you could refrain from stabbing Valterre's favorite new saint for just a little longer . . ."

He looked pained at the very suggestion. "I have a bad

feeling about him. About this place. The way he looks at you. The way he looked at *me*."

"That's because he knows what you are, Ransom."

"I don't fucking doubt it."

"You're worked up, that's all."

"Everyone in this place is worked up," he pointed out. "It feels like we're stuck on a carnival ride."

Huffing now, Sera dragged her fingers through her hair, anxiously pulling at the loose curls. She envied the dancers twirling around them. She wanted to laugh like the table of women nearby, wanted to drink something heady and strong, and damn the consequences.

"Maybe that's our problem." Thinking too much. Worrying about every little thing. For once, she wanted to lose herself in a moment, to breathe in the intoxicating fumes of Marvale and float above her worries. And she didn't want to do it alone. Feeling bolder, reckless, and aching for something she knew only he could give her, she slid her hands up his chest, raising her lips to his ear. "Maybe we both need to relax and enjoy the ride."

He blinked in surprise, some of that coiled tension rolling off him. "Are you intending to distract me from my own murderous thoughts, Seraphine?"

"That depends," she said, leaning in. "Is it working?"

"I'm not sure. Keep going," he said, sinking into that easy heat between them. All that aggression toward Andreas twisted, redirected now to other primal urges. Ones she was eager to indulge. He traced his thumb along her lower lip, smudging the rouging there. All around them, the sweet smoke thickened, the music pulsing along her skin until it felt like the entire dance hall was pressing in on them. Pulling on the chain of his waistcoat, she dragged him further into the alcove.

She laid her head back against the wall, spell-struck by the ravenous look in his eyes. "You're the only one I ever want to touch me, Ransom."

Lust snatched the air between them, those eyes drinking her down. His broad hands circled her waist, tracing the boning of her corset. "Where, spitfire?"

A gentle tug made her feathered scarf give way. It made a puddle between them, revealing the creamy slope of her shoulders and the column of her neck. "Here," she said, arching for him.

Sliding his hands through her hair, he leaned down to kiss her neck. Sera's lids fluttered, a familiar heat gathering inside her as he deftly worked his way up, tonguing the spot beneath her ear.

All thought eddied away. She forgot all about the prince and the king and the small matter of her own destiny. Her breath grew harsh and fast as he dragged his mouth down the column of her neck, lightly nipping, then laving with languid strokes of his tongue. He was teasing her, and she was melting for him, desperate for his hands on her body. Just a couple of minutes to feel—*just feel*—and not think. And, oh, she *felt.* So much that she found herself unravelling, her own hunger taking over as she reached for the buttons on his shirt.

Not here.

She gripped his waistcoat. "Let's go back to the Paramour. Now."

"Spitfire." His eyes darkening, he pulled back to look at her. "I am dangerously close to using Shade to clear this whole place out."

She nipped at her smile. "Less murder, more kissing."

"What about the prince?"

"Later," she said. There was no telling when Andreas would be back, and now that that they were acquainted, she had time for this. Time for Ransom.

They abandoned the alcove. Sera grabbed Val on the dance floor, telling her she was heading back to the inn. Let the others follow at their leisure, though it seemed they were sinking into the spirit of Marvale just as keenly as she was.

Tomorrow, they could be rebels.

Tonight, they could be free.

The journey back to the Paramour was really more of a feverish sprint, both of them barely able to keep her hands off each other as they raced through the winding streets.

Time skipped and swirled and then they were alone, holed up in Ransom's bedroom at the Paramour Inn. Moonlight slipped through the drapes and fractured across the walls as Sera crossed to the window. She was suddenly nervous, her heart so full, she could feel it in her throat. There was a sense of destiny about this night. She couldn't help feeling like they were teetering on the precipice of something new and vital, that their time at Marvale was going to change everything.

Parting the drapes, she watched the red mills turning high on the hills, those red lights casting a crimson glow across the town. She could hear the music all the way from here. It sounded like freedom.

Treading softly, Ransom came to stand behind her. "Everything dances here." He pressed a kiss to the back of her neck. "Even the moonlight."

Smiling, she turned her face up to his. "Feels like a good omen."

His hands skimmed her bare shoulders, each feather-light stroke firing every nerve ending in her skin. A familiar warmth rippled down her spine, her magic unfurling in her chest like a preening cat. It was enamored with Ransom.

She was enamored.

"Thank you for standing down tonight," she murmured. "For trusting me. For waiting for me."

He canted his head to look at her. "I'll always wait for you, Seraphine."

She blinked up at him, the words tripping out before she could stop them. "I thought that once before."

His brows knitted. "Things are different now."

"Are they?" she said, her hope a whisper between them.

"Now I know what it's like to go without you." The world dimmed to the honeyed light of his eyes, and the way his thick dark lashes cast shadows on his cheeks. "There is no Order, no allegiance, no amount of power that's worth that." He lifted a strand of hair from her face and tucked it behind her ear, trailing his finger along her jaw. Voice hoarse, he said, "I am not a good man, Seraphine, but I can be good to you."

She felt the truth in every word. Fingering the skull ring on his left hand, she said, "What will you be, if not a Dagger?"

His smile was slow and secretive, a flicker of white in the moonlight. "Bastian, I suppose."

Yes, her heart screamed. She loved the way he said his own name, as if he was reclaiming it. It felt like a new promise between them.

"You might miss it, you know," she teased, letting him turn her from the window. "Being my enemy."

He rested on the sill, pulling her into him. "I was never really your enemy, though, was I?"

She tugged on that silver chain. "I can distinctly remember a time when you *definitely* tried to kill me. Back when I was a thief."

"Then you stole the heart right out of my chest."

Shameless flirt. "Maybe *you* are the real Silver-tongue of Marvale."

His brow furrowed. "Enough about the prince. I'm only interested in one saint tonight."

"Please don't ever call me that," she chided.

"Do you prefer 'spitfire'?"

Laughing now, she nodded. "I think I do."

Outside the Paramour, the night mist thickened, blowing in from the west in lofty silver ribbons. It felt like a curtain was falling over them, hiding them away from the rest of the world. He moved his forefinger beneath her chin, tipping her mouth to his. She kissed him once, soft and slow. Then again, her lips parting to welcome his tongue. He groaned at the first brush, like a dying man slaked of thirst.

She arched toward him, and he deepened their kiss, the hungry press of his mouth dizzying her thoughts. He pulled her closer, and she crawled onto his lap. Pressing her hands against the window behind him, she claimed his mouth, wrenching another deep moan from him. No sweeter music.

He grew hard beneath her, the press of his desire sending heat spiraling through her core. When he gasped against her lips, she stilled, snapping her eyes open. In the reflection of his heavy-lidded gaze, she saw herself shining.

Smiling, he pressed his lips against her jaw. "You're glowing, Seraphine."

And he was not afraid.

Nor was she. She was something else entirely—a lit flame, burning under his touch. Ripping off his waistcoat, she parted the buttons on his shirt, revealing the scarred planes of his broad, muscled chest. Every last inch marred with shadow-marks. A reminder of what he was. Dagger. Killer. Lover.

Mine.

The word throbbed like a second heartbeat.

Her hands moved, spanning the black whorls. All this irrefutable evidence of a killer, a blemished soul. She lowered her mouth to them, kissing the one on his left shoulder. He clutched her head, muttering unintelligibly as she used her tongue.

With his free hand, he deftly worked through the laces of her corset, tugging it free. It fell away, leaving them skin to skin.

Pressing his forehead against hers, he looked down. The marks on his chest were so dark against the soft glow of her own. She traced the darkest of them, following it down to the scar above his liver. The one she had given him.

With feather-light touches, she traced that too.

His voice was a throaty whisper now. "That one's my favorite."

How far they had come already. How far they would go.

"Bastian," she whispered, as her hand inched lower. *"Bed."*

Springing up at her command, he lifted her from the windowsill and carried her to the bed. There, he took her mouth again. The world faded, leaving them alone in the hazy glow of her magic. She sighed, letting it flow through her.

Their kiss grew frenzied, as though time itself was running out. Like there would never be enough of it. Greedy for friction, she ground herself against him. His hands found the swell of her breasts and he thumbed her in lazy decadent circles. Light erupted from her, the pureness of her pleasure burning away all inhibitions.

"Saints." He dipped his chin, replacing his deft fingers with his tongue.

She stifled a cry, her gaze rolling back to the ceiling. He murmured against her skin, his kisses punctuated by throaty gasps as she ground against him, chasing the swell of her pleasure.

"*Yes*, spitfire," he groaned, guiding her hips. "Just like that."

It wasn't enough. How could it ever be enough?

She was a flame, and he was burning for her. Begging for

more. She pressed herself against him. "Bastian, I need *more.*"

Her skirt hit the floor, like a pile of discarded rose petals, his trousers following in quick order. Then their underthings until there was only a slip of moonlight between them, and the glow of her magic and the dark shadow of his marks. He maneuvered her until she was beneath him, the silver light making a silver crown around his head. With his jaw clenched and his lids heavy, he looked like a dark god drinking her in.

"Saint or spitfire, let me worship you, Seraphine."

With pleasure.

This time, when he kissed her, his fingers slipped between them, offering instant, unspeakable pleasure. Crying out, she arched her hips, and he grinned as he found her ready for him. His lids were low, her breath catching at the perfect pressure of his fingers, each masterful stroke making her heart gallop.

She shifted under him, until she could feel him, too. They couldn't go all the way, not without a tincture of herbs for protection, but they could have this pleasure—their hands moving feverishly against each other, their moans growing deep and frantic.

She quickened her pace, edging toward her own release.

His breath shallowed, chasing hers.

Words failed her. She couldn't think beyond the thrum of his fingers, the wet heat of his mouth moving on her. "Ransom, I'm going to . . ."

"Look at me." He drew back, resting his forehead against hers. "I want to see you."

She held his gaze, the pleasure climbing until it felt like a wave breaking under her skin. A cry built in her throat. His own breath stuttered, turning to a low animalistic moan.

"Seraphine." He cried her name like a prayer, his back bowing as they both crested the wave together.

Magic erupted from Sera's chest, flooding the bedchamber like molten sunlight. The walls turned gold, a blanket of fresh heat falling over them. And with it—a perfect punishing bliss.

Eons passed, the world slowly coming back together. He kissed her shoulder, murmuring soft words of adoration, before reluctantly drawing back and ducking into the adjacent bathroom.

Sera lay in a puddle of moonlight, her body and mind thoroughly sated. And yet, that heat inside her refused to recede. Somehow, it felt like her magic wanted more.

Maker, keened that ancient rippling voice.

Now is the time.

Frowning, she sat up. *Behave.* She tugged the bedsheet around her, dampening the eerie glow of her skin while she waited for Ransom to return. She could hear him humming to himself in the bathroom. Spotting a notebook and pen on the bedside table, she had the sudden urge to write him a note. Something funny and sweet, and absent of their usual overt hostility.

She reached for the journal, meaning only to tear a page out but it fell open on the centerfold, revealing a spread of tortured drawings.

It was a corral of terrifying beasts inked in black. There were wolves with scythe-like fangs and blood-soaked curling claws.

Snakes with jackal heads and winged monsters plucked of all their feathers. Sera couldn't tear her gaze away. Turning page after page, she stared in silent horror at Ransom's innermost nightmares, the wretched things that haunted him whenever he closed his eyes. The monsters that snapped at his heels. Was this the work of his Shade-ravaged mind, or an artist's imagination that had been honed in the catacombs of Fantome? Fed on terror and bloodshed, and given no freedom to thrive?

"Enjoying the hidden reaches of my mangled soul, Seraphine?"

A whole new wave of horror gripped her as she snapped her head up. There was no greater embarrassment than to be caught snooping, but to look upon something so personal . . . so *haunting* . . . it was an unforgivable intrusion.

Ransom stood over her. His chest and feet were bare, and he was dressed in loose trousers. His hair was dripping wet, water beads sliding down his cheeks and pooling in the hollow of his collarbones.

She slammed the journal shut. "I'm sorry. I was looking for a piece of paper. I wanted to write you a note."

His brows lifted, the tension seeping from his jaw. "Of what sort?"

All thought left her. "Um, the nice sort?"

"I find that hard to believe." A corner of his mouth ticked up. He was teasing her, not angry but perhaps embarrassed. As she stared up at him, like a deer caught on the hunt, she noticed the smooth expanse of his olive chest, and a new realization struck.

The words came on a gasp. "Your shadow-marks. They're gone."

He was smiling now. Of course he had noticed already. Even her shameless snooping couldn't banish the relief on his face, the fact that her magic had healed him.

And still it purred in her chest.

What more could you possibly want?

Maker, it crooned.

She shook it off, a new thought belatedly occurring to her. "Did I hurt you?"

He shook his head. "How could you hurt me, Seraphine? You are my antidote."

Flopping backward, she grinned up at him. For the first time in months, she didn't resent her magic. She was grateful for it, wonderstruck by its restorative power. Maybe it was Marvale, or her meeting with another saint, or her growing feelings for Ransom, but she was starting to feel excited about her power. Hopeful about what else it could do.

Ransom set his journal back on the nightstand. "And these . . . my nightmares . . . they didn't frighten you?"

"Of course not," she said, quickly. "I'm just sorry you have to see those monsters whenever you fall asleep."

"It helps to draw them. Gets them out of my head." His smile was rueful. "Makes room for more, I suppose."

"Maybe that will change now," she said, softly.

"Maybe."

He lay down beside her, and she turned into him, thinking of her life far beyond this night.

He gazed down at her. "A kingdom for your thoughts."

They had been here once before. Now they were here again.

"Run away with me, Bastian." The imploring look on her face said the rest, the enormity of the plea too heavy to voice. *Leave your old life behind—the skulls and the catacombs, the marks and the guilt, and the pain of the past. Run away with me, and be the man you were always meant to be.*

His reply came at once. "I'm already running, spitfire. Tell me where to go."

Giddiness suffused her, a laugh pealing through her chest.

He tugged her against him, enfolding her in the warmth of his strong arms. "Marvale. Halbracht. The frozen tundra of Borea. Just name the destination."

"You'll have to win Pippin over."

"I'll bring treats." She heard the smile in his voice. "Whatever it takes. Wherever you choose."

"You," she whispered, as her lids drooped. "Wherever you are, is where I want to be."

"Then we'll work out the rest." She heard the smile in his voice as she dropped off. "So long as we're together."

Chapter 27

Ransom

Ransom couldn't remember the last time he'd watched someone sleep. Not since he was a boy, standing guard over his younger sister, Anouk, on the nights his father came home steaming drunk, smashing up everything—and everyone—in sight. As a Dagger, he always slept alone. Deep and fitfully, his head full of monsters, as if some primal part of him was still rebelling against what he had become.

In the waning moonlight, he watched over Seraphine. Years had passed since he'd felt contentment like this. Like everything he cared for was still within his grasp. Like, maybe, just maybe, it wasn't too late to have it. As he slipped off the skull ring he had inherited from Dufort and placed it on his nightstand, along with his book of nightmares, he wasn't thinking about before, or what was yet to come, only the warmth of Seraphine's body curled inside his, and the slow thud of his own settled heartbeat. It lulled him to sleep—this creeping sense of possibility—and when the darkness found him, for the first time in forever, he didn't dream at all.

He woke to the sound of weeping. Dawn was sweeping across the sky, misting the clouds pink. Seraphine was sleeping on her back beside him, an arm slung over her eyes to block out the encroaching light. Following the unsettling sound, Ransom slipped out of bed and went to the window. There was a woman crying on the street below. Barefooted and bent double on the curb, she held her head in her hands like she was afraid it might shatter. Further on, by the shoemaker's, a man in a top hat was slumped on his side, the street around him painted with vomit.

In the dawning light, the cobbles were stained and strewn with fallen rose petals. The garlands above were withering. The music had stopped sometime in the night, replaced now by the distant cawing of a crow.

Up on the hills, the red mills were still turning, but all the laughter had died away.

Gone was the night magic of Marvale.

Here was its true face. The starkness of it made Ransom's stomach churn.

You're being paranoid, he told himself. *Looking for cracks already.*

Can't you ever just be happy?

He crossed to the bathroom to examine himself in the mirror. The planes of his chest were still smooth. His arms and hands, too, the whorls there washed away in the tide of their pleasure. Much of the heaviness inside him had lifted, so why, then, did he feel so on edge?

Seraphine had scoured his soul clean, taken the deepest pain from his body and scattered it to the wind. She'd reached beyond the Dagger to find the man beneath it. His spitfire. Flame or saint, he didn't give a rat's ass. He'd spent his entire adolescence worshipping at the altar of Saint Calvin. Now he had someone else—someone true—to love. To protect.

It was that vital, keening instinct, and not the creeping mist of his own pessimism that sent him back to the window. The hairs on the back of his neck rose when he saw the streets were empty now, the people there wiped away as if he had imagined them.

The vomit remained.

Something wasn't right.

Leaving Seraphine to sleep, Ransom got dressed and slipped out of his bedroom. He went first to Nadia's room and then to Caruso's, but there was no sign of either of them. That grumble of suspicion quickly rising to a roar, he took the stairs two at a time.

Down in the lounge, he came across Caruso. Still dressed in last night's outfit, he was wide awake and sitting on one of the couches. Val was curled up against him in her gown, her head resting on his shoulder. She was snoring.

Ransom frowned. "Well, this is odd."

"Keep your voice down." Caruso was stiff as a statue, either from the sheer discomfort of actual human touch, or in an attempt not to disturb her slumber.

"What's going on here?"

"Too much drinking and dancing. Val took a rest against the stairs when we got in. Insisted she had to sit down first."

"When was that?"

Caruso rubbed his forehead. "Hours ago."

"Did you speak to the prince?"

"I found myself in better company." His eyes flicked to Val. "Nadia did. She made a point of it, actually."

Unease churned in Ransom's gut. "Has she come back yet?"

"Isn't she in her room?"

"No, Caruso. She's not in her room."

"Well, don't look so narky about it. You fucked off long before I did. And I had my hands full with this one."

Ransom looked at Val. "She's drooling, by the way."

"It happens."

"All hell," he muttered. "You *like* her."

He spluttered a laugh, a familiar sneer curling his upper lip. "I don't like anyone."

There wasn't time to needle Caruso about it. Ransom's thoughts were on Nadia now, his feet already leading him out onto the dawn-lit street. More revelers appeared as he headed north, bodies drifting aimlessly through the town as if they'd forgotten where they lived. Their eyes were glassy and, despite the rising sun, they were shivering.

The closer Ransom drew to the red mills, the more disquieted he felt. He had seen enough hangovers—hell, he had endured enough himself—to know that whatever this strangeness was stretched far beyond alcohol and tainted smoke. It reminded him of the comedown after a Shade-heavy night, the creeping panic that twisted magic so often left behind long after it had run you through.

As quickly as they were swept off the streets by plain-clothed mercenaries, more appeared, with bare, bleeding feet, wandering around like lost children. When Ransom tried to speak to one—a man not much older than him—his words came out garbled, his eyes unfocused.

Ransom broke into a run, the mills soon rising to meet him. They were shabby in the morning light, the wooden blades cracked down the middle, their red paint chipping away. The smell of stale alcohol mixed with fresh vomit was even worse up here. Ransom held his breath as he ducked inside the Rose Garden, scanning the dim, airless interior. There were bodies on all the couches, revelers groaning as they tried to sleep off whatever strange magic was still coursing through them.

Raised voices filled the cavernous hall, echoing back at him. Keeping to the shadowed alcoves, Ransom crept closer, eyeing two figures standing by the stage. Despite the low lighting and distance between them, he could tell one was the prince by his golden mane of hair and the outfit he had been wearing the night before.

Still pristine.

The blond woman beside him bore a passing resemblance to him. Ransom recognized her as the same one who had briefly sat with Andreas and Seraphine last night.

". . . to come to us. Or you'll scare her off," Andreas was ranting.

“To where?” She threw up her hands. “I’m tired of waiting, Andreas. I’m getting bored.”

“So dance, Talisa.” The prince’s voice was hard and low, the words more a threat than an invitation.

The woman whimpered. “Andreas, *please*. I don’t want—”

“I said, dance,” he hissed, his eyes flaring gold. “Dance and be merry, and stop breathing down my fucking neck.”

To Ransom’s horror, the girl began to twirl. And twirl and twirl and twirl. She slipped, losing a shoe, then crashed into a glass table. Picking herself up, she twirled again. Her dress had ripped and her leg was bleeding, and still she danced. Crying out, she begged him to let her stop.

The prince swished his hand about, waving her off. “Dance away from me. Until your feet give out and you remember which of us is in charge here.”

Wailing now, she moved like an unsteady spinning top, staggering toward the doors. She passed Ransom, but her eyes were glazed, looking right through him. And then she was gone, crying and twirling into the harsh dawn light.

Now the prince stood alone on the dance floor.

Without turning in his direction, he called out, “I don’t care that you saw that, Dagger.”

So much for pleasantries. Ransom had already downed his vial of Shade anyway. He stepped out of the darkness, dragging the shadows with him.

“What the hell did you just do to her?”

“I asked her to dance,” said the prince, flatly. “Would you prefer I backhanded her? I’m really not the violent sort. Despite what my uncle told you when he placed that bounty on my head." He tapped his chin, amending his answer. "Or rather, I don't like to *do the violent part* myself. Such is the purpose of rebels and mercenaries." He gestured casually to the shadows pooling around Ransom. "I suppose we are unalike in that way."

"We're unalike in every way, Andreas." Glancing around, Ransom counted at least forty bodies, struggling to come to. There must be hundreds more strewn across Marvale, like wind-up toys that had sputtered out. "They're in your thrall. All of them. Last night was a farce. None of it was real."

"It was real enough for sweet Seraphine."

Ransom's fists curled.

"Unlike you, Dagger, she understands my grand vision."

Ransom might have laughed if he wasn't so close to throttling the smarmy bastard. Shaking his head, he said, "She would never want this."

An irritating shrug. "I suppose we'll see."

Not after I fucking kill you.

"Where's Nadia?"

"Sleeping somewhere around here, I suppose." He couldn't have cared less. "We had a long talk. After a little persuasion, your friend sang like a canary."

Ransom spotted her just then out of the corner of his eye. She was slumped in an armchair by the dance floor, her chest rising and falling. The tightened strands of her ponytail had come undone, and her brow was furrowed. She was twitching in her sleep.

"She looks like she's in pain."

"They get used to it. The worm will work itself out soon enough." Arrogance oozing from his voice, the prince didn't even glance in Nadia's direction. Ransom wondered if he even remembered which one she was. "It can be exhausting having to think for yourself all the time."

A sense of urgency gripped Ransom. Andreas had to die. And fast. But the prince was smarter than he first appeared, and armed with the kind of magic that could bring a village to its knees. And, in time, maybe even a kingdom.

"I owe your Second a great debt. And I intend to pay it soon enough. In telling me all about my final missing saint, Sister Marianne, she's saved me weeks of legwork."

Well, fuck.

Ransom had completely forgotten about the acolyte.

"All this time, I was wondering what was taking her so long to get here." Laughing now, Andreas threw up his hands, like they had just stumbled upon a funny blunder together. "How could my Marianne make her way to Marvale when she's trapped on that godforsaken island with a bunch of simpering acolytes?" His face changed in an instant, disgust twisting his features. "Imagine dedicating your entire life to praying to the meekest, least interesting of our dead saints. *Starving* for Saint Alisa! *Kneeling* at the altar of her memory! And when another one *finally* comes along after a thousand years of yearning and waiting and simpering, crowned in your *very priory*, instead of celebrating her, you lock her up and go crying to your king!" He spat on the floor. "Hypocrisy at its worst. The very core of this kingdom is rotten."

"Are you done talking?" Ransom flexed his fingers, sending his shadows skittering across the floor.

"Not remotely." Andreas walked right through them, grinning as they dissolved.

Fine, then. He could bleed the old-fashioned way. Cloaking the action, Ransom withdrew the knife in his waistband.

The prince was ten feet away now. Then eight. Six. Four.

Ransom was just about to lunge when he said, "Drop that knife."

His eyes flared bright gold.

For a fleeting moment, Ransom felt like he was staring straight into the sun.

His thoughts scattered.

The knife clattered to the floor.

He bent down to grab it.

"Leave it. You are not going to harm me."

Ransom froze in a crouch.

The prince stood over him, those shining eyes commanding every morsel of his attention. "I'll have your loyalty, even if I have to wrest it from your Shade-mottled mind, Dagger."

Snared in that all-consuming magic, Ransom could only stare up at him dumbly. He felt its power move through him, like a worm wriggling through his mind.

"In time, I'll have the rest of your Order, too," Andreas went on. "You see, I have plans for the Daggers, Ransom Hale. A rather unique army of soldiers, don't you think? And my dull-witted uncle only ever thought to use you one at a time. To scatter you like marbles across Valterre, hoping to catch me. It's almost insulting."

Ransom's legs began to ache. Reminding himself to stand, he rolled to his feet. "What are you doing to me?"

"I'm commanding you, like the dutiful soldier you are." Andreas smiled, the brightness of his teeth echoing the spell-binding sheen in his eyes. There was something maddening about that stare. It disturbed the deep waters of Ransom's soul, made them roil and thrash inside him.

Run, screamed a voice inside him. *Run and don't look back.*

"It hurts less when you don't fight it," Andreas remarked, with a casualness that belied his complete annihilation of Ransom's willpower. "You can remind your friend of that when she finally comes to."

It took every ounce of Ransom's attention to eke out his next words. "Fuck you."

The answering pain in his skull was worth it.

"I made a grave error in overlooking you last night." Tucking his arms behind his back, the prince circled him. A lion assessing its prey. The fine embroidery of his shirt glinted in the dim lighting, drawing Ransom's gaze to the roses emblazoned on his shirt sleeves. "If I go straight for the rose, I'll prick my eager fingers on the thorns."

He stopped in front of him, tilting his chin to account for their difference in height. "Seraphine is my rose. But you, Dagger, are the thorn that will keep me from plucking her for my court. From using her, as Saint Oriel intended."

Murderous thoughts filled Ransom, his vision narrowing to a keen red mist. His fists hardened, a dangerous heat gathering in his chest.

You are not going to harm me.

That thought alone stayed his hands, his head throbbing as he strained against it.

"You are the one who guards her."

Yes.

"Covets her."

Yes.

"You think of her as yours." His smile was indulgent. "Which means you are going to be a problem for me."

Ignoring the horrible pain in his skull, Ransom said through his teeth. "Bet on it."

"I'm afraid you have to go." The prince combed his hair back, skewering him with that blinding gaze. That cloying power suffused Ransom, like vines crawling over his mind. "But it just so happens, I need a very urgent favor from you, Dagger."

With mounting horror, Ransom found himself nodding. His thoughts were becoming a fog, the logical voice inside him quickly fading. "You are going to take your fellow Daggers away from Marvale and travel at once to the Isle of Alisa. You will find my missing saint and kill her, just as the king commanded."

Dimly, Ransom was alarmed by the stiffening of his spine, his shoulders rolling back like a soldier standing to attention. He pushed his next words out. "You're going to kill another saint?"

Andreas shrugged, the cost of betrayal hardly weighing on him. "More will arise in due course," he said, vaguely. "I prefer to work with known quantities. Preferably ones that don't murder their own."

"But Oriel—"

"Oriel is dead. Her will has no power over me."

Ransom opened his mouth to argue, the effort of pushing through that fog turning his tongue to lead in his mouth. The prince stepped closer, the magic in his eyes casting a golden sheen across his skin. Blanching the rest of Ransom's free thought.

"Find the acolyte. Kill her. Bury her body. And return at once to the catacombs of Fantome. I will find you there when the time is right."

Ransom felt himself nod.

"You will tell no one else about this conversation. You will simply disappear from here, as though you had never come to Marvale at all."

Seraphine, called that distant voice inside him. *You have to warn Seraphine.*

But the cry soon faded, lost to the dazzling brightness of the prince's magic as he leaned close—much too close—and said through those pearly white teeth. "Now *go.*"

So Ransom did.

Chapter 28

Seraphine

The storm was here again, howling like a beast. Lightning shattered the blackness, illuminating a sky full of heaving purple clouds. They pressed in from all sides, the white stone floor shaking under her slippers. Looking down at herself, she saw the pale blue of her prayer robe had been drenched to navy, the wool clinging to her sopping skin. Vaguely, Sera knew this was not her body, but the dream was as real to her as a memory.

And she was trapped inside it.

A bolt struck, much too close. In the spiral of flashing light, she saw she was standing at the top of a tall white tower.

Prayer tower, some distant part of her whispered.

But the storm was so fierce, and the stones were trembling under her feet. She didn't want to be here tonight, by herself, and so far from her sisters in the priory.

But tonight is my vigil. I must give thanks to Saint Alisa.

Thunder roared, and she fell to her knees, her shaking hands coming together in prayer.

Saints, she was so very frightened.

Why had Mother Madeline made her come up here tonight?

Couldn't their prayers wait for the sky to settle?

Wouldn't the sick of Valterre last until dawn?

It was madness climbing the tower when the sky was in such a state. And she was madder for doing it. Where was her backbone, that crucial sense of survival that had gotten her this far?

Run, you fool.

Run, before the storm takes a bite out of you!

Her inner voice grew as loud as the wind, urging her to return to the winding steps that would lead her back to earth. To safety. It was late now, and the others would be asleep. She could slip in through the back door and hide under her bed, like she used when she was a child. Honoria was such a heavy sleeper, she wouldn't even notice.

A fine mist gathered around her. The lightning was so close now, it raised the hairs on her arm. Fear won out. To hell with Saint Alisa, and the enduring sorrows of the sick. They only ever prayed for the rich ones anyway. She turned to run, tripping on the first of the five hundred stone steps. The world spun, the clouds so close, they dizzied her.

Don't look down.

Don't look up.

Ten steps, and then ten more.

Quickly, now.

The storm is at your back.

The next strike turned the world silver. She stumbled again, her knees meeting hard marble. Scrabbling to her feet, she reached blindly for the railing. She was screaming now, cursing madly, but she didn't care. She had far bigger worries than the hard rap of Mother Madeline's cane.

There came a dull ringing in her ears, and beyond it—utter silence. The sky raged but she could no longer hear it. Then a ragged pain in her back, like a hot poker skewering her spine. She couldn't feel her feet. She looked down, just in time to see the tower cleave, the steps falling away beneath her.

She fell too. So storm-struck she couldn't hear her own scream, not the heavy thud of her body landing on the sodden earth, or the hail of white stone as it buried her.

When death came, she reached for it with both hands.

I am tired, Saint Calvin.

Take me home.

Sera woke with a gasp. Sunlight poured over her, scorching away the nightmare she had just endured. All but the fear still pounding in her heart.

Not her fear.

Not her memory.

But she thought she knew that ivory tower, and where it stood: Ra'azule, home of the Priory of Saint Alisa, and the saint called Marianne who had been imprisoned there.

Strange that she would dream of her now. Last night's

meeting with Andreas must have unlocked her connection to another saint. The fog of destiny was slowly clearing but Sera still couldn't see her way through.

Or perhaps it had been Ransom who had unlocked her magic last night, deftly coaxing it out with a lover's touch. Maybe that was the secret to understanding it. Not fear but tenderness. Patience.

Last night came flooding back all at once. Sitting up, Sera looked for Ransom. Morning light cascaded through the open drapes, sparking off the skull ring on his bedside table. Dufort's ring.

Ransom had taken it off.

Was it intended to be a sign of his commitment to her? A gift of freedom to himself? He would tell her soon enough.

Smiling now, Sera grabbed her clothes from last night and got dressed in a hurry. She doubled back to pocket the ring. They could throw it in the river on their way to find Andreas again. There was still so much to learn, and to plan.

There was no sign of Ransom in the hallway, no echo of his footsteps in the stairwell. Where the hell was he?

When she returned to the suite she shared with Val and Theo, Val was fast asleep in their bed. Theo was standing by the window. A silvered brow arched as he looked her up and down, silently noting her badly laced corset and crumpled red skirt. Mercifully, he kept his mouth shut. Likely too tired to tease her. She could tell by his ruffled hair and puffy eyes that he hadn't been awake long.

"What time is it?" she thought to ask.

"An hour or so after dawn." Concern flitted across his face. "Are you all right?"

"I'm fine," she said, glancing at herself in the nearby mirror. Sure, she was a bit rumpled. She needed to wash and change but she hardly looked like roadkill. "Last night went well. The prince seems reasonable. A better man than the king." Not that the bar was high. "He's agreed to help us rescue Bibi. And help me with my magic, too."

Theo's frown deepened. "Good. But I was talking about Ransom."

"What about him?"

"He's gone, Sera."

She blinked, sure she had misheard him. "What are you talking about?"

"The Daggers left not long after dawn broke. I was asleep when Caruso showed up at our door, carrying Val, like a snoring sack of potatoes. Said the Daggers were leaving, and we were on our own now." At Sera's look of alarm, he turned back to the window, pointing to the empty street as though that was supposed to mean something to her. "They took the carriage and fled. I watched them go."

She joined him by the sill, a horrible tremor rattling through her chest. Clearly, Theo was mistaken. "Why didn't you come and get me?"

"I figured you two had a fight," he said, shrugging. "And that you had finally seen some sense. He wasn't exactly an ideal ally."

"No." She was shaking her head now, trying to shrug off the heaviness that was crawling into her heart, her bones. "We didn't fight. We just fell asleep. It was good. We were good." She started to pace, vaguely aware of the hysteria bubbling inside her. It was a mistake. This was a mistake. "He'll come back. There's obviously some kind of reasonable explanation."

Theo watched her go from one end of the room to the other and back again. Ever so gently, he said, "There is an explanation, Sera. This is what Ransom Hale does."

She stopped pacing to glare at him.

"He makes promises to you. And then he breaks them."

She resisted the urge to fling a cushion at him, to wipe that god-awful look of pity off his face. "This time is different."

He canted his head. "Is it?"

"Don't look at me like that," she snapped. "Like I'm some kind of maddened fool."

He huffed a sigh. "That's what love does, Sera. It makes fools of us."

She flung the cushion.

He took the hit.

"You're wrong. And I'll prove it to you." Throwing one last withering look over her shoulder, she grabbed a change of clothes, stomped into the bathroom, and slammed the door.

When Sera emerged from the bathroom Val was awake. Theo was perched on the bed beside her, speaking in hushed tones. Prickling at their sheepish looks, Sera went to shrug on her boots.

"I'm going out to find Ransom." Theo opened his mouth to respond but she went on quickly, "I know what you think you saw, but there's an explanation for it."

"Hey, I get it," said Val, blowing a curl from her eye. "Caruso ditched me too, *and* he owes me three whiskeys and a pack of cigarillos."

"I was *not* ditched." Sera grabbed the gaudy skull ring and held it up. "Ransom made a choice last night. And he chose me. Us. This. He was going to give Andreas a chance."

Val and Theo exchanged a loaded look.

"Ugh. Forget it." Sera pocketed the ring and stormed off.

Outside, the streets of Marvale were eerily quiet. Crows perched along the roofs, watching as she went to check on their horse and carriage.

They were gone.

Doubt crept in.

She shoved it down, walking to the bend in the road and then down the main street, where the wind grew cold and biting and the sound of weeping wafted from the dark alleys. There was something unpleasant about Marvale in the harsh morning light, a sense that the fanciful mirage of yesterday had faded, and what remained now were bouquets of rotting rose petals, the acrid scent of vomit and a lingering sense of regret. The few people she spotted looked strangely desolate, their glassy eyes filled with a kind of sadness that made her own heart ache.

Or maybe that was a result of another dawning reality . . . Ransom Hale was no longer in Marvale. And neither were his Daggers. A fact confirmed by the innkeeper at the Paramour who said they had all paid up in full before leaving an hour ago.

Why, then, had Ransom left his things behind? Dufort's ring, his journal, his satchel . . . Was he really in such a hurry to get away? Or was he afraid of saying goodbye to her again? Having to admit that he had sold her a false promise before yanking it out from under her feet.

It belatedly occurred to Sera that he might have gone to find Andreas. To meet the prince—and judge him—for himself. The thought sent her back out onto the street. With renewed hope, she headed in the direction of the red mills.

She had barely made it halfway there when a carriage trundled down the street, pulling to a stop beside her.

Andreas ducked his head out of the window.

His eyes lit up when he saw her, the sunlight bouncing off his hair. Unlike Marvale, the prince held up well in the morning. He seemed to shine, even as the village around him dimmed.

"Where are you off to?" he asked, with the casual nature of a friend.

Sera hesitated a beat. "I'm looking for Ransom."

And clearly wasting my time.

"Ah, your Dagger."

"I don't suppose he's made an attempt on your life in the last hour?" She was only half joking.

Andreas's chuckle warmed the air between them. "If he did, he was entirely unsuccessful."

Sera summoned a wan smile. It was a foolish thought in the first place. The simplest explanation was probably the truest. Ransom and the others really were gone. She blew out a breath, feeling like a colossal fool.

The prince's eyes darted, no doubt reading the shadows on

her face. "Do you want to go for a ride? There's much to talk about."

It was certainly a better offer than wandering around Marvale like a lost fool, searching for a man who clearly didn't want to be found. And anyway, wasn't that why she had come here in the first place? Her questions about Ransom Hale would keep. Her magic had waited long enough.

"All right," she said.

He popped open the door, and she clambered in, settling herself across from him. "It's not for everyone, you know," he told her. "These grand matters of magic and destiny. When your own people are threatened by your power, they either fight you for it or they leave you."

Her brows lifted. He was talking about Ransom, too easily sensing the hurt behind her smile, the bruise blooming on her heart.

"Just look at how my own family abandoned me. My own uncle wants my head on a pike."

"Do you blame him?" she asked without judgment. "Your rebels are ransacking Fantome, burning effigies of the king across Valterre."

"Perhaps my situation is a little more complex." He gave a mirthless chuckle. "In any case, it is the king's grand folly thinking a handful of Daggers could ever put a stop to a thousand-year-old prophecy and the saint who means to see it through."

Outside, the streets flew by. Gathering speed now, they passed the inn and continued east. Vaguely, Sera wondered where they were going, but she was too invested in the vital direction of their conversation to ask.

"My uncle and I never did see eye to eye," Andreas went on. "Not that it was a problem before I was remade. Now the power balance has shifted. It frightens him that I have a different vision for this kingdom and the means do something about it."

"What kind of vision is that?" she asked carefully.

"One without a king." There was no apology in the prince's words, rather, a sense of impending inevitability. "One where soldiers don't swarm the country like insects, threatening and harming whoever they like without fear of the consequences. One where our prisons don't heave with innocent folk. A place that allows no room for monsters, nor the man-made shadow magic of thieves and assassins." Curling his lip, he looked out of the window, his voice taking on a hard edge. "My uncle rules with fear. His iron fist holding tight to the noose above our kingdom. Without the might of his sword and his royal coffers, he would be nothing. No one."

Wasn't that what all powerful men were, though? Money and brute force? Wasn't that a kind of power of its own? She kept these thoughts to herself.

Andreas's voice swelled until it echoed from every corner of the carriage. "I will chase the terror from our kingdom. Destroy the Age of Darkness that has haunted our capital for centuries, keeping the people there kneeling under a shadowed boot, living every day in fear for their lives, for their children's lives. Their fear has been sown deep, but we are entering the Second Age of Saints."

A certain wildness gathered in his gaze, a kind of mania that made her nervous and excited in equal measure. "The future will be beautiful, filled with dancing and music and laughter and *freedom*." That word stirred the pool of her magic. "We will remake the kingdom as a place absent of pain and greed and corruption."

Sera thought again of Fontaine's tarot rose. Of new beginnings. A new kind of kingdom. A land without darkness, stripped of Shade and needless suffering, of assassins and thieves. How desperately she wanted to be part of that world. In Lightfire, she had discovered the magical antidote to Shade, had brewed and bottled it all winter long, but would that be enough for the prince's grand vision? Was there more she could do? Was there more she was *supposed* to do?

"I want to help," she said, and she meant it, truly, with every thud of her eager, pounding heart. "But I don't know how. I don't even know what kind of saint I am."

The carriage came to a sudden stop. Teeth gleaming in the dimness, Andreas leaned forward in his seat, and whispered, like he was confiding in her a grand and life-altering secret, "That's because you are no saint, Seraphine. *You* are my rose."

That word again, the tarot flashing in her mind. But still, she didn't understand, not the gravitas in his voice nor the hunger in his eyes. "Your rose?" she said weakly.

"We're here." The carriage door swung open, and he hopped out, beckoning for her to follow him. Ruled now by her own insatiable curiosity, Sera had no choice. It wasn't until the door closed behind them that she realized they had returned to the graveyard.

She hesitated at the gate. "I don't exactly have fond memories of this place."

He grinned at her over his shoulder. "That's about to change."

Sera remained where she was, a thread of unease taking hold of her. "What do you mean when you call me a 'rose'?"

"I mean you are the key to the rebirth of Valterre." He said it so casually, as though he was commenting on the rain clouds moving in from the south. "You are the hand of Saint Oriel, Seraphine. The grand arbiter of the Second Age of Saints."

Such wild words. So utterly unhinged. A laugh spluttered out of her. "You sound mad."

Seeing that she was refusing to follow him, Andreas stopped walking. They stood with a row of tombstones between them, but Sera couldn't take her eyes off his smile. The sureness in it when he told her, "You are not a saint, Seraphine. You are a maker of them."

Sera didn't know when it had happened, but her magic was wide awake now, streaming out from that door inside her. It climbed the notches in her spine and vibrated in her fingertips, like it was reaching for that word: *Maker.*

The one it had been whispering to her all along. In that moment, she couldn't face it, refused to admit it. "What the hell are you talking about?"

The world had fallen strangely quiet. The trees were no longer swaying, the wind dying out to listen in. Even in the sprawl of the graveyard, her own breath echoed back at her.

"Maker," said Andreas, his voice hardening. How did he

know that secret word, the one her magic whispered to her in the dark? "The storm began something *you* must continue. A handful of saints is only the beginning. *You* are the key to creating the rest. *You* are the force that will allow our new kingdom to truly bloom."

"You're wrong." *You're out of your mind.* Sera's throat was bone dry, her magic painting golden rivers under her skin. It was writhing, no, *dancing* to the prince's words as though some ancient, distant part of her was telling her they were true. That she was not one of the saints in Madame Fontaine's cards but the Rose itself—a force greater than the might of the king, of the swords that covered the flower on the kingdom's crest.

But she couldn't square herself to the idea. It was too absurd. "I can't make anything. Or anyone. That's not what I am."

"Why don't we ask our necromancer?"

She saw him then, coming through the trees. Robed in red, and with that eerie golden mask hiding his face. At a nod from the prince, he discarded it like a flying disc.

It landed at her feet.

But Sera's eyes were riveted to that face. Shock stole her voice away, made her knees tremble as she pulled the gate closed, making a paltry barrier between them.

No.

No.

It wasn't possible.

He was here again. The figure that had haunted her dreams for months now. The Dagger she had killed on top of the Aurore.

Lark Delano. *Saints above.* Here he stood in flesh and blood and bone. Only he looked different; his face was unnaturally gaunt, his gait was slow and dipped to one side, and his once pale skin had taken on an eerie gray pallor.

Around his wide green eyes, the sockets were shadowed and deep. When they met hers, they glinted like golden coins.

Saint.

"Hello, Seraphine." He greeted her like an old friend.

Blood roared in Sera's ears. "I don't understand," she whispered, gripping the gate between them. "You're dead. I *killed* you."

His smile grew, his teeth too white against the gray of his skin. "You *made* me."

"Saint-maker," said Andreas, with all the reverence of a prayer. "The might of a sword can make a king, but a rose in full bloom can make a saint. Here is your proof."

No.

No.

"Your body disappeared," said Sera, a touch hysterically. "Someone dug you out of your grave."

Lark said, "I dug myself out."

"That means . . . No." Stumbling backward, she released the gate. Part of her wanted to run, to bolt for the Paramour. But another part of her . . . that ancient, secret part was burning like a bonfire in her soul. Begging her to stay. To look and see. To *listen.*

Her feet won out, backing her onto the narrow street, away

from the graveyard and the carriage and the undead Dagger currently smirking at her. "How is it possible?" she breathed. "How is any of this possible?"

Andreas didn't follow her. That perfect smile gleaming, he simply called after her. "It's a new age, Seraphine. Anything is possible!"

For the second time in two days, Sera turned on her heel and bolted from the graveyard.

Chapter 29

Ransom

There was a worm in Ransom's head. A writhing, niggling thing that nibbled away his thoughts until only one remained.

Find the acolyte.

Kill her.

Bury her body.

Every time his mind strayed to the red mills of Marvale, to the woman he had left sleeping in his bed, and the dangerous, malevolent saint who had charmed himself into her good graces, a searing pain spiderwebbed through his skull. The worm returned.

Find the acolyte.

Kill her.

Bury her body.

They were almost at Ra'azule, and Ransom was sick to his

stomach. Nadia wasn't faring much better. Both of them had spent much of the journey trying to sleep off the terrible rattling in their skulls, the sense that something was amiss, without a sense of what it might be.

Caruso had taken their impromptu getaway in his stride, driving the carriage for much of the day's ride west under the assumption that they were still following the king's orders. Albeit with a sudden, inexplicable urgency.

It was nearing dusk by the time they reached the trading village of Ra'azulet. Ransom was riding out front with Caruso by then, hoping the fresh air would ease the fog in his head. A hush came over them as they crested the western hills and watched the town appear below them. Streetlamps flickered like a sea of golden stars, illuminating a patchwork of tall, narrow houses painted in every color of the rainbow. They formed a crescent around a gray lake that seemed to go on forever. The mist there hung low and thick, like froth skimming the surface.

Somewhere beyond floated the Isle of Alisa. And on it, their target. Ransom's fingers twitched as they drew nearer, the job so close at hand that the worm in his head grew bigger, until he could feel the weight of it pushing out against his skull.

As the sun set, the mist became a dense silver fog. Down on the strand, they commandeered a small rowing boat and pushed it into the water. They sat facing each other, Ransom on one side, and Nadia and Caruso on the other, their knees touching as they moved away from the dock and into the belly of the wide gray lake.

Ignoring the endless water at his back, Ransom kept his

mind on the task and not the yawning hollow in his heart, the sense that he had left something vital behind him. It was starting to hurt this feeling, the pain now spreading from his head to his chest.

"Nervous?" said Caruso, watching him as he rowed.

"No." That wasn't it.

"Is it the whole murdering-a-saint thing that's got you on edge? We can always toss a coin to the Alisans on the way out. Let them pray for our doomed souls." He snorted at his own joke.

Nadia punched him. "Shut up and row."

"Fine." Mumbling, Caruso picked up the pace. "What is up with you two today? You're miserable company."

That's because I am not in control of myself. The thought was gone before Ransom could catch it, gobbled up by the slimy black worm in his head.

Find the acolyte.

Kill her.

Bury her body.

The water whispered as they moved through it. Deep into the fog they went, the lights fading until Ransom could scarcely trace his friends in the moonlit mist. And then lights began to flicker, the Isle of Alisa winking at them.

The island was smaller than Ransom expected, populated by dense thickets of trees and crowned by the priory itself, a somber-looking building hewn from gray stone. Candles guttered in its arched windows.

They docked at a small wooden pier and made for the priory,

this mournful monolith that stood alone in the moonlight. Soon, they found themselves standing before a pair of large wooden doors. On either side, stained-glass windows portrayed Saint Alisa. In the first, she was a young girl, washing the feet of a plague victim. In another, she was old and hunched, holding the hand of a sickly child.

"We should have stayed in Marvale," muttered Caruso. "This place is giving me the creeps."

"Is it weird that I feel closer to hell here than down in the catacombs?" remarked Nadia.

Find the acolyte.

Kill her.

Bury her body.

Ransom swung the door knocker.

Thunk! Thunk! Thunk!

The echo carried across the island.

Caruso slipped a vial of Shade from his pocket.

"Easy," said Nadia, grabbing his wrist.

"What if one of the sisters starts trouble?"

At this, Nadia snorted. "They're acolytes, not Daggers. They don't know the definition of *fun*, let alone danger."

The door creaked open. A tall reed-thin woman with a pale pinched face occupied the frame. Her blue robes were embellished with gold thread, and she wore a structured veil that added several inches to her height. Around her neck, dangled a thick gold necklace that Ransom recognized as the bleeding heart of Saint Alisa. A more ostentatious version than the one his own mother used to wear beneath her vest, only taking it out to pray when he or Anouk fell sick.

By the innate imperiousness with which the old woman looked them over, Ransom assumed she was the Mother Superior. With a hideous scowl, she said, "You're late."

Ransom's brows shot up. The pious old bat had some nerve.

"We're Daggers. We arrive when we arrive," he said, endeavoring to be somewhat polite, though the urgency of his task was pulsing in his ears.

Find the acolyte.

Kill her.

Bury her body.

"You're Mother Madeline, I take it," he said, noting her impatient nod. "We're here about the saint."

She hissed through her teeth. "Do *not* call her that. There is only one saint on this island and it is Saint Alisa. We hold her spirit eternally close. All others are arrogant pretenders and shameless vultures."

"Tell us how you really feel," mocked Caruso.

"It makes no odds to us how you think of her," said Nadia, matching the old woman's impatience. "We'd like to get back to the mainland in time for supper, though."

Humming in disapproval, Mother Madeline glanced over her shoulder. "Come away from the priory. You'll set the sisters on edge. I'll show you to the girl." Ducking inside to fetch a lantern, she quickly shooed them off the doorstep, locking the door behind her.

Faces watched them from the windows as they followed Mother Madeline across the little island. She led them west, to where the trees thinned and a peninsula jutted into the lake like a crooked finger. It was there that the famed prayer tower of Ra'azule had once stood. A fact confirmed by the mounds of ivory rubble now winking at them through the mist.

The wind howled, shoving at their backs and chasing the fog across the water until the sky cleared. Silver-spun moonlight splintered through the clouds and danced along the marshes. With a bolt of jarring clarity, Ransom was reminded of last night, how the moonlight had slipped in through the window in his bedroom and danced across Seraphine's body, joining with the soft sheen of her skin until she glowed like a fallen star.

Seraphine.

Spitfire. Lover. Saint.

His.

A gasp stuck in his throat, his heart hitching painfully at the realization that she was not here. That he had left her without a word. That she didn't know where he was. The wrongness of their cleaving was a barb in his chest, poking, piercing—

Find the acolyte.

Kill her.

Bury her body.

And then go home, laying waste to the promises they had made in the moonlit dark and instead returning to the catacombs, where he would await the prince's next command.

Fuck.

That pain came again, like a pickaxe in his skull. Instead of his own voice, he heard another. Smooth as silk and dark as night.

Find the acolyte.

Kill her.

Bury her body.

Mother Madeline looked over her shoulder at them, the lantern casting eerie shadows across her creviced face. "I tried my best to help her, you know." Not that any of them had asked. Or cared, particularly. Perhaps she was speaking simply to fill the yawning quiet or distract herself from the trio of Daggers skulking at her back. "When I found Sister Marianne in the rubble after the storm, I dragged her back here myself. I nursed her with my own hands, offered up my own prayers. But as time wore on, it became clear the girl was changed. And not for the better." She shuddered at the memory. "She was . . . *dangerous.* The walls would tremble in her wake. When she had a nightmare, debris would fall from the ceiling. Too many nights, I woke choking under clouds of dust. Even the windows would rattle and break."

The whites of her eyes shone too brightly in the moon, the dread on her face making her look like a ghost. "You must understand why I could not let her leave. Not after she put her hands on Honoria. Not after the damage she did to our tower. To our priory." Again, the Daggers didn't speak. Matters of morality were not part of their remit and Ransom had no comfort to offer the Mother Superior. He was focused entirely on the task at hand. Once it was done, he could find his way back through the fog in his head. Back to himself. "Our world does not need more saints. It needs order. Discipline. *Humility.*"

Caruso gave a huff of laughter. "And the coin of rich people who will pay any amount for a few of your precious prayers," he sneered. "I'm sure it would upset your little island commune to have another dozen or so saints wandering around Valterre after all this time. Who would pay you then?"

Chastened, or perhaps too livid to respond, Mother Madeline turned and did not speak again until they reached the peninsula. There, she stopped walking, gesturing for them to go on ahead of her, to where the remains of the prayer tower stood.

The lantern in her hand began to tremble. "Take care not to speak to the girl. She'll beg. She'll weep. She'll use every tool at her disposal to try and free herself. The faster it's done, the better. And whatever you do, do *not* take her chains off," she added starkly. "Marianne's temper is a hazard. She'd rip the stars down if she could. You need only look to the fate of Sister Honoria to know it."

"We'll take it from here," said Ransom. "You can return to your priory."

But Mother Madeline lingered, her eyes on the broken tower. "I have an Order to run. And it already has a saint to worship," she said with a sniff. "Marianne has changed. The hand of destiny has struck her, and the wound cannot be mended. The matter is out of my hands." She took a careful step back. "The anchor stone should be enough to sink her but if you require more, there are loose rocks down by the shore. When it's done, fill her pockets and dump her body in the lake. The graveyard here is for our sacred sisters. I would rather not sully our earth."

"Charming," muttered Nadia.

"Thanks for the tip," said Ransom.

"Now fuck off," said Caruso.

Turning from the Mother Superior, they made for the end of the peninsula. The lake sloshed alongside their footsteps as they reached the sorry remains of the prayer tower. The base of it jutted up from the ground in uneven slabs of pale stone, reaching to just above Ransom's head. The rest of the tower was scattered across the strand, where huge white slabs stuck out of the earth like teeth.

Inside, a single oil lamp flickered, illuminating a slight, dark-haired woman. Wreathed in heavy metal chains, she was sitting on a threadbare rug with her back against the hard stone that anchored her. Her head was buried in the crook of her arms.

She must have sensed them standing there, six feet away and openly gawking at her, but she made no sound nor movement. Nothing beyond the barest twitch of her fingers.

"She's so small," said Caruso.

Another twitch.

"Underfed," said Ransom, frowning.

And another.

"And filthy," added Nadia. "Look at all that hair. It's like rattlesnakes."

Find the acolyte.

Kill her.

Bury her body.

The girl gave a derisive snort.

Stepping inside the tower, Ransom said, "Well, at least we know she can hear us."

"No shit," came the acolyte's reply. Lifting her head, she added, "Who knew assassins were so fucking rude?"

Ransom opened his mouth to respond but the words died on his tongue. Shock coursed through his body, snatching the air from his lungs. He blinked furiously.

Impossible.

Impossible.

The acolyte stared up at him, her hazel eyes growing. They were shot through with red and rimmed in the dark shadows of endless sleepless nights, but he would have known them anywhere. They had chased him through a thousand nightmares, haunted him for ten long years.

Haunted him even now.

Her chains twisting and clanging, the girl pitched forward, her voice so small the wind almost snatched it away. *"Bastian?"*

That name—the *sight* of her—was like an arrow through his heart. "Anouk?"

Ransom was on his knees before he realized he was falling, the whole world spinning until it was just the two them crawling toward each other, across the endless aching chasm that had been yawning between them for ten long years. And now he was here. And so was she. Remade by fate itself, and thrust into his path. He felt those unseen gossamer strands tightening around him, Oriel's hand falling heavily on his shoulder. He welcomed it, welcomed all of it, this grand game of destiny where the people he loved the most were, by some divine sense of irony, the key players.

Impossible.

Impossible.

"Anouk," he said, trembling as he reached for her. Desperate to know that she was real, even as he felt the truth of this moment thrumming deep in the waters of his soul.

The same question rolled from her tongue, both of them whispering to each other in the moonlit dark. *"How?"*

Chapter 30

Seraphine

How is this possible?" said Theo, the minute they stepped into the Rose Garden and saw who awaited them there. Sitting in an armchair beside the dance floor, as though he had been holding court all morning in the deserted mill, Prince Andreas lazily waved them over. Maskless now, Lark was perched on his right, as stiff as the skeleton glimmering under his taut, graying skin, while Talisa Mondragon—the prince's cousin—occupied the chair on his left.

An hour had passed since Sera had bolted from the graveyard at the sight of the Necromancer, overwhelmed by the startling realization about what it meant about her own magic. About *her*. Enough time to find her friends back at the Paramour and tell them everything she'd witnessed in a half-garbled hysterical rant that made Val rush to fetch her a shot of whiskey, while Theo took her pulse, sure she was about to keel over.

After a fruitless return trip to the graveyard, they had come to the red mills to see the truth for themselves.

However out of place Lark Delano had looked in the cemetery, he looked even stranger in the empty Rose Garden, an apparition conjured from the worst of Sera's nightmares, occupying a high-backed velvet armchair like the king of death.

"Told you I wasn't crazy," she said now.

Val bit off a curse as they drifted closer. "I really thought you had hallucinated him. But that is definitely Lark Delano, undead Dagger."

Theo shuddered between tentative steps.

"I prefer the term '*saint,*'" Lark called across the empty dance floor. "I do have feelings, you know."

"Well, at least being dead all that time hasn't affected your hearing," Theo called back.

"Not for Seraphine's lack of trying," parried Lark. "I feel for you, Saint-maker. I can't imagine there's anything more infuriating than going to the trouble of killing someone only to have their corpse rise from its fancy coffin newly imbued with unfathomable magic." He flashed his teeth. Despite the rest of him, his smile was pearly white, that shit-eating grin all but blinding under the low lighting. "All things considered, I'm grateful for the accidental sainthood. Even despite the unfortunate downturn in handsomeness."

Val wrinkled her nose. "That's one way of putting it."

Andreas rolled his hand, gesturing impatiently. "Enough squabbling. Come in and be civil. We're all on the same side. And we have work to do."

Sera marched across the dance floor. In the last hour, she had had some time to digest this shocking turn of fate, and she had a bone—or in fact several—to pick with Lark Delano. "You tried to kill me in that graveyard yesterday. You tried to kill Nadia. One of your own."

Lark raised a warning finger. "Ah-ah. I think you'll find you are mistaken."

Sera's fingers twitched into fists. If she had any idea how she'd accidentally made this prick in the first place, she'd be unmaking him right now.

"I was trying to speak to Nadia. *Alone*," Lark clarified. "The bones were a misguided attempt at distraction. I was hoping to chase *you* off. I didn't think she'd spook so easily."

Sera curled her lip. "Next time, try using your words."

"Andreas told me not to speak to you until we were together," said Lark, sounding petulant. "He said you'd need time to adjust to my identity."

"Insofar as it revealed your own," Andreas supplied.

Accidental saint-maker.

How could she forget?

"And I suppose he was right about that, considering you bolted from us only this morning like a frightened rat," Lark went on. He pulled a long, gruesome face. "Am I really so hideous?"

"Yes," said Sera through her teeth. She would not soon forget the skeleton he had sent after her, or the bones that still littered that graveyard.

"How the hell did *this* guy get to become a saint?" Theo despaired. "Saint Oriel must be laughing at us."

Lark winked at Sera. "Ask her assistant."

"I have no idea," she said quietly, the full repercussions of what she had done still dawning on her. She wondered if she'd ever get used to it. "It was a mistake."

A colossal mistake.

"I was confused at first too," said Lark, shrugging. "When you scoured your handprint into my chest and sent a thousand bolts of pure white-hot magic right into my heart, I was sure I was dead. I *felt* myself die." He flinched at the memory, roughly scrubbing at his jaw. "For months, I lay in the frozen earth of Old Haven, caught somewhere between life and death with my memories flitting just out of reach. And all the while my magic grew inside me, flickering, writhing, *begging* to be used. I just . . . didn't know how."

Sera hated that she recognized that sense of power and powerlessness, the endless push and pull of fear and confusion.

"*Wake*, it whispered to me over and over again," said Lark. *"Rise."*

She knew that feeling all too well, the echo of another's voice calling from somewhere deep within.

"Over time, it got louder. It became the only thing I could focus on, the only thread binding me to this world. One night, in the thaw of a vicious winter, I opened my eyes and I knew what I was. What I could do." He turned his face up to the light so they could better see the shadows around his eyes, the full horror of what he had become. "I knew I was a Saint of Death. Not quite like Calvin. Something new. Something… even more powerful." He huffed a mirthless laugh. "I suppose, after all those years of being a Dagger, how could I be anything else?"

"Why did you run away?" challenged Theo. "Why didn't you return to the catacombs instead of leaving an open grave and a shit-ton of questions behind?"

"Are you familiar with the concept of emotional adjustment?" Lark shot back. "The first time I glimpsed my own face in a moonlit puddle, I nearly crawled back into that grave. If I could barely face what I had become, how could I expect my oldest friends to accept me? How could I face the woman I love as this . . . this *monster* dredged up from the earth? This corpse who thinks himself a saint. Nadia would have lost her mind." His voice quieted and he looked away. "By then, she had already lost enough."

"So you ran away instead and decided to play walkabout with other people's corpses?" said Val, incredulously. "That's so . . . *gross*."

Lark tensed at the accusation. His grip on the armrests tightened, his sharp fingernails digging into the fabric. "I kept to the shadows of Fantome, listening to whispers of the People's Saint. Another who sounded just like me. Someone I hoped would understand what I had become." He looked now at Sera, as though searching for a shred of empathy.

Hadn't she come to Andreas for the same reason? Didn't she know the fear he spoke of?

She looked away, catching Talisa's eye. The Mondragon princess was smiling broadly, a strange look of eagerness on her face, as though something else was coming. Something big.

"With Andreas's help, I grew to fully understand what I

had become." Lark opened the top of his robe, baring the pallid planes of his chest. The outline of Sera's golden handprint shone out from it like a beacon. Even now, it seemed to smolder. "What *you* had made me."

Maker. Her magic purred in answer, its languid heat unfurling in her chest. It was pleased with her, pleased with this . . . this unholy accident. Yet all Sera wanted was to take it back.

"Lark found his way to me just as you did," said Andreas, as pleased as the hum of her own magic. "All of this, you see, it was for you." He splayed his hands, looking to the ceiling. "These long nights of laughter and dancing, of freedom flowing like fine wine . . . I chose the birthplace of Saint Oriel, made Marvale bloom like a rose of the north, hoping if would draw you out. Hoping you would come to me."

And she had come, like a moth drawn to a flame. Knowing that the spectacle last night, and all the ones before it, had been carefully designed for her—like a glittering snare—made her stomach clench. Had she already been caught in the prince's trap? Was it too late to wrench herself free?

Andreas was still smiling, oblivious to the war in her head. "We are, after all, bound by the same destiny."

Again, his words struck true, but they didn't feel right to Sera. They felt . . . *foreboding.* A warning rather than an invitation. One look at the grimace on Val's face confirmed she was not alone in her discomfort.

Andreas stood up. "Do you see how special you are now? Do you understand the role you're meant to play? My precious rose. My saint-maker."

Sera took a careful step back. "I don't belong to you, Andreas. And neither does my magic."

"Don't be scared," he said, those gold eyes flashing. Whatever magic he was using slid off her like water. "It's time to begin."

"Begin what?"

That smile again, so sure and wide. "Building our kingdom."

Another step away, her hand finding Val's behind her. "What are you talking about?"

It was Theo who answered. Theo who had been watching their exchange with rapt attention. Theo who hadn't moved an inch. "He wants you to make another saint."

There was a loaded silence, broken by the rustle of Talisa's dress as she rose to her feet. She floated toward Sera with all the grace of a ballerina, her eyes wide and hungry. "Well? Are you ready?"

"You can't be serious." Sera might have laughed if the mood hadn't turned so stark. "I have no idea how to make a saint!"

"Well, that's not strictly true," remarked Lark.

She glared at him. "You don't count."

"I'll help you," said Andreas, unerringly calm, like they were talking about making a pot of raspberry jam, and not completely rethreading the tapestry of someone's soul. "Talisa has volunteered herself for the experiment."

Sera spluttered a refusal, even as her magic gathered new heat, the fire inside her licking at her bones. Crooning to her.

Maker, the time has come.

"You're mad. You're both mad."

She tried to step back again, but this time Theo stopped her, laying a bracing hand on her back. "You could try it," he said quietly. "What's the harm?"

She turned to stare at him. "I could hurt her. I could hurt myself."

"Or worse. You could turn a Mondragon princess into a powerful weapon," hissed Val. "Who knows what kind of magic she'll end up with if it works?"

"We can all hear you, just so you know," said Lark drolly. "Sound carries in these old mills."

Sera turned back to Andreas. "The saints belong to Valterre. They are part of this kingdom." She looked pointedly at Talisa. "Not Urnica."

"Then try me," said Theo, coming forward. "Use me."

"No," said Andreas, beating Sera to her own refusal. It was one thing to harm a foreign royal, but another to risk the life of her best friend.

"It has to be Talisa," said the prince. "I have chosen Talisa."

"Why?" pressed Val. "Because she's under your thumb?"

Those golden eyes flashed. "Careful, Valerie. We are all allies here." He turned on Sera, a challenge in his voice. "Are we not?"

No, whispered her intuition. Her allies were the Daggers, and the Daggers were gone. She was starting to wonder what had caused them to flee so suddenly. If perhaps the prince had had a hand in their disappearance. After all, without Ransom and the others, their position here had weakened. If they tried to run, Lark could raise every corpse in Marvale. As a maker of saints, Sera had no true power of her own.

"It's Sera's magic," said Theo. "That makes it her choice."

Andreas's frown was a sharp, twisting thing. Gone in a blink was the handsome affable saint he had pretended to be last night, replaced in the harsh light of day by a spoiled, petulant prince. "Just as it is my choice to help you rescue your friend, Bibi." With a heavy sigh, he looked at her the way Mama used to whenever she fed Pippin under the dinner table or tracked mud in through the backdoor. "Tell me, Seraphine, why would I share the gift of my magic with you when you won't do the same for me?"

Sera's heart sank.

Here was the deal: a new saint for her friend's freedom. An experiment that could go horribly wrong in ten different ways for a life that meant as much to her as her own. Even Val was silent now, chewing up her bottom lip.

With the Daggers long gone, Seraphine could see no other way but this. "You win, Andreas. Blackmail it is."

"A saint of charms has no need of blackmail, Seraphine. This is simply a negotiation. I want to help you," he said, adopting an earnestness that tried to loosen the knot in her chest. "I want us to help each other."

"And *I* want to become a saint!" Talisa clapped her hands, bouncing on the balls of her feet.

Steeling herself, Sera rolled her shoulders back and welcomed the molten flood of her magic. "Let's do it," she said to the prince and his cousin. To herself. And her own magic.

It trilled in answer.

As the afternoon sun dragged itself over Marvale and the streets swelled with bleary-eyed townsfolk, Sera knelt on the floor of the deserted mill, trying to look like she knew what she was doing. Andreas was on his knees beside her, the sleeves of his fine silk shirt rolled up to his elbows. The others sat in armchairs around them, a rapt audience for whatever came next.

Andreas had summoned his mercenaries. Armed with impressive longswords that had likely once belonged to the king's soldiers and terrifying grimaces honed by years of brutal warfare, and later incarceration, they patrolled the outer walls of the mill, as well as either side of the only entryway. It was for their own privacy, the prince had assured them, and even despite the sincerity of his tone, Sera couldn't help but think these men were there as much to keep them in as to keep curious onlookers out.

Dressed in a long white linen dress and with her feet bare, Talisa lay on the rug below her. Her pale hair fanned out like a halo around her head, a purposeful pose that had made Sera's eyes roll so far back in her head she momentarily lost sight. The Mondragon princess was so eager for her sainthood, she probably would have swallowed a bowlful of worms if Sera asked her to.

It was that hunger that gave her pause. What was the measure of this spoilt royal from Urnica who seemed to have little personality to recommend her besides the utter adoration of her cousin?

What kind of saint would she make when it was done?

Did it even matter now?

Shoving her concerns aside and thinking only of Bibi, Sera tied her hair back from her face and tried to steel herself.

"Don't overthink it." Andreas leaned in, his voice a guiding whisper in her ear. "Just let your magic flow. It will know exactly what to do."

She muttered, "That makes one of us."

Talisa cleared her throat with a pointed squeak. "I'm ready."

It was the third time she'd declared it in as many minutes.

Saints, she was a pain in the ass.

Glancing up, Sera locked eyes with Theo.

He dipped his chin. *You've got this.*

Recalling what she had done to Lark atop the Aurore, she gingerly placed her hand in the center of Talisa's chest. The princess's heart thrummed under her fingertips, excitement making her breath hitch.

Sera's magic leaped at the contact, a flurry of heat racing to the surface of her skin. Inhaling slowly and deeply, Sera welcomed it.

I am not afraid.

I am in control.

That door inside her opened. First a crack. And then a foot, that frightened little girl crawling away from it.

I am not afraid.

I am in control.

She pictured her magic unfurling from within, not an uncontrollable bonfire but a ribbon of gold. She spooled it around her, coaxing it up and up and *up.* The warmth under her skin was familiar but Sera had never been so deliberate about it before, had never beckoned to her magic and felt it answer with such gentleness. Eager to be used. To be freed, at last.

"She's glowing," whispered Val.

"Beautiful," murmured Andreas, his breath hot against the shell of her ear. "Look at all that potential rippling under your skin, just *aching* to be used."

And I haven't done a single thing with it.

Guilt nipped at the edges of her thoughts. Her magic seized upon the change in emotion, that careful ribbon lashing out like a whip. Her hands began to sizzle. She reeled backward, pulling her hand away from the princess.

Talisa's eyes flew open. "What are you doing? It's not done."

"Sorry. I thought I was going to—"

"Put it back," snapped Andreas. *"Concentrate."*

Shaking off the upset, Sera returned her hand to Talisa's chest, feeling her pulse thrum in time with the princess's heartbeat. Her magic warmed, gathering into that easy familiar flow. Perturbed by the golden sheen of her own skin and the look of ravenous hunger on Talisa's face, Sera squeezed her eyes shut, just wanting it to be over. Impatience gnawed at her, making her magic thrash.

Another distraction.

Focus, Sera. Just get it done.

Talisa huffed, beginning to squirm. How badly the princess

wanted this—a font of her own magic, a new fate.

But does she deserve it? whispered Sera's conscience.

Would Saint Oriel approve?

Again, she faltered, her magic stuttering in her fingertips. Surely, this wasn't the way it was supposed to go. A new Age of Saints made and traded in clandestine deals and accidental fits of terror. What about worthiness? *Goodness?* Doing it like this—out of fear and panic—made a mockery of Oriel, and the saints of old, those ordinary, unassuming people chosen because of their pure hearts, their innate selflessness.

This was wrong.

It was *all wrong.*

Sera's fingers curled into a fist.

Talisa harrumphed. "Come on. I don't feel *anything.*"

"Seraphine." Andreas's voice became a low growl. "Get out of your own head."

"I c-can't."

"You *must.*" Cool fingers encircled the back of her neck, squeezing there. *"You will."*

Again, she flattened her palm. Again, her magic flowed, quick and hot and violent, as if a volcano was spewing inside her. There was fear there too, guilt and uncertainty and panic all melding into a dangerous maelstrom. Terror and magic tangled.

Her hand flared bright gold. White hot.

This is wrong.

This is wrong.

This is wrong.

Her power faltered, her magic turning back on itself as if in retreat. Too late. Too hot. Too close to the surface now. There was nowhere for it to go—all that heat. All that panic.

There came the scent of burning flesh.

Talisa screamed.

"No!" Sera tried to rip her hand away, but Andreas covered it with his own, pressing all that angry, spitting magic into Talisa.

Wrong.

Wrong.

Wrong.

The princess bucked. "MAKE IT STOP! IT BURNS!"

Silent tears streamed down Sera's face as she wrestled with the prince. "Let go, Andreas! It's killing her!"

"Fight through it!" yelled the prince. His eyes were wide and wild, sweat beading on his brow. "You have to fight through it!"

There was smoke now, the wound so deep it burned away the linen of her dress, charring the skin beneath. Talisa's heartbeat stuttered, her pulse fading under Sera's palm. Desperate now, she slammed her head backward, finding the prince's nose with a sickening *crack!* just as Theo lunged from his chair, tackling Andreas by the shoulders. He knocked him off Sera, his fists already swinging as he pinned him to the floor.

Then Val was there, dragging Talisa out from under Seraphine.

Mercenaries swept in, drawing their swords as Theo and Andreas swung at each other, spitting and cursing as they rolled across the ground. The connection finally severed, Sera crawled away from Talisa. Curling her fists, she willed her magic to recede, for the raging heat inside her to pass—and quickly.

Remarkably, the princess was not yet dead.

She could only whimper now, her small pale hands feebly clutching at her charred chest. It had split open, and between the burned ridges of her skin, Sera could see the white of her ribcage. Blood trickled from her nose and mouth, adding a gurgle to her labored breaths.

Lark alone remained unruffled by the sight. Rising slowly from his chair, he stepped over the keening princess and walked right off the dance floor, like the spectacle had simply bored him. He returned, carrying a pitcher of water, just as the mercenaries managed to drag Theo off Andreas.

Standing over Talisa, Lark said, "This might sting a little, princess."

He poured the water over her chest.

Screams erupted from the princess like a terrible aria, rising all the way to the ceiling.

Flinching—and entirely disheveled now—Andreas staggered to his feet. Dismissing his mercenaries with a wave of his hand, he turned on Theo.

"Remember this kindness, Versini. By rights, you should be dead for putting your hands on me." Then, looking down on the writhing, screeching figure of his own cousin, he said, simply, "Be quiet, Talisa."

Talisa's screams cut out. Though her mouth remained slack and gasping, she didn't make another peep. But Sera could see the agony in her eyes, the blood vessels there bursting until there wasn't a speck of white left.

Crawling back to sit by the princess, she turned her ire up at Andreas. "What the hell have you done to her?"

"You're the one who maimed her," he said, viciously. "I merely saved us all a headache."

"She's dying. She's going to die here."

Andreas scrubbed a hand across his face. "Talisa," he said, his eyes glowing. "Go and get yourself to the healer."

"Have you lost your mind?" demanded Theo. "Her chest has been scoured down to the bone. She can't just—"

Talisa sat up, like a puppet yanked by an invisible string. With obscene effort, she managed to drag herself to her feet. She swayed once, twice, and then collapsed. Theo caught her before she hit the ground. Her lids fluttered closed.

They didn't open again.

A yawning chasm of dread filled Sera, and she pitched forward, retching.

Andreas frowned. "This could not have gone worse."

No grief, only frustration.

Theo was still holding Talisa's body, staring vacantly at the chalky slats of her ribs, the pink ridge of her unmoving heart.

Val hissed in disgust. "She's your cousin, you callous prick. And now she's *dead*."

"Thanks to your friend." Andreas's voice was clipped, cold. "Here lies the price of your cowardice, Seraphine. Let this be a lesson to you."

Those cruel words struck true, slicing through Sera like a knife. She was too horrified to respond, too busy trying to hold herself together. She hadn't meant to kill the princess. She had tried to save her, tried to warn Andreas, but what did it matter now? It was her hand that had scoured her, her fear-addled magic that had ripped through blood and bone and sinew to snatch away the last handful of her heartbeats.

All for nothing.

If this was power, she didn't want it.

Take it back, she pleaded with Saint Oriel.

Smother it.

Give it to another.

At a snap of the prince's fingers, a mercenary rushed over. "Get her out of here. And be discreet about it."

"Aye, sir." The mercenary moved as if in a trance, taking the girl from Theo's arms, turning on his bootheel, and running across the empty dance hall and out of the back door.

Raising her head, Sera watched him go, then turned to study the other mercenaries in their midst. How they all stood, straight-backed and blank-eyed against the walls, like wind-up toy soldiers. She thought back to last night. All that raucous laughter that refused to die out, revelers dancing until their feet bled, twirling and twirling until they vomited. What Andreas had done just now to Talisa, plucking her from the floor like a broken stem and making her stand. How she had somehow managed it, taking those final tortured steps even as her heart gave out.

"They're enthralled." Her voice was a broken whisper. "You've enthralled all of them."

Lark snorted. "Well, obviously." He flopped back into his chair. "This is painful, Andreas. Why did Saint Oriel choose the dumbest one to lead us?"

"She's not a leader," said Andreas, turning back to them. "I am the leader. Seraphine is our maker."

"Looks more like a murderer to me," said Lark.

Another barb that found its mark. How could she deny it?

It was Val who spoke up. "She told him it wasn't going to work. It was Andreas who forced her to do it."

"It was working," said the prince. "I felt the hum of your magic. I watched it flow from your hand into Talisa's chest. You did something to twist it."

Sera was shaking her head, emboldened by Val's words. "If it doesn't feel right in my bones, there's nothing I can do about it. It's not *supposed* to happen this way, Andreas. Sainthood shouldn't be bartered or negotiated. How would we ever know that the right ones have been chosen?"

There was a short, strained silence.

It was broken by the rasp of Lark's laughter, joined shortly by Andreas's silky chuckle. "You must have crawled out from under a rock before that storm struck you down," he said, openly sneering now. "Long gone are the days when the simpering saints of old would walk among the people, doling out favors for goodwill and cheap prayers, Seraphine. Ours will be a new era of power. One where *we* do the choosing *and* the taking for ourselves."

At her look of abject horror, his smile grew indulgent. Talisa was barely a thought to him now, the callous suddenness of her death lost to the swell of his own ambition. Like it was only a blip, a kink in the grand tapestry of his plan. "How do you think I ended up on top of that clock tower in the grip of Oriel's storm? If I left the future of this kingdom up to fate, some other cowardly do-gooder would have *my* magic right now. Oh no, no, no." He clucked his tongue. "I knew what I was made for. The moment I found that prophecy, I knew there was a place for me in it. A way to twist the future, to mold it to *my* dreams." He was pacing now, excitement quickening his steps, carelessly smearing the still warm blood of his cousin across the floor. "I just had to find the right storm, wait for the right conditions. A hundred times I must have climbed that damned clock tower. A hundred times I waited for magic that never struck. But I did not grow discouraged. No. I became *emboldened*."

He stopped, looking up at the vaulted ceiling like he could see the storm clouds beyond. "And when that fated tempest finally struck, I was there, waiting for it. I reached up to that angry sky and I wrenched my destiny from the splitting clouds and swallowed it down like a hot poker, welcoming every aching, screaming beat of my heart."

"You weren't chosen." Sera shook her head in disbelief, as the threads of his plan came apart before her. The portrait of a charming prince replaced by the grasping, power-mad narcissist beneath. She could see it so clearly now she wondered how she had missed it last night. "You were never truly made."

He bared his teeth, a fevered look flashing in his eyes. The gold blood of his sainthood rose to the surface, making a mockery of the old saints, of all things that used to matter in Valterre. "I made *myself*. Just as I will remake this land." There was an edge to his voice now, a dark thrum to the power flaring inside him. Behind Sera, Val and Theo had fallen stone silent, the only sound the careful shuffle of their footsteps as they edged away from the prince. Like that could save them now. They had stumbled unwittingly into the belly of the beast, and it was all Sera's fault.

Andreas raised a prodding finger. "And *you*, my pious little saint-maker, are going to help me."

Over your dead body.

Sera pressed her lips together, swallowing the rage that had replaced the sharp edge of her grief, wordlessly weathering the prince's maddened soliloquy. Lark snorted at her poor efforts, but Andreas went on, caught in the grip of his own grand vision.

"*You* will make who sits alongside us, and *I* will keep them under control." Again, those eyes flashed—a bright menacing gold. They possessed no sway over her—for it was clear now that her strange, mercurial power outranked Andreas. And everyone else in the kingdom. Not that she could use it to help herself out of this mess. Or, more pressingly, her friends.

Andreas took a moment to gather himself, raking a hand through his hair. When he looked at Sera again, his eyes were clear and blue. "Together, we will build a kingdom like no other. One where every thought, every word, and every knee bends to us." His lips curled, that bright, pearly smile bringing a wasted measure of charm with it. "And you will like it, Seraphine. Trust me. Absolute power has a way of growing on you."

Her mind reeling, Sera wiped the disgust from her face and relaxed her shoulders.

Careful now.

She had to tread so very carefully.

"That's quite the vision," she said, in a stilted tone. "It may take me a little while to digest."

Grabbing her shoulders and squeezing hard, Andreas pulled her close, until she could see the scattering of freckles on his cheeks, smell the cinnamon on his breath. "You must bury the ideals of the past, Seraphine. You are not the storm that made you. You are the conduit. The power that thrives here is not yours to claim. Only to gift. You *need* me just as I need you. We need each other."

She made herself nod.

"We'll try again tonight. On another follower. And another. And another. As many as it takes."

She knew he meant it.

"All right." The word was hollow, her every thought screaming at her to *run*. Now, *fast*, and don't look back. But first, she'd have to play the Silver-Tongue herself, give the prince whatever he asked for, so they could slip away, unharmed. "I'll do better tonight. Now that I know what's at stake."

This seemed to please him. "Go back to your inn and rest." His eyes turned as gold as coins, as he moved his gaze over her shoulder, to where Theo and Val were standing in muted horror.

In a voice like velvet, he addressed them. "You will return to this mill at nightfall. You will not try to escape. You will not inquire after Ransom Hale and his Daggers. You will not leave the Paramour, except to come back here. And when you do, you will defer to me and any requests I make."

Sera's heart sank at the prince's silky command. She could

feel the threads of his magic twisting around her, reaching toward her friends.

Standing back, he asked them, "Is that clear?"

"Crystal clear," said Theo, at once.

Blinking slowly, Val nodded.

The prince clapped his hands, applauding their acquiescence. "Wonderful," he said, through that blinding smile, before spinning on his bootheel and striding toward the bar. "Now someone get me a fucking drink."

Still watching them closely, Lark Delano rolled to his feet. His eyes slid like oil from Val to Theo and back again.

"Until tonight, then," he said, that irritating smirk curling, as he sauntered off after the prince.

Chapter 31

Ransom

Find the acolyte.

Kill her.

Bury her body.

Ransom was in the grip of a nightmare. On his knees in the dark, his little sister was finally within reach. Smiling. Trembling. All grown up. It was a gift of fate, a kindness from Oriel herself, but there was a worm in his head telling him to kill her.

He had to kill her.

Anouk's hands were achingly cold, the chains around her wrist rattling as she gripped him. Her nails dug into skin, like she was afraid he would disappear. "Are you real?" she whispered. "Bastian, is this real?"

The fog was creeping in again. Head splitting. World turning. Breath hissing. Like a puppet, he felt the strings around him tighten. No. *No.*

Kill her.

Bury her body.

Through his teeth, Ransom begged, "Anouk, let go of me."

She shook her head, a familiar fierceness returning to her face. "Not a chance. Not after ten long years."

Kill her.

Bury her body.

"Anouk, you have to let go." Sweat beaded on Ransom's brow as he fought the urge rising in his chest. His fingers twitched beneath hers, his eyes drawn to the column of her neck. How easy it would be to snap. And then it would be done.

He just needed it to be done.

"Caruso," he groaned, fighting his own will. "Restrain me."

The Dagger, who like Nadia had been observing their reunion in confused silence, stepped into the tower. "What are you talking about? Have you lost your mind?"

"Yes," he ground out.

Kill her.

Bury her body.

"CARUSO! NOW!" An anguished scream ripped out of Ransom. Too late Anouk released him, scrabbling backward. He was already lunging at her, but Caruso was faster, collaring his neck and dragging him backward. Holding his elbows behind his back with one arm, he drove his knee into Ransom's back, pinning him to the cold stone floor. There was just enough space to raise his head.

Anouk, who had flattened herself against the far wall, struggled to catch her breath. Her eyes were so wide in her narrow face, the olive pallor all but drained. She looked like a frightened doll come to life, her cheekbones sharpened by weeks of starvation, her narrow limbs mottled with bruises.

And somehow, he still itched to kill her.

He *had* to kill her.

Nadia came to her knees beside Anouk, and in as gentle a voice as she could manage, said, "Are you all right?"

"Of course not," huffed Anouk, drawing upon that innate bravery she had had since she was a girl. "My own brother is trying to kill me!"

"Was," corrected Nadia. "I'm predicting a change of plan."

"And if it makes you feel better, Ransom tries to kill everyone," said Caruso. "He's Head of the Order of Daggers."

Anouk grimaced. *"All hell."*

Nadia threw Caruso a withering look. "Against all odds, you've actually made it worse."

"I thought she'd be impressed."

"She's a fucking acolyte, Caruso. What part of her incredibly pious vocation makes you think she'd rejoice at having a prolific assassin for a brother?"

"Well, excuse me for trying, Nadia. I'm new to family reunions."

"There's something wrong with him." Anouk turned her attention back to Ransom. Her dark brows lowered as she studied him. In her worry, she looked so like their mother. Even more so now that she was almost eighteen. "He's in pain."

Ransom wasn't in pain. He was in hell. Still thrashing against Caruso, he slammed his forehead against the ground, trying to destroy the worm inside him. Twining his fingers in his hair, Caruso yanked his head up. "Seriously, what the fuck is going on with you? You've been praying for this moment your whole damn life."

Chains clanging as she crept closer, Anouk canted her head to study him. When their eyes met again, hers flickered burnished gold. The faint scent of lemon blossoms filled the air, tickling Ransom's nose.

Sister.

Saint.

Helper.

Understanding softened her features. "There's a darkness in your head, brother."

Nadia and Caruso exchanged a glance.

"It moves like a shadow," said Anouk, coming closer still, straining against the chains pinning her to the wall. "A burrowing sickness that veils your free thoughts." She shuddered, clutching at her hollow stomach. "I can see it behind your eyes. I can *feel* it. It's a kind of magic."

Kill her.

Bury her body.

"Yes," Ransom eked out.

"Is this how your power works?" said Nadia, peering closer at Ransom. "Some kind of magical sight?"

Anouk's lips twisted. "Depends on who you ask. Sister Madeline says I'm a Saint of Ruination. That I destroy everything I touch. But I can mend too. I rebuilt every wall I tore down on this island. I would have put this prayer tower back together if she hadn't chained me to it." Anouk's voice grew stronger, her eyes shining with conviction. "I can mend. I know I can. She never let me try with Honoria. I wanted so badly to try, but she took her broken body away."

"Try now," urged Nadia. "Fix the wrongness in his head."

Caruso maneuvered Ransom closer. This time, when Anouk reached for him, she laid her hands on his head. He felt her fingers twitch against his scalp, searching, prodding . . . and warmth trickled through his skull. It was a peculiar feeling, like honey drizzled over his mind. Slowly, painlessly, the dark fog lifted, fractured by a creeping golden light.

Find the . . .

Kill . . .

Bury . . .

The voice dissipated. The worm destroyed.

Ransom opened his eyes and was himself again. The world shifted into stark focus, his friends kneeling at his side, his sister looking down on him with such tenderness, it made his eyes prickle.

Offering a wan smile, she sat back, folding her hands in her lap. "Better?"

"Better," he rasped.

Caruso eased off Ransom, keeping his hand twisted in the back of his shirt as he rose from the floor. With relief came the full, unvarnished truth of what had happened back at Marvale. And with it, a rage so quick and violent, Ransom could taste it between his teeth. *"Andreas,"* he hissed. "That malevolent prick got inside my head." A silver-tongue indeed. With a few choice words, he had tied invisible strings to Ransom and used him like a puppet. "He compelled me to flee Marvale. To come here and kill you at all costs." His own flesh and blood. And *saints*, he had almost done it too. He scrubbed his face, horror making his stomach lurch. "I almost killed you, Anouk."

"Andreas almost killed her," said Nadia, with her own dawning disgust. "You fought it, Ransom. You fought against his thrall with everything in you."

And still it had taken Caruso to restrain him.

Hell's teeth.

"Lucky I'm so damn strong," said Caruso, puffing out his chest.

Nadia rolled her eyes.

"Lucky I'm a saint," Anouk said, pointedly. "This could have been one hell of a shitshow."

"For an acolyte, you sure curse a lot," said Nadia.

"I'm a dab hand at lying, too." Anouk smirked. "Since I'm not Marianne Adina, either."

In the ruins of that damp prayer tower, a hundred and more questions crowded in on Ransom—there were stories to be traded, histories to be told. How had Anouk come to be in this place all by herself, living under a fake name, a fabricated vocation?

But this was not the place, nor the time. Not as the night darkened and the mist around them thickened. Nadia was on her feet now, examining the anchor stone behind Anouk, yanking at the rusted chains that bound her there.

Anouk reached for his hands once more, the light in her

eyes filling him with hope. "Look what fate has done for us, Bastian. It brought you back to me. After all this time, brother." Gripping him by the shoulders, she pulled him close. "Now we can leave this place together and begin again."

"That might be trickier than you think." Frowning, Nadia turned from the anchor stone. "I don't suppose the Mother Superior gave you a key?"

Ransom shook his head.

"We were supposed to dump her with the anchor stone," supplied Caruso.

"Callous old bat," muttered Anouk.

Eager to be of use—and to get his sister the hell away from this creepy place—Ransom got to his feet. "Leave the anchor stone. It'll only sink us on the way back. I'll go and get the key."

Caruso stepped out of the tower, joining Ransom.

They didn't have to go far to find Mother Madeline. She was standing where they had left her at the end of the peninsula. Illuminated by her dying lantern and with the rising wind tossing her robes around her, she looked like an angry ghoul.

"Is there a problem?" she called out. "I told you that girl was trouble."

"We need the key," said Ransom as they marched toward her. "Hand it over and return to the priory."

Mother Madeline took a step back, gripping a brass key that hung around her neck. "What do you need it for? Just dump the body along with the stone."

"No," said Ransom, fast losing the only shred of patience he had managed to conjure. He hated this woman for chaining up his sister—for beating and starving her, before marking her for dead—just as fiercely as he hated the prince who had chained up his mind, casting him from Marvale like a skipping stone. "Give me the key. I won't ask you again."

She looked between them, aghast. "*Sweet Saint Alisa*, you intend to free her, don't you?"

"I'm getting bored," warned Caruso. "You won't like me when I'm bored."

Ransom extended his hand. *"Now."*

Her lips thinned. Again, she backed away. "I refuse to let you help her. I *refuse* to allow you to take what belongs to this priory. I *refuse*—"

Crack!

Caruso snapped her neck. Her body crumpled in a heap, the lantern cracking as it rolled away, extinguishing the last of the oil. Mother Madeline stared up at them with blank, unseeing eyes, still clutching the key.

Ransom sighed. "That's one way of doing it."

"Don't act like you weren't fantasizing about it." Caruso leaned down and yanked the key from around her neck, pocketing it without so much as a second glance. "Let's go and spring your sister."

Leaving Mother Madeline where she had fallen, they returned to the prayer tower, eager to be free of the Isle of Alisa. Tonight, they would save the saint they had come to kill.

And tomorrow, Ransom would kill the one who had commanded it.

And he would do so with deep, abiding pleasure.

For Anouk, and for Seraphine.

For himself.

And the knife edge on which the future of this kingdom now rested.

Chapter 32

Seraphine

Back at their suite at the Paramour Inn, Sera locked the door behind them and went to the window. Outside, the town had come alive again, only now that she was looking more closely at it, she could see the people here weren't quite . . . *right.* They milled about in a daze, some stopping in the street to stare at nothing, while others scrubbed their streaming eyes, unsure of why they were crying. Even the dogs were disquieted, skulking like rats in the lanes or whimpering at their masters' feet. The red mills loomed over it all, like a row of menacing guardians, while the prince's mercenaries stood on street corners, armed with stolen weapons and those unnerving blank-eyed stares.

It was all a show. A farce. A changing portrait of lies. Last night had been a grand spectacle, put on for her benefit. And she had fallen for it, hook, line, and sinker.

Cursing her own naivety, Sera laid her head against the windowpane. "This is all my fault." Why hadn't she paid closer attention in the Rose Garden last night? Why hadn't she looked beyond the silver-tongued prince and examined the trappings of his lair, the revelers that he made twirl for him over and over again?

Absently, she fingered the skull ring in her pocket, wishing she could make Ransom appear. Why didn't she listen to him?

Because you are an idealistic fool, Seraphine Marchant.

She had pinned her loyalty to a corrupt saint and lost her strongest ally in the process. Her Dagger. Her protector. Her heart.

Thanks to the prince's compulsion, they would have to return to the red mills tonight, and Sera would either scour another brain-addled follower right down to the bone or make a saint for the prince to control at his own leisure. Another weapon for his arsenal. Another puppet for his rebellion.

"I'm sorry it's come to this." Feeling feverish with panic, she turned from the window and began to pace. "I'm so sorry. I'm so—"

"Sera." Suddenly, Theo was beside her, his hand heavy on her shoulder. She turned and his turquoise eyes were less than a foot from her face. "Slow down. You're going to ruin this nice carpet, and we can't afford to fall out of favor with the innkeeper right now. We need him to arrange a getaway carriage for us."

She stepped back. "What are you talking about?"

"It didn't work." Falling onto the bed, Val flung her arms

out like she was making a snow angel. "Andreas's stupid little compulsion has no effect on us."

Sera stood over her. "How do you know?"

"Because I have no intention of going back to that shithole tonight," said Val, blowing a curl out of her eye. "And because of this." Reaching under the collar of her shirt, she pulled out her necklace, revealing the precious bead of Lightfire they wore whenever they had to travel beyond Halbracht.

The Lightfire was meant to provide protection against Shade. Sera had never imagined it might shield her friends from something even more insidious; the poisoned-honeyed words of Prince Andreas Mondragon Rayere.

Theo pulled out his own then, the bead dangling from a loop of dark blue twine. "I was hoping it might work, but I couldn't be sure . . . Not until he tried to compel us."

"When he turned those creepy golden eyes on us, and spoke in that awful cloying voice, I swear I felt this strange shadow worm into my head," said Val, sitting up now. "I felt it trying to latch on to my mind, but it couldn't find the way in." She clutched her necklace, kissing her fist. "When the bead warmed under my shirt, I knew that must be why."

A hysterical laugh burst out of Sera. "So you lied?" she said, looking between them. "You both looked him in the eye and lied?"

Val shrugged. "Easy, really. I was a Cloak, remember? I've been double-crossing people my whole life."

Theo grinned. "Of course the arrogant fool fell for it."

This time, when Sera resumed pacing, it was in pursuit of

a plan. "We need to get out of here before Andreas figures out what happened. He won't make the same mistake twice."

"He's already sent the Daggers away," said Theo, echoing her own burgeoning suspicions. "Otherwise, why would he order us not to ask about them?"

It was a relief to think that Ransom hadn't abandoned her after all. But while it lessened the weight in her chest, the question of his whereabouts still prickled under her skin. Was he under Andreas's power? And to what end? She was worried about him. More than that, she wanted to be with him, to tell him that she would be at his side when they faced the prince together and killed him.

It was too late. She knew by the bleak look on Theo's face.

"We can't go after them, Sera. Even if we knew where to look, we might never find them."

"I know," she said quietly. And there was still Bibi to think about. They couldn't abandon her just because their plans had fallen to ruin. "We can't return to the Summer Palace empty-handed," she said, slumping onto the bed. "We might as well put a noose around Bibi's neck ourselves."

"Well, we can't kill Andreas, either," said Val. "Not like this, and not without the Daggers' help."

"Unless we had a saint of our own . . ." Theo was looking at Sera, his eyes glimmering. She recognized the light there, the silver threads of a plan forming. "You could always try again. On me."

The suggestion was so startling she shot to her feet. Hadn't he witnessed what had just happened to Talisa? Traced the contours of her ribs through the hole in her chest, held her broken body in his arms? Wasn't he *afraid*?

"No way," she said, folding her arms. "Theo, *no*. It's far too risky."

"It won't be like it was with Talisa," he insisted. "We won't force you. We won't hold your hand down."

"No," she repeated, firmer now. "It's not worth the risk."

He refused to back down. "You've already done it once. Delano is living proof."

"Lark Delano is a walking skeleton. Hardly a recipe for success. And look what happened to Talisa." The reminder of it made her retch, regret raking its claws down her spine. If Theo met the same fate at her hands, she'd never survive it.

He waved off her concerns, like they were talking about burning a batch of muffins and not accidentally killing a royal princess of Urnica. "You didn't *want* to make her. You were in your head about it."

"I don't know how to get out of my head," said Sera. "With Lark, all I felt in the moment was pure, bone-deep terror. The certainty that I was going to die. I flung my hand out as a reaction to that fear. It was just . . . *instinct*."

"So let this time be instinct. We might be dead by nightfall. At least this way, we'd have a fighting chance."

"Unless you end up with some shitty power," countered Val. "Like . . . I don't know, a Saint of Books."

He turned on her. "A saint of *books*? What does that even mean?"

"It means you're no killer," said Val, pointedly. "You're soft,

Theo. Studious. You care about knowledge and philosophy and invention. The odds of you being able to weaponize your power against Andreas in any kind of meaningful way—that is, if Sera doesn't accidentally *burn you to cinders*—are slim. It's not worth the risk."

He glared at her. "Consider me offended."

"If you ask me, *I'd* be the better bet."

"Stop arguing," said Sera. "I'm not betting on either of you. Not here. Not like this."

Stewing now, Theo went to the window, a muscle ticking in his jaw. "You'll have to try sometime, Sera," he said, in a low, frustrated voice. "It's your gift. Your duty. Not just to Saint Oriel, but to the kingdom."

"I will," she said, and despite what had happened with Talisa, she meant it. "Just not now. Not here."

He glanced at her over his shoulder. "Swear it."

Bristling, she said, "I shouldn't have to swear it. I don't break my word."

Turning back to the street, he sighed. "You're right. I'm sorry. It's just this place. Everything. It's getting to me."

It was deeper than that, Sera knew. Theo wasn't angry. He was jealous. Sometimes, when they spoke about these grand ideas of magic and fate and the true cost of power, she felt like she was talking not just to her friend but to his ambition, too, to that hunger inside him that crackled like an ember.

She could sense it in him now, that edge of frustration, that growl of need.

It reminded her of the Versini brothers. And if she was

honest with herself, after learning the truth about Andreas, she could admit that a part of her worried about pouring her gift into Theo, not because of how it might harm his body but of how it might harm his soul. What it might become when it sparked off that ember inside him.

Lark and Andreas were living proof that the Second Age of Saints was already a far cry from the first. Gone were the likes of tender-hearted Saint Alisa, dauntless Saint Maurius, and valiant Saint Cadel. Provost Ambrose was right. In this new world, power did not guarantee goodness.

If Sera was to be the conduit for a new Age of Saints, then she owed it to Oriel to be careful with her choices.

"I have a plan." Val's announcement knocked Sera from her thoughts. "Sorry to scoop you, Theo. I know how you like to be the problem-solver."

That earned her a dimpled smile, the lingering tension fading as they gathered close.

Val spoke fast and low. "We'll leave Marvale and go north to Halbracht. With any luck, Othilde will have finished the new batch of Lightfire. We'll take a wagon, and take a full shipment back to the king, telling him what we've learned about his nephew's power. Instead of a dead body, we'll offer him shields made of Lightfire. The ultimate protection against the prince's thrall. If he agrees to release Bibi, we'll outfit his entire army with them before Andreas turns up at his door and enthralls him, too."

It was a solid plan. A clever workaround, and the best hope they had now of saving their friend. Even if it did mean siding with the king.

"Screw the king," said Val. "Once we get Bibi back, I don't care what happens to him. If you ask me, both sides are bad. We just need to get out of this mess alive."

"At least under the Rayeres, we know what we're getting," reasoned Theo. "Andreas will be worse than his uncle ever was. A power-grasping tyrant who would enslave his own people to keep himself in control. Just look at Marvale. Imagine an entire kingdom like this, without free will, without free *thought*. For all we know, he's planning on serving Valterre up to the Mondragons on a platter. We could soon fall under the banner of Urnica and their bloodthirsty king."

"Unless Andreas enslaves him, too," muttered Sera, thinking of Talisa, and how callously he had discarded her broken body. Who knew where the true scope of his vision would lead the kingdom, or how the far-reaching strands of his power might affect the continent at large?

They were moving now, a sense of urgency taking hold as they began to stuff their satchels.

Outside, the sun was already sinking, the sky blushing to a deep rippling pink. Soon, the streetlamps would flicker to life and night would be upon them. Andreas would be waiting, watching. Hell, he could be watching them right now. Drawing the drapes, Theo said, "I'll speak to the innkeeper. Get a carriage arranged as fast as I can. We'll sneak out the back."

As the sun set on the red mills of Marvale, the darkening sky hummed with music and laughter tripped through the streets.

The familiar sounds raked their nails down Sera's spine. Just another one of the silver-tongued prince's lies. Another reminder to get the hell out of town.

Crouched between two burlap sacks of letters on the floor of the small postal coach Theo had managed to procure, Sera locked eyes with her friends. Fear hung like a cloud between them, no one daring to speak as they pulled out onto the main street and headed south toward the arch that marked the entrance to Marvale.

The postmaster rode out in front, his old workhorse clip-clopping far too slowly for Sera's liking. They had agreed he would drop them at the next town over, and from there, they would continue their journey north to Halbracht.

As they turned downhill at the end of the street, gathering speed, Val reached for her hand, squeezing it tight. Sera squeezed back.

Almost there.

Almost free.

Through a gap in the curtains, she spied the stone arch up ahead. The bodies of nightguards were still strung up like garlands, the scent of their rotting flesh stinging tears in her eyes.

Theo turned his face into her collar to silence his gag.

Eyes streaming, Sera dropped her head, counting the seconds until they were out.

Three more minutes until Marvale was behind them.

Two more minutes.

One minute.

Just *one more* minute.

The carriage slowed as it passed under the arch.

Then stopped.

Voices sounded near the front of the coach.

"Guards," hissed Theo, his eyes wide with panic.

Mercenaries.

Andreas must have stationed them at the gates.

There was a kerfuffle, the weight of the carriage shifting as the postmaster climbed down from his perch.

No.

No.

"What do we have here?" Andreas's face appeared at the window, graced with a frown as gruesome as the bodies swaying from his arch. "Three gutless turncoats about to ruin my fucking day."

The door swung open.

Val pounced like a wildcat, throwing herself at the prince. He reeled backward, and they fell in a heap on the ground. Theo went next, grabbing one of the prince's mercenaries by the throat. Sera dived to the right, running for the closest corpse. She pulled its sword free, swinging just as the second mercenary advanced on her.

A wide gash sliced through his right shoulder. Clutching at it, he stumbled backward, allowing her to gather her wits. With the postmaster cowering behind his wagon, it appeared to be three on three.

Val was holding her own with the prince, spitting and clawing and kicking for her life. Theo was still swinging from his mercenary's neck. Sera's assailant stalked toward her now, drawing his own sword.

"Do not dare harm my saint-maker!" Andreas yelled from the ground, before Val landed another punch. She earned two in return, the force knocking her head backward.

Sera raised her sword, sensing the odds shift in her favor. Her friends were fair game, but right here, in this moment, she was untouchable. She swung again, wild and fast and violent. In place of any kind of innate skill, she went for momentum. And complete recklessness. Running full tilt at the nearest mercenary, she slashed at his arms, his legs, bringing him to his knees. She reached the other just as he managed to dislodge Theo from around his neck.

When he drew his sword, she met it with her own, shoving her blade against his. She was slighter, weaker, and completely outmatched, but the magic simmering inside her meant her thoughts were still her own, and the poor bastard had been enthralled not to hurt her. Which meant she could be both a weapon and a shield.

She could save Theo's ass.

"Go!" she hissed, over her shoulder.

Her opponent dropped his sword, breaking the tension between their weapons. She stumbled into his chest, her blade biting into the hard leather of his vest. It fell away, leaving him free to grab onto her shoulders. Anchoring herself onto his beefy arms, she drew her knee up, sharp and fast, catching him between his legs.

Huffing out a curse, he fell to his knees. But when she

turned to help Val, he grabbed her collar, dragging her back to him. Those massive arms circled her chest, creating a steel trap. *Shit.* No matter how she bucked or kicked, she couldn't get free.

Still struggling against her captor, she could only watch as Andreas pinned Val to the ground. Choking her with one hand, he used the other to reach inside her collar and yank her necklace free. Holding it up to the dying light, his eyes grew in understanding.

A cruel smirk curled his lips. "And here I was afraid my power was waning." He smashed the bead of Lightfire beside Val's head, causing a quick flash of golden light.

Hinging upward, Val spat in his face.

He backhanded her.

"STOP!" Sera screamed. "If you lay one more finger on her, I swear I'll—"

"What?" he hissed, turning on her. "Run away like a frightened rat? Throw my kindness back in my face? Spit on the future of this kingdom because you're a gutless coward who can't handle the weight of her own destiny?" Grabbing Val's jaw, he dragged her nose right up to his. "And as for you, you feral little bitch, you will not harm me again. You will not run from me again. When I tell you to do something, you'll do it. Understood?"

Val went eerily still. Eyes misting, she nodded rigidly.

Sera's heart sank.

It was no trick this time.

Satisfied, Andreas peeled himself off her friend and stood

up. His brows knotted as he looked around. "Where the fuck is the other one?"

It was then that Sera noticed the fading thrum of hoofbeats. When she looked over her shoulder, she caught the silvered glint of Theo's hair, riding fast and far away from Marvale. A giddy laugh gathered in her chest. She swallowed it back.

Palming his sword, Andreas came to stand over her. "Do you think you've won, Saint-maker?" he sneered.

Looking up at him, she said, in all honesty, "I don't think either of us has won, Andreas."

His eyes darkened. "Not yet."

Behind him, Val sat up in a daze. "There's a worm in my head," she groaned. "It *hurts*."

Andreas kept his eyes on Sera. She kept her eyes on him. Hostility chilled the air between them, her magic igniting at his nearness and the hatred it stoked in her.

The prince sighed. "Since I can't enthrall you, we'll just have to do this the old-fashioned way."

Sera was about to ask him what the hell he meant when the hilt of his sword came crashing down. Pain exploded, snatching the world away. Then darkness devoured her, her magic winking out like light.

Chapter 33

Ransom

"Are you ever going to speak again?" Anouk asked her brother as they rowed through the gathering mist, toward the shores of Ra'azule. "If you think I'm angry about Mother Madeline, I'm not. She can rot on that island for all I care. Let the lizards have her. If they can chew their way through all that gristle."

On the bench across from her, Caruso and Nadia exchanged a bemused glance. "You really are nothing like your brother," remarked Caruso.

"You say that like it's a compliment."

"It is," they chorused.

"You're way less broody," said Caruso. "Look at him. He's even brooding right now."

Ignoring the jibe, Ransom turned to his sister. She looked so small wedged onto the bench beside him, her frame so slight that a brisk wind might topple her overboard.

Anouk was seventeen now, but those wide hazel eyes still hinted at the wonder they'd held when she was a little girl of seven dying to be a ballerina that danced across the world, and although her adult teeth had come in—as straight and white as pearls—he could still see hints of that crooked mischievous grin he used to sketch on long nights down in the catacombs. The dimple hidden in her right cheek. Her olive skin had turned wan from her secluded life in the priory, her life on the Isle of Alisa snatching the scattering of freckles from the bridge of her nose. And the way she looked up at him now—with quiet admiration—that was the same, too. As though the years that once separated them had concertinaed down to minutes, and the love that bonded them was as strong and sure as ever.

Tucking a matted strand of long dark hair behind her ear, Ransom said, "I'm not sorry about Mother Madeline either." Not when he looked at the manacle scars around his little sister's wrists, the bruises on her arms, the faint outline of her ribs jutting through her fraying blue robe.

He wanted to say more. The truth was, he had a hundred questions, but the first of them—the one that sat like a weight on his tongue—was too heavy for this moment. And he was afraid to ask it, afraid of the answer that sat like a dark shadow in that little boat with them, so he said instead, "We'll talk more on the shore, just you me."

Anouk nodded, then rested her head against his shoulder,

the movement like second nature to her, even after all this time. Ransom's thoughts drifted as he rowed, and the others fell quiet, welcoming the silence.

Back on the shores of Ra'azule, Ransom waited for Nadia and Caruso to walk on ahead, toward the lakeshore inn where a hot dinner beckoned. Gesturing for Anouk to sit beside him on a bench overlooking the gray lake, he summoned his courage and asked, "When did Mama die?"

Anouk sighed, casting off the bravado she'd worn back on the island. "Just over a year ago."

Although he'd known it was coming, the news punched him square in the chest. Winded, he doubled over, curling his arms around his middle to hold himself together.

Mama was *gone*. She'd been in the ground for a year and he hadn't even known it. How could he not have known? How could he not have felt her cleaving from the world, like a piece of his own heart falling away? He felt it now, like a blunt knife cutting through his chest.

She was dead. He would never again see the light of her smile or feel the warmth of her arms around him. Tears pricked his eyes, falling like raindrops on the shore. He had wasted all these years serving the darkness, kneeling at the feet of bitter, grasping men. Killing and killing and *killing*, and all for what? There would be no reunion now, no grand farewell.

"How?" he asked.

"You didn't hear?"

He snapped his chin up. "What do you mean?"

Her dark brows knotted. "It was a Dagger, Ransom."

Utter stillness now. Over the dull roaring in his ears, he said, "*Who?*"

"Gaspard Dufort."

Of course. *Of course* it was Dufort.

He might have laughed if he wasn't holding himself together, trying not to break from the cyclone of grief and rage inside him. All those years Dufort had promised Ransom he would help him find his family, and when he managed to track them down, he had struck from the shadows, removing the only thing that could ever tempt Ransom from the Order.

Anouk's voice was soft, her hand warm on his back. "We were down in Mauranus by then, living in a little cottage by the sea. After years on the run, we found a way to make a life there. A small one. But it was peaceful. Free of *him*." Their father and his cruel fists. His dank, liquored breath. "I was weaving baskets at our neighbor's house. Dufort was there when I came home. I recognized him from the penny papers. Mama used to pay a paperboy to go to Fantome every Sunday to fetch them. She read every single one, hoping to hear news of you, where you had ended up after Everell. It drove her mad—the wondering.

"At night in bed, instead of fairy tales, we told each other stories about you. We imagined where you were, eagerly sketching in the details of your new life." A smile brightened her voice. "We decided that you went to school to study art, and that one day, we'd see your paintings in the local gallery and know you had gotten out too. We'd know you by the stroke of your brush and the colors you used, and we'd find your new name right there in the bottom corner, your landscape like a map waiting to lead us home to you."

Ransom looked at his hands, thinking of all the stoppers they had removed over the years, all the vials of Shade he had swallowed. A part of him was glad Mama hadn't found him, that she had died with her dream of him intact, thinking he was an artist and not a murderer.

"That day, when I came home, Mama screamed at me to run. I dropped my basket and fled."

Silent tears striped her cheeks, smearing the dirt there. "I ran even as her scream cut out. I ran and I didn't stop until I made my way here, to Ra'azule. I couldn't think of anywhere else to go. I just knew I needed a place where the Daggers wouldn't find me. So I came, and I chose a new name and I got on my knees and I pledged myself to the Order of Alisans."

"You became Marianne."

"I wasn't very good at it," she admitted. "The priory was so . . . *stifling*."

"You never did like to be bored."

She pulled a face. "Prayers always make me fall asleep."

"You were right to hide. Dufort was like a dog with a bone. He would have killed you, too," said Ransom, with unerring certainty. There was no line of depravity he wouldn't cross.

"I thought it was Papa who sent him."

"No. Papa is dead." Ransom took a breath. "I killed him the day after you fled Fantome."

Silence, then, the lake whispering in the moonlight.

Anouk's hand on his back grew heavier. "Good," she said, more to herself than to him. *"Good."*

It was a bleak moment—an exchange of sorry news, but where Ransom was grief-stricken at the loss of his mother, Anouk was relieved to hear that Papa was gone.

"We're free now," she said eventually, and there was a kernel of hope in her voice. "And look what fate has done for us, Bastian. After all these years, it sent you here, to me. Saint Oriel has brought us back together again."

"And it has made you a saint." Ransom was still struggling to believe it, to see beyond the wraith his little sister had become, to the power swirling within. The kind that had threatened the king himself, that had nearly cost her her own life.

"A happy accident," she said, only she was frowning now. "I've never given much thought to the saints. Even when I prayed on my knees in that tower, my mind always strayed beyond the white walls, beyond that small cloistered life that never suited me. Even the *robes* are drab." Pulling a face, she plucked at the threading on her sleeve.

"But then the storm came, and the tower fell, and I couldn't run fast enough. I was inside it when it crumbled, buried in the heap of its rubble, and I would have died there if I hadn't felt something spark to life inside me. I lifted the stones, Bastian. I was half dead, and I found a way to move them." She turned her hands over in the moonlight. "Before that, I could barely carry the well water back to the priory. We were so weak from lack of food. And the bucket was so heavy I'd have to stop every twenty paces to catch my breath. Sister Honoria used to laugh at me." She tensed at the name, a shadow falling over her face.

"At first, I was too ill to understand what had happened to me. As I began to come to, I would have these awful nightmares. Panic would strike in the dead of night and I'd wake in my bed, screaming and thrashing, my magic like a bonfire in my chest. Mother Madeline started to chain me to the bed, but it didn't stop the panic. It only made it worse. It made everything worse." She looked away, guilt coloring her voice. "I tore down the walls. I shattered the windows. One night, half the ceiling caved in. Honoria tried to wake me, and she got struck. When I saw the blood on the floorboards, I turned cold. Utterly still. And I heard a voice inside me for the first time, so clear, it was like a bell ringing."

She stood abruptly, frustration making her pace. "I *knew* I could mend her. I could have healed her. I'm not just meant to take things apart, but to put them back together. To build. To make. To *fix*. I knew I could stop the blood and knit her wound back together, but Mother Madeline refused to unchain me. She called me a Saint of Ruination, a curse on the priory, an *unholy abomination*, and struck me as I pleaded with her. They took Honoria away. By the time I was dragged out of that room days later, she was already buried."

Stopping, Anouk curled her fists. She closed her eyes, but not before Ransom caught the golden glint behind them and felt the bench tremble underneath him.

"Breathe," he said, softly. "It's not your fault, Anouk."

She puffed her chest up, her breath whistling through her nose. Once, twice. The bench stopped trembling, and when she opened her eyes again, they were clear. In a quiet voice, she said, "I don't understand why this has happened to me, Bastian. I didn't want it. I still don't want it."

"I think that might by why," he said, gently. "You have power precisely *because* you don't covet it."

"What am I supposed to do with it?" She looked so lost now, as young and uncertain as that day she had fled from Everell.

"You'll find out, Anouk," he said, and he was suddenly sure of it. "We'll find out together."

Ransom couldn't guess at the inner workings of destiny—he had stopped trying months ago—but he no longer believed in coincidences. The threads of fate were growing stronger, moving faster, getting tighter, like gossamer strands shimmering in the air, binding him—binding all of them—to a future that was yet to unfold. He could see now that he could leave the Daggers but he could not outrun the change that was about to befall Valterre, not when the two women he loved most in the world were tied to the very fate of the kingdom.

In being chosen by Saint Oriel, Anouk and Seraphine were a part of something grand and vital and urgent, and if this kingdom truly was to be remade under the Second Coming of the Saints, he would have his own part to play in it.

For their sakes, and for his own.

There was no walking away now.

Fate had claimed his sister and his lover.

It could have him, too.

Edging closer, Anouk looked down on him, her expression turning quizzical. "Have you been a Dagger all this time, Bastian?"

He nodded. "Since the day we parted."

"You don't look like one." Her brows knitted. "The others . . . Nadia and Caruso. They have those marks all over their hands. I know what they mean." Each one, a death. The shadow of every vial they'd swallowed. "But your hands are clean."

A part of him wanted to laugh but when he lifted his hands to the moonlight, he remembered that she was right. "They weren't always like this," he told her plainly. "For a long time, they were worse than most. Deep and dark and painful."

"But now they're gone? How?"

"There's a woman, Anouk." He smiled without meaning to. "Another touched by fate. Her name is Seraphine, and the day she stumbled into my life, it exploded into color. She saved me, heart and soul."

And now I have to save her.

Anouk's face lit up. "Tell me."

"Come," he said, rising from the bench. "I'll tell you everything on the way to Marvale."

After eating their fill in a nearby inn and telling Anouk of the insidious threat of Prince Andreas and the rebellion he was brewing in the heart of Valterre, they returned to the carriage, eager to be free of Ra'azule and the island skulking in the mist. Having seized the opportunity to wash and change at the inn, Anouk gratefully accepted a spare outfit from Nadia, before chucking her own ruined robes in the lake.

Now, with her long dark hair clean and braided away from her face, and her cheeks scrubbed of silt and dirt, she looked more like herself than ever. She was older by some years and changed by the hand of fate, but was still the same Anouk. Soft yet fearless, and ever eager to be at her brother's side. They rode out front together, Ransom taking the first shift, while Caruso and Nadia polished off a bottle of wine and slept in the back of the carriage.

They journeyed on through the night. Guided by clear skies and a generous moon, they were kept awake by the chatter of their own voices as they swapped stories of their last ten years, painting in the edges of each other with the kind of giddy excitement Ransom hadn't felt since he was a child, swapping fairy tales with Anouk under the duvet.

And when Anouk said, "Tell me about Seraphine," an entire world poured out of him. He barely took a breath, frustration pricking at him as he tried to put into words the very music of his soul, to explain that insistent thread in his chest that always tugged when she was near. The searing sense that she was his, and he was hers.

Talk of his spitfire only made his desire to return to her greater, his eagerness to face the prince making his throat tight.

Never again would he let Andreas twist the fabric of his mind, not now he knew what the Silver-tongue was capable of. Not while he had Anouk at his side.

Sister.

Saint.

Secret weapon.

No. When Ransom returned to Marvale, their meeting would be quick and bloody.

It was a relief when dawn came, the waning moon fading in the sun-blushed sky. The red mills crowned the distant hills, farmland spilling out on either side of them, knitting a patchwork of green and gold. Sheep and cows slumbered in the yawning quiet, which was punctuated by the occasional cry of a rooster and Caruso's gruesome snores.

Ransom's sense of urgency gnawed at him, his heart pounding when the archway to Marvale finally appeared before them. He had forgotten to warn Anouk about the nightguards that hung from it. Retching at the sight, she leaned over the side of the carriage and vomited. "What *is* this?" she managed between heaves.

"Andreas has a flair for dramatics." Ransom could forget sometimes how startling a dead body was to someone so unused to seeing them. Making them. "Sorry. I should have told you."

The horse slowed as they drew closer. There was another body on the ground. Not a nightguard, but an older man in a flat cap, brown trousers, and a crumpled work shirt. He was slumped on his side in the middle of the archway, blocking the way ahead.

Hopping down from the carriage, Ransom made his way toward the body. It whimpered as he approached. Coming to his knees, Ransom said, "You're alive?"

Another whimper.

He rolled the man over, noting the deep bruises on his face, the bloodshot vessels in his eyes. He had been beaten to a bloodied pulp. With a struggling wheeze, he answered, *"Barely."*

"Ransom." Anouk was standing behind him. "There's blood everywhere."

Blood on the stones. Blood near the bridge. Blood dripping from the arch. "I know, Anouk."

He turned back to the man. "What happened to you?"

He took three breaths to answer. "F-f-failed g-getaway."

"Ransom." Anouk's voice was shaking now. It took him a moment to realize the cobbles were trembling too. Something groaned overhead. He looked up in time to see a crack fissuring down the middle of the arch, the stone on either side slowly giving way. "I c-c-can't stop."

"*Breathe*, Anouk," he called over his shoulder. Her eyes were bright gold. "It's all right. Just *breathe*."

Too late. The nightguards fell, crumpling on either side of him. The archway shook, the joins in the grooves coming apart. Grabbing the old man under his arms, Ransom dragged him backward with barely a heartbeat to spare. The entire structure came down with a deep, rattling boom.

Covering his head with his hands, Ransom threw himself

on top of the old man. Dust showered them, shards of rock and shale nicking his arms, his hands.

Anouk's cry rang out, her footsteps thundering closer. "I'm so sorry! I didn't mean to! I saw the bodies and I panicked!"

Somewhere over her shoulder, Caruso stuck his head out of the carriage window. "Some of us are trying to sleep!"

Sitting up, Ransom swept the dust from his hair and sighed. "You're really going to have to get a handle on that," he told his sister. "Preferably sooner rather than later."

"I just . . . I got spooked." Her forehead creasing, she knelt down beside the old man. "You don't look so well, sir."

Gross understatement. The man was half dead.

She flexed her fingers. "Maybe I could try and help—"

"Wait." Ransom eyed him with mounting suspicion. "He could be one of Andreas's mercenaries."

The old man puffed out a denial. *"Postmaster."*

"A postmaster! That's hardly sinister." Anouk laid her hands on the man's chest, swatting Ransom away when he tried to stop her. "Just let me try. He's at death's door anyway."

Closing her eyes, Anouk began to breathe deeply and slowly, her fingers twitching as they skated across his ribs, as if drawn there by some invisible magnet.

While she worked, Nadia and Caruso emerged from the carriage in matching states of bewilderment. Leaving his sister to her mending, Ransom stalked to meet them.

"Remind me to never get on her bad side," said Nadia, surveying the ruined arch. "That's quite an entrance."

So much for the element of surprise.

"We'll have to go in on foot. Find the shadows and keep to them." It was early still, the streets beyond the shattered arch eerily silent. High on the hills, the red mills were still turning but Marvale was fast asleep.

"Ransom." Anouk's voice drew him back to her. The old man was sitting up now. His face was still every shade of purple and he was clutching his ribs, but there was color in his pallor now, and strength in his wheezes.

"Punctured lung." Anouk beamed. "This makes up for the arch."

"That depends on how useful he turns out to be," said Caruso, coming up behind Ransom.

"You saved my life, girl," said the postmaster, ignoring them entirely. "Let me thank you. I have to thank you." He patted his pockets frantically and, before Anouk could stop him, he pulled out a large silver ring and folded it into her hand. "Take this. Please, just take it. Too big for those dainty fingers, but I was told it'd fetch a pretty penny in the market. Belonged to Hugo Versini, so it did."

With blood roaring in his ears, Ransom stared at the skull ring in his little sister's hand. The one he had worn for months already, binding him to a life of death and shadows. The one he had taken off and left on the bedside table the morning he walked out on Seraphine and didn't look back.

The one she must have found when she'd awoken alone in that bedroom, wondering where he was.

In a low voice, he said, "Where did you get that?"

"They gave it to me. Three runaways, they were. Said they had to get to the next town right quick. Bartered it for safe passage out of Marvale, so they did."

All those gruesome bruises on the postmaster's face were starting to look a lot more sinister now. "Looks like you didn't get very far," said Ransom, carefully.

He shook his head. "Surprised I got away with my life."

Ransom's heart climbed up his throat. "What about the runaways?" It was a struggle to keep his voice even, to push back the sudden clamor of his panic. "What became of them?"

The postmaster shrugged, looking back toward the slumbering village. "They're all gone now. Everyone is gone."

"Gone where?" chorused Caruso and Nadia.

"South. To the Summer Palace." At their looks of confusion, he added, "The People's Saint has gone to kill the king."

Part IV

"The Age of Kings is at an end,
The time of the saints has come again.
For there to be change, there must be sacrifice.
For there to be peace, there first must be war."

ANDREAS MONDRAGON RAYERE,
THE PEOPLE'S SAINT

Chapter 34

Seraphine

In the depths of slumber, where no thought or worry stirred, Oriel found her. The saint's face was grave, worry pinching the smooth brown skin around her mouth.

"Hear my voice, Seraphine."

Sera stared up at the saint, marveling at her closeness. She was almost real enough to touch, though she didn't dare disturb the mirage by reaching for her. How beautiful Oriel was, even in her anxiety. How bright her dark eyes shone, the pearlescent beads at the ends of her long black hair swaying in an unseen breeze.

"There is a wrongness in fate's tapestry. A thread that does not belong." Oriel's voice grew low and urgent. "You must pull it out."

The saint drew closer, those doleful brown eyes filling up the world. In them, Sera watched three towers fall, over and over again. She saw a fair-haired man throw his arms wide, gathering up the storm. Claiming all that magic for himself.

Oriel brought her lips close to her ear. "You must pull him out."

She drew back, looking so much older now. Frail, and small, and frightened, in a way that frightened Sera, too. "Or it will all unravel, and the world as you know it will fall to ruin."

The words spun round and round, echoing inside Sera's head.

And the world as you know it will fall to ruin . . .

Fall to ruin . . .

Ruin . . .

Oriel clapped her hands, creating a thunderous crash.

The dream shattered.

Sera woke with a gasp.

Brightness engulfed her. She blinked, trying to clear her vision but the eerie glow remained. It was rolling off her skin. Shining through her bloodstained shirt and glowing underneath the hem of her damp trousers. A cold trickle of air caressed the back of her neck, the scent of brine sticking to the inside of her nose. There was something dreadfully familiar about it.

"What will unravel?" Bibi's voice sounded from somewhere beyond the light. "Sera, were you dreaming just now?"

"Bibi? Is that you?" Slowly, softly, the light faded, Sera's magic settling back under her skin. It was dark then, the dimness feathered by distant wall lamps. Just enough of them to illuminate the thick black bars that separated her from Bibi.

Her friend was in the cell across from her, her pale fingers white around the bars, her face pressed against the metal like she was trying to wrench them apart. "It's me." She summoned a shaky smile, but the hell of these past few weeks was written all over her face. The natural rosy hue had been drained from her cheeks. Her once bright eyes were sunken, and her beautiful red hair was lank and knotted. "You've been glowing in your sleep. Murmuring the strangest things about threads and tapestries. I've been waiting for you to wake up."

"How long was I out?"

"A day or so. Almost twice as long as Val. She filled me in on everything before dropping off again." Shifting to the left, Bibi offered a glimpse of Val, who was sleeping on a bedroll behind her. While they had been confined to the same cell, there were two sets of bars and a narrow passage separating them from Sera. And her magic, she supposed. Unfortunately, someone had had the good sense to confine the resident saint-maker to solitary confinement. Not that she really knew the first thing about making a saint. At least without scouring a hole in their chest.

Dropping her voice, Bibi said, "Whatever Andreas did to her mind has exhausted her. It's like she's been wrung out like a dishrag. She's been trying but she's not truly herself, Sera. I don't know how to get her back."

Sera didn't have the heart to admit she didn't know either. And worse, she couldn't tell what commands the prince had buried in Val's thoughts, or how they might manifest. Though the reminder of Andreas's eerie elastic smile jolted Sera back to her senses. And the white-hot edge of her anger. The last thing she remembered was being at the archway to Marvale, caught in the grip of a failed getaway and kneeling beneath the prince's fury.

Now she was trapped in his uncle's dungeon. *Again.*

A cold slick of dread came over her.

"Where is the king, Bibi?"

Bibi huffed a short laugh. "How on earth should I know? It's not like he's ever visited me. Not that I'm complaining. Only the soldiers come down here, and they're usually too brash or too busy to hold any kind of intelligent conversation with. Although one did slip me a pack of playing cards when he heard me singing." A small sad smile glimmered in the dimness. "If it wasn't for that morsel of kindness, I think I'd have gone mad by now."

"I'm so sorry, Bibi." Guilt nudged Sera closer to the bars. She wished she could wrench them apart too, crawl to her friends and throw her arms around her. "You don't deserve this."

"None of us deserves it," said Bibi fiercely. "All we ever tried to do was help the kingdom. Why should we be punished for it?"

"Because bad men are afraid of good magic." Saint Oriel's face flickered in her mind, the echo of her dream still whispering faintly. *There is a wrongness in fate's tapestry. A thread that does not belong. You must pull it out.*

"We're not giving up, Bibi."

They couldn't afford to cower now. Not after everything she'd witnessed at Marvale. The king was one kind of poison, but Andreas Mondragon was a snake coming up from the long grass. A lethal, powerful charmer who had to be stopped at all costs. Left under his care, the entire kingdom would fall to ruin.

"Do you have a plan?" said Bibi. "Please tell me you have a plan."

Sera did not have a plan.

But she had hope, and clarity of mind, and that was not nothing. She might not have the prince's favor, but she knew she had his attention. His interest. He *needed* her to make his court, to empower his chosen minions. All she had to do was turn that need to her own advantage. Charm the silver-tongued saint, while sticking a knife in his back.

"You've got that wild look in your eyes." Bibi's voice was wary. "The kind that means you're about to do something reckless."

Damn right. "I'm going to kill the prince, Bibi."

There was a strange spluttering sound. *"How?"*

"I don't know yet," she admitted. "First, I have to find him."

"He has to be here," said Bibi. "The soldiers changed the night you arrived. Not their faces, but their eyes. How they move. It's like they're all trapped in a fog."

"All saints," muttered Sera, trying not to shudder. If Andreas had already installed himself at the Summer Palace, then what had become of the king?

And more importantly, what would become of them?

Days passed with maddening slowness, the constant dark making it almost impossible to keep count of the hours. They kept time by the meagre meals that came three times a day: cold porridge in the morning, a bread roll with cheese for lunch, and a sliver of fatty meat and boiled potatoes for dinner. The howling wind was worse at night, stealing under their blankets and filling their cells with the fetid tang of seaweed.

Val slept on and off, often waking in such a fog that at times she would have to sit in the darkest corner of her cell with her head in her hands, waiting for the pain to pass. Andreas's commands wormed through her thoughts, surfacing whenever they spoke of the prince. It was then that she would retreat, unable to speak against the Silver-tongue or conceive of a plan that would lead her to harm him.

Though Sera missed the physical closeness of her friends, the ability to hold their hands, to hug them during the cold howling nights, she was glad that Bibi and Val could offer that comfort to each other. That they weren't alone in their fear and uncertainty. That whatever came next, they would be able to face it together.

In the meantime, they waited, and they listened to the patter of footfall overhead. The palace was growing busier, a rising chorus of voices echoing through the damp stone walls as servants scurried about at all hours of the day and night.

Outside, whenever the ocean quieted to a gentle hush, Sera heard the palace gates groaning open to let carriages through. Wheels trundled across the grounds, punctuated by the excited chatter of voices and the telltale thrum of heels striking the polished floors.

"Something's happening," Val said to her one afternoon,

when her eyes were clear, and she was sitting at the front of her cell. "I swear it sounds like a party up there."

Bibi, who was shuffling their playing cards between games of rummy, went to the back wall to count the chalk markings there. "Oh," she said, in a strained voice. "I think it's King's Day."

The king's birthday.

An annual kingdom-wide celebration of Bertrand Rayere IV. Ordinarily, there would be banners hung in every town and village of Valterre, the children wearing paper crowns, colorful ribbons in their hair, while lively music spilled out of the taverns onto the streets and revelers gathered to toast another year turning. Another year of their king.

Even back in the plains, Mama always made a butter cake for the occasion, letting Sera stay up well past her bedtime to sip wine and watch the stars, imagining themselves as queens for the night. Mama never cared much for the king or his ilk, but she never passed up a reason to eat cake.

Sera wondered what King's Day would look like today in the rebelling heart of Fantome. Whether Andreas's followers were burning their pyres and tossing nightguards into the Verne. Whether people were watching the royal flags go up in smoke from their windows, fearing what the following year might hold.

When four stern-faced soldiers arrived an hour later, she was expecting them. The first of them, a tall imposing woman with a crop of white hair, said, "You three are invited to tonight's spectacle."

Spectacle.

Not party.

Not good.

"What's this spectacle all about?" asked Bibi, warily.

"You'll see soon enough." The soldier sniffed, then wrinkled her nose. "For now, you'll come with me. The maids will have to scrub the terrible reek off you and dress you in something presentable."

Chapter 35

Seraphine

The grand ballroom at the Summer Palace was alive with color and crowds and music. And Sera was the guest of honor. High on the dais that occupied one end of the room, she sat in a velvet chair on the right-hand side of the king's throne, which was empty. Lark occupied the chair on the other side, dressed in his long crimson robe and that eerie golden mask.

Sera herself wore no mask. At Andreas's instruction, she had been separated from Bibi and Val not long after they were ushered from their cells, then scrubbed until her skin was raw and dressed in a gown fit for a queen. A gown that probably *did* belong to the queen. Dyed the deep crimson of a winter rose, it hugged her corseted waist, before tumbling to the floor in delicate tiers resembling petals. Her hair fell in loose ringlets down her back, swept away from her face with fine golden pins that better revealed the dark red of her lips and the kohl smudged around her eyes.

Yes, here was the beginning of the prince's grand spectacle, and she was to be a part of it. The others milling about the ballroom might have looked upon her with envy if it wasn't for the ruinous scowl on her face and the chafing ropes binding her wrists to the armrests of her chair.

"Don't dare try anything funny tonight," the stern-faced soldier had warned her before prodding her up the stairwell. "If you ruin this moment for Andreas, he'll see to it that you suffer, saint-maker or not."

That she could well believe. But she'd made no promises to the soldier. She might be dressed like a dream, but tonight she had every intention of becoming the prince's worst nightmare.

Seated and quietly seething, Sera scanned the room for her friends.

Minstrels were playing on the upper balcony, which ringed the sprawling ballroom. The checkered floors were gleaming, the domed ceiling hung with glittering chandeliers, which were, in turn, decorated with bunting—the cornflower blue and sunflower yellow of Valterre to celebrate King's Day. Banners adorned the cream filigreed wallpaper, glimmering faintly under the moonlight that streamed in through the tall arched windows. At the other end of the ballroom, a pair of wide double doors sealed off a generous white-stone balcony that overlooked the South Sea.

The more she gleaned, the deeper her unease burrowed. Though the ballroom was bedecked for celebration, unease hung thick in the air. Judging by their gowns and finery, the guests here were clearly noble folk. The king's people—courtiers and confidants, wealthy merchants and traders, and favored guests, come to celebrate his birthday—but they were plainly confused at his absence, and becoming anxious at the sheer number of guards that surrounded them.

The room was thick with soldiers. They paced by the dais and lined the walls, scanning the crowd with military attention. Although they wore the colors of Valterre, the crest on their uniforms had been replaced by that of a single golden rose. The prince's symbol. An omen of what tonight would bring.

When she finally spotted Bibi and Val in the fray, Sera hardly recognized them. They had been primped and preened to an absurd degree, their hair curled in tight ringlets and pinned high on their heads. Bibi was wearing a satin emerald dress with a high, beaded neckline, while Val wore a deep purple sheath dress that expertly brought out the violet sheen of her hair and the dark fuchsia of her lips. They were loitering to the right of the dais, trying to blend in with the other nobles—but it was Bibi, with her clear eyes and wringing hands—who stood out to Sera.

Pressing a hand to the secret bead of Lightfire she wore beneath her collar, she looked up at the empty throne and then back at Sera, a question rippling across her brow. *What on earth is going on?*

Suddenly, a horn sounded, casting a rippling hush over the ballroom. As if summoned by the force of her curiosity, Prince Andreas arrived, arm in arm with his uncle. The king was dressed finely, even wearing his ceremonial sash and crown.

Never one to resist a flair of theater, Andreas had styled himself like a king too, wearing a high-collared golden frock coat inlaid with crimson filigree. His thick hair fell in loose waves around his face, as bright and shiny as the high gold boots that covered his black trousers.

His grin was as wide as Sera had ever seen it, and there was a subtle malevolence in his expression he didn't bother to conceal.

With a wave of his wrist, he ushered the king onward.

King Bertrand IV lumbered onto the dais with slow unsteady footsteps, eventually seating himself with a labored grunt. He didn't acknowledge Lark or Sera sitting on either side of him, nor did he seem remotely perturbed by their presence on the dais. In fact, he didn't notice them at all. Not that it bothered Sera. He was plainly under the prince's compulsion.

This was Andreas's stage, after all, and these were his players.

As still as a statue on his throne, the king looked toward the balcony doors at the other end of the room, that blank gaze passing over his roomful of guests as though they weren't there at all. They began to murmur among themselves. Some even tried to approach the king but were shooed away by the soldiers stationed there.

Tucking his hands behind his back, Andreas made his way into the middle of the room. With mounting unease, the noble houses of Valterre parted to let him through.

The music ground to a sudden halt.

Eyes blazing gold, Andreas turned on the heel of his boot, looking over the gathered crowd. "Esteemed noble folk of

Valterre and guests of the king, you will kneel on the ground until I say otherwise," he announced.

There was a fleeting breath of confusion, a simmering of outrage and then—

All across the room, guests fell to their knees like dominoes. Only Bibi knelt a half-second too late, but mercifully the prince didn't notice. He was too busy enjoying the tide of frantic whispers, salivating over the unique terror he was sowing among the most powerful families in the kingdom. A shudder passed through Sera as she read the anguish on the guests' faces, how their spines stiffened and their fists clenched as they fought in vain against the prince's thrall.

Licking his teeth, enjoying the view. "As it goes, I prefer my subjects on their knees in supplication."

Monster.

Sera's temper flared, stoking the well of her magic.

There is a wrongness in fate's tapestry. A thread that does not belong, it whispered Saint Oriel's words to her. *You must pull it out.*

Heart thundering, she strained against the ropes binding her wrists. They bit into her skin, leaving deep red welts.

His voice arcing, Andreas turned toward the dais. "Tonight, in celebration of my uncle's birthday, we will welcome him into retirement and celebrate a new golden era in our kingdom. Here sits the first members of my royal court. My fiery Valterran rose, Seraphine Marchant, and the Hand of Death itself, Lark Delano. My maker and her saint. The first of many more to come."

Murmurs of unease rippled through the crowd as the meaning of his words sank in.

"Rot in hell, Andreas!" The cry tripped off her tongue before she could help it. "Your silky words won't work on me."

"We'll see about that." Andreas moved to stand in front of his uncle. "Are you enjoying your farewell party, Uncle?" he asked the stone-faced king. "It's growing quite stuffy in here, is it not?"

The king gave no answer.

The prince snapped his fingers at a nearby soldier. "Open the balcony doors. Let some fresh sea air in."

A moment later, the doors groaned open, revealing a breathtaking view of the moonlit South Sea. Marred by four hanging bodies.

Cries of horror filled the ballroom.

"SILENCE!" shouted the prince.

The nobles choked on their whimpers, at once wrangled into unnerving quiet. Sera recognized those hanging bodies, even from a distance. The king's royal advisers. His *silent quartet*. How true that was now. The kills appeared fresh, the men dangling from the ledge above the doors by their necks.

Sera glanced at the king. His eyes had turned glassy, his skin so pale he looked bloodless.

"Do you regret your callous treatment of me yet, Uncle?" Andreas called out. "Your selfish disregard for your only nephew? Your barely contained disdain for my dear mother? All these years, you've held Valterre in the palm of your greasy hand, leaving the capital at the mercy of the twisted festering magic of Shade. Content to sit in your palace and gorge yourself on your own people's fear. The tides of fate have changed. Valterre no longer bends its knee to greedy, cowardly kings but to blessed saints." He canted his head. "Today, I will take what is mine."

The king said nothing, only watched in passive silence as the prince crooked his finger. "Come. Give me your crown."

Rising on trembling legs, the king stood like a puppet yanked on a string. He drifted down the steps toward his nephew. In one fluid movement, he ripped the crown from his own head and placed it on his nephew's. It shone as golden as his eyes.

Andreas removed the sword from his belt and handed it to his uncle. Looking directly at Sera now, he crooned, "And now, your heart."

There was a collective intake of breath.

The king hesitated, confused.

"Andreas," hissed Sera. "If you do this, there's no going back."

Through his teeth, Andreas said, "Cut. It. Out."

With ruthless efficiency, the King of Valterre took the sword and drove it into his own chest. Falling to his knees, he continued his impossible task, attempting to cut through muscle and bone and sinew, but there was so much blood pouring out, his grip slackened.

The sound of retching filled the ballroom. Guests began to faint, hitting the floor in a chorus of dull thuds. Bibi was hyperventilating, clutching onto Val for dear life.

Digging her fingernails into the armrests, Sera fought to

hold her nerve. Even as her magic became a furnace in her chest, burning hotter than ever before.

Pull it out! Pull it out! Pull it out!

Wrinkling his nose at the growing pool of blood, Andreas stepped backward. "Watch the boots, uncle."

The king swayed, his hands falling to his sides. He looked up at his nephew, and with his mouth full of blood, drew a final, wet gasp.

His body hit the ground like a sack of grain.

There was a deep, dread-filled silence.

Returning his attention to Sera, Andreas canted his head. "Changed your mind yet?"

"End this horrible spectacle, Andreas," she urged him. "Let these people go. You and I can talk in private."

And I swear I'll find a way to kill you.

"But wait . . ." He feigned a sigh. "What good is it removing the king if I let his bastard heirs live on?"

Sera heard their whimpers before she spotted them. The king's young sons were being shoved through the crowds by a pair of soldiers. The queen was with them, her beautiful face stricken as she pushed her boys behind her, trying to hide their view with the swell of her skirts.

Her gray eyes were wet, the noise that burst from her at the sight of the dead king halfway between a howl and a sob. *"Oh blessed saints!"* she cried out. "What have you done?"

"Andreas, *don't.*" Sera bucked and thrashed against her binds. "They're innocent!"

In the chair across from her, Lark stiffened behind his mask, revealing a hint of his own discomfort. “Stop him,” she hissed. “You’re not bound to that chair. You can take him. You can stop whatever he’s about to do.”

But the Necromancer simply shook his head. The minute movement signing three more death sentences in Andreas’s bloody theater. The prince could not be stopped. He was about to murder the king’s heirs in full view of his court, and smile while he did it.

The question of *how* was answered by the name he called out. “Come out, Lisette,” he crowed. “Let us put the loyalty you have pledged to me to the test.”

The doors to the ballroom opened. An icy-looking blond woman arrived in a gown of glittering silver, leading a crowd of thirty or so people. Not soldiers, nor nobles. Not mercenaries nor would-be revelers. Dressed in black, and prowling among the kneeling guests with predatorial ease, they gathered in the middle of the ballroom. If they noticed the king’s bloodied corpse or his four hanging advisers, they made no sign of it. Not a flinch among them, but then, Sera supposed they were used to the casualness of murder.

They were Daggers, after all.

There was no mistaking the silver of their eyes, or the sinister black whorls darting across their skin. Shadows gathered where they stood, poised like adders waiting to strike. Sera vaguely recognized the icy blond and assumed that in Ransom’s absence she had been the one left in charge. Lisette, the prince had called her.

Lisette, who, under no obvious compulsion and at the lure

of ever more power, had turned her Order over to the silver-tongued saint.

"Andreas." The queen's voice broke. She rushed forward, grabbing onto the front of his frock coat. "Andreas, they're just boys. You were like them once."

Uncurling her fingers with exaggerated slowness, he said in a voice dripping with scorn, "Yes, I was, Odette. And you weren't very nice to me, were you?"

"Andreas! *Please!*" The queen was screaming now, begging on her knees, desperately clutching at the hem of his coat. Behind her, her sons stood stock-still, staring horror-struck at their father's dead body.

Sera's magic was in her throat now. She couldn't talk. Couldn't think. Every inch of her pulsed with a dangerous mix of panic and rage, the force of a tornado quickly rising inside her. Power gathered in her hands, sizzling across her palms. She dug them deeper into the armrests. The wood of her chair began to smoke, her magic desperate to be free at any cost.

Andreas shoved the queen off him. "If you want mercy, crawl to my Daggers and kiss their feet. You will find none here."

With an anguished cry, the queen turned for Lisette.

A shadow crested from the floor, drowning her on her hands and knees. Her scream cut out with chilling abruptness.

Lisette didn't even blink. But she smiled like a serpent when, after ten quick heartbeats, she tugged the shadow away. There lay the Queen of Valterre, devoured by Shade. As dead as her husband.

Her sons' screams echoed from every corner of the ballroom.

The ropes around Sera's wrists went up in smoke as the boys rushed to their mother.

"NO!" With an anguished cry, Bibi lunged from the crowd and threw herself on top of them, making a shield of her body.

Another wave crested—and shattered in a hail of golden light.

"For fuck's sake," fumed Lisette. "Get that Lightfire off her."

Ripping her hands free, Sera leaped off the dais. She went instead for Andreas, seizing upon the momentary distraction. In the absence of thought—all those old festering fears that so often held her back—Sera gave herself over to emotion. To that gathering tornado of rage and pain and determination.

Her magic bellowed from the far reaches of her soul.

Maker! it cried.

But Sera's target was already made. By his own hand, he had cheated fate. Taken something from that storm that did not truly belong to him.

Unmake him, she cried to her magic and to Saint Oriel.

Pull out the thread.

Take out the pretender.

Power emanated from her like dragon fire, her body glowing like a lit flame as she landed on the prince. They fell to the ground together. Ignoring the rising shouts behind her, Sera pinned him there, pressing her hands into his face. He bucked and screamed, the scent of his burning flesh invading her nostrils.

Not enough.

Take his power.

Unmake him.

Plunging her fist into his mouth, she reached for that serpent's tongue. She caught his scream in her fist and crushed it with her magic. It was wet and slimy in her grip, even as it sizzled.

Hands on her shoulders now.

Almost there.

More around her neck.

So much blood.

A blade at her throat.

Rip it out.

She was dragged away, into a swell of soldiers.

No.

No!

Convulsing from the pain of their encounter, Andreas rolled onto his side. Soldiers alighted on him like fretful butterflies, using their coats to mop up the blood pouring from his mouth, holding his head steady as he retched and vomited.

Wild-eyed and panting, it took Sera a moment to get her legs beneath her, to realize that Lark was the one restraining her.

"Fool," he hissed in her ear. "Don't you know a beast that can't be trained will be put down?"

She slammed her head backward, shoving that gaudy mask into his nose until it crunched. "Enjoy your leash, dog."

"At least I know how to keep my friends alive," he sneered, spinning her around.

Sera saw Val first. Bent double on the floor, she was keening like a wounded animal. Reaching toward a familiar slip of emerald satin.

It took Sera longer than it should have to follow that green ribbon. To bring herself to look at the body lying next to her own feet. The body she had abandoned when she threw herself at Andreas.

Bibi.

There was such a tearing in Sera's chest. A deep, sucking sob burst from the puncture wound in her heart. She gasped for air but there was only pain.

Bibi was *dead*.

The bead of Lightfire at her throat lay shattered on the floor beside her, her once vibrant blue eyes turned black from Shade. Curled up on either side of her, as if they were simply sleeping, were the young princes of Valterre.

All three of them gone in ten heartbeats.

Sera's knees buckled, but Lark only tightened his hold. Refusing to let her kneel by the body of her friend. Refusing to let her hold Bibi one last time, to whisper to her *I'm sorry*, and pray that somewhere in the heavens she could hear her.

When she raised her chin, Lisette was smirking at her.

In the space of one breath, Sera imagined ten different ways of killing her. "There goes the fate of the kingdom," she said, her voice cracking through her teeth. "I hope it was worth it."

Lisette's silver eyes were cruel and taunting. "It's called survival, Seraphine. You never did get the hang of it, did you?"

With a pained grunt, Andreas dragged himself to his knees. His face was a gruesome patchwork of red and blackened skin, that once-sneering mouth now bloody and swollen. It was a beautiful sight, but Sera was too broken to enjoy it.

The prince's rage pulsed like a heartbeat between them. As cold and deadly as the look in his eyes.

She let her own rage lash out, the taunt coming through her teeth. "What's the matter, Andreas? Fate got your tongue?"

His fists curling at his sides, he shifted his gaze past her, managing to eke out a single garbled word. "Cull."

It was not a compulsion but an order.

"With pleasure," purred Lisette.

With ruthless efficiency, the Daggers went to work. The shadows obeyed their silent commands, peeling off the walls and slipping from the second-floor balcony. They dripped from the chandeliers and crawled out from under the dais, reaching toward the oldest and most powerful families of Valterre.

On their knees on the floor, they could only watch in muted horror as death came for them.

Saints above.

Andreas hadn't welcomed in the king's guests to witness a changing of power. He had corralled them all here to kill them. And the cull was starting *now*.

Lark gripped Sera in a vise as death filled the king's ballroom. When the shadows struck, the first line of nobles fell in tandem, twenty bodies swallowed up in a black wave. Still compelled to her knees, Val met Sera's eyes over the rising swell, the look of crushing defeat on her face saying what her lips could not.

So this is goodbye.

No.

No.

Screaming out, Sera twisted and thrashed, clawing uselessly at Lark. The angle was all wrong, the magic razing along her skin unable to touch him. To harm him.

More nobles fell. Ten bodies, then twenty more, strewn like gilded petals across the black-and-white tiles.

Sera couldn't stop it. Not with all the magic in her blood.

"HELP!" she screamed, desperately. "SAINT ORIEL, HELP US!"

The *BOOM!* came out of nowhere, so loud and close it shook the floor. The shadows faltered, the Daggers snapping their chins up as a series of loud *pops!* rang out. Fireworks exploded across the ballroom, shattering the darkness, replacing death's reaching shadows with a fanfare of searing golden light.

The scent of lemon blossoms filled the room, the air glimmering with the sparks of magic. Good magic. Familiar magic.

Lightfire.

The Daggers staggered backward, the last of their shadows dissolving as the hail of Lightfire leeched the silver from their eyes. The walls trembled, sending oil lamps across the floor. More fireworks went off, arcing over them like shooting stars. The Lightfire shattered the binds of the prince's compulsions, returning his victims' free will.

Screams erupted throughout the ballroom as the surviving nobles scrabbled off their knees. They scattered in panic, the chaos so sudden and acute that Lark slackened his hold on Sera. Spinning on her heel, she punched him square in the jaw, making his head snap to the left. Shoving him off her, she threw herself at Val, both of them grabbing onto each other for dear life.

"Are you all right?" they said at the same time.

No, no. Not even close.

But they were alive, by the skin of their teeth. By the grace of destiny, and all those blinding fireworks. Chandeliers tumbled from the ceiling, their lit candles rolling to meet the growing puddles of spilled oil. Fires sprang up in every corner and thick smoke began to billow.

Releasing Sera, Val fought her way through the sea of bodies to get to Bibi, leaving her to find Andreas in the fray. To finish what she'd started before those shadows struck.

There was no sign of the prince. But someone else appeared like an apparition in the smoke. There, on the other side of the ballroom, Sera spied a telltale glint of silver hair. Theo.

Theo had come back for them. Armed with a daring plan and a crate full of Lightfireworks, and he had not come alone.

Ransom was here, too. Stalking through the smoke like a predator on the hunt, Sera had never seen such rage before. But when their eyes met across the room, and he saw that she was still standing—still breathing—relief blanched the violence from his face. Raising a hand to his chest, he clutched at the space above his heart, like he was trying to stop it from leaping through his ribcage.

With tears streaming down her face, she went to him. Through fire and smoke, and death and chaos, following that insistent tug in her chest. The one that filled her with new hope.

The one that whispered, *Mine.*

Chapter 36

Ransom

Ransom was pacing on the shores beneath the Summer Palace when the minstrels began to play. Music wafted from the upper balcony, casting a merry lilt across the strand.

Another of Andreas's well-crafted lies.

The hour was late, and Ransom's heart was sitting in his throat. It had been there ever since they'd left Marvale, riding fast and hard until they met the River Verne. From there, they followed the river to the west of Fantome and all the way down the shoreline, where the grand white palace speared out of the bluffs like a snaggle tooth. For days now, they'd been watching the king's residence for signs of Prince Andreas, but the black gates never opened, and from the outside, the palace itself had remained eerily still.

As though it was holding its breath.

Now King's Day was upon them. All evening, the noble folk of Valterre had been arriving in droves, their carriages passing through militant gate inspections before being ushered inside. On the surface, the burgeoning festivities appeared entirely normal, but these were no ordinary guards standing at the black gates. They were mercenaries, marked by their frightening builds and battle scars, and the golden roses that had been emblazoned on their uniforms. A break with the king's own crest, a call to a new era.

This was Andreas's army.

Which meant the prince was already inside.

And so was Seraphine.

Every time the thought of her struck him—which was every three minutes or so—Ransom was seized by the sudden, violent urge to charge across the strand, rip those black gates apart, and kill everyone in his path until she was safe in his arms again.

"Easy," Nadia said now, like she could sense the beast prowling inside him. "We need to wait for the opportune moment."

Ransom clenched his hands in and out of fists, straining for calm. The party would soon be in full swing. Just another few minutes and they'd slip inside and go to work.

Quick, gruesome, bloody work.

"Yeah, we're losing him," remarked Caruso, who was passing the time by building and then immediately demolishing sandcastles.

"If Bastian had his way, he'd be dead ten times over by now," said Anouk, who was sitting on a rock beside him. "Even a man in the throes of true love can't fight his way through hundreds of hardened mercenaries!"

Try me.

"Don't tease him or he really will get himself killed," warned Nadia. "We'll go in after that last carriage. Look. Most of the soldiers are starting to head inside."

They were creeping up the rocky shoreline when Ransom caught a glint of silver in the distance. A lone figure skulking in the royal graveyard. They were just visible over the old stone wall, which was not far from the palace.

Stifling a curse, he took off in that same direction, slipping a vial from his pocket as he went. The others hurried after him. Somewhere behind them, the music cut out.

Ransom was just about to down his vial of Shade when Theo Versini popped up from behind the graveyard wall, wearing a large black rucksack and a look of alarm.

Reaching over the wall, Ransom grabbed him by the collar. "What the fuck are you up to?"

Shaking him off, Versini hissed, "Rescuing my friends, you brute. What are *you* doing here?"

"Same idea," said Nadia, coming up behind him. Caruso and Anouk arrived just as another figure popped up from behind the graveyard wall. Silver-haired, and with the same annoying smirk, he was a carbon copy of Versini. Only younger.

The Shadowsmith, meanwhile, fixed his gaze on Anouk. "You're new," he said, with some bewilderment.

"And *really* important," said Anouk.

Ransom jabbed his finger at the Versini the Younger. "Who the hell is that?"

"Tobias. My cousin. Don't be a prick. He's here to help."

Tobias rolled back on his heels. "The light-fireworks are *my* idea. I'm really the smart one."

"I immediately believe you," said Ransom, wondering what the hell light-fireworks were, and already liking the sound of them.

Versini was still staring at Anouk. "You look a bit like Ransom."

"I know," she said, smiling. "He's immeasurably lucky."

"Anouk is my sister. Stop staring at her. We rescued her from the Isle of Alisa."

Versini's brows shot up. "*You're* the other saint? That's not possible."

"Every time we say that something increasingly impossible happens," said Nadia. "Fate is definitely messing with us."

"Speaking of," said Versini, growing uneasy, "we have some . . . developments to catch up on."

A blood-curdling scream cut through the night.

They all snapped their chins up.

"Later," said Ransom, his blood chilling as he turned back to the gates. Mercenaries still swarmed the inner courtyard, though not half as many as before. It was now or never.

Hitching up their rucksacks, Versini and his cousin hopped over the graveyard wall. "Can you get us inside?"

By way of answer, Ransom raised the vial to his lips. "Stay behind me."

He swallowed the Shade in one go, this time welcoming its power. As Seraphine's scream poured out of that upper balcony, a wall of shadow erupted from the graveyard to the shore. A thing of rage and murder, a kind of fury Ransom had never known. He flung his hands out, driving the dark forward in a menacing tidal wave. The black gates twisted back on themselves, the carriages beyond crushed and flung aside.

Andreas's mercenaries scattered as the darkness bore down on them. The fools that stayed and drew their swords were dead in an instant.

Ransom never hesitated. Never flinched. As the cries of the woman he loved echoed through the night, he gave himself to the darkness, to that impulse to kill, and kill, and kill, until his body was scoured deep with shadow-marks and there was no one left to stand in his way.

Death swept across the courtyard. They followed its path into the mouth of the glittering Summer Palace and up the grand stairwell. When the doors to the ballroom were flung open, Ransom glimpsed a black wave just as deadly as his own. A thing he could not remedy, only worsen. Corralling his shadows, he stepped back, silently ushering Versini forward. A plea blazed in his silvered eyes.

Make it count.

Dipping his chin, Versini charged ahead, a firework already crackling in his fist. "Watch and learn, Dagger," he said, hurling it into the ballroom.

The explosion was a marvel. Followed quickly by ten more, the force of the crackling Lightfire was so quick and bright and violent, it blanched every speck of darkness from the ballroom.

Ransom hurled himself into it, letting it eat away the last of his Shade.

Screams erupted as guests fled for their lives. Flames danced along the oil-slick floors, spitting smoke into the air. Moving quicker now, Ransom shoved his way into the fray, frantically scanning the ballroom. As if fate itself had tapped him on the shoulder, he turned, finding her gaze in a sea of others. The realness of her, standing there, unharmed, was like a fist around his heart. He was suddenly aware of its weight in his chest, of every painful thump that pushed him forward.

Seraphine.

My Seraphine.

She stumbled as she went to him.

They were halfway to each other, wading through a tide of fire and death, when a figure lunged from the left, grabbing her by the throat. She hit the floor with a strangled cry, pinned by the mangled, seething form of Prince Andreas.

Ransom roared for her, caught in such a blinding fury that he barreled straight into the King of Valterre, who rose up from the floor in the space of a single jarring heartbeat.

Staggering backward, Ransom tried to make sense of the man who now stood between him and Seraphine. It was not the king but his corpse. Suspended there like a doll cursed to life. Still bleeding from its chest and mouth, eyes rolling back in its head, the dead king hovered before him on pointed toes.

"Guess who?" crooned an eerily familiar voice.

Ransom froze, the word soundless on his lips: *impossible.*

Fate was not letting up. Here it was again, only now it wore the face of his best friend. When the king's body dropped and Lark Delano appeared where he had been hovering, with eyes of burning gold, and wearing the same shit-eating grin he always had, Ransom didn't know whether to pull Lark into a hug or run him through with a sword.

It *was* Lark, but not as he used to be. His skin possessed an odd grayish hue and it was tight across the bones of his face, the shadowy sockets of his eyes making him look half skeleton, half man. For years death had ambled alongside Lark Delano and he had worn it lightly. Now death wore him like a second skin.

"*You're* the Necromancer." Ransom's head spun at this new unsettling truth. "How?"

"A kiss of fate." Eyes wild and gleaming, Lark grabbed him by the shoulders. "The kingdom is changed. Join us, brother. There is a place for all of us in the prince's court."

Seraphine's scream knocked Ransom back into himself. There wasn't time to take a breath, to face the astounding, earth-bending impossibility of his best friend's resurrection while the woman he loved fought for her life.

He pivoted around Lark, but his friend tightened his grip, holding him back. "Let them work it out," he said, as if Prince Andreas wasn't ten feet away, choking the life out of her. As though his mercenaries weren't closing in on them.

Yanking his friend's collar, Ransom pulled him close. "It's good to see you, brother, but I need you to move the fuck out of my way. *Now.*"

Lark squared his shoulders, and Ransom might have decked

him right then if Nadia's voice hadn't rung out at that very moment.

"Lark?" she cried. "*Hell's teeth.* Tell me I'm not dreaming."

Lark's attention shifted, the fight leaving his body like a sigh as Nadia ran to him.

Shoving him aside, Ransom ran for Seraphine.

The pillars in the ballroom began to crumble as Anouk went to work. Her laughter soared above the fray as she tore chunks of stone right out of the ceiling, flattening soldiers like flies. Methodically breaking down the wall of muscle that kept Ransom from the prince.

Vaulting over rubble, Ransom snatched up the nearest sword he could find. Without Shade, he'd have to rely on his own strength and his middling skill as a swordsman. Rage would make up for the rest.

As the prince's soldiers descended on Seraphine, Andreas sprang to his feet and slid into Ransom's path, his sword raised in warning. "The rebel returns."

The words were slow and garbled, accompanied by a lop-sided sneer. The skin of his left cheek was peeling off his face, and his jaw was covered in angry red blisters.

Ransom struck, meeting his blade with his own. "I've been meaning to butcher you."

Those golden eyes flashing, Andreas attempted a command. Ransom punched him in the throat, killing it. Better this way anyway, more personal. He slammed his fist into the prince's face, over and over again, until they were both splattered in blood. It was messy and primal and violent, and Ransom couldn't stop. Even as flames surged around them, licking at his feet.

Ducking his next assault, Andreas staggered backward with a ragged cry.

Ransom returned to his sword, meeting him clash for clash. Everywhere he looked, the fire raged out of control. Seraphine was lost somewhere in the smoke. The rubble had stopped falling, and Anouk's laughter had died out too.

Panic nipped at Ransom.

The prince swung again, their blades meeting in a deafening clash. A red mist came over Ransom as he fought, hard and fast, with everything he had.

Back, back, back, he pushed the prince, weaving between the bodies on the floor, trying to see through the gathering smoke. The walls flickered amber and gold, the thickening smoke making him light-headed. His thoughts spun away from him as he struggled to suck down clean air. There was so little of it left.

Andreas was struggling too. The prince swayed, his grip on his sword slackening.

Blinking heavily, Ransom struck again.

Too slow.

Too low.

Too hazy in here now.

Soldiers swarmed the tightening space, appearing as if from nowhere. They floated through the smoke, making a circle around them. Ransom turned, coming face to face with the Queen of Valterre. Her eyes were black.

Dead.

Already dead.

Fuck.

Not soldiers but corpses. Bodies impervious to fire and smoke. They advanced on him, dead arms flailing as they swung in every direction. He ducked a flying fist only to crash into another one, the sickening crack of a dislocated shoulder nothing to a man who was already dead. Ransom weathered the blow to his jaw, righting himself as more corpses came, fast and swinging.

Somewhere nearby, Lark was laughing.

The prince had disappeared, hidden behind the wall of the dead.

Ransom had to get away from them. His thoughts slowing, he turned and stumbled straight into Bibi. Her blank, black eyes looked right through him.

Fuck.

Bibi raised her fist. He caught it with his own, stilling her assault. She began to sway. The corpses around them seemed to be running out of steam. Lark must be fleeing too.

"Seraphine!" Ransom yelled between wheezes. "SERA-PHINE!"

As the fire surged, bodies fell one by one. Snapping his head up, Ransom spied a hole in the ceiling, where the stars shone through.

Air.

Clean air.

He sucked down a breath, his eyes streaming from the

smoke. The moon was on his side. Silver shards slipped through the cracks in the stone like torchlight. Across the ballroom, he spied Versini staggering back toward the doorway. Anouk flopped like a doll in his arms, while Val hobbled close behind, leaning heavily on Tobias.

Ransom's surge of gratefulness was short-lived, his thoughts tunneling to one single pounding thought: *Seraphine.* He would go up in flames if he had to, crawl the length of this room on his hands and knees until his lungs gave out, but he was not leaving here without her.

Because she *was* here.

He could feel it in his blood and bones. In every painful beat of his heart. And that's when he felt it—that insistent tug in his chest.

There.

There.

Look and see.

He raised chin, as if to follow it.

He saw her then, as plain as a fallen star. In the middle of the ballroom, half buried beneath the bodies of two mercenaries, lay the body of Seraphine Marchant.

High above her, the ceiling was starting to collapse.

Chapter 37

Ransom

Smoke seared Ransom's eyes and licked his skin as he crawled to Seraphine. Frantically calling her name, he dragged the bodies away, then cupped her face between his hands.

"Come on, spitfire. Wake up," he said against her lips. "Wake up and fight."

She groaned, slowly coming to.

"Hey," he said, lifting her arms around his neck. "Stay with me. We're getting out of here."

Nodding dazedly, she held on to him, and he hoisted her up from the floor. She stood on shaking legs, and he curled his arm around her waist to keep her upright. Both struggling for air, they made for the entryway, only to meet a wall of flames. The back half of the ballroom had caved in entirely.

It was only a matter of time before the rest of the ceiling

came down. If they didn't suffocate before that. The flames lashed out, forcing them back toward the only place that wasn't burning. Choking badly now, they had no choice but to make for the balcony.

Ducking between the bodies hanging there, Ransom swung her out onto the balcony, putting her as far from the hungry flames and raining rubble as he could. They staggered toward the stone balustrade, tipping their heads back to gasp at the clean sea air.

The sea wind rushed over them, chasing the smoke away. Ransom inhaled, filling his lungs. Far below, the last of the king's guests spilled like rats from the palace, wailing as they scattered into the night.

Seraphine sagged against him. "You came back," she rasped. "I knew you'd come back."

"I never meant to leave you," he said, sliding his hands through her hair, falling into the moonlit light of her eyes. They were trapped in a nightmare, but this moment—these precious seconds—felt like a dream. "Forgive me, Sera."

"Forgiven." Her eyes streamed. He wiped the tears with the pads of his fingers. Her smile wobbled. "For an assassin, you are really good at saving my life."

Only yours.

"I'm afraid now we both need saving."

She turned around, her back flush against his chest as she took in that searing wall of flames. And those four hanging bodies now burning to a crisp. They snapped and fell one by one.

"We have to jump."

"We will die," said Ransom, with unerring certainty.

Her frown said she knew it too. She raked her hair back, tying it into a knot at the base of her neck. It occurred to him that if he jumped first, it would better her chances of survival.

"I have an extremely reckless idea," she said. Darting over to the palace wall and braving the encroaching heat, she ripped down the last surviving King's Day banner. It stretched to at least sixteen feet. Not enough to bridge the descent, but it would get them close. They went to work, securing one end of their makeshift ladder to the balustrade.

"This is either the best idea you've ever had, or the worst," he said, sending up a silent prayer to Saint Oriel.

Let it hold. Let it work.

Seraphine tossed the banner over the side, and watched it unfurl toward the gardens. "If it's the worst, at least I'll be too dead to care."

Ransom had wanted to go first to cushion her fall. But the banner wasn't strong enough to guarantee two descents and the odds of survival were better for the first climber.

"After you," said Seraphine, standing back.

He summoned a smirk. "What's the matter, spitfire? Are you afraid of heights?"

Wrinkling her nose, she hissed, *"Never."* She swung her leg over the railing. Ransom held her arms, lowering her down. She wound her feet around the banner, grabbing the material with both hands.

"Go steady," he said, as she slid from his grasp.

Heart pounding furiously, he was more terrified of that drop than the heat surging at his back. The flames were licking his ankles now. He kept the discomfort from his face, holding her gaze as she slowly lowered herself down.

"Good, spitfire. Just like that."

The wind picked up, tossing her about.

Voice trembling, she looked up at him. "How much longer?"

"Not long now. Keep your eyes on me."

His legs were burning.

"Ransom?" The banner twisted back on itself, and for a heartbeat, she lost her balance. The rope at the top was fraying.

"Keep going, Seraphine. You're almost there."

She squeezed her eyes shut, sliding hand over hand, tugging at the weakening rope. He tightened his fists around it, holding it taut. Breath ballooned in his chest, the flames now lashing his back. Menacing amber flickers crowded his periphery, but his eyes were on her.

"Just a few more feet."

She opened her eyes. "Ransom, the *fire*."

"Never mind about the fire."

Too late. She let herself go, falling the rest of the way. Darkness enveloped her, the distant thud heralding her fall.

"Fuck."

"Still alive," she croaked, before his heart stopped entirely. "Hurry."

Ransom swung himself over the balcony, throwing himself at the mercy of the fraying banner. He didn't dare look up again, his palms burning as he slid fast and hard toward the ground.

He was halfway down when the rope gave way with a fateful *snap*. He pitched backward, the fire glimmering above him as he plummeted down, down, down—

"Oomph!"

The landing was softer than he was expecting, owing to the crushed rosebush underneath him. The pain in his shoulder told him it was dislocated. Seraphine, who had landed in the flowerbed to his left, was cradling her ankle.

"How bad is it?"

"A bit mangled," she huffed. "I think I can walk."

Shouts sounded in the distance, the clatter of bootsteps heralding nearby soldiers.

"Running would be better," he said, urgently. After grabbing a sword from a dead mercenary and hooking it to his waist, he helped her up, tucking his good arm around her waist.

They made for the gates, staggering down the steep hill to where the Verne flowed toward the midnight sea. Ransom spied twin glints of silver hair up ahead. The Versinis, Val, and Anouk were a quarter of a mile away, heading west along the riverbank. Most of the others had fled east, scattering across the rocky shoreline. No sign of Nadia or Caruso, or Lark.

They turned west too, following the river. Darkness enfolded them, the sea wind dragging clouds across the stars. Up ahead, the younger Versini had spotted them. He stalled downriver, waving his arms back and forth.

Ransom quickened his steps. "Almost there."

Seraphine grunted. "So tired."

They stumbled on.

Behind them, the Summer Palace was ablaze, a mighty torch against the darkening sky. Its reflection turned the river water amber, the flames dancing in the far-off sea. Gone was the king and his favored seat of power. Who would replace him in the cold light of morning? Would Andreas heal and live to terrorize Valterre? To chase Seraphine, his coveted rose, to the ends of the continent?

Doubt gnawed at Ransom. A part of him wanted to turn around and see his mission through. To look for the friends he had left behind.

"Old friend . . ." As though summoned by the thought, Lark's voice echoed through the night. "Where are you running to?"

Ransom halted. Tucking Seraphine into his side, he scoured the darkness, finding Lark just up the hill. He was standing by the entrance to the royal graveyard, that sacred wedge of land that flanked the Summer Palace and looked out over the South Sea. Even in death, the revered kings and queens of Valterre still had the best view.

In the darkness, Lark's golden eyes were like torches, illuminating the Daggers at his side. Lisette was there, along with half the Order, the thirty or so power-hungry assassins who had chosen to side with the untried People's Saint. Ransom expected it of Lisette, but the sight of Nadia standing at Lark's right-hand side struck him like a blow. Caruso, too, had chosen his side, though he hovered apart from the others, unusually quiet.

"Why aren't *you* running?" Ransom called back. "You're alive. You're *free*."

"Why should I run?" Lark parried. "I'm a saint now, thanks to your little firecracker. This is where I belong."

"In a graveyard?"

"In a palace." Lark laughed. "Haven't you been listening? The Age of Kings is at an end. The kingdom is ours for the taking." He gestured to the Daggers that crowded him. "It's time to crawl out of the man-made dark and seize our place on the throne of Valterre."

"There is only room for one person on that bloodstained throne," said Ransom. "And he has no interest in sharing it."

"We'll see," was all Lark said.

Ransom shook his head. "So this is where your loyalty ends."

"You're one to talk about loyalty." With a derisive snort, he pointed at Seraphine. "*She* fucking *murdered me!*"

"She made you a saint!"

"Which you figured out all of one hour ago," scoffed Lark. "How long were you screwing her before that? Enjoying the taste of your best friend's murderer?"

Ransom bared his teeth. "Tell yourselves whatever you need to, but tonight, you've sold your souls to Prince Andreas. And trust me when I tell you, he will mangle them—and *you*—as he sees fit."

Nadia was the only one who flinched. But still, she refused to step away from Lark, to sacrifice that decade of loyalty they had built down in the catacombs. The love they'd fostered in secret. A part of Ransom understood. The other part hated her for it. For making him feel like a traitor.

Lark clucked his tongue. "And you sold your soul to the

Saint-maker. If you think Andreas is more of a danger to Valterre than *her*, then you're a shittier Dagger than I thought."

"I'm done being a Dagger."

Angered by Lark's taunt, Seraphine found a modicum of strength, and with it, called out, "Stay here and worship your tyrant. Bow to the man who intends to control the free thoughts of Valterre. If you think I'm worse than Andreas, I promise you I *will* be. Move against me or my friends and I swear to Saint Oriel, I will do everything in my power to *unmake* you, Lark Delano. I will put you back in the ground."

"Fighting words." Lark sauntered forward, his steps lazy and unthreatening, but there was a predator behind those eyes, the glimmer of some new, deadly ambition that set Ransom's teeth on edge. "Call it now, Ransom. You're either with us or against us."

Tightening his hold on Seraphine, Ransom backed away from his friends, his family, the people who once meant everything to him.

"Don't make us chase you." Frustration rippled in Lark's voice.

"Make your own choices. And I'll make mine."

"We need the girl, Ransom."

Seraphine raised her middle finger.

Ransom palmed the hilt of his sword. "Over my dead body."

Lark gave a small smile. The hairs on the back of Ransom's neck rose. He knew that smirk. It was the same one he offered a mark right before a kill.

There came a bracing sweep of wind. It didn't roll in from the sea or skim the river. It came from the graveyard. The earth there trembled, a low moan gathering in the breeze. Raising his sword, Ransom backed away, making a shield of his body.

"Run," he urged Seraphine. "Get to the others up the riverbank."

She gripped him tighter. "Not running. Not without you."

The night air filled with the sound of shattered stone and churning earth. Something primal stirred the air, a wrongness snatching at them from the yawning shadows. Nadia glanced over her shoulder. Whatever she glimpsed in the graveyard made her curl her arms around herself and shuffle closer to Caruso.

Jaw straining, Lark raised up his hands.

Seraphine stiffened, muttering, *"Saints above."*

Ransom smelled the skeletons before he saw them, the putrid rot of mulch and bone and maggots bleeding through the air. A cloud passed in front of the moon. When the light returned, all the dead kings and queens of Valterre were standing in the graveyard. An army of rotting bones still wearing their beautiful golden crowns. Some were dragging rusted swords behind them.

"Lark." Ransom said the name like a curse, moving quicker now. Putting as much space between them and the dead as possible. "What the hell are you doing?"

"Is it not clear?" Lark stepped aside, ushering his makeshift army through the gates of the graveyard. "I am necromancing."

Composures wavering now, many of the Daggers turned

away. Caruso braced himself against the low wall. Nadia doubled over, vomiting on the grass.

"All saints," whispered Seraphine. "We're screwed."

Still ragged with pain and exhaustion, they turned and bolted for their lives.

The dead chased them.

Chapter 38

Seraphine

Things were bad. Extremely, harrowingly, unavoidably bad. Not only had Seraphine not succeeded in killing Lark Delano that night on the Aurore, now the ungrateful bastard was sending a graveyard's worth of corpses after them.

Royal corpses. Not that it mattered, she supposed. A reanimated skeleton was just as terrifying without a crown. It just so happened that these ones were glittering in their horror. Like specters shot through with moonlight, the skeletal remains of the royal house of Rayere drifted toward them on bone-white toes.

"This is a nightmare," huffed Sera, as they retreated up the bank toward the others, who were watching on in wide-eyed terror. "Any minute now, we're going to wake up."

"I'll admit this is disturbing as hell," muttered Ransom.

"And I grew up in the catacombs of Fantome."

Sera risked a glance over her shoulder, instantly regretting it. The corpses were much closer now and gaining far too rapidly. She stumbled, coming to her knees. Pain lanced through her ankle. It was getting worse.

"Come on, spitfire." Ransom's voice was low and urgent as he hoisted her back to her feet. "We're almost there."

Almost where? she wanted to scream. They were languishing in the moonshadow of the Summer Palace. Miles from Fantome, and hundreds more from Halbracht, where she wished she was now with all her heart. Somewhere safe. Somewhere far, far away. Somewhere saints didn't exist.

Too late for all that now.

Keeping his hand on her lower back, Ransom urged her on. The land climbed, the riverbank growing sheer and rocky as the Verne slowly dropped away.

The corpses drew closer still. Sera could smell them, that unmistakable rot skating on the river wind. Somewhere beyond it, Lark Delano was laughing.

The land was too steep. Their strength was flagging. The third time Sera fell, she couldn't get up, even with Ransom's help. Her ankle was badly twisted now, too weak to bear her weight. Ransom wasn't faring much better. His shoulder had dislocated, and the backs of his legs were badly burned.

Cursing, he tried to lift her anyway. "Come on, Seraphine."

"I c-can't," she said, fisting the grass.

The corpses were at their backs, the smell overpowering. Her eyes streamed, her voice breaking. "I *can't*."

"Then crawl," he begged. *"Please."*

She knew it was a wasted effort, a three-legged deer trying to outrun a hundred mountain bears, but for the imploring look in his eyes she dragged herself up the hill on her hands and knees.

After a minute or so, she noticed Ransom was no longer with her. At the dull thwack of steel meeting bone, she stole another glance over her shoulder. He was standing alone on the riverbank, taking on an entire army of skeletons by himself. Swinging fast and violently, he lopped off skull after skull, sending them plummeting into the Verne.

For every skeleton that collapsed, another took its place, testing the last of his strength. Sera was frozen, too weak to stand up and fight, too stricken to go on without him. She could hear her friends up ahead.

"Move!" Val was screaming.

Tobias too. "Hurry! While they're distracted!"

"Don't look back!" yelled Theo.

Sera couldn't tear her gaze from Ransom. He was barely holding his own against Lark's macabre spectacle of power. Her heart thrummed with fear, and deep inside her spent and aching body, her magic sparked. A new strength gripped her, that tug in her chest growing stronger. Urging her back to him.

Ransom was still swinging. Bones were crumbling, skulls flying. Swords and crowns littered the high riverbank like discarded pennies.

Lark was still laughing. "Give it up, brother! Come back to us! See the fun we'll have together!"

It was all a sick game to him. And Ransom was fighting for their lives. Sweat slicked his hair and poured down his face, his shoulder so twisted, his left arm hung limply at his side.

The skeletons kept coming, some rising again even without their skulls. Moving in a circle, they pushed him back toward the river's edge.

Panic shoved Sera down the hill, fanned the spark of her magic into a flame. She gathered that strength inside her, and used it to haul herself to her feet.

Ransom stumbled on the slippery rocks. His own sword fell from his grasp. He kicked out, shattering the ribcage of an advancing skeleton, then swung, upending a skull and crown with his right fist. Six more came, making a wall of their bodies. He was teetering on the riverbank, too close to the water—much too close.

Plucking a rusted sword from the riverbank, Sera staggered on. Five steps, then five more, held upright by the furnace of her own magic.

Ransom was up again, the sword heavy in his hand. The river wind rippled up the back of his shirt.

Her heart lurched. "RANSOM!"

The corpses edged closer, no longer attacking. But taunting.

Lark's little power game.

Sera flung herself into the fray, swinging with everything she had. Bones shattered, falling around her like confetti as they went to work, fighting side by side. After a while, the bodies stopped rising. Unseeing skulls stared up from the grass, the odd finger twitching, before falling still.

Without an army of skeletons between them, Sera saw Lark more clearly now. Standing alone with his hands in his pockets, he looked out over the debris of bone and metal, and shrugged, as though he had simply gotten bored.

Was it a reprieve or another one of his games?

Sera was so busy glaring at the Necromancer that she missed the sight of Andreas leering at them from the outer parapet of the Summer Palace. "If you're not with us, you're against us, Saint-maker!" yelled the soldier at his side, acting as his temporary mouthpiece. "We won't let an enemy as powerful as you simply walk away!"

Andreas raised his hand, and a volley of arrows arced through the sky.

Sera dropped to the grass, covering her head in her hands. The arrows struck, plinking off metal and bone. But there came no pain. No wounds. Drawing a careful breath, she peered through the crook of her arms. Arrows littered the ground around her. Missed, all of them.

There was a deep, sucking gasp.

Sera's heart stopped.

No.

A few feet ahead of her, Ransom was doubled over, clutching at an arrow in the center of his chest. The one he had taken for her.

Sera's scream split the night in two.

He stumbled backward, blindly reaching for her. *"Seraphine."*

The word was blood-soaked and far too quiet.

It sounded like goodbye.

"No." She lunged for him, but he was already falling.

It only took a stumbling misstep.

He went over the riverbank.

She screamed again, reaching the edge just in time to watch him fall. Down, down, down into blackness and oblivion and cold, unforgiving water.

Chapter 39

Seraphine

Ransom was dead. If that arrow didn't kill him, the river would. He couldn't swim, couldn't breathe with that steel in his chest.

Andreas's general bellowed another command. More arrows flew, but this time, Sera didn't look up. She was looking down at that dark, churning water.

The thread in her chest went taut.

One minute she was on the bank, and the next, she was free-falling down into the swirling waters of the Verne. She barely registered the shock of cold or the tug of the current. Every fiber of her being was focused on Ransom.

Find him.

Save him.

In the water, she was weightless. Painless. Half numb by the time she broke the surface. Sera was a good swimmer—quick in a current and confident in the dark, thanks to summer nights spent in Ploughman's Lake, and river-swimming with Pippin.

Using front stroke, she let the current carry her downriver. She scanned the surface as she swam, grateful when the clouds fractured around the moon, letting it light up the river.

Thank you, Saint Maurius.

Or whatever saint of old was listening to her prayers.

A glimpse of something up ahead made her jerk to the left. Moving closer, she spotted the arrow shaft protruding from Ransom's chest. He was floating on his back.

Not swimming.

Not moving.

Fear shoved her under the surface, where she swam as fast as a merrow, surfacing just behind him. She threaded her arm around his upper chest, careful not to disturb his wound.

"I've got you," she said, swallowing a mouthful of water.

Ransom was silent in her arms. Too cold. Too still. A flash of moonlight revealed his pallid face, and the blood seeping through his lips.

No. He was not dead.

She was going to save him.

They had made a promise to each other. She was going to keep it.

She floated on her back, propping him against her as the current carried them toward the mouth of the river. The South Sea glistened up ahead, where the Verne broke off into a series of narrow tributaries that reached toward the ocean, like splayed fingers.

The current slowed as the river splintered. Sera swam for the closest sandbank, crossing the narrowing inlet with renewed determination. When the water shallowed enough for her to climb out, she pulled herself up onto the sand, dragging Ransom with her.

Stars swam in her vision as she labored for breath, but she didn't dare break her focus. Not while the man she loved was half dead in her arms.

No, not dead.

He can't be dead.

She laid him on his back, the river lapping at her feet as she clambered over him. The arrow in his chest was like a knife to her own. His eyes were closed, his face so pale she hardly recognized him.

"Ransom?" she said, trying not to cry. "Can you hear me?"

Nothing.

She turned him on his side. He gave a small wet cough. A stream of water trickled out. It was tinged with blood. There was blood on his clothes, too. She ripped open his shirt and nearly wept at the sight of the wound in his chest.

Too near his heart.

Was it too late to pray to Saint Alisa?

"Bastian?" The name was a plea, a broken whisper.

His eyelids fluttered but never opened. His breath was shallow. He was dying. She could feel it. She could *see* it. All that blood still pouring out of him. There must be so little of it left inside.

Panicking, Sera pried the arrow free, covering the wound

with her whole hand. She pressed down hard, willing the last of his blood to stay in his body, begging his heart to keep pumping. She could feel it giving out under her palm.

"Please, Bastian." She brought her forehead to his, her wet hair falling around them like a curtain. "You have to live. I need you to live."

His heart lurched, surrendering a slow thud.

"You promised." She was crying now, her tears falling on his cheeks, trickling into his mouth. "You promised we would be together."

Another weaker thud.

She wasn't cold anymore. The numbness was gone. In its place, a violent heat ripped through her body.

"I love you," she whispered against his lips. "Please, Bastian. I *love* you."

A weak flutter beneath her fingertips.

The final beat.

She closed her eyes, pressed a trembling kiss to his cold lips. "Please, come back to me."

Then silence. The wind ceased, the river quieting to a reverential hush. For a moment, it felt like they were the last two people in the world. One of them already gone, the other holding fiercely to that thread in her chest. The one that told her he was hers. And she was his.

I love you, she said again and again.

Come back to me.

Time stretched, the familiar ache of grief creeping in. She refused to let go of him. To take her hand from his quiet heart.

I love you.

Come back to me.

Something sparked. The darkness winking from black to gold.

There was a slow, deliberate thud.

A heartbeat.

Sera lifted her head, confusion warring with hope.

Light suffused them. Here in the dark of night, a bubble of warmth surrounded them. It was coming from her. Her palm on his chest was glowing.

She stared and stared, terrified to remove it.

She felt it again—that deliberate thud.

And another, stronger now.

A rhythm.

A beating heart.

Ransom's lashes fluttered, his chest bowing under her touch.

A breath!

And another.

Then a name. "Seraphine."

Sera let out a sob. "Bastian?"

He whispered, "I love you, too."

Slowly, so very slowly, she removed her hand from his chest, stunned at what she found there. Not a gaping wound, or even a scar. But a handprint.

"Bastian?" she said again, nervous now.

He opened his eyes.

They were a bright, burning gold.

Saint.

A gasp stuck in her throat.

All around them, the darkness rippled. Shadows swarmed the riverbank, creating a canopy of starless night.

And from within, monsters came.

Chapter 40

Ransom

Ransom had been dead. He was sure of it. One moment, he was as cold as ice on the riverbank, breathing in the scent of lemon blossoms that clung to Seraphine's skin for the final time. Feeling that tug in his chest growing weaker. Then his heart had stopped, the world dimming to the cracked whisper of her voice:

I love you.

Come back to me.

He would have given anything. *Everything.* But there was nothing left to offer. No air to breathe, no blood to pump. No spark of life.

And then—

Deep in the blackness of oblivion, the sun rose over the waters of his soul. It was a gift, this light. A second chance at life.

I love you.

Come back to me.

And something more. Something ancient and powerful waking in the deepest part of him—magic bloomed in the dark reaches of his soul. And it whispered, *Live.*

He woke to a wash of bright light, and the face of the woman he loved. Seraphine was more beautiful now than she had ever been, her face like a painting on the canvas of his heart. He hated the tears that marred her cheeks, the pain breaking her voice.

The strange power inside him grew, yawning through his blood and bones.

Saint, said the old voice.

Welcome to the game.

Shadows crawled over them, dimming the light of her handprint on his chest. Seraphine's eyes were wide in the sudden dark, the whites of them glowing like moons. She clutched his shoulders, pulling him upright. He wrapped his arms around her waist, anchoring her to him. He was surprised at his strength, at how easily he could pull her into his lap.

She trembled against him, some new fear stealing the color from her cheeks. Her gaze shifted to something over his shoulder, her mouth forming a soundless word: *monsters.*

Yes, purred that voice inside Ransom.

The darkness rippled, the shadows dividing into forms. Beasts. Each one, huge and strange and snarling. The largest of them prowled back and forth like a panther, with long, pointed ears and sharp, slender fangs. In the water, a serpent made of dark mist raised its dragon-like head to watch them. Wolves moved along the strand, stretching their wide shadowy backs, and overhead a shadow-falcon with razor talons circled lower.

Seraphine buried her face in his chest.

Ransom held her tighter, whispering, "It's all right. They won't hurt us."

"They look just like your drawings," she said, half muffled. "Your nightmares."

Ransom felt himself smile. "They *are* my nightmares."

Only he was not afraid of them now. Unnerving as they were, the shadow beasts bore no threat to him. They were woven from his own imagination. Their forms born from this new power in his soul.

Not light, like Seraphine.

But darkness. Dreams and shadow. The two halves of Ransom's existence, the good and bad, combining to form an entirely unexpected power.

A Saint of Nightmares.

Twin serpents curled around his ankles, hissing softly. The sound, the weight of them, was as real as adders, those black fangs just as deadly.

"They're mine, Seraphine," he said, against her hair. "They answer to me."

Slowly, she pulled back, raising her cautious gaze to him. He glimpsed the golden sheen of his own eyes in the reflection of her wide black pupils. Cupping her face with gentle hands, he brushed his nose against hers. "I promise, they will *never* hurt you."

But they will kill for you.

I *will kill for you.*

Already attuned to his desires, the shadows peeled away from them, rearranging themselves in a circle, facing the river and its tributaries. A wall of beasts, ready to strike at his command.

"They're yours?" she said, pulling back. "You *created* them?"

"With your help," he said, "Saint-maker." First Lark and now Ransom. A power so great that Andreas coveted it above all others. "I guess you didn't mean to do it?"

She shook her head. "I meant to save you. I've never wanted anything more in my life." She was crying again. He tugged her close, pressing his lips against her hair. She turned her face to his, seizing his lips in a soft, lingering kiss.

His heart thrummed, the beasts around them settling. Contented.

"Saint of Nightmares," she murmured, echoing in his thoughts.

"Are they growing on you?"

She paled as the serpent slithered toward her. With a flick of his finger, Ransom sent it away. "I'm sure they will," she said, a little sheepishly.

He turned from her, squinting into the darkness. "Andreas's soldiers seem to have retreated for now. It won't be long before they regroup."

"We need to keep moving," said Sera, gripped by the same growing urgency.

They rolled to their feet, their strength renewed by the

magic that had passed between them. Pulling her into the heat of his body, Ransom raised her hand to his lips and pressed a kiss there. "Ready, spitfire?"

Sera smiled, twining her fingers with his. "For this, and whatever comes after."

And then they were running, hand in hand, a swarm of shadow beasts gathering at their backs.

Chapter 41

Seraphine

Ransom was a saint. And he was *damn good* at it. Deep in the Cavern of the catacombs of Fantome, he sat at one end of a long wooden table, his golden eyes glimmering like a dark lord of hell. Shadows swarmed him, shaped into seething, snarling beasts. More occupied the north and south tunnels and stood on either side of the guarded entryway. There, at his insistence, and by the grace of his new power, this writhing darkness made from light.

Drumming his fingers along the wood, he locked eyes with Sera, a smile curling one side of his mouth. Seated all the way at the other end of the table, like a queen of her own, she returned his smile, ever aware of that tug in her chest. The thread that had saved him. The one that now bound them to each other.

Between them sat the members of their burgeoning new Order: Theo at Sera's right-hand side, and Val to her left. Paola had remained back at Halbracht for the time being, to oversee the production of Lightfire and keep a watchful eye on Pippin, who was nestled safely in the Pinetops.

There was an empty chair beside Val for Bibi. Bibi who had died as a result of Andreas's macabre spectacle of power. Bibi, whom they had failed to rescue after all. The guilt of that loss was a rock in Sera's chest. As sharp and heavy as her grief.

She swore she would avenge her.

If it was the last thing she did.

All hell, she would.

Anouk occupied the chair beside Ransom, the rest of them filled by the Daggers who had ignored Lisette's call to pledge their allegiance to Prince Andreas and had instead waited for Ransom to return.

They had not been expecting the saint that had walked through these doors three nights ago. Or the company he had brought with him. But they had stayed, and heard it all, free to make a new choice: stand with the saint-maker of Fantome or pledge themselves to a tyrant prince.

The time of the Daggers was over. So, too, was the Age of Darkness they had presided over for too long. Ransom and Sera had seen to it yesterday morning, using the latest batch of Lightfire from Halbracht to destroy the remaining stores of Shade in the catacombs.

"Andreas will strike again soon," said Ransom now. "And he'll come straight for us."

For me.

For as long as Sera lived, Andreas and his power would not

go unchallenged. She was not his rose, after all, but a thorn in his side.

"He'll have an army of unfathomable proportions," said Theo, starkly. "The living and the dead if Lark Delano is still in play."

"We have an army too," said Anouk, those hazel eyes flickering gold. "If he wants to fight for the soul of this kingdom, let him come. I'll bring this whole place down on him. Every skull and rock and bone, and all the rats, too. Let them gnaw through the ribbons of his intestines once I'm done playing jump rope with them."

The Daggers at the table stiffened.

Theo cocked a brow. "Did they teach you how to talk like that at the priory?"

A thin smile. "You'd be surprised what unending boredom does to a young acolyte's imagination."

Ransom scrubbed a hand across his jaw. "Right. Thanks for that."

"There are only thirty of us down here," Val piped up. "Two saints, and a bunch of impotent Daggers now that all the Shade is gone." She flashed her teeth. "No offense."

"We have Lightfire," said Tobias. "Protection against the Silver-tongue's compulsions."

A boon, certainly.

"But nothing to shield us from Delano's . . . *talents*," Theo reminded them. "It's hardly ideal to set up our headquarters in the graveyard district." And that was to say nothing of all the skulls in these walls. It's not like they had had much time to come up with a place, having fled the Summer Palace in the dead of night.

"It's temporary," Ransom reminded him. "We'll find a new place now that we've dealt with the Shade."

The mood remained somber, the odds of what they were facing as menacing at the beasts that prowled at Ransom's back.

"Let Andreas gather his forces," said Sera, as though it was nothing to her. "Let him have his corpses and his slaves. We'll make our own army. Our own saints."

Theo's brows shot up, that silvered gleam returning to his eyes. "You're ready to try again?"

Her magic purred in response, the glow of it warming her skin.

Yes, Maker.

It is time.

She knew it now. She could *feel* it, this sense of rightness, of inevitability. And she was not afraid anymore. She was the right hand of Saint Oriel, and she would save this kingdom from ruin if it was the last thing she did.

"When?" said Tobias.

"Who first?" asked Theo.

"Whoever is willing," said Sera.

Thirty bodies went rigid, the sudden silence palpable. Desire, trepidation, intrigue, fear. She felt it all filling up the spaces between them. Her magic sensed it too, that invisible force inside her reaching out like tentacles, brushing up against these eager souls as if to make its own choosing.

"Sleep on it," said Ransom, rising abruptly from the table. "Just as Seraphine will."

He cast her a meaningful look.

Sera stood too, excusing herself from the table.

The Cavern descended into animated chatter as she made for the north passage, following Ransom out into the tunnels. His beasts flanked them, his power working even now. Not a show of control but a sign of his anxiety, his fear of losing her again. Of losing Anouk.

Stopping halfway down the narrowing tunnel, Sera tugged him back to her, pressing a calming hand against his chest. His heart galloped against her palm.

"You don't need the shadows all the time," she said softly. "Rest a while. Take a moment to breathe."

He turned into her, gently pressing her back against the wall. "How else can I keep you safe, spitfire?"

"I don't need minding, Ransom."

"I know." He tucked a hair behind her ear, his fingers lingering on her cheeks. "Let me do it anyway."

Slowly, like a dying wind, she sensed the shadows behind her melting away, his eyes returning to their usual honeyed warmth as he sank back into himself.

"Better," she murmured, sliding her other hand up his chest. "What did you want to talk about?"

He dipped his chin, looking serious now. "I know you're eager to try again. But take your time, Seraphine. There can be no mistakes."

No more Larks.

"You say that like you have a particular *mistake* in mind."

"You know I do."

She glowered at him. "Theo saved Anouk's life back at the Summer Palace. He lifted her body out of the rubble. When are you going to let up on him?"

"When he stops badgering you about your magic."

"Easy for you to say, *saint*." She was teasing now, prodding at the stress he wore so heavily. Tugging his collar open, she traced the top of her handprint on his chest, the gold there shining faintly in the dimness. "I've already had my way with you."

He dropped his gaze, trailing his finger down her neck. "Don't tempt me."

"Why not?"

Deftly angling her head to the side, he dragged his lips along her neck. Arching her back, she twined her fingers in his thick hair. She pulled him closer, pressed his mouth harder until she could feel the nip of his teeth against her skin. Magic roared through her bloodstream, greedy for more. It tangled with his own, a blanket of shadows coming over them, as if to hide them away from the world.

Sera was so lost in him that she nearly missed the sound of the bell echoing down the passageway. Until it rang again. Longer. Louder.

Dragging himself away from her, Ransom stepped back.

His eyes were wild and bright. In all the time she'd known him, he'd never seemed more alive. More *hers*. A king woven from the darkness, with a soul as bright as the sun.

"Someone's here." Composing himself, he turned and stalked toward the entryway. His beasts ran on ahead of him, two broad-winged ravens flying overhead.

Sera hurried after him.

One glance through the peephole and Ransom stood back, twisting the skull on the wall. The entrance to Hugo's Passage groaned open, revealing a well-dressed young boy with a pale face and a dark mop of hair.

Ransom's voice was a growl. "I thought I told you never to come back here."

The boy's eyes widened as a raven shot out of the tunnel. Stumbling backward, he caught himself before he fell. He found his voice a beat later. "Had to, Mr. Hale. I've got a letter from my mistress, see." He pulled a dark green envelope from the inside of his smart brown jacket. Sera recognized the wax seal at once.

"Madame Cordelia Mercure," she said, noticing the cloak around the boy's shoulders. "You're from House Armand."

The boy nodded. "I'm Fabian."

Softening ever so slightly, Ransom took the envelope and ripped it open. His brows shot up, and when he spoke again, there was a hint of bemusement in his voice. "Cordelia's heard what happened at the Summer Palace. She seeks a new alliance."

Sera blinked in alarm. "With the *Daggers*?"

Ransom slowly shook his head. "With the saints."

"There are saints on both sides of this war," she said, warily.

Fabian piped up. "Fontaine said you're the good ones."

"Did she indeed?"

"Except for your attitude problem," he added.

She snorted. "That sounds about right."

Shuffling from one foot to the other, the boy said, "So what do I tell her?"

Ransom and Sera exchanged a look.

"Tell her we'll see her soon," said Sera. "And tell Fontaine I've missed her terribly."

With a rush of giddy excitement, the boy whooped, taking off into the night.

Ransom stepped back into the catacombs. As the doorway sealed shut once more, she turned into his arms. Sighing softly, he pressed his lips against her hair.

"This might be fun, you know," she said.

She felt him smile. "Well, it certainly won't be dull."

Holding hands, they ambled back to the Cavern. Walking into the darkness but looking, at last, toward the future. This new kingdom. This new freedom. Even if they had to fight tooth and nail for it.

They would.

Together.

Epilogue

As the sun rose over the broken shell of the Summer Palace, Prince Andreas Mondragon Rayere stood alone on the upper balcony, looking out over the glistening South Sea.

Four days had passed since the King's Day massacrer, when the top of the ballroom had been cracked open like an egg. Behind him, soldiers and servants scurried to and fro, working to repair the damage. The bodies were long gone, but the stench of smoke remained. The royal flags and banners had been burned to nothing.

Soon, a new crest would fly in every corner of Valterre.

Not long ago, Andreas had stood atop an ancient clock tower, grasping for greatness. This time, the tower beneath him was one of corpses—the bodies of King Bertrand and the rest of the royal family all piled under his feet.

Without its king, Valterre was rudderless. A kingdom languishing in the throes of uncertainty and rebellion.

Who better placed than he to take hold of it? To guide its people to their knees and let them bask in the full glow of his own anointed sainthood? He had already laid the groundwork, after all. Even now, whispers of the People's Saint were snaking their way through the capital, whispers about this man—chosen by Oriel's storm—who had promised to lead them out of the darkness.

Here he stood in a slant of glittering sunlight.

A smile curled along his ruined mouth. He had avoided his reflection in the days since the fire, revolted as he was by the gruesome burns on his face, the skin there still scoured and pink. His tongue was healing well, however, enough that he could talk in short sentences, though the effort of it still pained him. The process was slow, but Andreas was a patient man. He would come back to himself, back to his power.

Footfall sounded down in the courtyard. His prized mercenaries and newly won Daggers were assembling for their first war council. And somewhere among them, his secret weapon: Lark Delano, his necromancer. Andreas would have liked the acolyte too—now that he had seen the damage she could do—but the Saint-maker had got there first, stealing her away to her side.

In the coming war, Seraphine Marchant would be the first to die.

Followed by Ransom Hale, the Dagger who guarded her like a dog.

And then Versini. Unless, of course, he could be turned to the prince's cause . . . It remained to be seen whether he, like his ancestors, coveted power above all else.

Andreas turned his face to the river, watching it wind away from him like a slithering gray snake. It should have drowned the Dagger that night. Drowned the Saint-maker, too, but Oriel was still playing out her hand. She would not make it easy for him—this grand destiny he sought.

But then, she never had.

As his followers swelled below him, Andreas adjusted the crown on his head. An unnecessary adornment at such an early hour, but his court were gathering for the first time. Let there be no mistake about who was in charge here. In this new world, there could be but one ruler.

As the sun continued its ascent over the South Sea, a clock began to chime somewhere in the bowels of the palace. His smile stretched, pulling at the scar tissue around his mouth.

The bells of Valterre were ringing.

Soon, he would have his vengeance.

Then he would have his kingdom.

And in time, the world beyond it.

Acknowledgments

Bringing a story like *The Rebel and the Rose* to life requires a certain kind of alchemy (and a whole lot of caffeine) behind the scenes. Luckily, I'm surrounded by the most magical team in the business, who I thank all the stars—and saints—for every day!

Claire Wilson, agent extraordinaire, thank you, as ever, for your grace, clarity, wisdom, and whimsy.

Rachel Denwood, my enchanting editor, you are the fire that started it all! Getting to shape this world—and these characters—with you continues to be one of the greatest thrills of my career. Thank you, Pete Knapp, for working your indelible magic Stateside. Thanks, too, to Danielle Barthel and Stuti Telidevara at Park, Fine & Bower.

Thank you, Safae El-Ouahabi and the rest of the team at RCW. Sam Coates, thank you for spreading the love for this series all over the world and finding the most perfect homes for Seraphine & Ransom.

Thank you, Kate Prosswimmer, for adding your singularly magical touch to this story and championing it so wonderfully across the pond.

To the team at S&S Children's Books, you are a shining example of innovation, dynamism, and sheer uncompromising brilliance. Working with you all has been an enduring highlight of my twelve years as an author. Thanks especially to Hanna Milner, Olivia Horrox, Emma Quick, Jess Dean, Laura Hough, Danielle Wilson, Leanne Nulty, Kate Dewey, Hannah Taylor, Leah Bird, Basia Ossowska, Sophie Storr, Justin Chanda, Karen Wojtyla, Bridget Madsen, Andrenae Jones, Shannon Pender, Lisa Quach, Caitlin Sweeney, Samatha McVeigh, Tatyana Rosalia, Debra Sfetsios, and Irene Metaxatos.

Thanks to Nina Douglas for your incomparable passion, creativity, and friendship. I'm lucky to know you and even luckier to get to work with you.

Thank you to Micaela Alcaino for conjuring up another incredible cover and to Sean Williams for your continued design wizardry.

Thanks to Berni Vann at CAA and Emily Hayward-Whitlock at the Artists Partnership for working to bring this series to life on-screen.

Thank you to all the booksellers, librarians, teachers, and readers who continue to support my stories and spread the word near and far. I am forever grateful to you all!

Thank you, as always, to my wonderful family on both

sides of the Atlantic. To Jack for keeping me sane (and fed) and to Cali for keeping me covered in magical golden glitter (see also: dog hair). And lastly, thank you to my darling Jonah for keeping me company in your own quiet, hiccupping way, throughout the nine months it took to write this book and for the life-altering enchantment you have brought into our world since (albeit in a much louder way). You, little you, are magic come true.

CATHERINE DOYLE

is the award-winning and internationally bestselling author of the Twin Crowns series, The Storm Keeper Trilogy, *The Miracle on Ebenezer Street*, and *The Lost Girl King*. Catherine grew up in the west of Ireland, and her books have been published in over twenty-five languages. She holds a BA in psychology and an MA in publishing.